WINDOWS OF FARN
CHRONICLES OF BEAR – VOLUME 2

I0614999

Tim Hanner

WINDOWS OF FARN
CHRONICLES OF BEAR – VOLUME 2

DOUBLE DRAGON

A DOUBLE DRAGON PAPERBACK

© Copyright 2020
Tim Hanner

The right of Tim Hanner to be identified as author of this
work has been asserted in accordance with the
Copyright, Designs and Patents Act 1988

All Rights Reserved

No reproduction, copy or transmission of the publication
may be made without written permission. No paragraph
of this publication may be reproduced, copied or
transmitted save with the written permission of the
publisher, or in accordance with the provisions of the
Copyright Act 1956 (as amended).

Any person who does any unauthorised act in relation to
this publication may be liable to criminal prosecution
and civil claims for damages.

ISBN 978-1-78695-430-5

Double Dragon
is an imprint of
Fiction4All

Published 2020
Fiction4All
www.fiction4all.com

Cover Art by Deron Douglas
www.derondouglas.ca

Prologue

The world went to hell in a hand basket when the Earth lost its ability to produce and sustain electricity. Humankind found itself returned to the seventeenth century with no radio, television or any form of electronic communication. Cars sat abandoned where they were when their life-giving spark disappeared. Society rapidly descended into chaos. Gangs took over cities and militia groups formed in rural areas.

One group of individuals banded together growing into a small community named Rebel's Revenge. Before the loss of power, they were members of a gunfighter's organization putting on comedy shows across southern Texas. After the blackout, they banded together for support and survival.

The citizens of Rebel's Revenge had to defend themselves against a militia group to the south and a gang that had taken over the city of Austin, Texas. The survivors won the battle with unexpected assistance from mutants in the area. With the battle over, death and destruction lay across the area of Rollingblock, Texas. It was time for them to leave -- time for each to find a new life.

CHAPTER ONE

Raphael Edmonds finished saddling his horse and packed a second to carry the supplies he needed for his wanderings. He had no specific plans, but needed to leave. This was a place of too much death, too many painful memories and loss. Memories, which he knew would haunt him for years.

Rafe, or Bear as his friends knew him, retired from the Navy SEALs following twenty years of military service. Following retirement, he returned to school and earned two degrees in alternative medicine. To support himself through school, he owned and operated two martial arts schools along with his retirement pay from the military. Now, in his late forties, he had lost a number of close friends including Davata, the woman that had meant as much to him as any wife.

Bear looked out of the corral area that housed the horses of the now defunct Rebel's Revenge. Another man dressed in the fashion of the eighteen hundreds strode toward him. His appearance was that of a man who had lived in the mountains for years. He wore a beat up black felt cowboy hat and a dirty, white duster.

Spyder held out his hand. "Looks like you're headin' out." Bear knew from their history, there were at least four pistols hidden under that duster. Spyder's hair hung to the middle of his back. His beard was almost as long and served to complete the mountain man appearance.

Bear shook the man's hand. "Yep," he answered. "I figure it's time to go. There's too much

7

loss for me around here, too many bad memories. I'm not fit for man nor beast right now."

"I know what you mean man," Spyder agreed. "Ginny and me's leaving in a couple hours. Figured we'd go back to East Texas and try to set up home there."

Bear nodded. He knew Spyder's history well.

"Neither of us have people there, but I know the area and won't have to put up with the likes of those assholes yesterday. We'll be traveling with Hal and Sandy for a while and Wind's goin' with us."

Besides looking the part of a Mountain Man from long ago, Spyder was an ex-biker, ex-KKK member and, of all things, a Methodist Minister. His belief in God was the only thing of which he was unwilling to compromise. He was a walking, talking dichotomy who strode among the members of Rebel's Revenge with total acceptance.

"We're heading near the same direction as you," Spyder said, "Ya sure you don't want to travel a ways with us?"

Bear looked hard at the man, this friend who had saved his life many times. "I need some time alone," he said. "Nothing against any of you, but I need to work things out in my own way."

"I understand," Spyder answered nodding. He looked down scuffing the ground with the toe of his boot.

The two men were as close as any brothers could be. Spyder had adopted Bear as family during a rough period in his life. Bear had needed a friend and Spyder was there with no questions asked.

Now, in this place where scores of people died, Bear knew it was time to say good-bye to this true

8

and trusted friend. The two men hugged, Bear patted Spyder on his shoulder and said, "I'll see ya sometime, man. We'll run into each other again sooner or later."

"You'll always have a place with us," Spyder said, referring to him and his new wife Ginny.

"I know. I'll see ya soon," Bear said, and walked away, leading his horses behind him.

Rounding the corner of the only crossed streets in the "Ghost Town" of Rebel's Revenge, he saw Hal and Sandy standing across the intersection. He walked up, stopped his horses and started rechecking his load. The last thing he wanted was to say good-bye to either of them. They were both family to him and he felt as if he would be leaving part of himself behind when he left.

Bear and Sandy were as close as any two friends could get. Even though Sandy was married to Hal, she loved Bear like a brother, and Hal not only understood, but encouraged the relationship. Both men cared about Sandy and wanted only the best for her.

"I'm gonna miss you Bro." She said.

Bear looked up from his work, "So, you're going back to Tyler."

Tears filled her eyes and she struggled to speak.

"Yeah," Hal answered for her. "According to that mutant, Gail, there aren't many humans back there. I figure we'll go back to Sandy's mother's old house -- maybe grow a garden. There's plenty of game around there. We should be okay."

"No doubt that you will be," Bear answered needlessly fiddling with the saddle on his horse. Both his horse and packhorse stood patiently

9

waiting. They were fully loaded with supplies, ammunition and other necessities of the trail.

"Now just where is it you're heading?" Hal asked.

Bear looked up from his work on the saddle toward the trees eastward. "Over there," he said nodding in the direction he looked. "I've got no family to hold me in one place, so I thought I'd look around some."

"You've got us," Sandy said. "You know that."

"Yes ma'am I do," he answered. "I'll come back around sometime. I know where you'll both be."

"I love you Bro.," she said, put her arms around his neck and hugged him hard. "You take care of yourself." She stepped back, tears flowing down her cheeks.

"I love you too," he answered.

"Like she said," Hal told him and held his hand out. "You've got family with us."

Bear shook the man's hand. "I know and I'll be back. You take care of yourselves."

Tears stung his eyes as he mounted his horse, tipped his hat to both of them and turned his horses eastward.

CHAPTER TWO

Hal and Sandy joined Spyder, Ginny and Wind just after noon. They were all going to East Texas to start new lives. Hal drove a horse-drawn wagon. Unlike its predecessors, the wagon, now loaded with supplies, had rubber tires and would be able to get traction on the paved roads the entire trip.

"Not quite the kidney buster as the old ones," Spyder had said.

Sandy and Ginny sat in the wagon beside Hal while Spyder and Wind rode separate mounts. Four additional horses followed the wagon attached to leads as they traveled eastward.

Before the blackout, Wind had expected to go to college on a track scholarship. He had received his nickname because of the state high school records he set in Louisiana. As an African-American growing up in the south, he had experienced his share of racial prejudice. However, his mother had insisted that it was what was inside a person that mattered and not the color of their skin. When he and Spyder, an ex-KKK member, became the best of friends, it proved she was right.

It'll be slow traveling," Hal said. "But the use of a diesel vehicle might draw unwanted attention."

If modified, a diesel engine could run since it didn't require electricity. However, their use usually drew gunfire -- times had changed. It was a dog-eat-dog world now. Trust of a stranger was rare and people defended what was theirs.

The small group would use familiar roads for the first part of their journey. "With the gangs gone

11

and the militia destroyed," Ginny said, "we shouldn't have any problems."

"Maybe," Spyder answered. "But once we get past Austin, we'll be in an area we're not that familiar with. There'll probably be other groups or communities formed the same as we did."

"Yeah," Wind said. "Not to mention that there'll still be mutants that don't know Bo or Gail. We'll have to keep an eye out for them too."

"That's true," Hal agreed. "Even if there aren't many mutants over there, we'll probably still face some."

"Anyone know where Bear'll spend the night?" Sandy asked.

"He said he wasn't sure," Wind answered.

"He'll probably stay at the Bar-B-Q Shack," Spyder said.

"Why there?" Ginny asked.

"It's where I'd go. There're uncomfortable memories there for sure," he answered. But, not as bad as in Rebel's Revenge. It's where he and I found Libby and Kai - and it's on his way."

"Makes sense," Sandy admitted. "Will we be going by there?"

"Yeah," Hal said. "But, if he's there we'll give him a wide berth."

"Why," Ginny asked sharply.

"He needs room to think," Spyder said. "He needs to get a handle on what's happened."

"That's no reason for us to sleep in the cold," Ginny countered.

"There are a bunch of houses in the area for us to use," Spyder explained. "It's not a problem."

"But the restaurant is set up for cooking food and... "

"Ginny, there're other places," Sandy interrupted.

"I'd expect you to say that... "

"Ginny," Spyder said, "knock it off. You're just being argumentative for no reason."

Ginny closed her mouth and stared straight ahead from the seat of the wagon. It was no secret that she hadn't cared for Bear since they were in college together.

***

Keith, Amanda and Dr. Hamilton left Rebel's Revenge later that afternoon for Shreveport. Keith had relatives there and the area would probably need a doctor. Hopefully they could settle down and re-establish lives for themselves.

Dr. Hamilton arrived at Rebel's Revenge with Davata, Wind and a young man nicknamed Melon who died shortly afterward. He was a widower who had returned to the Texas Hill Country after his wife of many years, died of cancer. He was a dear, gentle man, willing to help anyone or anything.

Surrounded by violence, he remained faithful to the field of healing. When possible, he tirelessly treated illness and injuries, set bones and checked the water of the community for contamination, among many other duties. He even delivered two babies in Rebel's Revenge after the blackout. Life was sacred to him and he was a true hero to the people whose lives he'd touched.

The small group used another homemade wagon to carry their personal gear and the doctor's supplies. Dr. Hamilton took enough items to open a single treatment room knowing he could grow from that if needed. The rest of the supplies were food, clothes and the ever-present supply of weapons and ammunition.

They stopped at the same house where they spent their last night before arriving at Rebel's Revenge. "It still looks the same from the outside," Keith observed.

"Ben said the mutants took it over for a while," Amanda reminded him. "If we're lucky, they may have left some canned goods. I'm sure all the rest is gone."

"Be careful when you open the door," Dr. Hamilton said. "There still may be mutants inside."

Keith hesitated then slowly opened the front door. The living room was empty except for the furniture, which once sat orderly in front of the fireplace and now lay scattered about the room. Only the couch and two chairs remained undamaged.

In the kitchen, Amanda confirmed that the mutants had left the canned food, however it was scattered throughout the room. Some of the cans lay crushed, their contents spilled on the floor or squirted across the room and still others were ripped open. However, she was able to find canned vegetables and a canned ham in a cupboard.

"At least we don't have to use any of our supplies tonight," she called to the others.

While Dr. Hamilton and Amanda checked the rest of the house, Keith took the horses and wagon to the barn.

Amanda was preparing a meal while Dr. Hamilton built a fire in the fireplace. "We should be safe here for the night," he said as Keith closed the front door.

"I think so," Keith agreed. "Just the same, we need to lock the doors." He turned the latch on the front door and double checked it. "The horses are fed and in the barn with the wagon. I found some hay, but the grain had gone bad."

The doctor nodded without looking up from his work, "That's probably smart, locking the door," he said.

Amanda appeared at the connecting door between the living room and kitchen. "Is there any reason for hurry?" She asked. "We're ten miles from Rebel's Revenge. Isn't the danger over for a while?"

"I don't see any need to rush," Dr. Hamilton answered. "If you want, we can stay here a couple of days."

"I don't care where we stay," she explained. "I just want to take some time to adjust to what happened. I feel like a hollowed out shell."

"That's normal," the doctor said. "Everyone survivor will probably develop PTSD to some extent. Everyone will have to deal with their feelings in his or her own way."

"I did things yesterday, I never imagined I could do," Keith said. "Even as I killed people, I felt nothing." He removed his coat, hung it on a wall peg and sat in a chair before the fireplace.

15

"That's the 'fight or flight' syndrome," Dr. Hamilton explained. "All people have it, just some stronger than others. Since it's over, however, you have a grieving process to go through."

"You think I'm gonna grieve for those assholes?" Keith asked incredulously.

"I don't know for whom or what you will grieve, but you *will* grieve. If you don't, it'll turn you inside out."

Keith still looked doubtful.

Dr. Hamilton leaned forward, his elbows on his knees and his hands clasp before him. The young man before him looked ten years older than he did just two days before. He could see the experience had taken a physical toll. Amanda quietly sat on the other end of the couch from them.

"Look Keith," he said, "I can give you all the medical terms and fancy phrases. That'll only mean you know the names. It still doesn't change a thing."

"I wish I was more like Bear," Keith said looking at the floor. "He can handle things like this." He pulled his hat off, dropped it beside his chair and slouched to the side, his elbow on the chair's armrest, his hand hooding his eyes as if blocking an invisible sun.

"No you don't," Amanda disagreed. "Why do you think he refused to go with Sandy and that group? He was going the same way they were."

Keith took his hand away revealing tear filled eyes.

"In the last few weeks, Bear lost Davata, Ben and his home," she explained. "Spyder said they asked him to go, but he said he didn't think he was fit to be around people. He's hurting as bad as you,

16

me or anyone else. He covered it well, but now he has to heal. He knows that."

Tears escaped Keith's eyes and rolled down his face. "Maybe you're right," he said. "But, look at me, I am crying like a baby."

"That's nothing to be ashamed of," Dr. Hamilton assured him. "We all will sooner or later."

***

Spyder was right, Bear made his way to the Bar-B-Q Shack before settling down for the night. The building was once a restaurant. A couple of months before, he and Spyder had killed four men here for taking two young women hostage and refusing to release them. *There are some things a man simply won't stand for,* he remembered thinking.

The women became valuable members of Rebel's Revenge and both sang Amazing Grace in the Native American language at Davata's funeral for which Bear was eternally grateful.

He put his horses in an extra building beside the restaurant carefully avoiding the structure where he and Spyder had thrown the bodies of the men they killed before. He put his personal items and supplies in the restaurant itself and relaxed for the night.

I'll miss 'em all, he thought. *They were good friends, every damn one of 'em.* Bear allowed his mind to wander, *Davata's gone and it's time to let Sandy go. She has a husband and they don't need me around clouding things up. They're both wonderful people, but I'd just be in the way. They need to make a life for themselves. I'm gonna miss*

Spyder and Wind too. Both of 'em saved my life. Hell, the whole community did. Most of all, besides Davata, I think I'll miss Ben the most. He was a true and faithful friend.

People described Ben as one of the most talented actors and storytellers in the country. He and Bear were friends since meeting at an audition for a play many years ago. Ben died, shot during the battle the day before.

Rest well my friend, Bear thought as he slipped into a deep sleep.

18

CHAPTER THREE

"There's the Bar-B-Q Shack," Hal said. The sun, a glow just below the horizon, turned the edge of the sky into a dim rainbow of colors. A light flickered in a bank of windows. Someone was obviously in the restaurant and he had little doubt that it was Bear.

"Stay here," Spyder said climbing from his horse, handing the reins to Hal. In a couple of seconds, he disappeared into the surrounding trees.

Wind dismounted and Sandy, Ginny and Hal climbed from the wagon and allowed the animals to graze. As darkness gradually descended on the countryside, the sounds of the birds subtly changed from the call of Jays and Sparrows to that of night birds, bullfrogs and crickets.

About ten minutes later, Spyder emerged from the tree line. "It's Bear alright," he said. "He's settling in and has his stuff piled on one of the sofas."

"We'll go to that large house on top of the far hill," Hal said motioning in the distance. "We can stay there for the night."

Before Ginny could protest, Sandy was back on the wagon and getting ready to urge the horses on. Ginny climbed into the seat beside her, looked fiercely ahead and said nothing.

About fifteen minutes later, they entered the driveway to a two-story house. It was on top of a hill about a mile from where Bear slept.

Hal cautiously opened the door and looked inside. There was a spacious living room straight ahead and a kitchen to the right. After searching, they discovered the house, a rambling four-bedroom structure with a large fireplace, was roomy and actually more comfortable than the restaurant would have been.

Ginny and Sandy found cans of various vegetables and, mixed with the venison they had, created an outstanding meal for all of them. Wind found four kerosene lanterns, one in each bedroom upstairs. It seemed they had stumbled on the perfect place for the night. Light, heat and food, what more could they ask for?

"Music!" Wind exclaimed walking into the living room carrying a guitar.

"Oh my God," Spyder said looking at the instrument.

Wind sat down and placed the guitar on his knee. Tuning it he asked, "What do you want to hear?"

Spyder looked at him, "Wind, I swear, if you... "

"I'd like something soft, something mellow," Sandy said interrupting.

Wind strummed a chord. "This is something I wrote some time ago," he said adjusting a couple of the tuning knobs. As he played, the music lilted from the guitar and floated on the air suggesting feelings of sunshine, happiness, love and peace.

"My God, that sounds like the harps of angels," Sandy said. "You're a true artist."

When he finished, he said, "I like the modern music. But, my heart's in the classics and gospel."

"Well, I'll be... kiss my ass," Spyder said a look of wonder on his face. "Son, you never cease to amaze me."

Wind grinned and started another song. "This is a hymn my mother taught me." When he sang, his voice was that of a trained singer and after the events of the day before, seemed like a gift sent from God above.

Hal sat, lost in memories of times gone by; thoughts of a time when life was easier - when choices were simple, and life and death didn't hang on each decision. He remembered Thanksgivings and Christmas' with family and friends long past. The feelings were warm, but made him ache terribly.

They spent the rest of the evening by a roaring fire, relaxed, warm and comfortable. Hal, a good singer in his own right, sang a couple of songs with Wind accompanying him.

"I think we're safe tonight," Spyder said rolling a cigarette. "Still just the same, I think we need to lock the doors."

"Yeah, you're right," Hal agreed. "I doubt we have any real danger around right now, but it's better safe than sorry."

Wind began picking a tune in the background.

"It seems like we haven't had a break since day one of the Blackout," Sandy said. "I'm tired and I'm beat-up. I've never felt this way before." She paused and looked at the fire. "Hal and I have been through a lot in our marriage, but nothing like this. After yesterday, I feel torn apart. It's as if part of me is missing. I just wanna be whole again. I wanna feel like I did when my kids were young, and Hal and I didn't know what it was like to kill someone."

Again, as earlier in the day and as it would be for some time to come, tears overflowed her eyes

21

and rolled down her cheeks as Hal pulled her close and held her tight.

***

Bear awoke to a rumbling sound. The building shook around him. A number of the windows forming two walls of the restaurant shattered and fell from their frames. The wagon wheel chandeliers hanging from the ceiling swung violently side-to-side. Lightning flashed across the sky, lighting up the countryside.

We haven't had lightening for months now. He thought. The ground heaved. *An earthquake in Texas? What the fuck's going on here?*

As if proving the existence of the lightning, thunder roared as a bolt struck somewhere close by. Bear threw his blanket off and, hindered by the shaking of the building, struggled to his feet after twice falling back on his butt. For every step he took toward the front door, he staggered one or two to each side like a drunk on ice.

The door stood awry on its hinges. Bracing himself against the sill, he peered out. Beyond, he could see stars shining brightly in the night sky. There were no clouds, yet lightning, sheet and fork, followed by thunder, hammered the countryside as if a fierce storm raged. Trees swayed in unison with the undulation of the ground, looking like some insanely coordinated line dance in a macabre honky-tonk. It seemed as if the world was trying to rip itself apart.

Glancing to his left he saw a shimmer moving rapidly toward where he stood. It looked like a transparent curtain allowing everything in its path to pass through as it raced along. At a brief glance, it seemed to stretch from horizon to horizon. In only a couple of seconds, the thing covered the half-mile open field beside him.

It looks like a special effect out of some movie. That was the last thought he had before the wave slammed into the restaurant.

***

Hal's eyes fluttered open. The room swam into view as he tried to blink the sleep away. This wasn't right; the room was different than he remembered. Instead of wood paneled walls, there was straw. Instead of a bedroom, the room where he lay was a vast oval. The ceiling, also straw, had a smoke hole in the center and there was an opening in one wall for a door.

He sat up, Sandy lay beside him asleep or unconscious; he wasn't sure which. The rest lay in other parts of the room.

What the hell's going on? He wondered grabbing his hat and slowly rising to a knee, then struggling to his feet.

The floor was dirt. There were no separate rooms, no kitchen, no fireplace and no bathroom. The building in which he stood was a single, open room with a door to one side. A circle of stones was on the floor under the smoke hole with a pile of burnt wood inside.

He looked at Sandy. Her breathing was regular and she looked peacefully at rest. He felt her pulse as Bear had taught him. It was full and regular, she didn't seem injured.

Without waking the others, He cautiously walked out of the building. Outside, he noticed a difference in the undergrowth. Trees rose from lush bushes with grass scattered throughout, but something was wrong. He looked closer and realized that the trees were different - many were palm trees. *There're no palm trees in Central Texas,* he thought. *They're further south, along the coast, in Florida and California.*

Sandy staggered from the door of the building. "What's all this?" She asked looking around. "What the hell's with the house?"

He looked at her and shrugged, "Your guess is as good as mine," he said. "I woke up and this is what I found."

"Damn, I've got a headache," Wind said from the door behind Sandy. "Where's Spyder?"

Hal looked at him, a blank look on his face. "What do you mean?"

"I mean Spyder's not in the house and I don't see him out here. Where the hell is he?"

Hal looked back into the room. "I didn't miss him until now," he said. "I'll see if I can find him as soon as I'm stable on my feet."

"I'd normally say not to worry," Sandy said. "But with the change around here, we need to start looking soon."

Wind stepped from the door and peered around. His mouth hung open as he stared at the change in landscape.

"Where the hell is Spyder?" Ginny asked emerging from the building.

"We were just discussing that," Sandy told her.

"He was gone when we got up," Hal explained. "But by the looks of the scenery, I think we need to find him soon."

Ginny looked around, "Where did the road go?" she asked.

"That's not all that's changed," Hal said. "Look at the plants. There are palm trees and look at the bushes around them, they have wide fronds."

"The flowers are larger and brighter," Sandy said as Hal walked to the end of the building.

As Hal rounded the corner, he saw Spyder on his horse in the distance. "Spyder's over here," he called to the others.

They watched as Spyder negotiated his way through trees and bushes before reaching them. "Bear's gone," he said dismounting. "Even the Bar-B-Q Shack is gone."

"Who gives a damn?" Ginny asked. "I suggest we worry about our own asses. He's a grown man and can take care of himself."

Spyder spun towards Ginny.

"No sign of him?" Wind asked before Spyder could speak.

"There's some tracks," Spyder said glaring at Ginny before looking at him. "But, I wanted to get back here before I followed 'em."

"Wind you, Sandy and Ginny stay here. I'll saddle up and we'll see if we can follow him," Hal said.

While Hal saddled his horse, Spyder gathered food. "We may be gone for a couple of hours," he said. "All of you stay close and eat something. There's some weird shit going on here." He added a box of ammo to the supplies. "Wind, keep your rifle with you."

As Hal rode up, Spyder tossed him a bag. "Food," he said.

Hal nodded and tied the bag to his saddle horn. "We won't be gone too long," he said. "We should be back around noon."

"Be careful," Sandy implored.

"We'll get things ready here," Ginny said. Under her breath, she added, "Go find Bear and don't worry about us.

Wind looked at the men and nodded. He understood that once again, the rules of life might have changed overnight. He didn't know how or why and it didn't matter right now. Until they fully understood their current situation, he needed to stay on guard.

***

Hal and Spyder rode to where the restaurant previously stood. All they found were tracks from Bear's horse, which led in the direction of Rebel's Revenge.

There was no road or even a path for them to follow, the tracks disappeared into the woods and dense underbrush.

"Surely Bear knew something was wrong," Hal said.

"He knew things were wrong," Spyder assured him. "But, he didn't know we were in the area. Now, he's heading back to where he last saw people. If we don't want to travel all the way back to Rebel's Revenge, we have to catch up with him."

Hal nodded and urged his horse forward. The two men followed the tracks through tall leafy trees with short plants consisting of bougainvillea, Spanish needle and many others impairing their progress. Some, they recognized from Bear's herbal books while others were foreign.

"Very few of these plants grow in Texas," Spyder observed. "Most of them are from more tropical climates."

"I noticed that," Hal said. "I've got a feeling we need to get ready to accept another change, probably something just as global as loosing electricity was."

"This is more than losing electricity," Spyder countered. "This is a complete change of the land. Not to mention the temperature."

"You noticed too, huh?" Hal said with a grin.

"I'd guess the temperature is in the middle seventies, and it's early. It'll probably get up into the eighties or nineties by afternoon."

"Did you see or feel anything last night?" Hal asked searching for some sort of cause for the change.

"Not after I went to bed," Spyder answered. "I slept like a log."

"Me too," Hal agreed. "Between stress and being bone tired, I slept hard. I think we all needed it."

"But to sleep through something that could change the land itself? I can't imagine that," Spyder said shaking his head and urging his horse through thick foliage.

"Hold it a second," Hal said stopping his horse.

"What's wrong?" Spyder turned his mount to face him.

"Listen," he answered.

"To what?"

"Just listen a second," he insisted. From the distance, came the faint sound of surf. "Do you hear that?" He asked a few seconds later.

"I hear something," Spyder confirmed. "But, there's no way it's what I think it is. There's no ocean around here."

"Smell the air," Hal said.

"Salt," he said. "This is bullshit Hal," he growled digging his spurs into his horse.

Forgetting the tracks, he urged the animal toward the sound of waves, to emerge from the thick brush into a grove of palm trees. Some of the trees, with coconuts hanging in bunches, were straight and tall while others angled skyward, growing from pure white sand. To Spyder, the scene was as pretty as any picture he'd ever seen.

The beach stretched a half mile to his right and disappeared, curving out of sight. A pile of rocks to his left jutted from the shore into the sea producing the sound they heard. Otherwise, the waves smoothly washed up on the gently sloping beach.

Hal rode up beside him eating a banana.

"Where the hell did you get that?" Spyder asked.

"You rode right past a bunch hanging from a tree," he answered holding one out. "Want one? There's also some berry bushes back there."

"Hell no I don't want one," Spyder snorted. "I wanna know what's going on here."

"So do I," Hal answered taking another bite, "but no sense in letting fresh fruit go to waste."

Spyder climbed from his horse and tied its reins to a bush. Walking to the edge of the palm trees, he looked up and down the beach. The sand was smooth, with no footprints except his own, to disturb the pristine surface. The sun reflected off the white sand, and in no time, Spyder, still wearing his duster, began overheating. "Goddamn it's gettin' hot," he said pulling the duster off and taking it back to his horse.

"White sand'll do that every time," Hal answered. He had dismounted and was tethering his horse to a tree. "So far, there's a change in the land and a climate shift," he said. "Either that or we were picked up and moved during the night."

"Oh come on, Hal," Spyder argued. "You think something or someone picked us up in the night and transplanted us somewhere?"

"I don't know," Hal answered. "I'm sure this ain't Texas and we're here. Something happened. That's all I know for sure."

"We need to find Bear and then get back to the others," Spyder said. "We don't need to be trapped away from them."

"I think you're right about that," Hal agreed. "Actually, I... "

"I'm right here," a voice said from behind them. They spun around and Bear stood inside the edge of the trees taking a bite of fruit.

***

Keith, Amanda and Dr. Hamilton were on their horses riding south after having awakened in a grass hut of some sort. Outside, their horses wondered around with no barn in sight. They hurriedly gathered and packed the animals. Fortunately, the wagon was still where they left it and still packed for all the good it did them. They had to leave it behind, since there was no longer a road near the house, and they had to travel on horseback. They could return for it later after finding out what was going on. The only thing they knew to do was return to Rebel's Revenge and see if anyone knew what had happened.

Keith took the lead, Amanda followed next and Dr. Hamilton was last in line. They had only traveled a couple of minutes when Dr. Hamilton called for them to stop and Keith and Amanda turned their horses to face him.

"Look around you," he said. "What do you see?"

"It's not just what I see that bothers me," Keith answered. "It's what I don't see as well. Like we talked about back there," he motioned the way they had come with his head, "there's no road, the house is completely changed and there's no barn."

"Hold on a second," the doctor said. "I don't know any more than you, but look around. What do you see?"

"Trees," Keith answered the statement a little more harsh than he meant it to.

"What kind of trees?" Dr. Hamilton pressed ignoring the tone.

Before he could say anything, Amanda said, "I see what you mean doctor. These are Koa trees."

Keith closed his mouth and looked at his surroundings. She was right. He recognized them from the herbal classes Bear had held. "Koa doesn't grow in Texas," Keith stated flatly.

"You're right." Dr. Hamilton reached out, plucked a leaf and looked at it. "I don't know what, but something's happened. What was a house is now a grass hut. The road in front of it is gone." After a second's hesitation he continued, "Smell the air - feel the air. What's different about it?"

"It's hot," Keith said exasperated.

"Keith," Amanda urged soothingly, "put your training to work. Use your senses."

Keith opened his mouth to argue and closed it. If Amanda wanted him to calm down, he would. He closed his eyes and let his mind and muscles relax. Using a technique Bear had taught him, he brought his senses to the forefront of his attention.

Keith became a student of Bear's after arriving at Rebel's Revenge. Even though the young man had his black belt in karate, he had been willing to learn from Bear who was a master in the arts. In his classes, he had learned the internal aspects of martial arts as well as ways to apply them in his life. Because of this, he learned that the physical part of the art was only a minor element of everything he could learn and achieve if he kept an open mind.

Relaxed, with a clear mind, he identified differences in his surroundings. The air was warmer and heavier. It also felt softer. He could smell the salt of ocean air, also the sweetness of fruit and fragrances of the flowers around him. The birds in the trees were different. Their calls and squawks were nothing he had heard in Texas. Then he recognized a sound in the distance. As incredible as it was, he heard surf. He had only heard it in movies, never in person, but he was sure it was the same sound.

He opened his eyes. He looked first at Amanda, then at the doctor. "We're on a tropical coast of some sort. We'll never find Rebel's Revenge even if we do keep going south. It doesn't exist."

"What do you mean it doesn't exist?" Amanda asked.

"I don't know," he admitted. "We've either been transported to another planet or Earth has been completely changed."

"Let's not get carried away" Dr. Hamilton warned. "I doubt we're on another planet."

"Then how do you explain what's happened?" Amanda pressed.

"I can't," the doctor admitted. "It *is* possible we've been transported somewhere else, but I doubt it. It makes more sense that the world has changed somehow."

"How does that make more sense?" Amanda asked. I'm surprised that you would even entertain *either* possibility.

"Look at it this way," he explained. "Which is the most plausible possibility? A superior race picked us out of billions of people and transported us to another solar system, or some other change has happened. Something happened before, when we lost electricity. Something, an anomaly in space, a dimensional shift or something else we don't know about, changed our world. We may never understand it, who knows?" His gaze swept the area around him. "Who cares for that matter? Something else has happened and we have to accept it. We either learn to live with it or go crazy."

"Okay," Keith said, "we weren't picked out of billions of people and moved, I agree that's not realistic. But are you saying we should just accept what's happened and go along with it?"

"Can you change it?" The doctor asked.

Keith simply stared at him.

"I'll take that as a no," he said. "If it's out of our control, we either accept it or don't. Which do you want to do? Do you want to deny that it's happened?"

Keith looked uncomfortable. He couldn't deny what was happening, but his youth demanded an explanation. Besides, the doctor was sounding like Bear now. "No, it's happening," he said.

"Maybe something in the future will explain it, but for now, we need to accept and cope."

"Where do we go then, doctor?" Amanda asked.

"I'm no more the leader than anyone else," he answered. "Where do the two of you want to go?"

"South for a while," Keith said swiveling in his saddle to look around, "or toward the water."

"What water?" Amanda asked.

"There's water to the east," he answered. "It's a large body, either an ocean or a huge lake. From the smell, it's an ocean."

She nodded. "Is south okay with you doctor?"

"I have nowhere else to be at the moment," he said with a smile. "I'll follow your lead. Besides, the last time we saw people, they were that direction."

He was right. The last people they had seen were at Rebel's Revenge. They turned their horses southeast. If Rebel's Revenge no longer existed, maybe some of their friends were, at least, in that direction.

34

CHAPTER FOUR

When Hal left to get Wind, Sandy and Ginny, Bear took a blanket, from behind his saddle on Dusty and spread it on the ground. He searched through the vegetation picking fruits and berries, which he tossed on the blanket.

"Never figured you for a berry picker," Spyder said with a grin.

"Hell, wait until you see me as a fisherman," Bear answered grinning back.

"I could eat me some fish," Spyder mused.

"Then I'll get the fruits and berries while you get the fish," Bear suggested.

"I don't have any line to fish with."

"Okay," Bear said, "you pick the bushes clean and I'll fish."

"I don't know what's dangerous and what's not," Spyder answered sitting on the sand. "You're the one who knows that."

"You're not much good for anything then are you," Bear said matter-of-factly.

"That's what I got you for," Spyder said clasping his hands behind his head and crossing his legs. He leaned against the base of a palm tree and relaxed. "Let me know when you've got something to cook." There was enough shade that it felt warm but not too hot.

"That's fine," Bear answered. "But I'd be careful of the ants."

"What ants," Spyder asked pulling his hat down over his eyes.

"The ones on those coconut palms," Bear said. "Those trees are ant magnets."

Spyder sat up, looked at the tree and immediately started swatting at his clothes. The animals marched in lines up the trees and back down again, carrying food to their homes in the ground. When Spyder blocked that progress, the ants detoured onto his clothes.

"Goddamn," he yelled. "Bear get these things off me."

"Get in the water," Bear called back.

Spyder slapped and danced around trying to dislodge the ants from his clothing. There weren't many on him, but it was the one animal he couldn't stand.

"Get in the water," Bear repeated. "Salt water washes 'em off and kills 'em."

Before Bear could tell him to take his weapons off, he ran to and dove into the water. Surfacing, he sputtered and spit, searching his clothing. He looked at Bear. "Are you sure it kills 'em?" he asked.

"Yup," Bear answered. "It kills 'em quick." He hesitated; "Of course, I'm not sure what's in the water. With all the changes, there may be some sort of sea-monster in there or the water itself might not even be safe."

Spyder ran, as quick as all his weaponry and wet clothing would allow, to the shore. "Bear, you son-of-a-bitch, I could have been killed. Something could've got me or I could've drowned."

Bear tossed more berries on the blanket. "As long as you didn't go in over your head, I figured you were okay. You could walk back."

"Kiss my ass," Spyder snorted. "I'd shoot you here and now if I didn't think you could help us later."

Bear looked back at him seriously. "You mean you'd shoot me over that?" His hand moved down to his pistol.

Spyder finally stomped completely out of the water and stood on the beach. "Bear," he said, "we don't need a problem here. I won't back down from ya - you know that. But, we need to talk this thing out."

"What're ya gonna do?" Bear asked. "Are you honestly threatening to shoot me?"

"I don't want to," Spyder said. "I honestly think we can work this out without bloodshed."

"Good," Bear answered. "I'd hate to shoot a man with wet powder. He grinned and returned to the bushes for another load of berries.

Spyder realized he'd been had. Bear had gotten the ants off him, got a laugh and, at the same time, rendered his pistols on his hips useless. The powder in the weapons would be soaked. "Bear, you can kiss my ass twice," he said and stomped over to his horse for dry powder.

He's lucky I think of him as a brother, Spyder thought. Then a realization struck him. *We're lucky he's with us. He's been in a tropical setting before. That's why he knew about the ants. He was just fucking with me after that.* Spyder shook his head as he emptied and reloaded his pistols. *We're gonna need him. He fought in jungles and on islands in the military.* Spyder put his reloading supplies away. *Glad he's with us. But I'll get even with the son-of-a-bitch for this, sooner or later.*

"Yo Spyder," the yell came from the trees.

Hal was back with the others and Spyder felt a wave of relief. The group was no longer apart. If

37

something else happened to this reality, at least they would all be together.

"Where's Bear?" Hal asked.

"The motherfucker's over there," Spyder pointed to the trees where he previously stood. He was gone and only the blanket partially covered in berries and fruit remained.

"Oh hell," Spyder said, "he's probably out getting a vegetarian diet for us to eat.

Wind, Sandy and Ginny followed Hal to the edge of the trees and dismounted. "I love the beach," Sandy said. I don't know what happened, but I'm not complaining about the location."

"That's true," Hal agreed, "and if a storm blows up, we can go back to the shack. It's only about two miles, but that should put us far enough away to be safe."

"So would our shack," a voice came from the tree line to the north.

Everyone turned toward the sound and Spyder pulled a pistol. Keith rode his horse from the bushes, followed by Amanda and Dr. Hamilton.

Spyder re-holstered the weapon as he and the others erupted in a chorus of greetings and hurried toward them.

When things finally subsided, Hal said, "We didn't know who all was involved in this. So far, it's just been us, except for Bear, he's out there somewhere."

"We know, he pointed us this way," Keith said. "I don't know where he is now, but he got us to you."

Finding other survivors provided a release for emotions and everyone continued hugging and shaking hands. It seemed, some of Rebel's Revenge had survived another change and were together once again.

Dr. Hamilton explained what happened after they went to sleep the night before. Hal confirmed that their experience was essentially the same. No one had any idea what had happened, just theories. Everything was different, the birds, foliage, climate and countryside.

In the distance, they heard a gunshot followed by two more in rapid succession. "Maybe he's getting something other than berries and fruits," Spyder suggested hopefully.

"I've always told you I didn't have to worry about him shooting me," Hal said grinning at Sandy. "Whatever he shot at was probably only ten feet away and it took three shots to hit it." Hal hesitated, "I only hope he didn't shoot his horse by accident. I like Dusty."

I'm gonna take a look around," Keith said. "I'll be back in a couple of hours."

"Would you like some company?" Amanda asked.

"Not right now," he answered. "I'd rather you be with the others until we figure out what's going on."

"I'm not sure you should go off on your own," Hal said. "I know you can take care of yourself, but still... "

"I'll be okay," Keith assured him. "I won't be gone long."

Amanda nodded, she understood. She might be a little over protective, but it was because he cared and worried about her. She stood on her tiptoes and kissed him. "See ya in a little while then."

Keith smiled at her, placed his hand on her cheek, then mounted his horse and disappeared into the trees.

***

Keith rode toward a steep cliff about a half mile to the south. The cliff, the closest of many, rose at least five hundred feet straight up. The sides were green, covered with lush foliage. It reminded him of pictures he had seen of islands in the Caribbean and exotic tropical locations in the Pacific.

Without guidance, his horse picked its way through the thick brush with ease. It was almost as if the animal enjoyed the bushes running along its sides, massaging its skin. The horse broke into an opening and he noticed a path running away from it toward the cliff.

He dismounted and tied his horse to a tree. Following the path on foot, he searched for tracks. The trail, carpeted with grass and leaves, led to a sandy area a short distance away. There he saw footprints - human footprints.

Tracks clearly showed that humans and animals used the path. The animal tracks crossed while the humans traveled along it. Keith inspected at the animal prints to see what might have made them. Only one caught his attention. The sand was soft, and prevented identification since the sides had collapsed and partially filled them. However, he thought it was some kind of large reptile. It looked something as he imagined an alligator print would look.

It can't be an alligator, he thought. *There's no track for the tail, and the print is way too big.*

The print was not only big, but deep as well. Whatever produced it was massive and heavy. On closer inspection, he found that it traveled on four legs.

Feeling a little uneasy with the discovery, he returned to his horse. After mounting, he continued along the path a little more cautiously, eventually reaching the base of the cliff. The land he traveled, while covered in thick foliage, was level and the base of the small mountain sharply jutted toward the ocean in the distance.

Riding around the point of the cliff, he saw a tall, narrow waterfall. Water cascaded from the rocks high above into a clear pool below. Keith again dismounted and led his horse to the edge of the water.

He could see the bottom, which looked about ten feet deep. The water was crystal clear and ran into a small stream that continued toward the sea. Keith bent down and tasted the clear cool liquid. It seemed fresh and clean. However, he knew Dr. Hamilton would have to check it properly. If it were good, they would have all the fresh water they needed.

He searched the edge of the pool and found another path leading off in a different direction. He also located another clearing about twenty yards wide. *Maybe we can set up camp here.*

Remounting his horse, he rode toward the ocean.

***

Hal looked up as Bear dismounted and tied Dusty's lead rope to a tree. As he walked across the beach, Hal called to him. "Did you bring us some meat?"

"Nothing to eat," Bear answered. "But you might be interested in what I found."

"Whatcha got?" Spyder asked.

"A big cat," Bear said.

"A big cat?" Hal questioned. "You mean like a mountain lion?"

"Something like that," he confirmed, "but a little more interesting."

"What're you talking about?" Hal asked.

"Let's see the damn thing," Spyder said before Bear could answer.

Everyone followed him toward his horse. "It's back in the bushes a little way," he said. "Dusty wasn't too happy being around it."

A short distance into the brush, they saw a tarp with a rope attached. Bear had dragged the carcass wrapped in the tarp to keep from tearing it up.

As the rest approached, Bear took his canteen from his shoulder, unscrewed the cap and drank deeply. He recapped the container and slung it over his head and shoulder. He pushed his hat back off his head. Its stampede string looped around his neck held it against his back.

"Before you look at this thing," he said. "You'd better get ready for another reality check."

"What sort of reality check?" Sandy asked.

42

Bear looked at each of them in turn. "Do you remember when you studied world history in school? Do you all remember the saber-toothed tiger?"

"Bullshit," Spyder snorted, drawing the word out. "Are you trying to tell us you have an animal from prehistoric times in that?"

"Let's open this up," he said reaching for the tarp. "Then, you can tell me what it is."

They untied the rope wrapped around the bundle. After unraveling it, they pulled the flaps back exposing an animal. Lying on the tarp was a large mountain lion. It was light brown, with massive paws, a long tail and its face partially buried under its chest.

Bear pulled the head up. It was a mountain lion all right. However, protruding from each side of its mouth was a curved fang. The teeth were at least ten inches long, curved and tapered to points.

The group stood in silence - dumbfounded.

"I was riding Dusty, checking the area out," he explained. "There're pine trees to the northwest."

Amanda nodded. "We saw some on our way here."

Bear continued. "I was in the trees about five minutes when Dusty became skittish. We stopped and I saw something moving through a clearing. It was brown and moving fast and quiet. I pulled the M16 and waited. If it was a cat, and I thought it was, you don't want to try to track it. You'll only become the hunted."

"You got that right," Spyder said confirming the statement.

"A couple of minutes later, the cat came at me from the side. I hit it in the chest the first shot, but it kept coming, so I put two in its head, and it dropped like a rock."

"You're lucky," Hal said. "If you'd missed or it was closer, you might be dead."

Bear nodded. He failed to mention that the cat had dropped less than three feet from him and Dusty. He knew how lucky he was, but he didn't see any reason to lend more fear or nervousness to the situation. It was more than enough that they had no idea where they were and a prehistoric animal was laying on the ground before them.

They heard Keith calling from the beach.

"We're here," Amanda called out and started back.

"The rest of you go on with her," Hal said. "Bear and I'll take care of this."

When the others disappeared toward the beach, Bear looked at Hal. "Take care of this? What do you want to do with it?"

"I just wanted them gone," Hal answered.

Bear nodded. He figured that was the man's intentions.

"Does any of this seem familiar to you?"

Bear shook his head. "Nothing more than we're in a tropical environment, near an ocean or sea. The hills and mountains look like they're formed by volcanoes and the foliage is from almost any tropical setting in the world. Why do you ask?"

"No real reason," he answered. "I was just hoping you could possibly identify the region."

Hal stroked his beard thoughtfully and Bear ran his hand through his own long hair. He could make no more sense of the situation than Hal. They pulled one side of the tarp upward and the animal rolled from it. After folding the canvass, they silently returned to the beach, each lost in thought.

***

The rest sat on the sand, listening to Keith, when Bear and Hal walked up. "There's enough fresh water that we'll never go thirsty," he said. "That is, if it's okay to drink. Dr. Hamilton'll have to test it." He looked at the doctor. "You do still have the equipment to test the water don't you, Doc?"

"It's back at the wagon," he answered. "If we bring the supplies here, I can test it."

"I don't see how we'll get the wagon through all that," Keith said nodding at the tangled brush.

"We can't," Bear said. "We'll have to haul it on horseback. In fact, we'll have to haul all the stuff from both locations that way."

"We have enough horses to get everything from your wagon in one trip," Hal suggested. "You said we can reach the waterfall from the beach, right?"

"Right," Keith nodded.

Before Hal could say anything, Bear rose, pulled his stampede string and placed his hat on his head.

"Before everyone gets away," Keith said. "With all the excitement over the cat, I forgot to mention that I saw some tracks on a trail not far from here."

"What kinda tracks?" Bear asked.

"Well, I saw a bunch of animal tracks," he explained. "But I also saw human footprints in some sand."

45

"Human!" Spyder exclaimed. "... and you forgot to tell us?"

"When Bear came back with the... "

"Never mind," Hal interrupted. "There's a lot going on. Anyone could've forgotten."

"Besides the human footprints, I saw another track," Keith said. "I couldn't tell what it was, but whatever made it was big and heavy. I know it sounds silly, but it looked like something an alligator might make."

"An alligator?" Spyder questioned.

"I didn't say it *was* an alligator," Keith explained. "I said it looked something like what one might make. I've never seen an alligator track before. I've also never seen anything like this either. The problem is that there wasn't any sign of a tail dragging. It was strange."

"That's strange alright," Hal agreed. "I don't doubt that you found something, but I don't think it would be an alligator."

"Why not," Sandy protested. "We have no idea where we are. Why couldn't there be alligators?"

"It's just a feeling," Keith said.

Hal stroked his beard thinking. Looking at Spyder he said, "Ya know she may have something there. How the hell do I know what made the tracks?"

"We need to get going if we're gonna get those supplies," Wind said.

"You're right," Bear agreed. He was obviously ready to get moving. "We can figure the rest out later."

"Sandy, Amanda, Ginny and Wind should go with Keith to the waterfall," Hal said. "You can go

46

on foot along the beach. When you turn toward the mountains, mark your trail. We'll come back that way and follow it until we find you. Sorry, but we're gonna need all the horses to carry the supplies."

No one argued with the suggestion. It was the quickest way to get everything back. Bear lay the tarp out and said, "Put all the saddles on this. The horses need to be bareback. Keith, leave your horse saddled. Tie a couple of ropes from the tarp to the saddle horn and drag it on the sand."

Keith grinned wishing he had thought of the idea. His respect for Bear grew daily and he wanted to learn everything he could from the man. He was learning, but he also knew he had a long way to go.

When all the saddles, and what few supplies they had, were loaded on the tarp, Keith led the horse, accompanied by the women and Wind, down the beach. The rest of the men headed out to retrieve the supplies with Dr. Hamilton leading the way. They had to hurry if they were to get back before dark.

***

The men located the supplies, loaded them on the extra horses and return about thirty minutes before sunset. They traveled along the beach until they came across three branches stuck in the sand with palm fronds fluttering from their tops.

"Leave it to Keith," Bear said. "He's using his wits."

"You know he looks up to you," Spyder said.

"I hope he looks higher than that," Bear answered. "He's got more potential than any of us give him credit for."

They turned and entered the brush, traveling toward the rocky point of the cliffs. Keith had said they needed go to the right of that point.

"It's a shame we can't give him more of an education," Dr. Hamilton said. "He absorbs information like a sponge."

"We may not have the books, but we all have different knowledge," Hal said. "There's no reason we can't give it to him subtly."

"It's something to think about," Bear agreed. "I still have some of the Traditional Chinese Medicine and Naturopathic medical books."

"There are algebra, chemistry and two general medical books in my saddlebags," Dr. Hamilton offered.

"Doc, you're something else," Spyder said. "Everything falls down around your ears and you still keep educational material around. I can understand Bear having them, he hasn't been at it as long as you, but you know all this."

"I have to keep up with things," Dr. Hamilton told him. "My memory isn't what it used to be." He smiled and followed the others toward the waterfall.

CHAPTER FIVE

Night veiled the area beneath the high cliffs and the stars twinkled brightly overhead. Through the opening in the trees, Sandy watched as they came out one by one. The rest of the camp was set up and Dr. Hamilton declared the water safe to drink.

"In fact," he said, "it could actually be good for you. I haven't run proper tests, but from what I've found, there're minerals and nutrients in it that will supplement your food intake." Since the water ran flowed from the pool into a small stream, they could swim in the pool and bathe in the stream.

"Hal," Sandy called to her husband.

"Whatcha got?" he asked looking over where she lay.

"We're on Earth."

"How can you possibly know we're still on Earth?" Hal asked in a teasing voice. He understood she might have some information, but at the same time, he wanted to keep everyone's feelings upbeat. There was no need for more stress than they were already under.

"I'm looking at Orion," she said sitting up pointing.

Hal looked up. He didn't know the sky that well, but he had no problem recognizing the three stars forming Orion's Belt. "Outstanding Hon," he almost shouted. He looked down at the others to tell them what Sandy had discovered and found them all looking up as well.

"She's right," Wind said. "It's Earth."

"Exactly where on Earth, I don't know," Dr. Hamilton said. "But, we're still on the same planet."

"Folks, it's only stew and a little bread," Ginny announced. "But if you're hungry, it should fill you up."

The whole camp rose in unison. Ginny was one of the best cooks any of them had ever encountered, even her stew was a delight and would be a full meal.

The rest of the evening had a lighter feel to it. At least one mystery was behind them; they were still on Earth and hadn't been carted off by little green men and deposited on some distant body in the universe. None of them had actually considered that a viable possibility. Still, they weren't when or where they were supposed to be.

"We have to post watches," Bear announced.

"What for," Wind asked. "There aren't any mutants around we have to worry about."

"None we know about," Sandy corrected.

You're right," he admitted. "I forgot the cat bear killed. Shoot, mutants might be the least of our worries." He looked around at the faces of his friends. "Sorry, I didn't mean to cause more concern."

"You're right," Bear agreed. "We're near a fresh water supply and it may be used by the animals in this area. This place could be like a watering hole in the desert and we may get visitors during the night."

"Damn, he's right," Spyder agreed. "I hadn't thought about that."

"We need to keep watch just in case," Bear explained. "The person on watch doesn't need to raise an alarm unless something comes toward the camp.

The rest looked skeptical.

50

If it's a watering hole," he continued, "there is no telling what kind of animals will visit here. Some may be peaceful while others might be carnivores."

After agreeing to a watch schedule, the rest of the camp settled in for a night's sleep. It had been a long day and everyone needed rest. Engulfed by the warmth of the night, everyone was asleep in minutes.

***

Bear took the four to eight shift. He sat on a fallen tree trunk half way between the camp and the waterfall. Hal had awakened him and reported only a few animals moving around the area. Some were near the water and others out farther away from the camp.

Bear could hear a light breeze blowing through the trees, a sound that felt calming and comforting as it wrapped itself around his body. It reminded him of better times when he lived in Hawaii years before. He was married back then and times were easier. The work was easy and afforded plenty of time off.

Sitting on the log, listening to the breeze and the waterfall in the distance, almost allowed him to relax. He knew he needed to let his stress drain away, but until they were sure of their circumstances and surroundings, he would keep his guard up.

He recognized the call of most of the birds and the buzz of the night dwelling insects. The sounds, smells and feel of the surroundings indicated that this land was much as he had seen before in Hawaii and places in the West Indies.

He heard a loud thump in the distance and recognized it as a coconut falling from a tree. *I'll have to remember to warn the others about those.*

Something moved through the brush a short distance away. In a couple of seconds, he heard a grunt as the animal ran off. *Wild boar,* he thought. *We have meat on the hoof - Kalua Pig would be nice. At least we haven't seen any signs of mutants.*

His thoughts drifted to Davata. He remembered seeing a vision of her at her funeral. She was pregnant when she was senselessly killed. At the funeral, he saw a vision of her holding the hand of a young girl, her unborn daughter, as clear as if they had really been standing before him. Davata mouthed the words, "I love you," and walked upward as if on invisible stairs and disappeared.

Hal said it was the result of an overworked mind. Sandy simply smiled and nodded. She never questioned what Bear had seen. "God allows people to see what they needed to," She had said. "It was obvious you needed to see her again - to know she was at peace."

That sight, even if imagined, had eased some of the pain of losing her. Sandy was the closest thing he had to family and accepted him as he was. Davata was the same way. The two women had given him the closest thing to unconditional love he had ever experienced.

Bear rose and walked to the pool at the base of the waterfall. To the side, he saw a deer, its head down, drinking. The water pouring into the pool fell in a stream more than fifteen feet across and the curtain shimmered in the moonlight. *At least this world is at peace,* he thought. *I just wish we could be.*

A faint scream in the distance brought him back to reality. It was the sound of a mountain lion. *Probably one of those saber-toothed tigers.* It echoed again sounding almost human. Then the night fell silent again. The deer looked from side to side, took another drink and bounded away, satisfied for the night.

He wandered back through camp and then toward the ocean. The brush was thick, but they had made a path dragging their supplies to the camp. Another coconut fell and something moved quickly through the bushes. Whatever it was, was large, low and moved fast. The rustle of bushes indicated that the animal moved toward the ocean.

Bear increased to a trot until reaching the edge of the beach. In the light of the full moon, he saw a shadow slip into the water. The animal was huge. He waited silently for five minutes, but it didn't reappear.

It's amphibious, he thought. *Great, just what we need -another problem. It has to be what made the tracks Keith found. It's not only big, but fast as hell.*

He hurried back to the camp. The people sleeping there might be in more danger than any of them realized. Guards would have to be extra watchful. Things had just become a bit more complicated.

***

53

Ginny was the first to awake. She rose and stretched. Bear recognized her momentary disorientation and then she seemed to remember what had taken place and where they were. Almost as if everything was normal, she picked up a couple of pieces of wood and placed them on the fire he had started earlier.

Picking up a large coffee pot, she noticed him standing at the edge of the clearing. "Morning," she said. "I'll get some water for coffee."

He nodded at her and smiled, "Sounds good Ginny. I don't think there's any danger, but take a pistol with you."

She reached down, picked up a pistol and put it in her belt as she left for the waterfall. It was obvious that she did it only to keep the peace and not because she thought it necessary.

Bear knew she still had a problem with him. When they were in college together, he refused to let her cheat off his test once and she didn't seem to have gotten over it. It still seemed to be an underlying problem, hiding in the background, when they had dealings.

Their brief conversation was enough to rouse the rest of the camp. They all began their individual morning rituals. Some sat up and stretched, while others stood and walked around. "Gotta get the blood flowing," Spyder said. "Where's Ginny?"

"She's at the waterfall," Bear answered, "getting water for coffee."

"That's my little teacup," Spyder said. "I'll see if she needs some help."

As he left to join Ginny, Hal asked Bear, "Was it quiet after I left?"

"Yeah," he answered. "But there's something strange running around."

"A mutant?" Hal guessed.

"I don't know," Bear said honestly. "If you don't mind, I'll wait and tell everyone together. Let's all get some coffee and wake up first."

Hal understood, nodded and unconsciously checked the position of the pistols on his hips. Amanda passed by, walking away from the stream. "I don't mean to be crude, but we'll have to set up a bathroom area over there," she said pointing the way she was heading. "Dr. Hamilton says it needs to be away from the stream and our water source."

"Everyone's made it second nature to think of the group," Hal commented looking at Bear.

"We're still relying on each other," he replied. "We all still need each other."

"Everyone except you," Keith said from behind them. Stepping up he continued, "You can take care of yourself. I haven't seen anything you can't handle."

Bear knew the young man was trying to pay him a compliment, but he couldn't allow the misunderstanding. "Keith," he said, "I'm probably the one who needs the rest of you the most."

Keith looked shocked. "But you... "

"It was once written that no man's an island unto himself," Bear interrupted. "Nothing could be truer in a situation like this."

"I understand the saying," Keith countered. "I simply meant that you could survive without any of our help."

"What kind of survival would that be?" he asked. "What kind of life would I have without the rest of you? Sure, I can find food and water. I can make clothes and gather herbs for medicine." He looked around at the others, "But what good is all that if I'm only doing it for myself? Who would help me when I hurt inside? Who would tell me when I'd made a mistake? Who'd help me keep my humanity?"

Keith was stunned. He'd never thought of the man like this. Bear had always known what to do when a situation arose. Sure, he had needed help when the militia had shot him, but that was different.

"Keith, I want you to think about something."

"Sure," the young man answered.

"You understand that the ocean is made up of countless water particles grouped together, right?"

"Right," Keith said. "They're all combined to make a single mass of water."

"Just as the ocean is made up of different water particles," Bear continued, "each particle of water is made up of an ocean."

Keith's confidence slipped to confusion.

Bear smiled and placed his hand on the young man's shoulder. "Let me know when you've figured it out."

Bear and Hal walked off leaving Keith to consider what he had just heard.

"That's a hard lesson to learn in the beginning," Hal said.

"It's a lesson that could take a lifetime," Bear answered. "But, it's worth pondering."

As the men approached Sandy, she looked at Bear, smiled and said, "I see you've started teaching

Keith. Hal told me about your discussion yesterday."

"Good," he answered. "Keith's a good person. But, he has to learn with his heart and not just his head."

"Amanda can help with that," Sandy suggested. "He's close to her and she cares about him."

"That's a good idea," Bear agreed.

"Talk to her and see what she's willing to do," Hal recommended. "Just remember, we can overload him and that'd be a real problem."

Sandy smiled. "It'll be okay, she's good at teaching without preaching and he'll listen to her."

Wind came running into the clearing. "You gotta come see this," he said panting. He wore cut-offs, was wet and must have been swimming in the pool at the base of the falls.

CHAPTER SIX

With everyone at the waterfall, Wind dove in and swam to where the falls plunged into the pool. Choosing his hand and footholds carefully, he pulled himself up into the cascade. Almost instantly disappearing behind the curtain the water created. "Can you hear me?" they heard him call from behind the falls.

"There's a space behind the waterfall," Bear surmised. He started removing his weapons and clothing.

"You want some music while you do that?" Hal asked grinning. The man had a contagious smile, which was hard to resist.

Bear grinned back. "Anything but you singing," he said.

Hal, actually a very good singer, sang regularly at the community-gathering place when Rebel's Revenge still existed. "Well, I would. But, you're almost ready to go and I don't want to waste my voice on something like that." He said flicking a backhand at Bear dismissively.

Bear wore only boxer shorts, the rest of his clothes and weapons were in a pile near the water. He jumped in and swam to the base of the waterfall. Finding handholds on the slippery rocks was difficult. However, after a few tries, he too disappeared behind the falls.

As he surfaced near the falls and searched for a way to climb out of the water, Hal grinned, "Hope his shorts stayed on. We don't need a moon under the falls."

Sandy grinned back. "Don't worry," she said. "He can't put my man to shame."

Hal only shook his head still smiling.

Behind the falls was a dimly lit cavern. Bear could see around the room aided by the sunlight filtering through the water.

"Wind," he called looking for the young man.

"Over here," Wind answered. "Watch your footing. It's slippery."

He walked a few paces and found a tunnel to his left with a shaft of light a few feet further in. "Where are you Wind?" He called again.

"Just past the light," Wind answer.

Walking cautiously forward and inspecting the walls as he did, he figured the tunnel probably formed as the result of an ancient volcanic eruption. The walls were lava, all pocked with sharp edges surrounding small depressions. The floor seemed relatively smooth though, the sharp edges reduced, probably scoured by earth and water over time.

Then, stepping into the light, he looked up. Above him rose another shaft, about four feet in diameter and at least a hundred feet long, which allowed light into the cave. Stepping past the light, he found Wind standing in a cavernous room.

"There's more," Wind said. "But, it's too dark to go any further."

Bear looked around at the room. It was at least thirty feet long and twenty across. The ceiling was ten to fifteen feet high. The floor was dry and as smooth as the one he used to get here.

"Looks like we've got a place to set up home," Wind said.

"We need to search the rest before doing that," was all Bear said.

"But we can get in out of the weather, if it gets bad," Wind argued.

"We'll talk about it outside," Bear answered, turning he returned to the front of the cave.

"Of course it's not good enough," Wind mumbled to himself. "I found it."

Bear ignored the comment and disappeared past the shaft of light.

When Wind reached the opening, he had entered the water and swam away from the falls. Wind dove in and reached the other side shortly after him.

Bear picked up his things and strode toward the clearing. The rest asked questions, which he ignored. Upon reaching the camp, he dried off on a piece of cloth, dressed and was strapping on his pistols when Sandy walked up.

"What's wrong?" She asked.

"Nothing's wrong," he answered.

"I know you better than that," she insisted. "You and Wind disappeared behind a waterfall; you come out and ignore the rest of us. That's not like you."

"It has nothing to do with the rest of you." He looked around and took a deep breath. "I'm claustrophobic," he admitted. "Once I got inside, the place started closing in on me; I felt trapped and had to get out. There's a room that's large enough for us in bad weather. But, I couldn't stay long enough to check it out. Maybe Wind can tell us more. I don't know."

"I understand," she said. "I hate heights."

The rest entered the camp with Wind excitedly explaining what he'd found interrupted their conversation. As the rest gathered around the campfire, Wind told of the space behind the waterfall.

"The room's huge," he said. "It could hold all of us with no problem. We could pack all the supplies in there and still have room for everyone. There's also another passage to the back, but there's no light. I didn't want to go any further in case there was a hole in the floor. I don't need to fall down some crevice and kill myself."

"What do you think Bear," Hal asked.

"I'm not sure," he answered. "I didn't get a good look at it."

"Bullshit," Wind growled. "You saw it as well as I did. You just don't like the idea that someone else found it first."

Bear looked at Wind, smiled and slowly shook his head.

Before he could say anything, Wind continued, "Don't be condescending with me, man. I'm not like Keith. I don't need your approval. I found something good for us and you can't accept that it was me that found it and not you."

"Wind... " Sandy started.

Bear placed a hand on her shoulder. "It's okay," he assured her. He looked back at the young man. "Wind," he said. "I have no problem with the fact that you found the cave. I think it's great. It may be very helpful."

"May be helpful," Wind said gruffly. "It's a place to store things and we can stay in there if the weather turns bad."

"That may be true," Bear said pouring a cup of coffee.

"Why can't you accept that I did something good to help the group?"

The rest of the group listened intently. Both men were important to them, each in their own way. This was the first real dissention they had experienced within the group in a number of months. Even in Rebel's Revenge, they had agreed on almost everything with only minor differences.

Spyder, after checking closely for ants, leaned against a palm tree sipping a cup of coffee. Keith squatted near the fire, Sandy crossed her arms beneath her breasts and Hal sat on a rock and bit off a piece of jerky. No one concealed his or her curiosity.

"Wind, there's no doubt you do a lot of things good for all of us," Bear said. "I'm very glad we have you here."

"Then what's the problem?"

"I don't know," Bear answered. "You're the one who seems to have a problem with me."

"Why couldn't we have searched the cave more?" Wind asked. "You weren't even willing to check it out. You looked around and stomped off without even seeing if there was a possibility of using it."

"What should we have looked for?" Bear asked.

"We needed to find out where that tunnel in the back went. We should have checked the floor. If there was any dust on it, we could see if there were prints of animals of humans there. What if there were other rooms? We could divide where we lived

62

and where we stored things. There are a bunch of things we needed to find out."

"I agree, we need to know everything you mentioned," Bear said. He took another sip of coffee, impressed at the young man's attention to details.

Wind obviously had a problem with Bear's casual attitude and the way he treated the situation. "All you can do is stand there sipping your coffee, dismissing the possibility of using the cave as a home or even shelter," Wind said angrily. "Obviously, the rest think there is a possibility there. Why the hell are you so complacent?"

"How would we have checked the tunnel in back?" Bear asked. "You said you would have checked it, but you didn't have any light. Do you think I wanted to fall through some hole?"

"No, of course not," Wind answered. "But why couldn't we have checked the room out?"

Bear took a deep breath, let it out and wiped his face with his left hand as if removing a coat of sweat. "The room was about thirty feet long and twenty feet wide. The floor was smoother than the walls and ceiling. There was a discoloration of the ceiling in one of the front corners possibly caused by smoke from a fire of some sort. The light shining down through the shaft illuminates an area about ten feet on both sides. The shaft is around a hundred feet tall, four feet wide and the sides of it are smooth. It was probably formed by water." He took another sip from his cup and swallowed. "How do you get the supplies in through the waterfall? If there's another opening somewhere, maybe we can take them in through it."

***

Wind stood looking at him astounded that he had seen all that in a matter of seconds. *Then what problem does he have with me? I know it's not because I'm black. He's never done this before. He can't be prejudice.*

"I'm prejudiced," Bear said as if reading his mind. "I don't like black."

"No fuckin' way," Wind said, stunned at what the man said.

"You don't understand," Bear said with a smile. "The room was enclosed. Worse than that, it was dark, almost black in there. I felt like I was suffocating."

"You?" Wind exclaimed. "Claustrophobic?"

"That's why I didn't stay long," he explained. "I'm okay in a cave with a light, but it gets bad real, real quick in the dark."

Wind looked at the ground, then back to Bear. "I didn't know, man. I thought it was something to do with me. Goddamn, I'm sorry. Have you had it all your life?"

"We'll have to talk about it later," Bear said. "Right now, we need to find out more about that cave."

"But, what about... "

"Wind," Spyder interrupted. "How far back was that shaft?"

Wind looked at the waterfall. "About fifteen to twenty feet from the front of the cliff," he estimated. "But those cliffs are at least five hundred feet tall."

He stopped and thought for a second, "How could that be?"

"I'd bet there's a ledge hidden in the bushes somewhere up there," Spyder answered, "and we need to find out. I can try climbing. But, I ain't worth a shit at it."

"I think I can get up it," Bear said. "I've done some climbing. Not a lot, but some."

"I can climb it," Amanda offered. "My cousin and I used to do some rock climbing. It's been a while, but that doesn't look too bad."

"Are you sure?" Sandy asked.

"I've done tougher climbs than that," she said. She could see the cliff in the distance. In fact, she thought about climbing it earlier, but knew she didn't have time for simple enjoyment.

"I'd never try something like that," Ginny stated firmly.

"I've done this stuff before," Amanda assured them.

"We don't have any climbing tools," Hal reminded her.

"I don't need any," she replied. "In fact, tools would probably get in the way with all the vegetation. The roots won't be deep, but they should hold me."

"Do we have to do this," Dr. Hamilton asked. "The last thing we need is to have someone broken up from a fall. Isn't there some way to check for a back way up?"

"The doctor makes sense," Hal agreed. "Why don't we check the bottom of the mountains for a path up before we ask someone to take on something dangerous like this?"

"I can do it," she insisted.

"No one doubts that," Keith said. "But what if something happened and you fell? I don't mean to be a pain in the butt, but I don't want you to get hurt."

She smiled, understanding he was only thinking of her safety. Nevertheless, she wanted to do something to prove her value to the group. With no children around to teach, she felt like a fifth wheel. Besides, she would love to tackle the face of the mountain.

"Let's split up and search the base of the slopes and see what we can find," Hal suggested. "What do the rest of you think?"

"I'll take the north side," Bear said. "I think I saw some sugar cane over there and want to check it out."

"I'll take the south," Spyder volunteered.

"If it's okay with Bear, I'll go with him," Wind said.

"No problem with me," Bear answered.

"I'll go with Spyder," Keith volunteered.

"I would rather you stay here at the camp if you don't mind," Bear countered. "If he doesn't mind, Hal can go with Spyder."

"Fine with me," Hal answered.

"What's wrong with me going?" Keith asked disappointed.

"Nothing's wrong with you going," Bear answered. "But you haven't answered my question yet. Besides, we may need someone to go in the cave and Hal swims like a rock." Bear grinned. "He's real fast, but travels in only one direction --

straight down. I'm hoping you can stay here and help out with camp safety."

"No problem," Keith said. "I'll help take care of things around here."

Even after his statement about Keith wanting to please Bear, Wind couldn't help but appreciate the young man's desire to be a part of the teamwork required to make things work in this situation.

CHAPTER SEVEN

Dr. Hamilton joined Spyder and Hal, using the need for exercise as an excuse. In reality, he knew Bear would be checking out the different vegetation and he wanted to do the same. He had a couple of books on the subject, and wanted to bone-up on plant recognition.

Spyder led the way through the thick foliage. The cliffs on the left seemed to grow steadily higher as they proceeded. "Keep your eyes open for any paths or possible areas safe for climbing," he said.

"You're not gonna get me to climb any of these slopes," Dr. Hamilton declared. "They're almost vertical."

"I know the feeling," Spyder agreed. "I'm just looking for a way for someone else to use."

"You've got to be kidding me," Hal spat disgustedly. "You mean to tell me you're only looking for a way for someone else to risk their asses? What the hell's wrong with the two of you? How can you ask someone to do something you're not willing to do yourself? Shit, Amanda was even willing to take a chance on climbing up there."

The other two men stopped and looked at him.

Hal continued. "Finding a way up could save our lives sometime. Don't you think it's worth trying to find a safer place to live? You've gotta be kidding me."

Spyder and Dr. Hamilton both wore surprised looks at his outburst. They looked at each other and, after a few seconds, Spyder stammered, "Shit man, I don't want to put anyone at risk, but I know my limits. There's no way I'd climb any of these cliffs.

I'd wind up a casualty and the Doc here would have to patch me up."

A short hesitation and the doctor said, "I'm willing to help out if you want to climb up there. But I'm not about to leave the level ground unless I absolutely have to."

"Damn Hal, we're not saying we won't help. If you want to try a way up, just let us know," Spyder said. "We'll help you all we can."

"Hell no," Hal shot back, "I'm not about to climb anything like that. Are you kidding? I just thought that if I could get one of you to, I wouldn't feel so guilty. That's suicide for someone like me."

"Kiss my ass Hal," Spyder snorted. "You had me believing you were crazy enough to try something like that."

"You gotta be outta your mind," Hal said grinning. "Not only do I have a wife back there, but anything higher than a step-stool and I get a nosebleed. A man could get hurt doing something stupid like that."

"I'm glad to hear that," Dr. Hamilton said. "I only have minimal training in psychiatry and I wasn't sure how I was going to handle you being insane."

The men's mood lightened and they continued on, changing leaders about every fifteen minutes. In the dense underbrush, the person in front had to forge a trail for the other two, and the going was tough.

***

69

Bear and Wind walked in silence for ten minutes. "I'm sorry for causing a problem back there," Wind said.

"You didn't cause a problem," Bear answered. "In fact, by questioning what I did, you stopped a problem from developing."

"Yeah, but that was a lucky result, not the intention," Wind was obviously still embarrassed over the previous confrontation.

"Just imagine what would have happened if you had let a situation develop," Bear explained. "We could've wound up at each other's throats. You did the right thing."

"I just couldn't believe it when you said you were prejudiced against black people."

"I never said that," Bear corrected. "I said I was prejudiced against black. As worked up as you were, I figured you'd hear what you wanted to. I admit it was cruel, but I was just proving it to myself and I apologize for that. I shouldn't have done it."

"Don't worry about it, Wind said. "I learned a lesson too. I still tend to jump to conclusions and I need to knock that shit off."

Bear smiled and continued walking. A while later, they found the sugar cane he had seen before.

"You know what that is?" He asked.

"It looks like the pictures I've seen of sugar cane," Wind said taking hold of a slender stalk. "It's grown in Louisiana, but I never saw any."

"That's what it is," Bear confirmed.

Wind pulled at the plant. The outer part was a layer of smooth hard skin, almost bark, with joints circling it every eight or nine inches. The plant bent but refused to break. He pulled again, harder. This time the cane gave way splintering, but still not breaking away.

"If you break that off and eat it, you're gonna have a belly ache and the drizzlin' trots," Bear said. "It's still green. Look over here." He took hold of another stalk. "This one's ready to eat."

Wind joined him. The plant he tried to break had a greenish tint to its covering. The outside of this one was much more yellow. "Just look at the color," he said smiling. "It'll tell all you need to know."

Bear pulled his knife and chopped the cane near the ground. It looked like bamboo with segmented sections delineated by knuckles between each section. After cutting the cane from the ground, he put his knife back in its sheath and proceeded to break the plant at the sections. The parts that didn't break, he again used his knife to cut.

The cane cut or broken into sections, he proceeded to strip the outer sheath from the soft center. "This is what you eat," he said and handed a piece to Wind. "We'll take some back with us."

Wind tried to take a bite of the sugar cane only to find a thick, heavy fiber. There was no way he would be able to eat it.

"You chew it," Bear said. "You'll have to do a lot of spitting to get the fiber out of your mouth."

The taste of the plant was wonderful. It was like honey on a stick. Only in this case, you chewed the stick.

Bear handed Wind two pieces. "You don't want to eat any more than this," he said. "You'll get a stomach ache if you do."

71

He bent more stalks over and demonstrated how to cut them. The extra they stuffed in their packs, then continued on their way.

The day was warm, the breeze blew gently across the land and Wind found himself daydreaming. He remembered being with his family on the farm. Many of the summer days in Mississippi were like this. It was easy to forget the circumstances that brought him here, easy to forget the killing of recent days --and for that, he was grateful.

Bear reached down, picked up a piece of wood about six feet long, and used it as a walking stick. *He must not have his strength completely back yet,* Wind thought. *Shit, he's been shot three times in as many months. Damn, I forgot about that.*

Bear, shot twice in a confrontation with a militia a couple of months before and once only three days ago, astounded him with his recuperative powers. *He called it a flesh wound,* Wind remembered. *But you can bet I'd still be on my back if it were me. I'm not sure who's the toughest man alive, him or Spyder.*

Wind remembered being sent from Spyder to Bear with a message during the battle. While he was with Bear, Wind saw Ben shot and killed. He had never seen a change in a person like the one he saw in Bear that day. The man seemed to become inhuman. It was as if his soul left him. The entity remaining had no feelings and was nothing short of a killing machine driven by rage and revenge. Yet he was almost calm in his anger.

When he returned and told Spyder the news, Wind saw the change again. He had no idea humans

72

could change that way. He knew anger; he understood fear and anger combined to create rage. However, he had no idea how to describe what happened with the two men that day. *They lost their humanity,* he remembered. *Nothing mattered other than killing their enemy. The entire aspect of their being changed, they were like the mutants in human form.*

In front of him, Bear used a walking stick to keep going. "Are you okay?" Wind asked. "Do you need to take a break?"

"I'm fine," he answered looking back. "You need to stop?"

"I'm okay," Wind assured him. "But I wasn't shot three days ago."

"That's no problem," Bear said. "Did you see that trail to the right?"

Wind had been daydreaming, following the man in front of him instinctively. "No," he said. "I missed it, sorry."

"Don't worry about it," Bear answered. "Look up there." He pointed with the limb.

About ten feet up the cliff; Wind saw a path wandering through the brush. "How the hell did you see that?" He asked.

"I was looking for it," Bear answered. "It's angling down to a point just ahead."

They reached the place where the narrow path descended to the base of the mountain walls. "We're gonna have to go up it as far as we can," Bear said. "We need to see if it works its way anywhere near the top."

"I'll go," Wind volunteered. "If it stays a path all the way to the top, I can go quicker by myself than if both of us go."

"You're probably right," Bear agreed. He pulled the M16 off his back and handed it to Wind. "If it gets too steep for you to carry this, you need to come back. If you can't carry this with both hands, I want you to come back for now. We can go back and get others to go with you. Do you understand?"

"No problem," Wind answered.

Bear put a hand on his shoulder. "Wind, you have to give me your word that if it gets too steep for you to carry the rifle with both hands, you'll come back."

Wind looked at the other man. Bear knew if he gave his word, he would be bound to do as he said. He also knew Bear trusted him to do what he promised. This was Bear's way of keeping him safe.

"You have my word," Wind said. "If it gets too steep for me to carry the rifle with two hands, I'll come back here."

"Then you're on your way young man," Bear declared grinning and slapped Wind on the shoulder.

Wind was off, hurrying up the trail. He wanted to see where it went and was anxious to help his friends any way he could.

***

Keith sat on a rock on the outer edge of the camp when Sandy approached. "How's everything?" She asked.

74

"All's quiet on the western front," he said grinning. "Is everything okay in camp?"

"It will be during the daylight," she said. She wasn't sure why she said that, but it seemed right to her. It was funny; she had been able to sense things before. However, since finding herself here, it seemed to have increased. She could feel things that she hadn't noticed before. She fully realized it when she knew Wind would go with Bear before he volunteered. She also knew Bear was going to stop Keith and suggest that Hal accompany Spyder. None of it surprised her. She wouldn't question it, but go along with what was happening. *God has to have a hand in it,* she thought. *Through him, we'll survive this.*

When she approached Keith, she could tell he was deep in thought. She hated to interrupt, but something told her he needed to talk. "You looked like you were somewhere else," she said. "I hope I didn't interrupt you."

"Not at all," Keith answered. "I was just thinking about a statement Bear made."

"That can be a pain in the butt," she said. "Sometimes he can be confusing."

"I'm just not sure what he meant by what he said."

"What did he say?"

"Well," Keith paused, removed his hat and ran his hand through his hair.

He's taken on some of Bear's mannerisms, Sandy noticed. *He has no idea he's doing it, but he likes and wants to be like my bro.* She knew it would embarrass him if she pointed it out though and said nothing.

"He said the ocean is made up of water particles bonded into one large mass," Keith said. "At the same time, one water particle contains an ocean within it."

"What's the problem?" She asked.

"You mean you understand that shit?" Keith asked shocked that she might understand the wisdom of the ages. Then, realizing what he had said, "Sorry, I didn't mean to cuss."

"That's alright," she assured him. "We all do it sometimes -- and, I've heard stuff that would make you blush, believe me."

"But, you mean you understand what he's looking for?" Keith pressed.

"Maybe," she answered. "I may be able to ask some questions that will start you thinking along the right track."

"Go ahead," he said. "I need all the help I can get."

She smiled knowing his statement was a start. It was true she didn't have the answers. She didn't think like, or necessarily believe what Bear did. Bear's belief in spirituality and the world was a little different from hers. Even though it was similar, she couldn't get herself to look at it in the way he did. But, that was okay. He was a good man and she loved him.

Sandy thought for a moment and Keith fidgeted. "What makes up the ocean?"

"Water particles, minerals, salt and a bunch of other stuff I don't know," he answered.

"Okay, then this particle you are asking about is a small part of the ocean, right?"

"Yeah, sure," he agreed, "a minute part of it."

76

"What is the particle made up of?"

"Hydrogen and oxygen atoms," he answered.

"Then the atoms connect to form the water particle like the different elements of the ocean bond together to form it."

A look of understanding crept across his face. Before he could say anything, she continued. "Just remember, Bear wasn't talking about only the physical aspects of you or that particle. As he says, there's a yin and yang in everything. There are always give and take, highs and lows, light and dark, man and woman. Think about those things for a while and see if it helps," she said.

"I still don't understand," Keith said shaking his head.

"He believes that everything is the same, the Earth, the sky, the trees, people and rocks. We're all made up of the same energy," she tried to clarify. "This is only the basics. He believes that everything in the universe is the same. Therefore, we're all part of the universe and its part of us. We're all single entities inside a whole thing and, as such, contain the same thing inside as well as out."

Keith still shook his head and looked at the ground.

"That's the best I can do," she said. "The rest is up to you to figure out for yourself. Talk to Amanda, she may be able to help you."

She rose and walked away, leaving Keith to his thoughts. Bear never discouraged or argued her Christian beliefs and his seemed to suite him fine.

He always follows his beliefs and his heart, she thought. *I've never seen him put another down because of their religious or spiritual beliefs or try and push his on them. He accepts people as they are and their beliefs as what they need to make them good people.*

CHAPTER EIGHT

It was less than an hour before sunset when Bear and Wind returned to camp. Hal and his group had returned less than thirty minutes before. "What did you find?" Wind asked Spyder as they entered the area.

"More fruits and berries including a bunch of grape vines," he said. "We did come across two more waterfalls though. Both were half the size of this one. That's about it; did the two of you find anything?"

Wind smiled. He was anxious to tell what he and Bear had discovered.

"Did you find that sugar cane you thought you saw?" Hal asked.

"Yeah," Bear answered. "We've both got a load in our packs."

Wind was excited and wanted to tell the others about the trail.

"Any more big cats?" Hal asked.

"Nope," Bear answered. "We didn't see or hear anything like that. In fact, it was pretty quiet."

Wind was becoming antsy and no one would give him a chance to tell his story.

Before Wind could speak, Spyder asked, "What about any of those amphibious critters?"

"Nah," Bear said. "We didn't get close enough to the shore to see anything like that." Turning away from Wind toward Spyder, he asked, "Did you say you found some grapes?"

"There's a bunch of trees in a valley about a mile from here. Not only grape vines, but some apple and orange trees as well."

"Maybe we can get some of the grapes for some wine," Bear suggested.

"That's what we thought," Spyder exclaimed. "We've got a couple of those five gallon water jugs from the wagon."

Finally, Wind blurted out, "Does anyone want to know what we found?"

Hal looked at him with a surprised look. "Oh, did you guys find something?" He asked. "Bear didn't report anything. He said you guys didn't find any... "

Spyder, who could no longer keep a straight face, roared with great, long belly laughs. It was obvious Wind was about to burst with excitement as he squirmed on the rock where he sat.

"You all think it's so goddamn funny?" He asked. "You can all kiss my black ass."

At this, the entire group burst into laughter, no one could resist. Still chuckling, Bear stepped up and put his hand on the young man's shoulder. "Tell them what you found son," he said.

"You tell 'em," Wind said angrily. "Nobody wants to listen to me." He failed to see the humor in the situation and didn't like being the butt of a joke.

"I can't," Bear said, his amusement subsiding. "I didn't see anything, you did the exploring. By the way, you're taking yourself way too seriously."

That was when he realized what had just happened. Bear was right, He had taken himself too seriously, just like earlier that morning. His anger fell away as he joined in the laughter.

Eventually, Bear said, "Tell 'em what you found, man." To the others he said, "Wind followed a trail up the side of a mountain. He was gone

80

almost two hours before he came back and told me what he had seen." He looked at Wind and nodded.

"Bear found a path up the side of one of the mountains. I followed it for almost forty-five minutes switching back and forth before reaching the top. The trail went along the top of a ridge to the west." he hesitated, trying to find the right words for what he had seen.

"The cliff here, with the waterfall is the east end of a ridge jutting from the main range of mountains. It looked about a quarter of a mile wide. The mountain range beyond is massive and much higher. Some of the peaks must be thousands of feet high."

"What kind of mountains are they?" Hal asked. "Do they all look like they were formed by volcanic action?"

"With the steep sides and all the valleys between, I'm sure this place was formed by heavy volcanic activity," he answered and intentionally held some information back, wanting to give it to them last. "I'm not sure if we're on an island or a peninsula of some sort. When I looked to the north, the shoreline continued out of sight. Whatever the land is, it's at least fifty miles long. I couldn't tell about the width. The mountains blocked my view to the west."

"What about the south?" Dr. Hamilton asked. "Could you see anything in that direction?"

Wind smiled. "Whatever we're on, we seem to be at the southern end. The land to the south is a plain. It's covered in trees and all sorts of vegetation, bushes, flowers and tall grass. I could see the hut we woke up in yesterday and there seems to be four or five others dotted on the plain."

"Did you see any other people?" Sandy asked.

"No," he answered. "I didn't see any people, but if there are houses, they had to be built by someone."

"You said you saw valleys," Bear said. "What were they like?"

"I can't say," he admitted. "I could tell there were valleys between the ridges extending from the main range. I did see something unexpected though." He hesitated to make sure everyone was listening. He hadn't even told Bear about this next information.

"There's a smoking volcano about fifteen or twenty miles to the northwest." He looked around at his friends. They were interested, but didn't show the surprise he expected. "We didn't see the smoke because the wind seems to blow from east to west."

"Trade winds," Bear said. "It must be the prevailing direction, at least for this time of the year. It's probably year round."

"What makes you think that?" Ginny asked.

"I haven't seen any ash," he explained. "If the wind shifted to the east for any extended duration, there'd be ash. We only found out about the volcano when Wind saw it." He sat on a rock, put his coffee beside him and started rummaging through his pack.

As Bear pulled out short sticks of sugar cane, Wind continued. "The mountains and valleys look like a natural maze. Like I said, this place is huge. I did see more land to the east. It's probably fifteen or more miles across the water. I didn't get a good look and couldn't tell if it was attached to this, but it's there."

As Bear started passing the sugar cane to the rest, Wind removed more from his pack.

"Did you find out anything about the shaft in the cave?" Keith asked. It seemed that everyone had forgotten why people had gone out searching in the first place.

"The path didn't go that way," Wind answered, "and I followed it. I guess I got excited and forgot to check on the shaft, sorry."

"Don't worry about it," Hal said. "Any of us might have done the same thing. Besides, you found a way up the ridge. Maybe tomorrow a group of us can go up and look for the shaft."

"That's probably a better idea," Sandy said. "That way we can help each other out if we need to."

"We need to go back over the inventory," Bear said. "Combine our supplies and we'll have an idea of what's on hand and what we need to find."

"If we don't have it," Ginny said, "how can we get it? Wind said he didn't see any other people."

"We make it," he answered and walked over to the supplies.

It only took a couple of hours to re-inventory the supplies and as before, Ginny was in charge of the count and storage. She directed where she wanted each type of item and, with Hal, Sandy and Spyder's help, erected a cover for protection.

When everyone gathered to eat and relax, Bear said, "I'm gonna take a while and check the place out."

"What do you mean check it out?" Hal asked.

"I'm gonna take a few days to see what the area's like. If we don't know the land and its inhabitants, we don't know the dangers or advantages to our new home."

"Makes sense," Hal agreed. "The camp here seems to be as good as any for a base."

"This may be your new home," Ginny said, "but it's not mine."

Bear nodded. "That's fine, let me know when you find it," he said and turned away.

"I'll go with you," Keith volunteered.

"I need to go alone," he answered. "I need some time alone while I'm doing this. I appreciate the offer, but I need to take some time for myself.

CHAPTER NINE

Bear traveled south until night started to veil the land. He camped was near a small waterfall flowing from the face of a cliff. The pool at its base was small and filled with clear cool water. He had seen three other falls along the way -- the other reports were correct, fresh water was no problem.

After building a small fire and spreading a blanket on the ground, he lay down. It had been a long day, his shoulder was stiff and he needed to rest. With his weapons beside him and his hunger satiated by fruits and berries, he drifted off to a night of restful sleep.

***

A dark figure moved among the shadows of the night. In the dim glow of the remaining embers of the fire, a presence moved silently around the sleeping man checking his equipment and supplies. It seemed to have no problem moving effortlessly without waking him.

Opening the bag with his medical supplies, the figure sprinkled powder on his remaining gauze and closed the bag. It opened his canteen and sprinkled more of the powder in it.

The shadow moved to the far end of the clearing checking the rest of his supplies as it went, hesitated and melted silently into the foliage.

***

Bear awoke the next morning to a bright cloudless sky. *I can definitely learn to like this place,* he thought. *It's been a long time since I was in a tropical atmosphere. I love the peace and quiet here, and it's a far cry from what we've become accustomed to.*

The birds sang in their search of food. The small waterfall produced a relaxing happy sound as it splashed into the pool and the air was cool and moist. It was almost enough to give him an excuse for lying around a couple of hours.

He added wood to the embers of his fire for breakfast and noticed footprints in the camp. The prints were made by bare feet -- human feet. Someone was in his camp last night.

Examining the tracks, he knew someone had entered the camp, searched through his supplies and passed within a foot of him while leaving. *Either I slept like the dead, or they're good.*

A check of his pack showed nothing missing. It lay open with everything inside. Someone had gone through his supplies, left everything in place and departed. He thought about what had happened. *If I was in danger, it's too late now. Obviously, whoever did this was just curious. I'm probably safe. I'm also probably being watched right now.*

He made coffee over the fire, then sat with his back against a tree and changed the dressing on his shoulder. If someone was watching, he wanted them to see he wasn't worried about the tracks and in no hurry to start his day. It was the least threatening he could make himself for now.

After a breakfast of fruit and coffee, he cleared camp, put his trash in his pack and set out along the base of the mountains. The terrain reminded him of Hawaii but the fruit represented not only Hawaii, but parts of the Caribbean as well. Not all the plants were safe though. Unsure of what it was, he picked up a piece of fruit from under a tree. *It's manchineel,* he thought. He had seen the plant in the Caribbean. It looked like a crabapple, however if eaten, death occurs within a couple of hours. There was also danger from the leaves and sap.

He had already seen Akee trees. The fruit was nice to eat when ripe, but if eaten too early or too late, they were poisonous. "I gotta keep this trip short," he said to himself. "We may be in paradise, but it's still a dangerous place." He hadn't seen any of the plants near the camp, but there was still the possibility of someone finding something.

Instead of following along the foot of the mountains, he decided to travel half way between the mountains and the shore. This way, he could travel in a relatively straight line. He wanted to cover at least fifteen miles before turning back. However, after traveling about ten miles, he ran into an obstacle.

A body of water, at least a hundred feet wide, lay in his path. The water was salty, which told him it connected to the sea. The surface was calm indicating little or no flow and he figured it was an estuary of some sort.

After traveling toward the mountains a while, he suspected the water must reach the base and possibly continue into a valley between steep slopes. He would have to wait until he had more time to investigate further. It was mid-afternoon and he needed to get back to the others. He'd rest here tonight and double time it back tomorrow.

***

Bear set his camp at the base of a mountain. He felt like he was being lazy, but figured he deserved to do something for himself. He would lie around the rest of the day and tonight before traveling hard tomorrow.

He took his time and readying wood for a small fire. Koa wood burned hot, but required extra space between limbs to remain lit. He didn't need a raging fire, just something to keep the animals away -- animals and or humans that is.

He was more curious about the human last night than worried. It had passed up the opportunity to attack him. Nevertheless, he wanted to know who was watching. Whoever it was, they were good. While the sun was still up, he searched the immediate area and finding it void of human presence, set out a couple of trip wires. Maybe he would be lucky enough to catch them. If not, the wires would at least warn him of their presence.

Bear enjoyed being away from the others, not having the weight of responsibility for the group on him. It was nice to sit back and relax. He didn't have to worry about anyone but himself tonight. That would change tomorrow, but for tonight, he could enjoy the area, the gentle breeze and the smells of nature around him. He knew he wasn't actually responsible for the rest, but because they were friends, he couldn't shake the feeling.

It was obvious that something worldwide had again happened. The planet had somehow changed. He didn't know if it had anything to do with the previous loss of electricity and it really didn't matter. They were here and that was what counted. Now, they simply had to make the best of it.

It must be some sort of time warp, he thought. *I wouldn't have believed anything like that could happen if it hadn't been for that saber-toothed tiger. It wasn't a look-alike either it was the real thing. Also, that shadow I saw the other night was something from a different time and place. Not to mention, the mixture of vegetation we have here. We simply need to learn the rules so we can live by 'em.*

The sun was below the horizon and he had eaten an MRE and some fruit. From his pack, he pulled a small flask of rum. He took a drink; put it away and sat back to get some rest. He would have to let things sort themselves out. In no time, he drifted off into a deep, restful sleep.

The next morning, Bear awoke only when the sun climbed high enough to shine in his eyes. It must have been at least nine in the morning when he sat up and looked around.

***

Spyder and Wind decided they would return to investigate the top of the ridge. After eating, they set out with packs to see what they could find.

The rest remained at camp supposedly to make sure nothing happened to the supplies. In reality, they were comfortable to remain where they were and relax. Everyone was quite comfortable in their present location and began to think more and more of it as home. The ocean was only a couple hundred yards away, they had fresh water and in an emergency, a cave for protection.

They all agreed that sitting around the campfire, drinking coffee in the morning, was the best way to start a day. Even though they weren't where they were supposed to be, there was a lot to being a small group rather than being alone. They hadn't seen another person or any threatening animals other than the tiger. Still, they had no idea where they were or what to expect. At the same time, the situation didn't feel as enormous as it did back at Rebel's Revenge.

"We can stretch the supplies a long way," Ginny said. "With all the fruits and berries, they'll last a lot longer than we expected. If we find meat of some kind, we're set."

I'm gonna look around today," Hal said. "Maybe there're some animals we can use for food. I can't believe there aren't any rabbits, deer or even wild boar around here somewhere."

"I wouldn't mind trying my hand at some fishing," Dr. Hamilton said. "There should be an endless supply of food in the sea."

"You're right," Keith agreed. "We should always be able to get fish."

"When are you going hunting?" Dr. Hamilton asked Hal.

"As soon as I get off my butt and get moving," he answered.

"You mind some company?"

"I don't mind the company," Hal said. "I just don't want to leave the camp unguarded."

"We can take care of the camp," Keith stated. "The four of us can handle things here."

Hal was surprised at Keith's willingness to stay behind while he and the doctor hunted. "If you're sure it's okay," he said.

"It's fine," Keith assured him. "Besides I have some things to take care of around here."

Hal smiled at him, nodded and rose to his feet. "You ready to go, Doc?"

"Ready when you are."

"Let's do it," he said. To Sandy he added, "We should be back sometime after noon."

"Bring back food," she said. "I want a steak of some kind tonight."

"I'll be sure and bring something back," Hal assured her. He kissed her cheek. "I don't want to lose a horse just because you're hungry."

Hal and Dr. Hamilton left the camp walking southeast. Both men carried an M16. Neither of them thought they needed the weapons for safety. They were just lighter and easier to carry than the other rifles they took with them more from habit than anything else.

After just a couple of minutes, Dr. Hamilton realized Hal was out for a walk rather than actually hunting. He tromped through the bushes making no attempt to reduce or hide his noise. He was on a sightseeing expedition. It was obvious that this was an opportunity to get away. "Why don't we take a look over near the shoreline?" The doctor asked.

"What do you think we could find near there?"

"Oh, probably the sound of waves on the beach, sun, the sounds of birds and wind through the trees," Dr. Hamilton explained. "We might even see something we could shoot for food."

Hal smiled, "If we shoot a crab, there won't be anything left to eat."

"You say you're a good shot," the doctor countered. "Just shoot 'em in the head."

Hal's smile broadened into a grin as he made his way through the brush toward the ocean, "Doc, you can be a real pisser, ya know."

As Dr. Hamilton followed him, a small branch slapped him on the chest, "I know," he said, "and sometimes, it can be a lot of fun."

Hal grunted and led the way to the beach.

The water beyond the beach was calm with waves sliding onto the shore producing a soft swishing sound. Hal found a large piece of driftwood, sat down beside it and leaned back. After checking the wood, Dr. Hamilton joined him. "Now if you see any food walking by," Hal said, "you let me know -- wake me up if I happen to fall asleep. No offense to you Doc, I enjoy your company, but I'm gonna relax."

"No offense taken if you don't mind me doing the same thing."

Hal grinned and pulled his hat over his eyes. "I don't mind at all," he said, "not at all." The atmosphere of the beach was relaxing, the sun was warm and he wanted to let the stress flow away to the rhythm of the waves. With the events of the previous week, he knew everyone needed some time for themselves. The feelings they were all experiencing wouldn't simply go away. It would take time for the nerves to settle. As he lay on the sand, the stress slowly slipping away and Hal drifted into a light sleep.

***

Hal jerked awake to the sound of screams. Pulling his hat from his face, he looked around searching for the source of the sound. It sounded more like pain than fear and it was male.

Near the shore, a large creature dragged the screaming Dr. Hamilton toward the water. The animal's giant jaws gripped him across his body from the left shoulder to the right side of his stomach. Hal guessed by its description, it was probably the same thing Bear had seen the night before.

The doctor hammered on the animal's snout with both fists trying to get it to release him.

Jumping to his feet, he grabbed the rifle next to him and jerked it to his shoulder. He tried to take aim, but Dr. Hamilton's body blocked any shot. He ran toward them, but the deep, loose sand slowed his process, tugged at his boots and caused him to trip. He hit the ground and dropped the rifle.

The doctor tried to scream but the only sound he made was a gargle as blood spewed from his mouth.

Struggling to his feet, Hal saw Dr. Hamilton weakly trying to reach the creatures eyes. He struggled to his feet pulling a pistol and raced toward the struggle at the edge of the water. He reached the solid footing of damp sand just as the creature and its prey disappeared below the ocean's surface.

93

The water thrashed, bubbled and turned red. The death struggle just below the surface was causing a boiling effect. He knew the doctor didn't have a chance and fired into the disturbance again and again wanting to kill the thing that had him. When he stopped shooting, he had fired seven bullets and the disturbance ceased.

He's gone, Hal thought. *That fucking thing got him. He never did anything to anyone. All he tried to do was help people. He was a kind, gentle soul that only wanted to do good and that goddamned thing ripped him apart. If there's a God in Heaven, he isn't paying attention to this.*

He watched the water for some sign of the creature. The waves continued to wash up on shore. It was as if nothing had happened. Nature continued despite the fact that a person had just had his soul violently ripped from his body -- and the world spun on.

Hal stumbled back up the sand to the edge of the trees and half fell, half sat on the wood where he previously slept. *This isn't right. This can't be happening,* he thought. *It was hard enough before, but this is pure bullshit. Things like this don't really happen. You see 'em in movies, but not in real life.* He let out a scream of anguish and pounded the sand with both hands. This man dedicated his entire existence to medicine and the preservation of life died for no reason.

Another thought crept into his mind, reached deep and clamped down on his feelings like a cold vise -- none of them was safe. This could have happened to any of them. Bear saw one of the creatures near the camp the other night. Hal was immediately up and running.

***

"I understand the thing about the ocean being made up of water particles, but I have no idea what he means about an ocean in a particle of water," Keith said.

Amanda smiled. "Just consider what makes up a water particle," she said. "Is it just a single thing, or is it made up of other... "

Something raced toward the clearing, through the bushes. Keith rose and, in a flash, pulled a pistol. Amanda hurried toward her rifle. Seconds later, Hal burst into the camp.

He glanced around. "Where's Sandy?"

"Are you okay?" Amanda asked.

"Where's Sandy?" Hal repeated almost shouting. The look on his face was of pure panic.

"She's at the waterfall," Ginny said.

Hal sprinted toward the cliff.

Bursting through the foliage, he looked frantically around. She wasn't there. He spun in circles, "Sandy," he screamed.

She broke the surface; she had been swimming under water.

"Sandy," Hal yelled again.

She turned and looked at him with a smile. "You ought to come in," she said. "The water feels great."

He stood at the edge of the pool panting. "Sandy, come out of the water," he said. It was more of a demand than a request.

95

Sandy read her husband's face. Something was wrong, almost all its color was gone and he looked almost beyond panicked. She swam to the edge of the water and climbed out. "What's wrong Hal?"

"We need to get back to the camp," he said hugging her fiercely.

"What's wrong," She repeated the question.

He didn't say anything for a moment, but held on tightly, as if unwilling to let her go. "You're here," he said, "and you're safe." Eventually, he slowly released her.

"What's wrong?" She repeated.

"I'll tell everyone at the same time," he said shakily.

They turned around to return to the camp and the rest were standing behind them. They had followed Hal as he raced from the clearing.

"Let's get back to the camp," he said. "I need a drink."

Back in the clearing, Hal opened a box, pulled a bottle from it and took a long, deep drink.

It's gotta be bad, Sandy thought, *he rarely drinks*. She looked around the clearing. "Where's Dr. Hamilton?" She asked.

Hal recapped the bottle and put it back in the box. He looked from person to person. "He's dead."

"Dead," Amanda repeated staring at him. "What do you mean? What happened?"

"He was killed by some sort of fuckin' animal. It killed him and dragged him into the ocean. I was asleep and heard him screaming. When I saw 'em, they were down the beach and Dr. Hamilton was trapped in its mouth," he paused and ran both hands over his face. Reliving the incident was more than

96

simply painful; it chewed at him like a cancer. "He was screaming and pounding on the creature with his free hand. The animal backed into the water and took him with it. Before I realized what I was doing, I was shooting at the water." He looked completely helpless as he remembered the attack, tears leaving streaks from his eyes into his beard.

"That was when I realized none of us are safe. That could have happened to any of us. I started running and got back here as soon as I could -- and you know the rest."

"What did the thing look like?" Keith asked. "How big was it?"

"I'm not sure," He answered. "I need some time to sort things out. All I could think about was to get back here and make sure Sandy was okay."

"Of course that's all you would think about," Ginny said in an accusing voice. "The rest of us can just take care of ourselves."

Hal's head snapped toward her. "I'm not married to any of the rest of you, Bitch. You're friends, but none of you is the center of my life. None of you are the... "

"Don't worry about it," Amanda interrupted. "We understand. We're just a little shaken, that's all." She glared at Ginny who walked over to the fire where food was cooking acting as if she had done nothing wrong.

"Take some time," Keith said to Hal. "Sorry about all the questions. I know it has to be hard."

"I need to go back and get my rifle," Hal said. He was acting mildly drugged. "I left it back there."

"I'll get it," Keith told him. "You need to rest and get yourself together

97

"You're not going by yourself," Hal said snapping from his semi-trance. "I'm going with you."

"... And leave everyone else here alone, unguarded?" Keith countered. "No, I can get the rifle. I'll be okay."

"I'll go with you," Amanda offered.

"I'll go by myself," Keith stated firmly. "I can travel faster and easier alone."

"Careful," Sandy quipped. "You're starting to sound like Bear."

Keith grinned and headed into the bushes toward the beach. She knew she had just given him the best compliment she could, in his mind, and he had to live up to it.

Sandy stepped over to the fire beside Ginny. "Ginny," she said in an even voice. "I know you're upset. But, you're an ass. And if you ever pull another stunt like you just did, I'll kick your ass all over this island. I don't know who you think you are but... "

"I don't know who you think you are," Ginny fired back interrupting.

"Shut your fucking mouth," Sandy said. "If I want anything from you, I'll beat it outta you."

Ginny closed her mouth, surprised at Sandy's anger and the obvious sincerity of her statement.

"You're nothing but a self-serving, egotistical bitch. People think about things other than you. You're not the center of everyone's attention. You're Spyder's and you should be. But, don't expect that from the rest of us."

Ginny glared back. Then, without saying a word, returned to her cooking and Sandy went to sit by her husband.

CHAPTER TEN

About fifteen minutes after Hal returned to camp, Spyder and Wind came trotting into the clearing. "What was the shooting all about?" Spyder asked nobody in particular.

Sandy, Amanda and Hal had been discussing the group Wind had arrived at Rebel's Revenge with. He was now the only one left. Mellon, Davata and Dr. Hamilton were dead.

Hal rose to his feet. "Wind," he said, "we need to talk."

"What's wrong?" Wind asked. "What happened?" he looked around the camp. "Where's Doc... and Keith?"

Sandy took a couple of steps closer. "Keith's okay. He's gone down the beach. "It's Dr. Hamilton. He's... " she hesitated, "... dead. He was killed by some sort of amphibious creature."

Wind looked like someone had just punched him in the gut. He stumbled to a log and dropped clumsily to the ground. Amanda and Sandy hurried to him as Ginny went to Spyder.

Amanda and Sandy repeated what Hal had told them. At the same time, Ginny told Spyder her version of the encounter with Sandy when Hal came back. When she finished, Spyder looked at her. "She's right," he said. "Hal should have been worried about her. He should have come back looking for her. If it had been me, I would have come back wanting to know about you. I doubt that would have bothered her in the least." He paused not sure if he believed her actions, "Do you honestly believe he would let anything happen to any of you?"

Ginny looked like a child who had just been scolded. "You're right," she said to him. "I'll talk to her later. I just don't like what's going on. I don't like what's happening to us."

"None of us do," he answered. "But we still have to work together."

***

The sun stood above the two peaks he used to tell time. There were only four or five hours until dark. Keith had found the rifle and seen the marks Dr. Hamilton left on the beach. Briefly searching the spot, he found seven casings from a 9mm pistol.

He walked slowly through the thick vegetation remembering the doctor when a noise to his right alerted him to another presence in the bushes. He crouched, slowed his breathing and waited. Something moved in the direction of the camp. It made little noise, but moved steadily along.

Slowly, he rose and released the safety on the M16. He could see nothing in the darkening shadows. Bear was out, but they didn't expect him back for a couple of days. As he inched forward, another movement from beyond the first came rapidly toward him. The first immediately retreated toward his position. *Hunter and hunted,* he thought.

He stepped behind a tree and waited. A figure broke through the bushes in front of him. A human was running from the other source of movement. He swung the butt of his rifle at the head of the fleeing person and somehow missed. Spinning, he leveled

101

the weapon ready to fire but there was no one there. *That's impossible,* he thought. *I may have missed, but there was someone there to hit.*

Before he realized it, Bear stood beside him. "Don't let it get to you," he said. Keith jumped at the sound of the voice and quickly spun toward the other man. "I've been trying to catch whatever it is for over two hours."

Keith knew there was a second person when he swung at the one as it passed him. However, when he missed and his prey disappeared, he momentarily forgot about the other. Trying to regain his composure, he said, "I forgot about seeing you."

"That's understandable," Bear answered. "Did you see where it went?"

"That's what bothers me," Keith answered. "I saw a movement, had time to set up and still missed the thing when I tried to drop it with the butt of my rifle. It just disappeared -- I don't mean I lost sight of it, it disappeared." He emphasized the last word.

They started back toward the camp. "Like I said," Bear repeated, "I've been chasing it for a couple of hours. It was in my camp last night, the night before and seemed to follow along... "

"In your camp... " Keith interrupted, concern etched on his face.

"Don't worry about it," Bear said. "If the thing had wanted to hurt me, I'd be dead. I didn't know it was there until I woke up the next morning.

As they walked back to camp through the thick underbrush, Keith listened for the sound of another person or animal. There was none, but he knew it meant nothing; something might stalk them at a distance.

102

***

As they approached the camp, Hal stepped up to meet them. He held his hand out. "We didn't expect you for another couple of days."

"I found some things out I thought everyone needed to know," bear said.

"Plus, he's not alone," Keith said.

Hal looked around for someone else.

"They're not here now, but they were earlier," Keith assured him.

Hal looked at the young man. He knew they were under a load of stress, but still...

"I'll explain it to you later," Bear answered. "There's no need for you to think he's any crazier than need be."

As they entered the clearing, Sandy walked quickly up and gave him a hug. "We didn't expect you until tomorrow or the next day."

"I'm beginning to think I'm not wanted here," he said with a grin. "Maybe I should go away a couple of more days then come back."

"It's just that we're glad to see you," Spyder said from the side, "especially with all that's happened."

"What's happened?" Bear asked. "It seems like we've all got news to share."

"You might better sit down," Spyder said. "It ain't good news."

Bear saw the seriousness in his friend's face and sat on a large rock.

"There's no other way to say it, but Dr. Hamilton's been killed," Spyder said solemnly. "We think he was killed by one of those things you saw the other night."

"I saw it," Hal said. He ran his hand over his face. "It dragged him into the ocean." He was shaking his head as his gaze shifted to the ground. "There was nothing I could... " His voice trailed off as Sandy moved over and put her arms around him.

Bear shifted his eyes from Hal to Spyder. "We need to check Wind's cave out," he said. "Someone or some *thing* followed me back here. It got away from Keith and me a little bit ago. I'm not sure we're safe out here anymore."

"We need to check the cave," Wind said.

"You're in charge of that," Bear said. "I can't be in there any more than I have to. I'll stay out here while the rest of you check it out."

As the others quickly prepared to check the cave, Bear took up a position so he could guard the camp. *Things are piling up again,* he thought. They had been here less than a week and one of their numbers was dead -- killed by some sort of unknown animal.

***

Keith swam to the rocks at the bottom of the falls with Hal and showed him where the hand and footholds were. Hal went behind the cascading water and waited to help the others. One at a time, Keith assisted everyone else up the sharp rocks, through the cascade and into Hal's grasp inside the cave.

In no time, everyone had assembled below the vertical shaft that ran to the top of the cliff. Spyder removed some matches and cloth-wrapped limbs covered in grease from plastic wrap and lit the homemade torches.

"We'll need to stay within eyesight of each other," Wind said. "Watch out for any holes in the floor or slippery areas. The floor here is worn down, but may not be in other places. If it's not, the lava will slice like a razor blade."

Slowly, they made their way to the back of the large room. The opening at the rear gave access to another room, about the same size, that sloped gently to the right. There were three small openings about three feet in diameter, at the floor level, in one wall of the room.

"These were probably created by water," Wind said. Actually, he was guessing, but wanted to give the rest a feeling of confidence.

In the wall to the left of the one with the holes was a slit that appeared large enough for a person to slide through. As spider peered into the slit, a commotion erupted near the middle of the other three holes.

A large creature emerged and rushed toward Amanda. The thing looked like a giant armadillo with a horn protruding from the middle of its forehead. Two rows of short spikes ran the length of its armored back. Bird-like talons tipped each toe and clicked as it scurried across the rock floor.

Keith grabbed Amanda and pulled just as the horn on the creature's forehead hooked her pant leg. The material ripped and the animal spun with incredible speed, apparently ready to charge again.

Spyder pulled his bowie knife as Wind scooped up a rock. Wind was able to slip between the animal and Amanda and Keith. At the same time, Spyder charged from its rear.

Immediately, a tail emerged from the shell and swept Spyder's feet from under him and he landed hard on the rock floor. As the creature turned, Wind drew his arm back to throw his rock at its head.

A loud hollow thud sounded and the animal dropped immediately to its belly and its head turned awkwardly to the side. Sharp talons clawed at the floor for a couple of seconds, then it lay still as blood pooled under its head.

Wind moved cautiously to the head of the dead animal. He looked at Spyder and saw that the man had regained his feet and was moving close with his knife. Holding his torch near so he could see, Wind inspected the thing on the ground before him.

"You're not gonna believe this," he said.

"What?" Spyder asked.

"What is it?" Hal said irritated. He hated guessing games when things were serious.

"You gotta see it," he said and stepped back.

As they moved close enough to see the animal's head, Wind looked around the room. There was a rock embedded in the skull of the creature. From the looks of it, the rock had struck with enough force that it penetrated the skull and lodged in the animal's brain.

The problem was that no one had thrown the rock. He still held the rock he had picked up and Spyder still held his knife. Hal carried a long slender branch for a walking stick and protection, as did the women. None of them carried rifles or pistols because of the weight and the fact that they had to swim and climb slippery rocks to get to the cave. Someone else had killed the animal with the rock -- but who?

Amanda stepped back from the thing and continued moving until she reached the wall. "We're not alone," she said.

It was as if none of the rest had realized what Wind was talking about until her statement. Quickly all of them moved their dim lights around to illuminate the entire room. They appeared to be alone.

"I think it's time to leave," Wind said. "We can discuss this outside."

The rest agreed and started for the front chamber when Ginny said, "It ain't happening."

The others turned toward her.

"It may not be worth a damn, but I want this thing hauled outta here so I can see if it's worth eating. If it is, we need the food."

Spyder shook his head and grinned. "Leave it to my "Little Teacup" to be thinking about keeping us fed."

He and Hal carried the creature between them hanging from Hal's walking stick to the front of the cave. Using rope, they pulled it across the pool and carried it to the clearing.

***

Wind helped Ginny gut and prepare the animal so they could cook it and see if it was worth eating. Sandy and Amanda helped with the actual cooking. When Sandy tasted the first piece, she grinned and said, "Nope, it's not like chicken. It's more like turkey." The others looked at her skeptically. "I'm serious, taste it," she urged.

To everyone's surprise, it really did taste like turkey.

"There's enough meat here to help feed us at least a week," Ginny said, "and if I'm right, we can use the armor for plates and cooking pans."

About an hour later, with all the meat cooked along with some steamed vegetables, they sat down to eat.

"I still think we need to use the cave tonight," Spyder said,

"I agree," Wind said. "Hopefully, we won't run into any more of those rhinodillos."

"Rhinodillos?" Hal raised an eyebrow questioningly.

"Well it looked like a cross between a rhinoceros and an armadillo to me, so I call it a rhinodillo."

"It makes as much sense to me as anything else," Bear agreed. "As for staying in the cave, I think Wind's right. You can take some pistols in with you."

"Us?" Sandy questioned. "Not you?"

"There's no way I can stay in there all night." Bear said. "I'd be a raving lunatic before two hours. It's not really the close space, but the combination of confinement and absolute blackness."

"Then are you gonna sleep out here?" Amanda asked.

"I'll stay with him," Keith said before Bear could answer.

"I'll stay out here," Bear confirmed, then looked at Keith, "alone. I don't need a babysitter."

"I didn't think you did," Keith said defensively. "I just... "

"Everyone else will stay in the cave," he interrupted, "and I'll stay out here."

"Why argue with him," Ginny said, "He's gonna do what he wants anyway, he always does. Don't give him the satisfaction of giving him attention by arguing with him."

Sandy spun toward Ginny and Hal quickly grabbed her by the elbow. "Let it go," he said. "It's not worth a fight or any more drama than we already have." He looked at Bear. "You do what you think's best," he said. Then he looked at Ginny, "We understand."

Ginny picked up some pots and pans and left the clearing, walking toward the stream.

***

Following an hour of wrapping supplies in plastic and moving them into the cave, they had almost half the items stored away. There wouldn't be much for Bear to guard during the night. Having to reuse plastic bags and sheets during the move, they were careful not to care or rip any.

Spyder and Wind blocked all three holes in the second room by piling supplies in front of them. "If nothing else, it'll make noise if something tries to come in here," Spyder said.

Wind dropped a sleeping bag next to the supplies and began unrolling it.

"Good thinking," Keith said. "Something has to move you as well as the other stuff to get in." He reached over, grabbed another sleeping bag and laid it next to Wind's. "That makes two."

"Here's the third," Spyder said throwing another on the opposite side of Wind.

"We should only use one torch at a time," Hal said. "We can't afford to use up too much oxygen and create carbon dioxide since we don't know what kind of air circulation there is."

"True," Keith said. "One of those holes could even be the reason for any air circulation at all."

"That's not a very settling thought," Sandy said.

By the look on everyone else's face, they seemed to agree with her last statement.

CHAPTER ELEVEN

Bear was sure he heard or sensed someone in the water below the falls. However, at about five-thirty in the morning, it would still be dark for another half hour or so and next to impossible to see anyone among the ripples and waves caused by the cascading water as it entered the pool.

He had last spoken to Hal around midnight, who told him that everyone was going to bed. Although someone would be awake, they would be in the cave the rest of the night. After that, he spent some time constructing a trap to see if he could catch whomever it was moving around in the dark.

Unable to see anyone in the pool, he returned to the outside camping area. Most of the supplies still there were fresh food. For now, they would continue to only use the cave at night and do everything else in the open.

Settling on his favorite rock in the clearing, he heard a noise in the foliage to his left. Slowly reaching down, he unhooked the black-powder pistol on his right hip. He quietly pulled the 9mm from his waistband. The pistol on his hip didn't have as many bullets, nor was it as accurate as the 9mm, but it had considerably more knockdown power.

More noise and he slipped silently off the rock into a crouched position, pistol aimed at the spot. A familiar grunt told him his visitor was a wild boar. *More meat on the hoof,* he thought. *Maybe things are starting to look up.*

No sooner had the last thought crossed his mind, when a crashing sound erupted a couple of yards from the boar. Even though it was in heavy foliage and moving with unbelievable speed, he saw one of the amphibious animals he had seen before -- one of the goddamn things that killed Dr. Hamilton -- who knew, maybe the same one.

Bear stuffed the 9mm back into his belt and pulled the second 44 cal. Black-powder pistol from its holster. As he was about to fire, one of his traps sprung and yanked someone or something off the ground. Even as he began shooting, he was aware that a human figure dangled by a foot a short distance away.

Bear fired at the charging creature, striking it with every shot, yet it kept coming. Emptying both pistols, he dropped them, pulled the 9mm from his waist and one from its shoulder holster, and continued firing.

About eight feet away the animal stumbled, caught its balance and continued slower. However, the hesitation was enough for Bear to blow both its eyes from their sockets. At the same time, the bullets must have found a way into its brain and possibly ricocheted around inside its skull. The creature dropped less than a yard from his feet. To his left the boar was crashing away in the underbrush, to his right a human hung from an ankle among the limbs of the surrounding trees and in front of him lay at least a little revenge.

"That one's for Doc," he said as he walked away.

He approached the figure hanging in the tree from the east as Hal ran up from the west.

"You okay?" Hal asked. "I heard shots."

"I'm fine," Bear answered and continued to where a wire hung from a limb.

"You set a trap?"

"Yep," Bear answered.

Hal looked around. "What set it off?"

"A person."

"I don't see anyone," Hal argued.

"Look at the wire."

"Okay, I see the wire," Hal said. "It's that small cable you used as a string line for the horses before."

"That cable was coiled."

Hal realized what Bear was saying. The cable hung straight as if it held a weight. He stepped toward the loop above his head.

"Don't get too close," Bear warned.

"Hal stopped and looked at him.

Bear looked around found a branch, picked it up and without hesitation swung it at the area where he remembered the person's head should be. He connected with something invisible resulting in a loud "whack" and an unconscious female flickered into view. A young woman hung from the cable by her right foot.

Hal released the cable and eased the unconscious woman to the ground. He removed the noose from her foot and stood up straight.

Bear looked at the young woman on the ground. From what he could tell, she was in her late teens or early twenties. She had long black hair and was dressed in a short brown, one-piece animal-skin dress. Blood oozed from the side of her head where he hit her.

He turned the girl over and removed a knife from the sheath hanging on her belt. The eight-inch weapon had a wooden handle with a blade of smooth stone. Bear shoved the knife into his own belt for safekeeping.

Pulling a cloth from his pack, he soaked it with water from his canteen and put it on the cut. As he did, Keith came rushing through the bushes.

"Everyone's still in the cave," he said. "They're safe there. I said I'd find out what's going on and let 'em know."

That's when he noticed the young woman on the ground.

"What the... "

The girl slowly regained consciousness. As she became aware of the men, she sat up and tried to pull away. Bear spun her around and held her from behind. "Take it easy," he said soothingly. "We're not gonna hurt you." She continued struggling.

Keith knelt in front of her and said, "You're safe. We won't... " The young woman's leg flashed out, kicking him in the chest. He flew backward and landed flat on his butt then sprawled on the ground.

Hal leaned against a tree with his arms crossed across his chest. "Ouch," he said grinning.

Bear burst out laughing. He laughed so hard, he almost released his grip on the young woman. Regaining his composure, he slowly released her with his left hand. He again placed the damp cloth on the scalp laceration. "You're in no danger," he said still behind her. "We won't hurt you."

This time, she didn't move. He slowly relaxed his grip on her left hand and handed her the cloth. Gently, he released her and moved to the side where she could see him.

"Can you understand me?" He asked.

The girl looked at him blankly.

114

"Do you speak English?" he asked.

Slowly, the young woman nodded.

"What's your name?" He asked.

Again, she simply looked at him.

Keith regained his feet and slowly approached Bear and the young woman. The girl's hand dropped to the empty sheath. Realizing she was weaponless, fear again clouded her face.

"I've got your knife," Bear said. "I'll give it back to you when I'm sure you won't use it on me."

She looked at him appraisingly.

"My name's Rafe," he looked at Keith, "and this young man's name is Keith." Then pointing at Hal said, "... and that ugly thing over there is Hal."

She looked at the knife in Bear's belt. He saw her gaze and said, "I'll give it to you when you tell us your name, how's that?"

As they watched, the young woman faded from view. She simply disappeared from sight.

"What the... " Keith said.

Hal shrugged himself off the tree.

Bear stood and looked around in disbelief.

From the side they heard a female voice. "Palenaka" it said. "I am Palenaka."

The men spun toward the sound. The young woman stood five feet away looking at them. She was about five feet, six inches tall with long black hair and compelling almond shaped brown eyes.

Keith's jaw dropped and he stared at her as if she had two heads. Bear, surprised but not showing it said, "That's a good trick."

Palenaka smiled. "I mean you no harm," she said.

Bear nodded and pulled the knife from his belt. "In that case, you may want this back."

Palenaka stepped forward and took the weapon from him with both hands, placed it against her forehead and then placed it in its sheath. "I was following to learn more of you."

"You've been following me for two days," Bear corrected.

"That is correct," Palenaka said. "I stood beside you at the alawai. It is a place I love."

"So do I," Bear answered smiling.

"You know the place of which I speak?" Palenaka asked surprised.

"The place where the water reaches from the mountains to the sea," he answered. "Mauka to makai."

"You know my language?" Palenaka appeared very surprised.

"Only a few words," he told her. "There are other people over there." He nodded toward the location of the cave. "They're our friends."

"They are in the ana," Palenaka said. "I will follow you."

"Ana?" Keith asked.

"Cave," Bear answered, "why don't you get the others and meet us in camp?"

Keith was off in a split-second.

Hal joined Bear as he walk by and Palenaka remained behind them.

***

When they walked in the camp, everyone was already waiting there.

116

"Folks, we have a visitor with us," Bear said.

Keith walked into the clearing from the cave as Bear made his statement. "Some visitor," a man with a long beard said and grinned. "He only comes around at eating time."

Keith stuck one finger up from his fist and stepped to the side.

"Well, I'll be damned," the man with the beard said. "Where did you find this purdy young thang?"

"Hi," Sandy said stepping forward. "I'm Sandy."

"Everyone, this is Palenaka," Bear formerly introduced her. "She's from around here somewhere. You'll need to introduce yourselves."

Palenaka smiled. "Aloha," she said with a slight bow.

Bear noticed that she eyed Spyder cautiously. He leaned over and whispered in her ear. "His name is Spyder and he's harmless. He just covers his ugly face with hair."

"I heard that," Spyder retorted, then back to Palenaka. "I ain't that ugly ma'am. I just don't like to shave, that's all. You're as welcome here as a breath of fresh air."

Palenaka was surprised at the warm greetings of these strange people. Their dress was different from anything she had ever seen. They spoke the English language, but differently than she had ever heard. Some carried knives and all carried other things she intuitively knew were weapons, though she didn't know what kind.

Everyone introduced him or herself in turn and Sandy invited her to sit in the clearing with them. Palenaka sat on a log hoping she wasn't doing anything wrong. She left the large rock, the highest of the seats, for their leader. When Sandy sat on the rock, she was surprised.

Rising, she walked over, knelt before Sandy, crossed her arms across her breast and bowed her head. "I ask you to accept me as a humble visitor to your Ohana nui. I am Palenaka, kama'āina 'OHana O'Makemake. I thank you for your welcome and bid you Aloha."

Sandy surprised by Palenaka's actions, composed herself and said, "Palenaka, you're welcome here with us." When the young woman looked up, she continued. "I have to tell you that we consider everyone here equal. We hold no one higher than another."

Palenaka was surprised at this revelation. "But you sit in the place of honor. You are above all others are you not?"

Sandy looked around. "Yes, I guess I'm sitting higher. But, it has nothing to do with my position with the others." Sandy stood up. "Actually, if we were going to honor anyone, we would honor you. You are from here and can teach us much. Please, sit here." She motioned to the rock.

"I could not," Palenaka said. "It would not be right."

"Fine," Sandy said and sat on a log, level with the rest of the group.

"We're all equal here," Amanda explained. "We work together to survive."

"Like Ohana nui," Palenaka said.

The others looked puzzled.

"Yes," Bear answered. "Like a family or clan."

Everyone agreed nodding at the definition.

"Where is this place?" Bear asked. "Does it have a name?"

Palenaka looked at him surprised. "It is our home," she said. "It is Farn." She paused, "If I may ask, how is it that you came here and not know where you are?"

"We don't know how we got here," Hal answered. "We went to sleep in one place and woke up the next morning, here."

Palenaka nodded as if the answer contained nothing unexpected.

"How did you learn English?" Bear asked.

"The old ones tell of people, haoles, from the sea. They brought English here. My mother and I learned it because we are Kupua. It is expected of us."

"Kupua," Keith repeated. "What's that?"

Palenaka looked confused, as if she couldn't find the right word in English.

"A Kupua is a person with powers," Bear explained. "In English, they'd be called a witch or warlock."

"That's silly," Sandy said. "Don't tell me they believe in witchcraft."

"Don't scoff too soon," Keith cautioned. "Bear and I have seen some of her powers. They're real."

Sandy looked at Keith. "Now Keith... "

"Sandy," Bear interrupted with a tilt of his head. "She does have powers beyond what we'd call normal."

She looked at Bear and shook her head. The last thing she needed was for Bear to be buying into superstition.

"After we caught her, she turned invisible," Keith explained. "I'm not kidding," he said when the others looked at him in disbelief.

"He's telling the truth," Bear said. "I know it's hard to believe, but it happened."

"Show us," the one called Ginny challenged. "Show us how you can become invisible."

"There is no need for me to at this time," Palenaka said. "I did it before when I feared danger.

"Right, sure you did," Ginny said sarcastically.

"Then you only do it in times of danger?" Keith asked.

"Yes," Palenaka said. "Even then, I can only remain unseen for a short time. Afterward I am very tired. The longer I continue, the more tired I become."

"We used to have another member, but he was killed by some animal," Sandy said.

"What kind of animal?" Palenaka asked.

"The kind that was chasing that hog," Bear answered.

"Kalekona," Palenaka said softly and lowered her head.

Everyone looked at her questioningly.

"Kalekona means dragon," Bear explained.

"The Kalekona can live on land even though they prefer the water," Palenaka explained. "They can run like the wind and jump very long distances. The ones that live on Lua Pele are said to breathe fire."

"Lua Pele?" Hal asked.

"Lua Pele is volcano," Bear said.

"It was a lizard of some kind," Hal confirmed. "I couldn't get a shot at it; Dr. Hamilton blocked the thing's head."

"No one's blaming you Hal," Bear said. "Actually, I'm hoping the one I just killed is the one that got him. At least, I'd like to think it was. No one thinks you'd let anything happen to any of us if you could help it, you should know that."

Ginny rose to her feet. "Speaking of which," she hesitated. "I made a fool of myself today with Sandy and I want to apologize."

Sandy appeared shocked. "Don't worry about it Ginny. It's over."

"That's kind of you Sandy, but I said what I did in public and I want to apologize in public," Ginny insisted.

Sandy stepped up to her and the two women hugged. Even though they weren't close, Sandy admired Ginny for what she'd done. "It was just nerves," Sandy said. "Thank you for the apology and you know it's accepted."

"Thank you," Ginny said and sat down.

"That's my Little Teacup," Spyder declared.

Palenaka wasn't sure what was happening, but she could tell that it made everyone happy and that was good. She could sense that these people meant no harm; they only wanted to live in peace and care for each other. She was glad to have found them. However, she wanted to tell them about the Nāki.

"You are safe here for a time," she said. "But, you must avoid the Nāki."

Everyone looked at Bear. "The Nāki?" he asked.

121

"The Nāki is a clan of giants. They are 'Ai kanaka." She hesitated trying to find the right word. "Flesh eaters," she finally said.

"Cannibals," Bear said the word in disbelief.

The group looked at each other. A feeling of unease seemed to settle on them like a blanket. With this new revelation, even as the dark retreated, it felt deep and repressive. Each looked at the surrounding bushes, the surrounding shadows took on menacing shapes and Sandy tossed a log on the fire.

***

Sandy helped Ginny finish the food and everyone sat down to eat. Palenaka was unsure of the food. She had never smelled anything like it before. When she tasted it, she smiled and said, "It tastes like He'e".

Bear smiled. It was canned clam chowder with herbs and spices added. "Octopus," he said. "It's probably the closest thing they have to it."

"I love octopus," Keith said enthusiastically. "I used to eat it all the time."

"Sooner or later, we'll find some eggs and get some bacon and ham from one of the local boars," Ginny said. "Then we'll be able to have a normal breakfast."

"Speaking of eating," Bear said. "There're some fruits you need to stay away from. He pulled a piece of cloth from his pack, unwrapped it and produced a manchineel fruit.

"Karkoi," Palenaka observed. "It is dangerous to eat. Even the blood from the plants can injure a person."

Bear pulled an akee from the pack.

"Akee," Palenaka said. "If it is not ripe, it is poisonous. We also use it in ceremonies to see visions. You should not eat either of those."

"Are there any other things we shouldn't eat?" Sandy asked.

"Koa nuts," Palenaka answered, "Kooluu and lahiki from the water."

What is kooluu and lahiki?" Bear asked.

"They are I'a," Palenaka explained. "Kooluu looks like a large worm with a fin along the back, but it has six legs. Lahiki is like a large leaf that flies underwater, but it has two tails and four eyes. They produce death in less than a sunrise."

"Six legged eels and rays with two tails," Bear mused.

"A sunrise?" Spyder asked.

"The time it takes the sun to show fully above the horizon," Palenaka said.

"About twenty to thirty minutes," Bear estimated. "They're quick. Koa nuts come from all these trees around us. The wood is great for building, but the nuts will kill."

"Is there anything else?" Ginny asked.

"Nothing but some of the kuka in an ana," Palenaka answered.

"Kuka in an ana?" Sandy questioned.

"On the walls," Palenaka clarified.

"Algae," Bear guessed. "So, we don't eat anything scrapped off a cave wall."

"I won't be missing that," Spyder said, thought for a second and continued. "You said before you and your mother were... " he hesitated, "witches. Where is your mother now?"

"We are Kupua. We do not live with the others of our Ohana. We live alone, as is our tradition. As Kupua, we live away, but serve our Ohana nui."

"What do you do?" Amanda asked.

"We serve our Ohana nui as they need us. Kupua have many skills that may be used. As you have seen, my special skill is to be unseen. My mother can tell what a person is thinking when needed. Other advanced skills are becoming an animal and flying. Maybe, in the future, my mother or I may be able to do one or all of these."

"Now they're sounding like you Bear," Keith said.

"You are Kupua?" Palenaka asked.

Bear grinned. "No I'm not," he said. "I just believe it could happen."

"Of course it can happen," she said. "You have seen it."

As Bear nodded, Amanda said, "Is there any way we can see you disappear?"

"It is not needed now," Palenaka answered as before.

"Would you be willing to show us one time?" Sandy asked.

"For you, I will do it," Palenaka said.

Sandy didn't argue with her decision or point out again that she wasn't a leader.

As they watched, she faded from view. A few seconds later, she spoke from behind Bear. "That is what I can do."

Sandy looked behind Bear. She was stunned. What she had seen went against all logic. Yet, there Palenaka stood. She had disappeared in front of their eyes and materialized in another place. Sandy was speechless for the first time in a long time.

"I just remembered something," Hal said. "You knew where all our friends were before. How did you know that?"

"I was in the ana when the hao'amakila attacked. It was I that took its life."

"The rhinodillo," Wind said.

Bear only shook his head as if he had known it all along.

"I have been here since... " she looked at Bear. "Since Bear Rafe returned."

"My real name is Rafe," he explained, "but all my friends call me Bear. Since I think of you as a friend, you can call me Bear too."

"Thank you my new friend, Bear," she said.

"If it is permitted, I must talk to my mother," Palenaka said.

"Of course it's permitted," Sandy said. "You're not a prisoner here."

"Thank you," Palenaka said and rose to her feet. "I will return tomorrow." She gave a short bow, turned and in only a few strides disappeared into the dense foliage leaving the rest shocked and astounded at her abrupt departure.

CHAPTER TWELVE

Bear awoke, stood, stretched and added a log to the fire. Even though the place was beautiful, danger lurked on land and in the sea. It was agreed; everyone felt better keeping the fire going through the night.

He wanted his morning coffee. Taking both coffee pots, he went to the pool for water. No one liked his coffee, which suited him, but he could still get water for them.

Kneeling to dip the pots, he saw Palenaka sitting at the edge of the pond a short distance away. She sat cross-legged beside the water with her wrists resting lightly on her knees. With her obviously in meditation, Bear didn't want to disturb her.

After quietly filling the pots, he rose and turned to leave.

"My mother asks to see you," Palenaka said.

"To see me?" He asked.

"To see all of you," Palenaka corrected. "She asks that all of you come with me to our home."

"I can't make a decision like that," he explained. "I have to talk to the rest. If they vote to go, we will."

"I do not understand," she said. "Is there not one who leads among you?"

"Not in the way I think you mean," he answered. "We're free to make our own choices. No single person can make a decision for the rest."

"What do you do if all do not agree?"

"Then, the person must decide what's best for him or herself," he explained. "As long as it doesn't put the rest in danger, they'll do what they want. We always think of the group first."

"This is a strange Ohana nui. But, it seems to serve you well," Palenaka observed.

"Let's get back to the others and I'll talk to 'em about a trip to see your mother," he said. "By the way, how far away is she?"

"It is three daylight's travel from here to my home," she said.

"Can we travel by horse?"

"You may travel on your animals to the alawai. There is no way for them to cross. You must leave them there," she explained.

"I'll tell the rest," he said.

Back at camp, the others were up and moving around. As Bear and Palenaka entered the clearing Ginny walked by them on her way to get water for coffee. Bear raised the two large pots for her to see.

"I was looking for those," she said. "Glad to see we didn't lose 'em." She took the containers and returned to the fire.

"You're welcome," Bear said to her back as she left.

"She did not thank you for your effort," Palenaka observed.

"That's just Ginny," he explained. "She might not always act or talk kindly, but she does think of the rest of us."

Palenaka nodded.

Over breakfast, Bear explained that Palenaka's mother wanted to meet them. The first question was from Sandy.

"Palenaka, how did you talk to your mother if she's three days from here?"

Palenaka looked surprised. "We talk with our minds," she said. "All Kupua do this."

"Of course," Sandy said, "how silly of me."

"When I saw her, Palenaka was in deep meditation," Bear explained. "That's probably how she did it."

"All this magic and mysticism has me concerned," Sandy said. "How do we know she's not someone or something evil? I don't mean any disrespect, but we know nothing about you. Besides, I'm not sure pure magic exists."

"This place shouldn't exist," Bear reminded her. "We went to sleep in one place and woke up the next morning in another. Can you explain that? Can you explain the creature, the kalekona that killed Dr. Hamilton?"

"Sandy, as much as I hate to admit it," Spyder said, "we're under a different set of rules here. Things have changed, they're different and we have to accept them or die because of disbelief. I don't understand everything, but I'm willing to accept what I see and experience. Shit, Palenaka disappeared. I saw that. It has to be real."

Sandy understood what he meant. However, her religious teachings hadn't taught her to accept magic as a good thing. Obviously, it was real here. However, she would have to wait and see whether it was good or bad. "I'll do my best," was all she said.

Bear knew Sandy's statement meant that she would open herself to the possibility of new things. It might be slow in coming, but it would happen eventually.

The group voted to follow Palenaka to her home. As they began gathering their supplies to load on the horses, Palenaka approached Bear.

"Why do they take those things?" She asked.

"They're supplies. Things for us to eat, clothes to wear," he explained.

"Why would you need them?" She pressed.

"We don't know about gathering food here. We don't know what shelter there may be on the way."

"I know of these things," she said. "There is no need for worry." She pointed at a rifle. "What are those tools?"

"That's a rifle," Bear answered. "Don't you know about rifles and pistols?"

She shook her head.

"They make a loud noise," he pulled a bullet from a magazine, "and throw one of these a long distance."

Palenaka looked confused. "I do not understand." She reached toward the weapon.

Bear pulled it back, "It's dangerous," he said. "Until you know how it works, you could injure yourself or someone else. Follow me and I'll show you what it does." He called across the camp to Hal, "I'm gonna be firing a couple of shots. Don't worry there's no problem. I'm gonna show Palenaka how a rifle and pistol works."

Bear led Palenaka away from camp to the grove of palm trees beside the beach. A coconut lay on the sand about fifty yards away.

He pointed, "See that coconut on the sand?"

"Yes, I see it," Palenaka said.

"You'll need to put your hands over your ears." He showed her what he meant.

When she followed his example, he raised the M16 to his shoulder, took aim and fired.

Palenaka jumped as the rifle cracked. Fifty yards away, the coconut shattered in a small explosion.

Palenaka wore a stunned and slightly fearful look. "I have heard of such things, but I have never seen them," she said.

"Stories from the ancients told of this," Palenaka said. "But, I did not believe such was possible."

Bear pulled a 9mm from his shoulder holster. "This does the same thing," he explained. "It just doesn't work at as long a distance. Cover your ears again."

Bear shot another coconut. This time it shattered with less of a mess than before.

Palenaka looked from the coconut to Bear. "What kind of magic is this?"

"It's not magic," he said. "It's made by man."

"Such things could protect you from the Nāki," she said.

"Is that knife your only weapon?" Bear asked.

"No," Palenaka said. "I also have a ma'a."

"What's a ma'a," Bear questioned.

She unwrapped the belt from her waist. Bear was surprised to see that the short sheath holding her knife was also the pocket of a sling.

She picked up a rock and put the knife between her teeth. After loading the rock in the sling, she spun it over her head and released it. The rock struck another coconut on the sand. The coconut burst open with a loud pop.

Palenaka wrapped the sling around her waist, tied it in front and returned the knife to its pocket.

Bear grinned. "Not as loud, but still effective," he said. "That's how you killed that hao'amakila, in the ana, I like it."

Palenaka nodded. It pleased her that she could bring something useful to these people.

***

At Palenaka's urging, they packed only what they could carry on the horse they rode. Since no one wanted to be without a weapon or bullets in this strange new place, they were the main things taken. They moved rest of supplies into the cave and reluctantly released the remaining horses.

As they rode to the north, Bear described the saber-toothed tiger he had killed.

"Oli'i kika," Palenaka said. "They are great hunters. My mother has studied them most of her life."

Just before sunset, they reached the alawai. The water was calm and clear. Looking into its depths, Bear estimated it to be at least fifty feet deep.

Palenaka led them toward the mountains until reaching the spot where he stayed before. Once there, they set up camp. As they unloaded the horses, Palenaka disappeared into the surrounding forest.

"Where's she going?" Hal asked.

"I have no idea," Bear answered.

"I'll follow her," Keith offered.

"I wouldn't do that," Bear said. "If you lose her, you might get lost in the dark."

"It's not that dark," Keith argued.

"Not yet," Bear said. "But in another ten minutes it will be, especially in the forest."

"He's right," Wind said. "None of us needs to take chances around here."

They finished setting up camp and started a fire as Palenaka returned. She carried a young pig over her shoulder. She dropped it beside the fire and Ginny saw that it was already prepared for cooking. There was even a stick running through the animal lengthwise.

After gutting the pig, Palenaka had stuffed numerous fruits and berries into the stomach and sewn it shut with some sort of small vine.

"That's very kind of you," Sandy said. "Not only did you do the hunting, but you prepared it for cooking."

Palenaka nodded and smiled. "It is easier to carry as one."

"I'm the cook around here," Ginny mumbled as she picked up the suckling pig and walked away to the fire.

Palenaka looked at Hal.

"Don't worry about it," he said.

"We might as well let the horses go now," Bear said. "There's no reason to keep 'em tied up anymore."

"Maybe not," Palenaka said. "Mother says we may be able to take them with us. We will know in the morning."

"I thought you said there wasn't any way to take 'em across the water," Bear reminded her of her previous statement.

"There is no way," Palenaka assured him. "But, mother says we should wait until tomorrow."

He didn't know what she meant, but was willing to wait until morning. He and Spyder staked the horses in a large patch of tall grass for the night.

***

"I still can't believe the climate here," Sandy said lying beside Hal. Everyone had finished the meal, cleaned up and retired for the night.

"It's beautiful alright," he agreed. "Have you come to terms with the magic thing yet?"

"Hell no," Sandy answered. "I accept that it's happening. I'm just not sure if it's good or a trick to make us trust her."

"Don't you believe that God can save a person?" Hal asked.

"Of course I do," Sandy said. "You know that."

"Wouldn't that be magic of some kind?" He asked. "Wouldn't that be good?"

"I'm gonna stop talking about this for now," she said. "I need to think about it some more."

"Want to talk about that dragon thing?" Hal asked.

"Kiss my ass honey," Sandy said sweetly. She knew Hal was smiling beside her in the dark.

"There you go getting all romantic on me again," he said rolling onto his side.

Everyone slept well that night -- they all needed to. The loss of Dr. Hamilton had added to their stress and drained all their emotional and most of their physical strength.

CHAPTER THIRTEEN

Bear awoke with Palenaka gently shaking his shoulder. When he opened his eyes, he saw that she was smiling. "What's wrong?" He asked sitting up. The sun was barely above the ocean and its light only shone above the treetops.

Palenaka looked around. "I see nothing wrong," she said a frown furrowed her brow.

He looked around and saw Hal was awake and pouring a cup of coffee.

"Did you make coffee?" Bear asked Hal as he stood and stretched.

"No," he answered. "I think it was Palenaka."

Bear looked at her. "Did you make the coffee?"

"Yes," she said. "I watched Ginny and attempted to make it as she did."

"It's good," Hal said after taking a sip.

"It seems like an important part of the morning meditation ritual," Palenaka said.

"I don't know about the meditation part," Hal said grinning. "But, it is part of the morning ritual."

"Mother says I should help you keep your rituals while we travel."

"God bless the woman," Hal said raising his cup in a toast.

"Mother also says we should see the alawai mauka of here."

"What do we need to look for?" Bear asked.

"I do not know," she answered. "However, mother says help may be there."

"I'll get the others up," Hal said. Looking at Bear, he asked, "What's mauka?"

"Mauka means inland or toward the mountains," he answered. "Makai means toward the sea. It's used for directions from a point or place."

"Your friends are not needed for this," Palenaka said. "They are welcome to come, but it is not necessary."

"If it's okay, I'd like Keith to go with us," Bear said.

"If you wish," she agreed. "He is your student, yes?"

"He has talents and we're trying to give him knowledge to go along with 'em," Bear explained.

Palenaka smiled as if she knew something they didn't.

Bear woke Keith and told him to get ready to travel. Hal woke Sandy and told her he, Bear and Keith had something to do and they would be back later.

*****

Palenaka wove her way through the thick brush silently and effortlessly. After traveling a short distance, Bear moved Keith up to follow behind her and see how she did it.

"Watch what she does," he said. "She'll show you how to pick your way through the brush without resistance and noise."

They traveled westward for almost an hour following Palenaka before emerging beside the alawai, closer to the base of the steep mountains. The water was only about twenty-five feet wide. It seemed to be narrowing, the farther it extended from the sea.

Palenaka made her way away from the water, through another grove of trees choked with bushes. In a couple of places, she pointed out plants with large thorns. "Avoid these," she said, "they cause sickness."

About fifteen minutes later, they again traveled along the edge of the water. She smiled as she looked up the alawai toward the mountains.

When Keith, Hal and Bear emerged beside the water, they stood dumbfounded. A short distance away, a bridge spanned the canal.

"I thought you said there was no way across the water," Hal said.

"There was none yesterday," she answered.

"This bridge didn't just grow here," Hal argued.

"How could your mother build a bridge?" Keith asked.

Palenaka smiled at him. "She did not build it."

"That makes no sense," Hal said shaking his head.

"They're real here," Bear said softly to himself, surprised at what lay before them. "They actually exist here."

"What the hell are you talking about?" Hal asked.

"Magic," Keith answered for Bear.

Palenaka frowned. Why was the bridge so hard for these people to understand?

Bear looked at Palenaka and smiled. "Tell them who built the bridge."

"Menehune," she said matter-of-factly.

Hal and Keith didn't understand and looked at her questioningly.

"The little people," she said as if the statement should clear everything up for them.

Keith looked at Bear still confused.

Bear was still smiling. "They're myths in Hawaii," he explained. "They're like the leprechaun in Ireland. They have magical powers, but in Hawaii, they love to build."

Both men looked skeptical. Neither was ready to accept little people with magical powers could build the bridge they were looking at.

Bear grinned. "This is incredible," he said. Turning his gaze from the bridge, back to his friends, he explained, "They only work at night and in secrecy." A frown came over his face. He looked at Palenaka. "When a bargain is made, they'll willingly help humans."

She nodded.

"What agreement did your mother make with them?" Bear asked.

"She will tell you later," Palenaka said.

"Her mother made a deal with Leprechauns, Hal said, not believing what he was saying. He could understand if Keith was willing to go along with this bullshit, but Bear? He opened his mouth to further proclaim his disbelief, and then remembered *I watched her disappear. She vanished in front of my eyes and reappeared in another place. I tried to explain to Sandy that magic could be a possibility here. Why should I have any more trouble accepting Leprechauns?*

Keith observed the changed in Hal's expression. "What," he said. "What were you thinking?"

"Oh, nothing," Hal answered, stretched and ran both hands over his face. "But, how can I ask Sandy to accept the possibility of magic here, if I'm not willing to do it myself?"

"We must use the bridge today, Palenaka explained. "It will not be here at the second sunrise."

"I'm not gonna ask," Hal said, shaking his head with a sigh.

They walked to the bridge for a closer look at the structure. It was about twenty-five yards long and constructed of Koa wood. No one doubted that it would hold them and the horses. Except for the width, it would probably hold a car.

"There is no way this could have been built in one night," Keith said. "Even with modern technology, it wouldn't happen overnight."

"The Menehune only work at night," Palenaka explained. "This is a small structure for them. Unless one controls them, they will work only one night for a person."

"How do you control 'em?" Keith asked.

"You have to be able to recite the linage of the leader," Bear answered.

Again, Palenaka nodded in agreement. "You understand many of our things," she said to Bear. "However there is much you have to learn about yourself."

He simply nodded as if he already knew the information. "We need to get back and bring the others," he said.

The rest agreed and started back the way they had come.

"When she said you have a lot to learn about yourself, you didn't seem to have a question about that," Keith said.

"I have no doubt that she's right," Bear said. But with all you know... "

"There is no way anyone will ever know everything there is to know about themselves," he said. "We're always learning." Keith opened his mouth to speak and Palenaka angled away from the water. The men hurried to catch her and in a few minutes, entered a narrow clearing. The opening in the trees weaved out of sight to the east.

They followed the clearing for about thirty minutes then Palenaka led them to the left, directly into their camp.

"Why couldn't we've used that path on the way there?" Keith asked her as he entered the camp.

"I did not know where to look," Palenaka answered. "We needed to follow the alawai."

"We need to talk folks," Bear announced sitting down to wait for everyone to gather around.

***

Following an hour's discussion about the bridge and an explanation of the Menehunes by Bear and Palenaka, they packed up their camp and used the shorter route to get to the bridge.

"I suggest we dismount and lead the horses across," Bear said. "We don't need to have one spook and toss anyone in the water."

The rest followed as he walked his horse across. On the other side, Wind said, "That's a solid bridge, there's no way it'll fall down in just a couple of days."

"It'll be taken down," Bear said. "That's what Palenaka's mother meant."

139

"Who would do something like that?" Wind asked. "That's a sturdy bridge. It could be useful for a long time."

"It was made for our use only," Palenaka said.

"Why can't they leave it up for future use?" Sandy asked. "It would help everyone."

"It is the Menehune way," Palenaka explained. "Mother requested their help for us. When that help is finished the bridge will leave."

"How far is it to your home, little lady?" Spyder asked.

"It is less than two suns using these horses," she answered. "We will have to lead the animals at the end."

"Let's get going," Bear said.

"We must catch fish," Palenaka informed them sliding off her horse.

"We have enough supplies and can hunt for more if we need it, Ginny told her.

"We must catch fish," Palenaka repeated and walked to the water's edge. She stood facing the water and spread her arms with her hands palm up, her elbows slightly bent. Her chant began barely above a whisper and rose to the level of normal speech by the time she finished.

She untied the sling from around her waist and laid her knife on the ground. Standing at the edge of the water, she knelt and dipped the pocket of the sling under the surface.

The rest, after tying their horses to trees, watched with fascination. In less than a minute, she pulled up and out sharply on the lines. A fish popped from beneath the water, over her head and landed on the ground behind her.

"We can use spears," Spyder offered.

"They must be whole, without injury," Palenaka explained dipping her sling back in the water.

"I don't think these are for us to eat," Sandy suggested.

Palenaka smiled at her. "You are correct."

Bear walked up and nodded at Spyder as he unrolled the canvas he carried behind his saddle. Each man held an end and dipped the material in the water. About two minutes later, Spyder whispered, "Now." Both men pulled the canvas, now containing water from the canal. Inside were three fish swimming in the water dipped from the alawai.

"You are both good at this," Palenaka said smiling and nodding at the men. "I will get one more."

"I guess we needed five," Wind observed.

With a flick of her wrists, Palenaka flipped the last fish out of the water and onto the shore beside the others. She went to a Koa tree and pulled some small vines encircling it. With each fish, she ran one end of a vine into its mouth, out through its gill and tied the end back onto the vine.

She carried the fish to the end of the bridge, dropped them back in the water and tied the vine to a board. On her way back, she met Hal, Bear, Spyder and Wind, all carrying a fish tied to a vine.

"Thought you might like some help," Hal said, "We'll be finished in a minute."

With the last fish secured to the bridge, Palenaka said, "We may go now."

"Well, this was a waste of time," Ginny said mounting her horse.

141

Palenaka glared at her. "It was payment."

"I'm sure," Ginny said waiting for the others to get ready.

Back on her horse, Palenaka led the way along the base of the mountain range.

CHAPTER FOURTEEN

About noon of the second day, following their leaving the bridge, Palenaka entered a valley. "We will lead the horses from here," she said. "Stay in the stream and leave no tracks."

They traveled in single file for three hours. Palenaka insisted the horses remain in the stream even when they took short breaks. During the first break, she explained why they could leave no trail.

"Nāki sometimes pass this way," she told them. "They have not discovered my home. We are safe until they do. This is why we must keep the horses in the water and leave no sign of our passing this way."

After traveling the length of the valley, they came to a dead end. "Are you sure this the right place?" Ginny asked, she was tired and obviously becoming impatient.

Palenaka smiled sweetly. "It is the place," she said. "I was born here."

"There's no home around here," Ginny argued. "I think you're lost and don't want to admit it."

Palenaka looked at her still smiling. "You have much to learn," she said. The young woman turned and faced the cliff. Once again, she raised her arms with elbows slightly bent and her palms up. A few seconds later the rocks before her faded from view revealing a tunnel through the wall.

Without looking at Ginny, Palenaka led them through the short tunnel which was less than six feet long. Wind noticed the lack of animosity from the Palenaka toward Ginny. She had every right to be upset, but seemed unaffected by the woman's comments.

She's a calm person, Wind thought. *I'd have torn the bitch a new asshole by now. Maybe I can learn tolerance from her.*

"You must not pass this point without me or my mother," Palenaka said. "You will not be able to return."

She led them another fifteen minutes before entering a large clearing bounded on all sides by Koa, palm and other trees. Within the ring of trees were two stone houses and one small hut, all with thatched roofs.

A woman sat in a wicker chair on the porch of the smaller stone house. She almost looked like Palenaka's twin. She wore a floor-length, white cotton dress and an orchid in her long, black hair behind her right ear.

Palenaka dismounted, walked to the woman and knelt, bowing her head and crossing her arms across her breasts. "Mother, these are my friends from the point. I bring them in peace to Hana O'Makemake.

The woman rose, stepped forward and placed her hand on her daughters head. "Aloha, I am happy to see you home safely."

She returned to the chair and sat back down. Palenaka rose, turned sideways and looked at the group. Hal looked at Bear and nodded.

Bear stepped forward. He removed the M16 from his shoulder and laid it on the ground. He did the same with his pistols and lastly, his knife. Slipping his hat back off his head, he stepped up to the woman in the chair, knelt on one knee, crossed

144

his arms across his chest and bowed his head the same as Palenaka.

Looking up, he said, "We are friends of Palenaka and come to your Ohana Nui in peace. We are haole and greet you with aloha spirit."

The woman smiled. "Aloha," she said. "I am Weniki, mother of Palenaka. We are Kupua of the O'Hana O'Makemake. You are well met."

Bear stood and bowed. "Mahalo," he said pulling the stampede string and putting his hat back on his head.

"My daughter has told me of you," she said. "But, she did not tell me from where you come."

He hesitated. "We come from another time and place."

To Bear's surprise, she said, "You are not the first."

"Not the first?" He questioned.

"Aka is the first," she explained. "He came in the time of the ancients, long before I was born. He took over leadership of the Nāki and has ruled them since."

"How could he live for so long?" Bear asked.

"The Nāki have Kupua in their Ohana Nui," she explained.

"Magicians of their clan," Bear translated. "People used magic to keep him alive."

"It is said that he does not age," Weniki continued. "He continues to rule throughout time."

"What of the Nāki?" Bear asked.

"We will talk of these things and more later," Weniki said. "Now, you must gather your things and rest." She motioned at the other stone building.

145

"You mean that building is for us?" Bear asked surprised.

"It was built for you and your Ohana Nui," she answered, "except for that one." She pointed at Ginny. "She still has much to learn." Pointing at the small shack," she said, "You may stay there."

Ginny wore a stunned expression.

"She's my wife," Spyder said. I'll need... "

"It is our way," Weniki said. "When she learns, she may add to the Ohana."

"Goddamn," Spyder swore, "I'm not gonna give my wife up for any of these people." He looked at Weniki and Palenaka. "They can kiss my ass."

"Spyder," Bear said, "It won't take long. Ginny'll re-join us soon."

"Bullshit," he said. "That ain't gonna happen."

"It is our way," Weniki repeated. "We live in harmony with each other."

"I don't give a... "

"It's okay," Ginny interrupted. "It only means I sleep in a different place. We'll all be together during the day."

"I don't care... "

"It's okay," Ginny repeated placing her hand on his shoulder. "We're all safe here and the rest doesn't matter for now. It'll be fine." She looked at Weniki and said, "We'll follow your ways for now, no matter how stupid they are."

Weniki nodded and walked into the house.

***

The inside of the large stone house was one large room with five smaller ones surrounding it.

146

Grass-matted walls separated the rooms and the doors consisted of hanging cloth. The larger room had a rectangular table, a wooden bench, four chairs and a clay oven in a corner. The bench was large enough for four people. It was obviously the living and dining room. They surmised that the smaller rooms were bedrooms.

Palenaka stood with them in the large room.

"How did she know how many of us there were?" Sandy asked.

"I told her when we... " she hesitated, trying to think of the right word, "communicated," she finished.

"Is that how she knew our names without us telling her?"

"That is correct," She answered.

"Is this house always here?" Sandy asked.

"It is not, the structure was built last night," she said.

"Menehunes, right?" Wind asked.

"Yes," she answered. "They were pleased with our payment at the bridge."

"Do we owe them five more fish?" Amanda asked.

"No," Palenaka said. "Mother has taken care of the bargain. We are happy to have you here."

"We pay our own way," Spyder said. "Your mother shouldn't have to pay any bargain for us. We chose to come here."

"It is our way," Palenaka said, turned and left the house.

Spyder followed her out of the building. To his surprise, she went to Ginny's shack. At the door, she stopped him. "You may not enter," she said.

Spyder stiffened. He had no intention of abandoning Ginny. He didn't care what their way was.

"This is a structure of teaching. No one may enter but the student and the teacher. I may not even enter."

"That's a damn shame," Spyder said. "I'm sorry you can't go in, but you can't keep me out."

He stepped around Palenaka and reached for the cloth covering the door. However, an invisible barrier prevented him from touching it. He tried to enter and ran into something like a soft wall. It didn't feel solid, but he couldn't push past it either.

He stepped back as Ginny pushed the cloth aside and walked out of the building. He stood, looking at her dumbfounded. "How did you do that?"

"Do what," she answered with a confused look.

"I can't go inside there," he said.

"Oh," Ginny said looking at the door. "Sorry to hear that." She walked toward the ring of trees. "I need to answer the call of nature."

Spyder walked back to the large house. He wanted to let everyone know what had just happened. There was much more here than met the eye.

***

Bear stepped from the large house. He looked at the ring of trees around the large clearing. His gaze followed the surrounding mountain peaks. The walls were almost vertical and looked like the rest of the mountains he had seen. They looked as if

148

they were smooth at one time and rivers of water had cut deep grooves in the sides. The range was beautiful and reminded him of the Koolaus in Hawaii.

The mountains always looked to him as if some great monster had used its claws to dig furrows in their sides. Sharp ridges separated the fissures, green vegetation covered the whole thing and the overall effect was nothing short of stunning. *Who knows,* he thought, *in this world, maybe that's how it happened.* He smiled to himself, surprised at his own imagination.

The approaching night was warm with a soft breeze. Being in a valley, surrounded on all sides, he was surprised at the breeze. It was soft and almost caressed his skin as it passed by.

He walked along the ring of trees trying to learn the area. This morning, even though the valley had appeared to end, at least as much of it remained behind the barrier as outside. He was sure the barrier they had encountered was a mental image cast by Weniki or her mother. However, according to Spyder there was a similar barrier at Ginny's door. He didn't know what it all was and it really didn't matter as long as it kept them safe.

After walking the tree line, he turned back toward his new home provided by magical little people. Weniki stepped from her home and met him in the clearing between the structures. I hope you find your new home comfortable. It is not much, but I had little time.

"It's fine," Bear assured her. "We've been sleeping outside since coming here. We thank you for your hospitality."

149

Weniki nodded slowly. She looked at him, her eyes seemed to bore through him. A sad look washed over her face. "You are in great pain," she said.

Bear knew what she was talking about and looked at the ground. He had thought about Davata every day, since her dying in his arms. He looked back up into Weniki's eyes and smiled.

"Your soul is in pain," she said with conviction. "You are incomplete. This will change in time."

"No," he disagreed, "it won't."

"This soul, you encountered," she said, "was placed in your life to help you through a time of hardship. Your spirit is scattered, but it will repair. Even if you do not believe it now, this will happen."

"You're right," Bear agreed, "I don't believe it. She was my soul mate."

Weniki smiled, "We shall see."

Sandy stepped from their house. "Am I interrupting?" she asked joining Bear and Weniki.

"No," Weniki answered. "We were just talking of life." As she walked past Sandy she said, "Take care of your brother, he needs your help."

"What's wrong?" Sandy asked concerned. "Does your shoulder hurt?"

"It's not my physical condition she's talking about," he explained.

"You told her about our friendship, huh?" Sandy said.

"No, I didn't," he answered looking after Weniki. "I don't know how she came up with that."

"There's more going on around here than any of us understand," she said walking to a bench along the front of their new home and sitting down. "We

150

all have to adjust our thinking. We're living under different rules."

"There's more than that," he said sitting beside her. "The other day Palenaka said the name of the island is Farn. There is no 'F' in the Hawaiian language."

"What are you getting at?" Sandy asked.

"Someone else had to name the island," he answered. "It had to be someone whose language has an 'F' in it. Either they named it and left or other people live here."

"The Nāki," Sandy suggested concerned.

"I'm not sure," Bear said, "maybe."

They sat in silence, listening to the sounds of the night. The valley was a peaceful place. Something about it made him feel safe and relaxed.

At night, the area around the houses appeared exactly as portrayed in movies about Polynesian villages. Each house had a pair of torches on each side of its front door. Soft candlelight glowed through the windows of the buildings. The night was warm; the air felt soft and a gentle breeze was fresh, sweet and clean.

***

Keith and Amanda were in their room. "I think I've about reached my limit," Amanda said. "I can't handle much more."

"If we don't have a choice, what can we do?" He asked.

"Have a breakdown," she responded quickly. "In less than a week, we've been in a battle, sent to some other place, we've seen a saber toothed tiger, a giant man-eating amphibian lizard of some sort and lost a dear friend."

"It's only a problem if you try to make sense out of it all," Keith said soothingly, "only if you try to know the reason for things."

"Don't you want to know the reason why all this has happened?"

"I wouldn't mind knowing," he explained. "But, at the same time, it's not that important right now. All I want to do is keep you and everyone else as safe as I can. The rest, I look at as an adventure."

"As an adventure?" she questioned. "I wish I could see things that way." She had a faraway look in her eyes.

"I don't know if you ever will or not," Keith answered. "But, I'm sure you're not gonna have a breakdown. You'll find a way to deal with all of this." He looked at her.

Tears escaped her eyes and rolled down her cheeks. When he turned toward her, she buried her face in his chest and sobbed.

CHAPTER FIFTEEN

The next morning Bear walked outside to see Spyder playing with a small piece of metal and a string. "Got a new toy?" He asked.

"You're not gonna believe this shit," Spyder answered. He looked at Bear holding the string up toward him. "We've got poles again."

Bear frowned.

"I was able to magnetize the pin and it points north."

"Magnetize the metal?" Bear questioned. "That explains the lightening back when this new change happened. I'll bet we've got electricity back."

"Great," Spyder said sullenly. "What the hell good does that do us? I don't see anything around we need it for."

We're all finally reacting to everything that's happened, Bear thought. "You're right," he said. "It's just something to keep in mind."

"How did you get over killing a person?" Spyder asked becoming serious. "How do I come to grips with that? Don't get me wrong, they deserved killing. Still, I can't get used to killing that many people, no matter what the reason."

"When you find a way," Bear said, "you tell me. I still haven't found out how to accept it yet. Taking a life isn't like it is on TV or in the movies."

"I was ready for the death part," Spyder explained. "What people don't know about is the sounds, the screams, the smell, even the feel of death in the air. In real life, it's not clean like it is in books or on TV or in movies -- it's dirty it not only stains the hands, but it stains the soul."

153

"Spyder," Bear said, "I was in the military for twenty years and I haven't ever been able to accept the taking of another person's life. I live with it, but there isn't a week that goes by I don't think about it. Those memories will remain with me until the day I die."

Spyder was quiet for a moment. "I guess I just needed to talk to someone about it."

"That's normal," Bear assured him. "I appreciate talking to you about it. I need to get it out of my system as much as the rest of you -- it hurts."

"I can't imagine having something like that with me the rest of my life," Spyder said.

"You will," Bear answered. "You'll deal with it one day at a time. It does get easier, but it never goes away. I think we have a chance to deal with things right now. This may be our time to heal and we should all use it."

***

Wind saw Bear and Spyder talking. Avoiding them, he walked toward the back of the valley. Once in the trees, he let his emotions take over. His thoughts drifted. *All of my family's gone or dead. Davata was murdered, Melon's dead and Dr. Hamilton was killed by something here. They're all gone but me.* He wandered aimlessly through the valley. The foliage opened into another pool beneath a waterfall. He gazed around uncomprehendingly and sat beside the water, his thoughts still far away.

Without effort, some of his stress slipped away with the assistance of the melodic, soothing sound produced by the waterfall. The humidity was higher, the air softer and it seemed the ills of the world lost their effect here. It was as if they were unable to invade the serenity of the pool.

"May I join you?" Palenaka spoke from behind him.

Wind recognized the voice even as he rose. "Sure," he said. "You're welcome to join me if you want."

"Mahalo," she said and sat beside him.

They sat beside the water. "I was just thinking," he said.

"I do not mean to intrude."

"You're not intruding," he assured her. "I wasn't thinking of good times."

"You are all special people," Palenaka said. "I have never seen this number of special people at one time."

"There's nothing special about us," Wind said, "other than we care about each other."

"You all care about each other fiercely," she corrected. "It is hard to tell where one spirit ends and another begins. The universe has chosen all of you, as a group, to make changes."

"I don't know about that," he said doubtfully. "All I know is that these people are good. They treat me as good as anyone else even though I'm black."

A frown clouded her face. "Why would they not?"

This woman has no idea of racial prejudice, he thought. *She's never seen anyone of any other color and it means nothing to her.* "It's nothing," he said. "It's something from a long time ago, back where I lived before."

155

"You have all been chosen as travelers," Palenaka explained as if Wind should already know this. The Spirit of the Universe knows you can make a difference."

"I don't want to make a difference anymore," Wind argued. "I just want things to be the way they were and live in peace."

"You may someday," she said. "I cannot see the future. However, I do feel that your life will be a great one."

Wind shook his head. He had no idea what she was talking about; he also didn't care about being great. He only wanted to find peace and quiet for a while. "This is a beautiful place," he said changing the subject, looking at the foliage around him.

"It is a sacred place," Palenaka told him. "This is where mother and I speak with the Spirit of the Universe."

He realized that he might be interrupting some ritual and said, "If I need to leave and let you meditate, I will. I didn't mean to be in the way."

Palenaka smiled, "You are not in the way. I have already been here today."

"You've already been here today," Wind repeated. "How much do you sleep at night?"

"A Kupua only needs the time of four sunrises of slumber in a day," she told him.

Wind calculated the time as two hours. "How do you keep going with that little rest?"

"We rest during the day, between activities," she explained. "We are accustomed to it. It is our way of life."

Thinking about what she said, Wind was satisfied to sit in silence and listen to the waterfall.

***

Weniki was gone most of the day. A couple of times, she returned to her house for a few minutes then left again. Palenaka was in and out of the house a number of times. The aroma of cooked meat mixed with that of baked bread.

That evening, in the large house, a feeling passed through Sandy. She stood from the bench and walked outside. There she found Weniki waiting.

"If your people would like to eat," Weniki said, "there is food." A large mat lay on the ground between the houses. There were torches at each corner with plates, cups and bowls arranged as place settings for each of the newcomers.

"How did you call me out here?" Sandy asked. "I didn't hear you, but I knew that you wanted me."

"It does not matter," Weniki said. "I will bring the food." She turned and walked toward her home.

Sandy went back into the house and told everyone what Weniki had said. There was no question about them accepting the invitation. They were interested in what Weniki and Palenaka had fixed for them to eat.

Outside, Weniki and Palenaka stood waiting. Weniki wore a full-length white dress. Her daughter wore an identical style blue one. Both wore leis around their necks, flowers behind their right ears and carried leis draped around their arms.

As each person approached the mat, they placed lei around the neck of the women or a smaller one on the heads of the men. Along with the

157

leis, each person received a kiss on each of his or her cheek and a greeting of "Aloha."

Palenaka motioned for them to sit. Each sat beside a plate. The meal set before them consisted of seasoned fruits and berries, a green salad, potatoes, roast pork, spiced foul, fish and carrot cake for dessert. It was a feast fit for a king.

Before the meal, Weniki stood and, in the same manner as her daughter before, held her arms out. After a chant, she crossed her arms across her breasts and bowed slightly. Sweeping her hands toward the feast she said, "Please eat and enjoy our humble luau."

Keith looked around for a knife or fork. The only things before him were a plate, a bowl and a wooden cup. "I don't wanna be rude but... "

"There's nothing here you need utensils for," Sandy said interrupting as if reading his mind. "Everything is eaten with your fingers. Believe me, it's the best way to enjoy this food."

Bear looked at Weniki a little confused. He knew of the Polynesian way. They were wonderful people full of care, warmth and giving. However, something felt wrong here. He didn't know what, but something wasn't right.

As everyone began eating, he sat with his hands resting on his lap.

"You do not eat?" Weniki asked.

The fact that Weniki noticed him not eating, meant something. He wasn't sure of the meaning, but intended to find out what he could. "You've done much for us," he said.

Everyone stopped eating and looked back and forth from Bear to Weniki. They sensed something was amiss.

None of the men was armed, but all wondered if they should be. Their attention focused on Bear.

He continued, "... and we appreciate everything. You've provided us a safe place, a home, food and rest. I don't wanna seem rude, but I have to ask if there's something you need or want from us?"

The rest of the newcomers realized what he was asking. None of them had questioned the kindness of the two women, only accepted it as offered.

Weniki placed her hands in her lap. "May we talk of this after the meal?"

"I thank you for your kindness, but we must talk about it now," he said.

Weniki appeared relaxed and not the least threatening or scheming. "There is something we would ask of you. However, it is a request; we do not require it of you."

Bear nodded. "What do you need from us?"

"We ask for your help with the Nāki," Weniki said. "We do not wish you to do battle for us. We ask for your knowledge in defending ourselves from them. We do not ask for any of you to put yourselves in danger for us," Weniki paused. She knew this was a large and potentially dangerous request. "If you choose not to help us, you may return from where you came or stay here with us -- it is up to you. We will provide you passage back across the alawai if you wish."

"Tell us about the Nāki," Bear said.

"As Palenaka explained," she said, "they are a race of giants. They are 'Ai kanaka. Palenaka said your word for them is cannibals. They eat the flesh of other humans. After the arrival of Aka, they began to hunt in groups. Some of the people they took became slaves of Aka; the others used as food. He has many Nāki under his power."

Bear understood. Weniki was asking them to teach her people more ways to defend themselves. "Why can't you simply put a barrier around the village?" He asked.

"We are five villages. Some as much as five days travel apart. It is not possible to hide all of the villages and the people when they hunt and fish," she answered. Her voice was calm and soothing, almost as a parent patiently answers the questions of a child.

"We aren't warriors," Bear explained. "We had to fight before, because our lives were threatened. We only want to live in peace. We don't even know how we got to this place and the Nāki haven't done anything to us."

"None of us are violent people," Hal interjected.

"I have touched all of you," Weniki said. "I know each of you have strong feelings of recent experiences."

"Wait," Spyder interrupted. "What do you mean you touched all of us?"

"I have experienced your feelings," Weniki explained. "I have the ability to feel what others feel."

"Does that mean you can read minds?" Sandy asked.

160

"I can, but I will not without first asking. That would be wrong. To invade a person's thoughts is different from experiencing their feelings."

"How do you know the difference?" Ginny asked.

"As I explained before," Weniki said looking at her. "You must enjoy your meal in silence."

Ginny nodded and bowed her head. She had obviously forgotten the rule.

"Again, I don't know what we could do for you," Bear said.

"Aka knows things of battle beyond our understanding," Weniki explained. "We hope you can teach us ways to live safely. Like you, we are also peaceful people."

"This isn't something I can decide for the rest. We'll need to discuss it and get everyone's opinion," he told her.

"That is expected," she said. "For tonight, please enjoy your meal. Decisions can be made at a later time."

"I'm willing to do that," Wind said grinning.

Amanda stood. "I can't go through another war," she almost sobbed. "I don't have it in me. I can't take another life." She buried her face in her hands and ran into the house.

"I'll be right back," Keith mumbled standing.

"Please," Weniki said softly, rising to her feet, "let me go to her."

Keith looked at her a moment. "Okay," he said. "But call if you need me."

Weniki smiled, nodded and went to Amanda in the house.

Keith turned back to his friends. "She started last night," he said sitting down. "The attack at Rebel's Revenge was almost too much for her. Now, with everything else that's happened, she can't justify all of it in her mind."

"That's a normal reaction," Bear assured him. "I'd be worried if any of us weren't feeling stress. She's probably experiencing early signs of Post-Traumatic Stress Disorder. She'll get over it. It's not easy, but she'll do it."

"I figured it was something like that," Keith said. "But, I didn't bother her with an explanation. I think she should spend time working on her feelings and not be worrying about the name of the problem."

Bear nodded his head smiling. "Good thinking, you're probably right." Looking at the rest he said, "It'll happen to all of us. Symptoms can run from fatigue, to nervousness and sleeplessness, to anger and extreme fear or any number of others. None of us are immune to it."

"You are all welcome to stay here and heal," Palenaka said, "no matter if you decide to help us or not. For now, please enjoy your meal."

162

CHAPTER SIXTEEN

Amanda lay on a mat in one of the rooms crying. Her head buried in the crook of her elbow as her body shook with sobs.

"I ask your pardon for interrupting your feelings," Weniki said slightly above a whisper. She waited a short moment. "May I join you for a time?"

Amanda slowly looked up with tear-filled eyes, "Yes, thank you," she said and slowly, rose to a sitting position. "I'm sorry for what happened out there."

"You have nothing to be sorry for," Weniki said. "You must never be ashamed of compassion."

"What I regret," Amanda said, "is losing my family and my friends. Everyone I knew are either dead or gone and I don't know which. We seem to be lost here, wherever this is, and have no way of returning home."

"What you say is true," Weniki agreed. She waited a couple of seconds. "May I share your thoughts?" She asked.

"Share my thoughts?" Amanda questioned.

"Some Kupua have the ability to share the thoughts of others," Weniki explained. "I will not do this without your permission."

Amanda looked uncertainly at her. "Why do you want to do that?"

"I wish to know of your demons."

Something about this woman was comforting. Amanda felt sure she meant no harm. "What do I have to do?"

"Close your eyes, breathe deep and relax your mind," Weniki said. "You will feel light as if you float upon a cloud, do not let this disturb you."

Amanda closed her eyes and took a deep breath.

***

As Palenaka served the dessert, Weniki emerged from the structure and re-joined those sitting around the mat.

"Is everything okay?" Keith asked as soon as he saw her.

"Amanda is well," she answered.

Weniki moved regally, her body straight and head held high, as if floating over the ground.

"Where is she?" Keith asked looking back at the door.

"She is resting," Weniki said. "She will sleep the rest of the night."

"Are you sure she's alright?" Keith asked, a tinge of doubt in his voice.

"She is well," Weniki repeated. "She shared her thoughts with me. That is all I can tell you. If you wish to know more, you must speak to her tomorrow." Weniki gracefully lowered herself and resumed her place at the mat.

"But, what about... " Keith started.

"She won't tell you anymore," Bear interrupted. "You're asking about Amanda's personal thoughts."

Keith was growing impatient. He glared from Bear to Weniki and back.

"Think of it as talking to a doctor," Sandy explained. "A doctor can't tell someone about another person's health. It's the same with this."

Weniki nodded smiling. "My thanks mistress, you are correct in what you say."

Keith didn't like not knowing what was happening, this was Amanda they were talking about. *How does this woman know if she's okay or not,* he wondered. *Who knows, she might have planted something in Amanda's mind. How do we know she's alright and just sleeping.*

Drawing his attention back to the clearing, he realized that the others had returned to their desserts. He'd make sure she was okay later tonight and talk to her tomorrow.

***

It was past midnight when Bear approached the waterfall. As he entered the clearing, the falls shimmered in the moonlight. The water itself created a luminescence as it plunged from the cliff into the pool. He had seen the almost mystical light from the deck of a ship, but never in fresh water.

Weniki sat quietly at the edge. Upon seeing her, he turned to re-enter the forest, trying to avoid disturbing her meditation.

"The water is beautiful tonight," she said softly.

Turning back to her, he said, "I've never seen fresh water glow before."

"This is the only place on the island where it does," she told him. "Palenaka and I like it."

"Do you mean you do this?" He asked.

"Yes, we do," she answered. "We do it for our enjoyment."

"Your valley's beautiful," he said taking a few steps toward her.

"Please join me." She patted a rock beside her.

As he walked toward her, a thought flashed through his mind. *You are welcome here my friend.*

With a puzzled look, he asked, "Did you say something?"

Weniki smiled and patted the rock again.

He sat beside her. "What happened with Amanda doesn't surprise me," he said. "In fact, I'm surprised no one else has shown a reaction."

"Each of your friends is fighting a battle within," she said. "I know much of what happened by sharing with Amanda." She paused, a strange look on her face. "May I ask about some things which I do not understand?"

"Sure," he answered. "I'll tell you what I can."

"Amanda shared things of a terrible battle. When she did, I saw images of strange creatures walking on two legs. I felt no fear from her of these creatures."

Bear smiled, remembering Bo and the others. "We called them mutants," he explained. "Something happened to change people into what you saw. Their leader's name was Bo. He and others of his kind helped us out when we were attacked."

"Her feelings started as fear. However, the fear disappeared at a time while people died all around her," Weniki explained. "I witnessed everything but could not experience any of the other feelings she would have felt."

166

Bear sat thoughtful for a moment. "She probably didn't feel them herself," he explained. "During the heat of battle, many people experience what is described as a state of satori. It's when the thinking process stops and reactions take over. A person does things without thinking, reacting only to the situation."

"This satori sounds like part of our meditation," Weniki observed. "We have to release our thoughts before sharing with another or with nature."

"I understand sharing with another person," Bear said, "but what do you mean sharing with nature?"

Weniki looked over and motioned toward the sparkling waterfall. "The light in the water is done by sharing with nature. It is the same with the wall you came through to arrive here."

Bear nodded, understanding what she meant. It was a manipulation of her natural surroundings. He was sure there was more to it, but for now that explanation would do.

"We refer to it as the natural mind," she continued. "Everyone can experience it, in fact most do. They do not recognize it though. We Kupua practice every day and accept it as a way of life."

Bear smiled as he looked at her. "That's what you did as I walked up. You told me that I was welcome here."

"You are all welcome here," she said.

"... and you told me that without speaking, right?"

"Yes," she said, "I did. There are still many things I would like to know."

"All you have to do is ask," he smiled.

167

"It would be quicker if we shared," Weniki said.

She really doesn't do it without permission, he thought, *otherwise she would have known it was okay.* To her he said, "I have no problem with that. What do I need to do?"

***

Hal and Sandy sat around the fire with Palenaka, the rest had gone to bed. Along with the torches, the fire produced a warm glow to the area between the houses. With everything of the feast removed, they drew three chairs around the fire to relax and talk.

"That was a great meal," Hal repeated for what he was sure was at least the tenth time.

"I am happy that you enjoyed it," Palenaka assured him. "It is nice for mother and me to have visitors with whom to share our food."

"I was wondering something," Sandy said, "and you don't have to answer if you don't want to."

"I will tell you what I can," she said.

"How old are you?" Sandy asked.

Palenaka frowned slightly, "I am nineteen cycles."

"Nineteen cycles?" Sandy repeated. "What's a cycle?"

We have two seasons, which alternate. One is a planting season and the other is the harvest season. Together, they are a cycle."

"These cycles are what we call a year," Hal explained.

168

Suddenly, Palenaka slammed back into her chair, causing it to topple backward. A couple of seconds later, she sat upright on the ground, concerned look on her face.

"Are you alright?" Sandy asked.

"Mother needs my help," she said staring straight ahead. Her body jerked again and tears trickled down her face.

Sandy hurried to her and knelt before her, "Are you sure you're alright?" She asked.

"I am helping mother," Palenaka said tears flowing freely now.

Hal hurried over and knelt beside her as well. "Is there something we can do?"

"Mother is sending me feelings from your friend Bear," she explained. "They are very strong and fearful."

"Can we help?" Hal repeated.

"Are you willing to share his feelings?" She asked, her head held steady, her gaze never wavering.

"Of course we are," Sandy answered immediately.

"Then take my hand," Palenaka instructed. "But, beware the feelings are very strong.

Sandy took Palenaka's hand in both of hers. After only a slight hesitation, Hal did the same. Bear was his friend and he wasn't sure he should intrude on the man's feelings. However, Palenaka seemed to think it might be alright.

Hal and Sandy both felt a warm feeling wash over their bodies then feelings slammed into them. Neither saw anything, but was flooded with intense feelings. Occasionally, a single name or word would separate itself from the feelings.

The name Carla included an intense feeling of sadness, followed immediately by anger. Many more names and words followed. Each accompanied by intense anger, fear, happiness or guilt with the last one being love. When the feeling of love washed over them, it was as intense as the rest. Along with the feeling came the name Davata. The love was intermingled with hope, sadness and anger. Finally the words baby girl flashed with the feeling of sadness and all began fading.

When the feelings left, Palenaka released Hal and Sandy's hands. They struggled to their feet and returned wobbly to their chairs. Palenaka saw that they were both soaked with sweat. The sharing had lasted about an hour and Hal and Sandy were exhausted.

Sandy noticed that Palenaka was sitting serenely in her chair, her hands clasped in her lap. "How did you do that?" She asked trying to slow her breathing. Her heart was still hammering in her chest.

"Mother needed help sharing with your friend Bear. She sent me feelings, some of which I passed to you," Palenaka explained. "We are also spiritual healers. With your help, we were able to sort his feelings. We were able to help him make sense of them. Some were kept and some discarded."

"You mean what we felt weren't all of 'em?" Hal asked.

"What you felt were only a few," Palenaka said. "The strongest were dealt with by mother. She sent me the feelings he was in control of and some of these, I passed to you."

"You mean he had feelings stronger than what we felt?" Hal asked an astonished look on his face.

"Not stronger," Palenaka corrected, "but out of control. They could injure one who did not know how to control them. Others that have tried suffered many problems afterward."

"All this was in one person -- Bear?" Sandy asked.

"Yes," Palenaka said. "He worked daily, controlling a lifetime of emotions held deep inside. Mother has relieved many of those feelings. He has never been able to release them before now. It appears he had a life of war, anger, fear and strife held deep inside. Some of those are gone now. He will sleep by the waterfall tonight."

***

At the waterfall, Bear lay beside the pool. Weniki walked a few yards away from him and vomited in the bushes. What came from her mouth weren't the contents of her stomach, but the physical manifestations of negative feelings, a crimson and black glowing liquid.

For minutes, she expelled the liquid, pausing only to breathe. When the viscous liquid hit the ground, it rebounded and evaporated into tiny pinpoints of light.

When she finally rid herself of the mass, she stood unsteadily to her feet and started toward her home to rest. The man, Bear lay where he had fallen

171

after the sharing. Weniki paused, looked back at him and smiled.

CHAPTER SEVENTEEN

Wind stumbled from the house, still only half-awake. His sleep the night before was troubled with hellish shapes and feelings that something had hunted him.

Once outside, he saw Bear sitting in a chair beside the fire pit used the night before.

"Morning Bear," he said. "How was your night?"

"Slept like a baby," he replied, "yours?"

"Restless," he answered. "I'm having nightmares."

"Not surprising," Bear said picking up a cup and coffee pot. "Want some coffee?"

"Who made it?" Wind had tasted Bear's coffee and didn't want that experience again unless he had to.

"Either Weniki or Palenaka," Bear guessed. "It was done when I got back to camp."

"I'll have some then," he said grinning. "Maybe it won't eat the lining of my throat and stomach."

Bear poured him a cup and both men sat by the fire sipping the brew.

"So you went for a walk already this morning, huh?" Wind guessed from the man's previous statement.

"Nope, I spent the night at the waterfall," he answered. He didn't want to get into what happened the previous night. It would be too hard to explain. Besides, he wasn't sure exactly what had happened.

A short while later everyone had joined them to enjoy their morning coffee. Hal and Sandy were the last to emerge from the house.

Seeing Bear, Sandy asked, "Are you okay?" Fear tinged the question.

"I'm fine," he assured her. "I feel much better after last night." When he rose and went to the pot to get more coffee, Sandy noticed the only weapon he carried was his knife.

"That was a helluva deal last night," Hal said.

"What do you know about it?" Bear asked straightening up.

"Not much according to Palenaka," Sandy answered. "But we can talk about that later."

"No, let's talk about it now," Bear demanded sternly.

"Take it easy," Hal said sensing a rise of anger in the man.

"We were sitting with Palenaka," Sandy explained, "and experienced some of your emotions through her. According to her, it was very little. Though, I wouldn't have wanted to get the full brunt of it all."

"Palenaka only allowed us to experience feelings," Hal explained. "We didn't know what most of them were about, we just helped her deal with them in some way or another."

"What the hell did Palenaka have to do with all this," Bear demanded, his anger still evident. "What happened was supposed to be personal."

"I asked her for help," Weniki said from her front door. As she approached the group around the fire, she continued, "I shared none of your thoughts with her, only feelings."

"I don't care about that," Bear assured her. "I don't have anything to hide from you or the others. I just need to make sure I know the rules."

174

"This I understand," Weniki explained. "It is important, to us, that you know we would never share thoughts with others -- not even your friends."

"Did any of this have anything to do with my nightmares?" Wind asked looking at Weniki.

"It is possible," she answered. "The close friendship between you and the others may have allowed you to experience some of the stronger feelings."

"That would explain my dreams," Spyder said.

"After my experience last night," Amanda shook her head, "I was too tired to feel anything. I slept like a log."

"So did I," Bear said.

"Your bodies needed rest after the sharing," Weniki explained.

"What about you?" Bear asked. "You don't seem to be affected by the experience."

"I have done this many times," she answered. "Only one other has ever had feelings as strong as I feel in each of you. I think it is because of the experience before."

"Mother and I are willing to share with any of you, if you wish," Palenaka said. "It is a decision only you can make."

For the next three nights, the newcomers experienced strange dreams and even nightmares as their friends shared with Weniki and Palenaka. Each day someone else felt better, lighter and more energetic than he or she had in years. Their healing hastened, through the kindness of mother and daughter.

***

Inside their house, pistols hung in their holsters with rifles leaning beneath them against the front wall. No one felt the need to arm themselves with anything other than a knife, which was used as a day-to-day tool.

Bear, Hal and Sandy sat with Weniki sipping coffee. "Do you ever leave the valley?" Bear asked.

"Yes," she answered. "We visit our Ohana many times in a season. When we sense the need, we go and tend to people."

"Do you treat them with medicines?" Sandy asked.

"We have a Ho'ōla that heals their bodies," she explained. "We use some herbs, but mostly help with thoughts and feelings. Many problems are caused by the confusion of combining the two."

"Are all Kupua like you and Palenaka?" Sandy pressed. She wanted to know more about these Kupua women.

"No," Weniki said. "Some have taken the dark path. Except for three, they have no Ohana of their own. There are three more that have Ohana with the Nāki. Two of the three must follow the dark path or their sons and daughters will pay with their lives. The third is of the Nāki Ohana by his choice."

"How often does the Nāki attack your Ohana?" Bear asked.

"That is mostly when we go to the village," Weniki explained. "The Nāki will take food many times in a season."

"Don't your people fight the Nāki when they come?" Hal asked.

176

"The people try to hide, but the Nāki are hunters and always outnumber my Ohana," Weniki answered. "The Nāki Kupua is able to find the people, even if they are hidden."

"Why don't your people fight?" Hal asked again.

"The Nāki are not only hunters, but warriors as well." Weniki spoke matter-of-factly, she acted as if the taking of people for food was an acceptable practice. "People have resisted the Nāki only to bring more trouble upon us."

"What weapons do the Nāki have?" Bear asked.

"They use spears, clubs, arrows and long knives," Weniki said. "They only attack one village at a time."

"Move your villages together," Keith suggested as he and Wind joined them. "There's strength in numbers."

"Our Ohana Nui has lived the way we are for many generations," Weniki explained. "We are not willing to change."

"Not even to save your lives?" he asked surprised at not only her answer, but her attitude as well.

"My people live as they always have," she said. "We will not change. It is not our way."

Wind shook his head. "That's as ridiculous as some of my old friends' ideas were about their color," he said. "Some people simply can't see the forest for the trees."

Hal looked at Bear. "He's right," he said, "there is strength in numbers."

Bear nodded in agreement. "Would your people be willing to live in a single community for a

177

while?" As she started shaking her head, Bear continued. "It wouldn't have to be for long," he explained, "only until something is done about the Nāki. We can possibly help your Ohana Nui if they are all in one place, but not if they're separated."

Weniki thought for a while. "I cannot speak for the others," she said. "All I can do is tell them of what you say. They will have to decide."

"I have a problem," Sandy said.

Everyone around the fire looked at her. From the tone of her voice, she was about to become confrontational.

"How can you be so calm about all that's going on?" She asked looking at Weniki. "You act like it's normal for one group of people to use another as food and slaves. When you talk about it, there's no emotion in your voice. It's like you don't care."

Weniki looked up, a calm expression frozen on her face. "I care very much," she said slowly changing her gaze to Sandy. "However, I cannot help my Ohana Nui, if I do not control my feelings."

A look of recognition spread over Sandy's face. "When was the last time you shared your thoughts and feelings with someone else?" She pressed. Weniki had remained extremely passive since their arrival over a week before. She had assisted them with their feelings and emotions, but had remained unaffected by any of them.

"I share with Palenaka," Weniki said. "She cannot accept a full sharing with me. It has been too long since I last emptied myself through sharing. It would injure her if I failed to control our contact."

"So you help everybody else and have no one to help you." Sandy was astonished Weniki was

178

able to handle the emotions of everyone else; the situations of her people served as food for other humans, and mask the doorway to their part of the valley without help from anyone else.

"There is a Kupua with whom I could share, but she is old and many suns travel from here," Weniki explained.

"Is there any way you could share with us?" Sandy asked. She wanted to help Weniki if possible. Because of her, they all felt better than any could remember feeling in a long time.

"That is not possible," Weniki said. "None of you know how to share properly."

"What about Palenaka?" Bear asked. "Why can't we do it the same way as when I shared with you?"

Weniki sat quietly thinking about the possibility. "It is not possible for Palenaka... "

"We can do it in that manner," Palenaka said from the porch. Unknown to the others, she had been listening to the conversation from a distance.

"It is too intense for her," Weniki argued.

"We can do it," Palenaka insisted. "It will take longer. She has years of sharing to release. The only way she can do it safely is through another powerful Kupua. If she shared with us, she would have to do it slowly. There is danger only for us."

"I'm willing to take a chance," Wind said.

The rest of the group agreed in a rush of words, "We can do that, it's no problem, we owe you."

Weniki had helped each of them through horrible thoughts and feelings of the past and they wanted to return the favor if possible. None of them could begin to imagine the load she carried.

"I do not wish to put any of you in danger, especially my daughter."

"It's a risk we're willing to take," Sandy said. "You helped all of us and we're not willing to simply sit idly by and not help you if we can."

Weniki stood intending to leave and Palenaka blocked her way. Both women stood face-to-face, looking intensely into the other's eyes. The rest of the group knew mother and daughter were having an argument they couldn't hear.

Weniki looked down, some of the strength and resolve drained from her face. For the first time since her arrival, Sandy saw emotions cross her face. It was nothing more than a slight change in expression and posture, but it was a change, nonetheless.

Weniki nodded, turned and left the group. As she entered the door to her house, Palenaka said. "Mother is willing to allow us to try."

"That's great," Sandy said, happy for the chance to help.

"I must tell you what is to happen," Palenaka explained. "After which, you may all decide if you wish to continue."

"I think we all agree... " Sandy started, as she rose to her feet.

Palenaka interrupted. "Please let me tell you everything. It is important that you know all before you decide to do this."

The rest nodded in agreement and Sandy returned to her chair.

"As you know, Mother has many thoughts and feelings of others inside her. She cannot rid herself of these the same way she did with yours, it is different with Kupua." Palenaka lowered her head in thought, fiddling with her hands in front of her nervously. Looking up, she continued. "The sharing will take most of the night hours. It can only be done a little at a time."

"Why does it have to be done at night?" Amanda asked.

"Night is the time I am strongest," she answered. "It is then I can best control the sharing."

"When would she be willing to do this?" Bear asked.

"Tonight," she responded. "We must soon go to a village the Nāki is approaching."

"Wait," Amanda said. "How do you know the Nāki is about to attack a village?"

"I feel it," she said.

"If you know they are about to be attacked, why don't you warn 'em?" Keith asked.

"That is not possible," Palenaka explained. "The village is a two day journey from here. The Nāki will be gone before we reach it."

"What will happen to Weniki if she doesn't share?" Bear asked bringing the conversation back to the business at hand.

"I do not know," Palenaka answered. "No Kupua has ever gone this long without sharing. It has almost completely reduced her abilities."

"Almost completely reduced her abilities?" Spyder questioned. "You mean she normally has more abilities?"

"Many more," Palenaka assured him nodding. "I am still her student and even I have not experienced all that she can do."

181

Everyone sat in stunned silence. Weniki could read thoughts and feelings, make waterfalls sparkle at night and keep the valley in secrecy with a masking field of some sort. What else could she possibly do?

***

Weniki and Palenaka sat on the edge of the pool under the waterfall while the others formed a circle around the fire. Sitting beside each other holding hands, they waited for the warmth, Palenaka had described, to engulf them.

Before going to the waterfall to join her mother, Palenaka had told them the order in which they should sit. Bear, Hal and Sandy were to be on the end toward the waterfall. Continuing in line, were Amanda and Keith, then Spyder, Ginny and Wind.

Palenaka explained that, for their protection, they were to sit in family groups. It was not bloodlines that mattered, but emotional ties. If Weniki was as powerful as Palenaka described, they finally understood the need for protection.

After only sitting about ten minutes, they again felt the warmth settling down over them like a blanket descending, wrapping each individual in a cocoon. In a few seconds, emotions overwhelmed Bear, Hal and Sandy. The others experienced individual emotions, each having a different feeling with which to deal.

The emotions felt by Bear, Hal and Sandy came in waves like the ocean hammering the shore in a storm. A feeling of revulsion swept over Sandy. Mixed with the feelings were the words murder and children. The feeling increased in intensity until it was almost unbearable. Blood trickled from her nose as pressure built from inside. Her body shook and her head thrashed from side to side as she dealt with the storm raging within.

Images assaulted Bear and Hal's senses with scenes of battles, torture and deaths. Both felt revulsion caused by violence between seemingly unarmed people and an army carrying lances, swords, shields, bows, arrows and glowing staffs. Along with the feelings of fear, anger and grief were dark horrific shapes, some of which flew, while others remained on the ground -- all mercilessly murdered the people around them.

The ordeal continued throughout the night and only ended as the sun rose in the east.

CHAPTER EIGHTEEN

It was noon before Bear awoke and walked out of his new home. Weniki was in her chair, on the porch, sipping tea. Her entire aspect seemed impossibly more serene, more relaxed and calm. It was as if her whole body brightened with her smile. She looked like Palenaka's twin sister rather than her mother. The sharing had melted years from her appearance.

Bear tipped his hat to her as he walked toward the coffeepot hanging over the fire. Coffee or tea around the fire was now an important morning ritual followed by everyone.

As he poured the coffee, Weniki approached. "I am pleased that none of you were injured last night." She sat in a chair beside the fire.

"Palenaka was right," Bear said sitting in the chair beside her. "There is no way any one of us would have lived through that. It was hard enough for us as a group."

Weniki smiled with a warmth Bear had never before experienced. Truly, a changed woman, she exuded compassion and serenity. Much different from her previous aura, she was missing tension he had obviously failed to sense before. With the stress gone, the feelings from her were soft, more relaxed and calming. She was the most captivating person he had ever seen and that was saying a lot given the life he had lived.

"You seem to be feeling better today," he said trying to hide his surprise.

"I held the experiences far too long," she said. "I am grateful to all of you for helping rid me of them."

"Palenaka talked about the Nāki attacking a village." Is there anything we can do to stop it?" He asked.

Weniki's expression turned to sadness. "No," she answered. "It is happening as we speak." She spoke with a certainty, which left no room for doubt of its accuracy.

"Do you know where the Nāki live?"

"They live on Lua Pele."

"Isn't that where you said the Kalekona live that breathe fire?" He asked.

"Didn't you say Kalekona means dragon?" A voice asked from behind. Hal moved toward them, a cup in his hand.

"That's what it means," he confirmed, watching Hal pour coffee.

"You didn't make this, did you?" Hal asked with a worried look before taking a sip.

"You're outta luck," Bear answered. "Either Weniki or Palenaka did."

"It didn't come to me on its own, so I figured it was safe." Hal sat on the other side of Weniki. "Where's Palenaka today?"

"She has gone to the village," Weniki said.

"Aren't you worried about her safety?" Bear asked. "What if the Nāki take her?"

"Palenaka will not allow that," she assured him. "No single Nāki would live through an attack by her."

185

Bear remembered when he and Keith met Palenaka. She was resourceful, but no match for a warrior intending to kill or capture her.

"How's everyone?" Amanda asked walking out of the house.

"I'll bet they're drinking coffee," Sandy said following her.

"I agree with Keith," Amanda answered, "when he said never bet against a sure thing."

"You look good, considering how long last night was," Sandy said to Weniki.

"I am much relieved today," Weniki said smiling. "You have all proven to be good friends."

"I've never experienced... "

"Please," Weniki interrupted her. "It is not good to speak of a sharing."

"Sorry," Sandy said. She wasn't sure why it was a problem, but she was willing to follow the advice just the same.

"I see that you no longer carry weapons," Weniki observed.

"There's no need for 'em here," Amanda answered. "We only carry them when there is a possibility of danger."

Spyder and Wind walked from the house arguing about something as usual.

"They are good friends are they not?" Weniki said nodding at the approaching men.

"Very good friends," Hal said, "and they're both good people."

"As are all of you," Weniki assured him.

Ginny, carrying an armful of fruit entered the clearing from the direction of the waterfall.

"There's my little teacup," Spyder called to her.

186

Ginny smiled and continued walking. As she passed the group, she nodded to Weniki and carried her load into her hut.

"What the hell's wrong with her?" Spyder asked.

"She is working," Weniki explained. "She is not to talk until this lesson is finished."

"What lesson?" Spyder challenged.

"She has many things to learn," Weniki answered. "She has chosen to remain here and learn."

"What choices does she have?" Spyder argued.

"She may leave or stay and learn," Weniki explained, surprised at Spyder's questions.

"This is bullshit," Spyder snorted. "Where the hell would she go? You're the only one who thinks she has lessons to learn."

His attitude visibly startled Weniki "It is unfortunate there is not enough time to teach her everything. We must leave tomorrow for Hana O'Makemake."

"Where's that?" Wind asked.

"It's the valley where her clan lives," Hal answered.

"I know what it is," Wind said. "I want to know where it is."

"It is two suns travel from here," Weniki said.

"We're gonna need all our weapons and ammo," Bear announced. "The Nāki attacked the village today."

"Are we sure we want to get in the middle of this fight?" Amanda asked. "I know we owe Weniki and Palenaka a lot, but do we want to get into a war?"

"We do not wish you to fight for us," Weniki assured them. "We only ask for your knowledge of how to defend ourselves."

"How do we avoid being drawn in if we're in the area?" Amanda continued probing. "I was able to handle the previous feelings, through help from Weniki," she said. "I damn sure don't want to replace them with more of the same."

"There's no way I wanna get in another fight," Wind said. "But, I can't just stand by and allow people to be killed for food. That's barbaric."

"I agree something has to be done," Sandy said. "But, what can we teach 'em? Bear's the only one who has experience in battle strategy."

"Not in anything like this," Bear interjected. "I'm only trained in small group tactics. We're talking about primitive weapons and an army."

"Couldn't our rifles and pistols give us a big advantage?" Keith asked.

"Sure they could give us an advantage," Hal said. "But, we don't have enough to supply Weniki's people. We'd have to get involved."

"I won't fight for someone else," Amanda stated flatly. "It was bad enough when I had to take a life for my own protection. I won't do it for people I don't even know."

"I've been in a lot of fights," Spyder said. "But, I always had an investment in 'em. I'd have to know a lot more about this before I'd be willing to get involved."

Everyone sat in silence for a moment. "We've been talking about helping these people for a little while now. I don't know if anybody noticed it or not, but when someone agreed Weniki's people needed help, the next word they said was 'but'," Amanda observed. "It seems like we're all in agreement that they need help. It also seems like we all have reservations."

She was right. Bear and the rest of the group shifted uncomfortably in their places. There was no clear answer to the dilemma.

"I will leave you to speak of this," Weniki said, rose and walked to her home.

***

Spyder needed to think. He wandered toward the opening in the rocks Weniki and Palenaka somehow kept secret. The split through the rocks looked innocent enough. It was hard to believe a barrier hid the opening from an outsider. From this side, it simply looked like a path through the cliff. On the other side, the cliff appeared solid.

Spyder shook his head. Even though the place was a paradise, it held mysteries beyond his comprehension. He sat on a rock, picked a blade of grass and chewed on it absentmindedly. The taste of chlorophyll reminded him of peaceful times.

Even though Weniki had left us to talk things out, it was as if she was still there, he thought. *Nobody wanted to say anything that might insult or disturb her. There's no doubt she and Palenaka only want what's best for their people.*

There's also something about the way she treats Ginny I don't understand. Ginny can be hard-headed sometimes, but she's always tried to help with any group situation.

189

"Am I interrupting, man?" Wind stood a short way up the trail.

"Nah," Spyder answered. "Drag up a rock and have a seat."

Wind found three boulders, which almost formed a chair, climbed up and settled himself where they joined.

"What's going on back at camp?" Spyder asked.

"Everybody's resting," Wind answered. "Weniki said we have a long way to travel in the next two days."

"Something bothers me about all this," Spyder said. "I can't put my finger on it, but something's wrong."

"I know the feeling," Wind agreed shifting his body to fit his perch. "What are we supposed to teach these people? We're not soldiers, except for Bear that is."

"Bear was a soldier in the past," Spyder corrected. "He's not now though. He knows fighting, but it's not his way of life now." He paused, "... and what's all that shit with Ginny? I know she can be stubborn, but what lessons does she need to learn?"

"What does she say?"

"Nothing," Spyder snorted. "Every time I ask her about 'em, she says they're taught by sharing and we shouldn't talk about sharing. It's the same thing Weniki says."

"What if only a couple of us go with Weniki to the village and the rest stay here?" Wind suggested.

Spyder thought about the idea. The two sat silently listening to the breeze rustling the treetops accompanied by the chirps and calls of birds. He knew one of the reasons he didn't want to get involved in another fight was because he was happy here. He didn't want to give up that happiness and replace it with violence.

"That might just be what we need to do," he said after a while. "It's obvious that Bear should go with her. I hate to put more on him, but he's the one with the knowledge."

"I don't think he should go alone," Wind said. "Someone else should go with 'em."

"I was thinking that too," Spyder nodded. "It'll need to be Hal or me."

"Not really," Wind argued. "Keith or I could go."

"I don't think so," Spyder disagreed. "We'll need you and Keith's energies back here."

Wind sat back to think. Spyder plucked another blade of grass and nibbled. Just when they were getting comfortable, another problem had raised its ugly head to mess things up.

***

"I don't like asking you to take this on while most of us sit back here doing nothing," Spyder said after presenting the idea to Bear.

"I don't mind going," Bear said, "and I think you're right. Someone else should go with us."

"Like I said," Spyder explained. "Wind came up with the idea. He's got a good head on his shoulders."

"He's become a real friend to all of us," Bear said. "I'll talk to Weniki about it in a little while."

191

The men were beside the pool at the waterfall. To Bear, it was the most relaxing place in the valley. When Spyder returned to camp and found Bear absent, he knew exactly where to look for him.

"I hate to do this to you my friend," Bear said. "But, I think you're the person to come with us. I agree with you about Keith and Wind staying behind. Hal can keep them in line and work on the weapons while we're gone. But, honestly, I want the meanest son-of-a-bitch from this valley with me."

Spyder simply nodded. What Bear said made sense. He also figured he should be the one to go along. "I don't know about the meanest S-O-B in the valley, but I'm willing to take your back."

"Double check your weapons," Bear reminded him. "Take all the modern ones. We have to travel as light as possible and the black powder weigh twice as much. We need two boxes of shells for each type and have all the magazines loaded. We can carry the magazines in bandoliers."

"How's your side?" Spyder asked.

"It's healed," he answered.

"You mean it feels healed, don't you," Spyder corrected.

Bear shook his head, stood and raised his shirt. Where he was wounded a couple of weeks before, there was now only a scar. "I mean it's healed," he said.

Spyder shook his head. "This is a beautiful place," he acknowledged, "but, some strange things happen here."

"Weniki did it," Bear explained. "It took two sharing episodes to completely heal it.

Bear sat back down. He and Spyder could take a little more time here before getting their things ready to go tomorrow.

***

Night had fallen when Weniki joined Bear, now sitting alone, at the waterfall. He rose to his feet when he heard her approaching in the moonlight. Wearing a long white gown, she was radiant. He knew she was over forty, but she looked barely half that age.

"Thank you," Weniki said, joining him as he sat back down.

"You're welcome," he said. "I'm not sure what for though."

"I sensed your approval of me," she replied.

Damn, she's even more sensitive since the sharing, Bear thought.

"I also sense that you and your friends have a plan for us," Weniki added.

"Yes, we do," he agreed. "We think it would be best if only two of us go with you tomorrow. The rest can stay here until we get back."

"Why would that be better?" Weniki asked running her fingertips through the water, producing ripples across its surface.

"A smaller group can travel faster and quieter," he explained. "There'll be less chance of us being seen. Also, the rest can work on the weapons back here."

Weniki thought a few seconds. "As you wish," she said. "Who will go with us?"

"Spyder," he answered.

193

"A good choice," Weniki nodded. "He can travel swiftly."

Bear looked from her to the waterfall. Instantly, it glowed in the night. The cascading water shimmered deep blue and the luminescence, as it struck the pool, was a white radiance. The scene was beautiful and reminded him of waterfall paintings he'd seen in the past.

"I still don't understand how you do that," he said.

"Tonight, I do it for you," was her answer.

A little surprised, he looked at her and smiled. Sitting there in the moonlight, she was the most beautiful woman he had ever seen. He felt an attraction for her and a pang of guilt. He didn't want to betray the memory of Davata.

"You still grieve for the one before," Weniki said with certainty. "This is good. It tells much of you."

"It does?" he asked.

"Yes," she assured him. "It means you are loyal to those with whom you are close."

He listened to the sound of the waterfall without speaking.

"You are a man who holds his friends close to his heart," Weniki explained, "a man of feelings."

"I don't know what to say," he answered.

"You need say nothing," she said soothingly. "I can sense that you have feelings for me. Yet, you feel betrayal of the woman before."

"That's true," he said nodding.

"As long as you hold her in your heart, she lives."

"She's alive in my memory," he agreed, "but, she's not here with me."

"You may see her again in another life," Weniki said.

"I believe that too," he answered barely above a whisper, a mixture of emotions tumbling inside him.

"I can allow you to see her once again if you wish," Weniki offered.

"No," he said quickly. He didn't know why he said it, but he knew it wasn't something he should do.

"As you wish," she answered. "You have learned much here."

"Not enough," he countered.

"We should swim," Weniki said standing. "It is good for the soul."

"Swim?" Bear questioned rising with her.

Without hesitation and with no sign of self-consciousness, she slipped the dress from her shoulders and let it drop and pool around her feet. She stood naked in the pale light and he couldn't help staring. Her breasts were those of a young woman. Her long black hair flowed down her back and accentuated the curves of her body.

She turned her head toward him and her almond-shaped eyes glistened in the moonlight, her lips soft and inviting. Before he could speak, she dove into the pool, submerging from sight. She remained submerged until he began to worry for her safety.

Surfacing, she turned toward him. "The water will strengthen your energy," she said and again disappeared beneath the surface.

A modest person, he was hesitant to undress. *What the hell,* he thought trying to get his courage up. *She did it.*

As he removed his clothes, she resurfaced and watched him with a peculiar interest. Unnerved, he had to force himself to continue under her gaze. He hadn't been skinny dipping since high school. Back then, he didn't have an almost fifty-year old scarred body that, at times, ached with stiffness from a lifetime of injuries.

Naked, he dove in the water and surfaced close to her. "What is this skinny dipping?" she asked effortlessly treading water. When he looked surprised, she added, "It is a thought you gave me."

His nervousness had been a strong feeling. *That must be why she sensed the thought.* Aloud, he said, "It's swimming without clothes."

"You swim with clothes?" she asked, a confused look on her face.

Before he could answer, he heard a splash nearby. It was a distinctive sound separate from the waterfall. He spun around as quickly in the water as he could looking for the source.

Understanding his actions, Weniki said, "Menehune."

"Menehune?" he repeated. Behind her, he saw a person climb out of the water. It was a man about two feet tall. He was naked and immediately began effortlessly climbing the slick face of the cliff. He climbed quickly and effortlessly up the shear wall.

"They love to dive," Weniki explained. "If you watch them too much, they will leave. They are here because they trust you and me."

"They trust you, you mean," he corrected.

196

"The Menehune know of you and your friends. They trust all of you."

Bear looked up to see the small man had climbed to the top of the waterfall. Standing with him were two other men and two women of approximately the same size. He posed on a rock and sprang out. After a perfect one and a half flip, slipped into the water with almost no splash and only a ripping sound indicating his entry.

Bear looked back to Weniki, "They're good divers."

"They are excellent divers," she corrected. "Follow me," she said with a smile and descended below the surface.

Bear took a deep breath and followed her to the bottom of the pool where she waited for him. Even though they were almost fifteen feet below the surface, the water around them was illuminated. She waited effortlessly on the bottom as if standing on dry land.

He swam to her and felt a soft embrace surround his entire body as he approached. *It has to be from her,* he thought. *She's helping me stay down.*

Facing each other, less than a foot apart, he felt emotions radiating from her with affection and desire engulfing him. His mind told him it was time to go to the surface, but his lungs felt comfortable with no need for air yet.

Weniki moved closer and the feelings intensified. Becoming aroused, he reached for her. She pulled away and held her hands out, palms toward him.

197

Somehow, he knew he should place his palms against hers. He reached out and she interlaced her fingers with his. His mind exploded in a burst of bright colors. Feelings rushed through him. The feelings were sexual, but stronger than he had ever felt. Radiating warmth grew in the center of his chest, spreading outward to all parts of his body, the feeling so intense, it engulfed his entire being to his very soul.

He had never experienced anything such as this in his life. Not simply sexual, but every positive feeling and emotion he had experienced in his lifetime flooded and flowed through his being.

Weniki moved forward and, placing her arms around him, pulled him tightly to her. Unbelievably, the emotions rose even more, to a crescendo. He felt like his very soul was lost in hers. Not lost, but intermingled, mixed beyond recovery.

When Bear awoke, he was lying beside Weniki at the water's edge. The sky glowed in the east. If asked, he would never be able to explain what had happened or how long he was underwater. The entire experience had a dream-like quality, yet he could remember it all. Feeling totally rested, he turned to Weniki. She lay on her side beside him, her head in her hand, propped by her bent arm.

"It is time to get your friend and leave for Hana O'Makemake," she said. She remained undressed and lay unconscious of her body and its effect on him.

He didn't want to move. She was beautiful and had performed some profound act with him. "What just happened?" He asked.

"The thing that happened was a bonding," she answered. "But, it did not just happen. It happened when the moon was overhead."

He couldn't believe what he was hearing. The bonding, as she called it, ended more than five hours ago. Yet, he felt as if they had just finished. "That's impossible," he insisted. "We were just in the water."

Weniki smiled and rose to her feet. Stepping into the dress as it lay on the ground; she pulled it up her body and onto her shoulders, the reverse to how she removed it the night before. "We must go," she repeated.

Bear stood and began dressing. Remembering the feelings, he asked, "How long were we underwater?"

"Not long," she answered. "Only two hours, if I understand your time correctly."

"Two hours," he repeated astounded. "That's impossible; I can't hold my breath more than a few minutes."

"I helped you," Weniki said and set off along the path toward the clearing leaving him to finish dressing.

CHAPTER NINETEEN

Weniki, Spyder and Bear stood, once again, at the edge of the pool. Spyder told Bear that Hal and Sandy had informed every one of the plan for them to travel to Weniki and Palenaka's village. Hal also assured him that he would clean and check all the weapons before their return.

"We will go through there," Weniki pointed toward the cliff to the right of the waterfall.

"Here we go again," Spyder said. "There's something there we can't see."

"Actually, we see something that isn't there," Bear corrected.

"Whatever," Spyder snorted. "We're going where she pointed and there's a rock wall there."

Weniki faced the wall next to the waterfall, raised her arms in a now familiar motion, closed her eyes and slowly nodded. The wall shimmered and faded. As it did, a cave came into view. "We go through there," she said motioning toward the entrance.

The three of them walked around the pool, along a path at the bottom of the wall and entered the cave. Once inside, Weniki's body radiated a soft white light, the light extended at least five feet around her. "Please follow me," she said and proceeded into the darkness.

As Spyder followed Bear and her, he looked back at the entrance. It appeared as it should. He could see where the cave opened to the world, across the pool to where the path from the water's edge began. *We're at her mercy,* he thought and continued. *I hope we're right in trusting her.*

200

About two hours later, they emerged into bright daylight. After walking a few feet, Spyder looked back at this end of the cave. They had just emerged from what now appeared to be a solid rock wall. "Well, I'll be kiss my ass," he said.

"That is two times I have heard you speak of this," Weniki said. "Is there something special I should know of this action?"

"Don't pay any attention to him," Bear interjected. "It's just a manner of speaking some of our people use. It's only an expression of surprise."

Weniki eyed Spyder inquisitively.

"He is surprised the cave can't be seen from here," Bear explained.

"If it could be seen..."

"Never mind lady," Spyder interrupted. "I should've expected it." He motioned for he to continue and shook his head.

She started a slow trot into the thick brush as if nothing had happened. She accepted this Spyder person as he was, a friend of Bear's.

***

After traveling ten hours, according to Bear's estimation, the trio set up a small camp beside a stream, at the base of the range of mountains. They had only taken four breaks throughout the day. Weniki seemed tireless as she slipped her way through the thick vegetation.

The area where they stopped was lush and green and dotted with colorful flowers of all kinds. Fruit, pine and other trees mixed with various types of grass to produce a relaxing aroma.

201

Weniki had advised Spyder and Bear to carry only their weapons. "We can gather food along the way," she said.

With mats laid out, Spyder and Bear sat down to rest. "She keeps a hell of a pace," Spyder said relaxing against a rock.

"That she does," Bear agreed. "I've done more, but it was a long time ago."

"Where is she anyway?" Spyder asked looking around.

"Probably off killing an elephant," Bear answered and laughed. "I've got a feeling this was nothing for her."

"We need to get some rest," Spyder said. "We're gonna need to stand guard tonight."

"Guards are not necessary," Weniki said approaching from beside the stream. "There are no Nāki here and I will keep the animals away."

"You don't have to tell me twice," Spyder said smiling. "I could do with a good night's rest."

"We have traveled slower than I expected," she said. "But, we will still reach the village tomorrow."

Spyder shot a surprised look at Bear who shrugged, "I told you it was probably nothing to her. We only covered about thirty miles over rough terrain in ten hours."

Weniki seemed to be paying the men no attention as she prepared birds for each of them. "Please start a small fire," she requested looking at Spyder. Shifting her gaze to Bear, she pointed, "I will need berries from those bushes."

Bear looked at the three bushes she pointed to and nodded. "I can do that," he said, rose and went to pick the berries.

With the fire going, she showed Spyder where to find wild potatoes. Soon, he returned with a double handful.

In less than an hour, Weniki mixed the berries for a basting sauce and used it while cooking the birds over the fire. Seasoning for the meat came from a pouch she carried on her belt. They boiled potatoes in the cups from the men's canteens. It was obvious they would eat well tonight.

The food was excellent and the men's appetites immense. Weniki had saved the day with her hunting and gathering abilities, not to mention her cooking.

"You carry seasoning for food with you?" Spyder asked.

"It is not only seasoning for food, but also protection for poisoning and injuries," she explained. "Many are combined into one. I must carry little when I travel."

"This woman's a keeper," Spyder said to Bear grinning. He didn't understand what was going on with Ginny back at the main camp. However, Weniki seemed to be good for Bear and he was willing to give her the benefit of the doubt for his sake.

"When tomorrow should we reach your village?" Bear asked.

"After midday," Weniki said.

"Do the Nāki ever come this way?" Spyder asked Weniki.

"Yes," she answered. "However, I do not sense any nearby."

"How far from your village does the Nāki live?" he questioned.

203

"The Nāki live in a valley along Lua Pele. It is a long, two day travel."

"I would feel safer if we kept watch," Spyder said, after rethinking their position.

"We will not be visible to anyone," Weniki assured him. "You should both rest."

"I trust her," Bear said seeing Spyder's doubtful look. "I've got a feeling, we're gonna need all the rest we can get."

"I've got no trouble with rest," Spyder said. "She's relentless when she travels."

***

The previous night and the rest of their trip to the village were uneventful. The village, they found, was nestled at the base of three cliffs, the setting as beautiful as any Bear had seen before.

A stream flowed along the valley floor with huts, constructed of grass and other natural materials, placed on either side. The largest structure was near the center of the village.

Palenaka met them as they entered the small community. "Five were taken," she said. "Lopaka has called for a meeting tonight."

"Who's Lopaka?" Bear asked.

"Lopaka is our leader," Palenaka explained. Then back to her mother, "Kimo is working with three injured in the attack."

"Kimo must be your... " Spyder hesitated, trying to think of the right word. "Healer," he finished.

"Yes, he is," Weniki said. "He treats their bodies."

"Do you ever work together?" Bear asked.

"Why would we do that?" Weniki asked surprised at the question. "I treat the spirit, he treats the body. One has nothing to do with the other."

Bear couldn't believe what he was hearing. They didn't believe the spirit could influence the body's healing process. The idea went against everything he knew, also against his wound healing with Weniki's assistance. His belief was that healing came only through the combination of treating body and spirit together.

Obviously reading his thoughts, Weniki said, "You do not understand our way of healing. This, I will explain at another time."

"Can I see the injured?" he asked. "Maybe I can help."

"I will ask him," Weniki said and walked away leaving the men with Palenaka.

"Can we go with her?" Bear asked looking after Weniki.

"There is no hurry," Palenaka said. "None of the injuries are serious."

He nodded and continued watching Weniki until she entered a hut. Turning back to Palenaka he asked, "How many people live here?"

"About one hundred families," Palenaka answered. "There are many others living away from the village though."

"I understand," he said. "Can we take a look around?"

"You are free to go wherever you wish," she said. "However, you must remember. This valley is not protected as ours is. There are Oli'i kika and sometimes Kalekona."

205

Spyder looked questioningly at Bear.

"Saber toothed tigers and dragons," he translated. "We need to keep our weapons with us." To Palenaka he asked, "Can you come with us?"

Palenaka shook her head no. "I must check on people outside the valley. To do that, I must leave now. I will return before night tomorrow."

"Shouldn't one of us go with you?" Bear asked.

"I will be safer traveling alone," she said.

"If she's anything like Weniki," Spyder interjected, "we'd just slow her down."

"You be safe," Bear said.

Palenaka smiled at both men and nodded. "Aloha," she said and trotted away through the village.

"I hope Weniki knows she's leaving," Bear said as he walked along the stream.

"She probably told her as she ran by," Spyder said grinning. He still couldn't believe these two women.

As they walked along, Bear noticed each hut had a fire or place for a fire situated in front of it.

When he pointed it out, Spyder said, "A fire inside could catch the building ablaze."

"You're probably right," Bear agreed. "Plus, it'd get hot as hell in there."

Each fire area had a spit across it for cooking meat. Each hut also had at least a couple of baskets in front containing fruit.

Palm, fruit and Koa trees grew among the huts producing shade and food. The area, completely void of brush and spotlessly clean, had no debris of any kind. It appeared the villagers worked vigilantly to keep it that way. If a villager saw an errant piece of bark or trash of any kind, he or she would stop and pick it up.

As they passed a villager, they always received an 'Aloha' and a warm smile. "These people seem unaffected by the attack yesterday," Bear observed.

"I was noticing that myself," Spyder agreed. "How can people accept something like that and go back to normal the next day?"

Bear shook his head. "I've got no idea."

The village extended along both sides of the shallow stream about a hundred yards and as many huts were situated away from the water as along it. Most of the buildings were identical in size and shape with only a few variations.

When they reached the far end of the structures, the growth of the area became as thick as a jungle. A small path continued to wind its way into the thick underbrush.

"Let's stay in the village for now," Bear suggested. "We don't know what's out there."

"I agree," Spyder said. "I want to know more about the place before we go out exploring."

When the men approached the only large building in the middle of the village, Weniki met them. "Kimo says it is acceptable for you to join him in the treatment house."

Bear nodded, "Where's that?" He asked.

"It is that building," Weniki said pointing straight across the stream.

"I'll be there," he said and crossed the stream jumping from rock to rock to keep his feet dry. Weniki led Spyder toward a group of huts away from the water.

207

Bear knocked on the door to the treatment house. A man at least sixty years old pulled a flap back. "Aloha," he said and stepped aside to allow Bear entrance.

"Aloha," Bear answered. "Do you speak English?"

"Yes," the man answered. "My name is Kimo."

"I'm Rafe," Bear answered. "But my friends call me Bear."

"I will call you Bear, if it pleases you." Kimo said.

"It would," he answered with a nod.

Two windows allowed sunlight from the outside and he saw four mats spread on the grass floor. Numerous people lay on the mats with, what he was sure were, injuries from the attack.

Three of the people had minor wounds. The fourth's arm was missing from the elbow down. He looked at Kimo questioningly.

"His injury is mild," the older man said. "He will be able to leave at first light tomorrow."

"Minor?" Bear questioned. "His arm's missing below the elbow."

Kimo looked surprised. "Of course his arm is missing. It has been for many seasons."

Bear smiled and shook his head. "I saw the wrap on the stump and thought it was recent."

Kimo looked down at the man and realized what Bear meant. "I see," he said. "That would... "

Three shots, in rapid succession, echoed in the distance. Bear could tell, from the sound, it was a 9mm. Pulling his pistol, he sprinted from the house.

***

When Keith awoke the day before yesterday, Weniki, Bear and Spyder were gone. According to Hal, they should reach Weniki's village by sunset today. For those remaining behind, the valley should be safe as long as they remained within its borders.

He wanted to use the down time, as he thought of it, to work on himself. Martial arts katas were the best way he knew to center his mind and bring the world back into perspective. The kata he now practiced was Kusanku. As he performed the movements, his muscles relaxed and his mind cleared. He let his feelings reach out attempting to become more in touch with nature.

He practiced in slow rhythmic movements. Control was the essence of the physical motions and after performing the kata for many years, he was able to do it without conscious thought. As he moved, he meditated about their situation including Palenaka and Weniki. Something about this place bothered him. It was almost as if the land itself was alive. Bear had said he felt the same thing.

Sensing a human presence behind him, Keith spun in its direction and slipped into a defensive stance.

"You seem to be working hard," Amanda said a few feet away.

Seeing who it was, he relaxed as she continued.

"You've been here over two hours," she said. "I was wondering if you were okay."

"I'm fine," he assured her, "just trying to think some things through.

"What things?" she asked.

"Nothing serious," he answered.

"Bull," she argued. "You practice katas all the time. But, I was standing over there trying to get your attention for a couple of minutes."

"Let's go to the waterfall," he suggested.

"Sounds good to me," she agreed.

At the pool beneath the falls, Keith stripped down to a pair of shorts and, without a word, dove in. Amanda wasn't sure what he was doing and sat beside the pool.

"What's going on, Keith?"

He swam to the edge of the water and lay on the shallow bottom. Placing both hands on a rock, he rested his chin on them as they talked. "I'm not sure," he said. "Have you ever had weird thoughts flash through your mind? I mean thoughts about things totally unrelated to what you're doing."

"I'm not sure I understand," she answered. "I've had all kinds of random thoughts while I was teaching something I knew well. I have it when I'm bored or teaching something simple."

"That's not what I mean... " Keith thought a couple of seconds. "I'm not sure how to explain it. Fragments flash through my mind and yet, they don't seem to mean anything."

"What kind of fragments?"

"That's just it," he tried to explain, "I can't remember exactly what they were. It's like a snapshot of something and a single word or concept, but the two don't always go together."

"When did you start feeling this?"

"When we arrived here," he explained. "The first time was when I knew there was an ocean to our east. That was when we woke up in the hut that was a wooden house the night before."

"Is there a theme to the thoughts?"

"I don't know," he said frustrated. "I'm telling you, it doesn't make sense."

"Okay, okay," Amanda tried to soothe him. "Don't get upset about it. You still seem to be the same Keith I know and love."

His expression brightened. "I love you too," he said. "I don't mean to drag you down. I'm just thinking out loud."

In the past, Amanda was a schoolteacher. She had run into Keith after the blackout and they had remained together ever since. Even though not married, they considered themselves a couple as did all their friends.

Amanda leaned forward and kissed him. He had changed from a teenage boy to a young man of great depth. Circumstances caused him to set aside the self-myth of a boy who thought he would live forever. In its place was the knowledge that life is fragile and happiness is to be cherished and protected.

Amanda pulled back. "You know we'll probably have to help Weniki and her people."

He climbed out of the water and sat beside her cross-legged. "We may have to," he said, placing his hands in his lap. "There may be no way to avoid it."

"I know you don't want to fight any more than I do," she conceded, "but how can we avoid it?"

"Bear told me of two karate masters forced to face each other in combat by their lords. The people of the village knew of the fight and gathered at the appointed time. The two masters stepped into the circle formed by the onlookers.

Both men squared their shoulders to the other, bowed, relaxed their bodies and waited for the other to move. As time passed, they remained in the same position even as the representatives of the lords screamed for combat. The masters stood motionless for eight hours until finally one of the representatives jumped in the ring and struck one of the men on the back with a staff. Not to be outdone, the other representative followed the actions of the first and struck the other master across the back.

Instantly, both masters spun on their attackers and killed them. Having completed their task, they turned, bowed to each other and left."

Amanda looked at him, waiting for more. When he said nothing, she said, "That's a nice story, but what does it have to do with our situation?"

"Our group is like the masters," Keith explained. "We only fight in self-defense. We won't go out looking for a fight. We'll only fight those who attack us first. We'll have to see who, if anyone, is the enemy. Then if attacked, we'll defend ourselves."

"Sure, I understand that," Amanda said, "but... "

"That," Keith interrupted, "is what we have to teach Weniki's people. They can defend themselves with what we teach them, but never attack others. Power is a dangerous thing."

Amanda understood what he was saying. She just didn't understand exactly how it applied to them. *He's getting to be more and more like Bear,* she thought. *He applies his training to everything now.*

***

Bear splashed through the stream and rounding a building, saw Weniki standing over a body. A teenage girl lay on the ground with three deep gashes across her chest and blood pooling around her.

"What happened?" Bear asked scanning the area for danger.

"Two Nāki attacked your man, Spyder and Kapane. They killed her and took him."

"Where's the body?" Bear asked.

"She lies there," Weniki said motioning at the girl.

"I mean the Nāki body," Bear said. "I heard three shots. Spyder doesn't miss."

"I have seen nothing. I was with Lopaka, in his home, when I heard the disturbance. When I arrived, this is what I found."

Bear eyed her closely. Something didn't sound right. Looking around the area, he found a puddle of blood. *Spyder didn't miss after all.*

"I've gotta go after him," Bear said looking for tracks.

"That would not be wise," Weniki said. "They will go to their village."

"It may not be wise," he countered. "But, it's what I'm gonna do. I won't just let 'em take him without doing something about it if I can."

"I cannot go with you," Weniki told him. She wore a worried look on her face. "When you go, I will not be able to protect you."

"I'm not asking you for protection," he said. "I can take care of myself."

She nodded, "As you wish," her eyes filled with tears. "They will not let you live."

"Then I'll return to the Power of the Universe where I came from," he said and followed the tracks away from the village.

CHAPTER TWENTY

At the time Bear ran toward the sound of Spyder's shots, Sandy was walking beside Hal. She stopped and grabbed his arm. "Something's wrong," she said.

"You okay?" Hal asked concerned.

"I'm fine," she assured him. "But something's going on with Bear and Spyder."

"Going on?" Hal asked. "What do you mean going on?"

"I don't know," she said trying to sort out the feeling settling over her.

They walked a few feet further toward the houses and Amanda ran up to them. "You've gotta talk some sense into Keith."

"What's wrong?" Hal asked. "What the hell's going on?"

"Come on, we gotta get back fast," Amanda said and ran back toward the house.

As they arrived, Keith walked out wearing two 9mm pistols, two bandoliers of ammunition and carrying an M16. To everyone's surprise, he was dressed in camouflage and had a Ghillie suit rolled into his backpack.

"Keith wait," Amanda called to him. "Listen to Hal and Sandy a second.

"I can't wait," he said. "I need to get going."

"What the hell's going on?" Hal asked. "Where're you going?"

"I'm going after Bear and Spyder," he answered.

"You've got no idea where they are," Hal argued.

215

"It doesn't matter," he stated flatly. "I'll find 'em."

Hal pulled his hat off with one hand and ran the other over his face in frustration.

Before he could protest further, Sandy said, "He has to go."

Amanda looked at her in disbelief. "Are you crazy? He'll get himself killed."

"That may be," Sandy said. "But, he has to go, something's happened. If he doesn't we'll all be in danger soon."

"How can you know that?" Amanda asked. "I don't understand."

Hal, surprised at Sandy's statement, stared at her. Before she could answer, he said, "If she says he's gotta go, I believe her."

"That doesn't mean I have to," Amanda snapped at him.

"I can't explain it," Hal told her, "but I trust Sandy's feelings."

"I have to go," Keith said softly.

She turned to him and the others walked away, giving them privacy.

"When will you be back?" She asked.

"I don't know," he answered. "I have to find both of 'em. After that, we'll do whatever we have to so you're safe back here."

Amanda rushed forward and threw her arms around him. Something told her she would never see him again. It wasn't just worry, but a feeling of impending loss.

"I love you," she whispered. "You have to come back to me."

"I love you too," he said. "I'll be back when I can."

"Promise me you'll come back."

"I promise I'll do my best," he promised.

"Promise me," she urged.

After a hesitation, he said, "I can't do that. All I can say is that I'll do my best."

They held each other close for almost a minute before he pulled back. "I gotta go." He kissed her and trotted away.

She watched him run down the path. As he disappeared from sight, her soul ached.

***

From the onset, Bear understood he was tracking members of a physically larger race of beings. From the tracks, he knew there were two, however, he noticed a number of differences in the tracks. The tracks were made by shoes or boots. He was used to seeing tracks here of people barefooted or wearing slippers. These tracks had heel impressions, unlike those made by soft soles. In addition, the length of the stride was that of a regular sized person. Nothing about them indicated a race of giants.

As he followed the signs, he was aware that his prey made no attempt to hide their passage. Looking closer at the tracks, he noticed sprinkles of blood dotting the ground here and there.

I wonder if that's Spyder's or if he shot one of the bastards? There was no way to tell.

Thunder rolled in the distance and he looked toward the mountains. Dark clouds hung ominously,

217

shrouding the peaks from view. "That's all I need," he mumbled to himself.

Beginning to trot, he increased the speed of his pursuit. The tracks would soon disappear with the rain.

Somewhere up ahead, his friend was in serious danger. There was no way he could allow that to continue. Fear edged into his determination. Relaxing his body, he slowed his breathing, making the breaths longer and deeper. He cleared his mind and allowed himself to enter a state of moving meditation.

He entered a small clearing and instantly flew sideways, slammed by something traveling perpendicular to him. Flung off his feet sideways, his head struck a rock as he landed roughly on the ground. Red flashes pierced his vision just before darkness swept over him.

***

Keith hurried forward, following the feelings leading him to somewhere or someone else. From deep inside his consciousness, he saw flashes of scenes. People died and war raged. He couldn't tell if they were premonitions or an overactive imagination.

He heard thunder and saw the clouds on the mountains. Neither of these mattered. He was following something inside, no tracks, no trails, just feelings.

After three hours, he found a rock beside a small stream and sat down to rest. From a pouch on his hip, he pulled a tincture of schisandra, licorice and ginseng. After pouring some of it in the liquid in one of his canteens and shaking it, he drank deeply. The tincture would help fight fatigue and stress as well as give him energy.

His attention quickly focused on a feeling of something in the bushes ahead. Something raced toward him, no longer stalking, but attacking. He pulled the M16 to his shoulder and fired three rapid shots as a saber-toothed tiger leapt from across the stream.

The first shot caught the cat in the head jerking it up and back. The second two plowed into its chest making it fall to its back short of him. The animal hit the ground and clawed at its underside as if trying to extract the hot lead through self-mutilation. In a few seconds, the muscles ceased to work and the animal lay still.

Seeing the animal dead, Keith's attention turned to his surroundings. *Forgot about those,* he thought surveying the area for further danger. Another thought flashed through his mind. This time, he knew it was from somewhere outside himself. *It was sent to stop you.*

Where this came from, he didn't know. Still, it felt real - and he trusted it. It was a warning of some sort from someone else. *Enough of this shit,* he thought. *I gotta get going.*

He stood, rearranged his pack, slung his rifle and set out again to help his friends.

***

When Bear awoke, night had settled in. He was soaked to the skin by what must have been a heavy rain. As he looked at the mountains, there was no sign of the sun. Obviously, he had lain unconscious for three or four hours.

Clambering to his feet, he found the stump of a tree to sit on. His head ached from where it struck the rock. Thinking about the incident, he didn't remember flying sideways from the impact. *It was more like something pushing me sideways in the air,* he thought. *The impact wasn't like someone running into me. It was more like a solid, but pliable wall hitting me, almost like a solid cushion of air.*

As his senses returned, he realized he might still be in danger. He quickly removed his rifle, from his shoulder, and scanned the bushes surrounding him. *Don't be stupid,* he scolded himself, *if something wanted to kill me, I'd be dead.* This last thought did little to assuage his unease. Something had attacked him.

Combing the area produced nothing he could use to identify his attacker. It was as if something had flown in, hit him and flown away. He located the spot where whatever it was hit him and where he landed. Other than that, there was nothing.

Even though it was night, he knew he had to push on. There was no doubt; his prey along with Spyder was far ahead of him now. He would keep on traveling all night and all day if he had to. Spyder was like a brother and he wasn't willing to let the man down.

The only trail he had to follow was broken and bent limbs. The rain had washed away any footprints his enemy might have left. He could only hope he was going the right direction.

Around midnight, he stopped to rest.

CHAPTER TWENTY-ONE

Amanda, Sandy and Ginny sat around the fire. Hal and Wind were at the waterfall. They wanted some time to mull over what was happening. Keith had been gone two hours before Wind returned from a hunting trip with birds for dinner.

"Doesn't this seem strange to you?" Amanda asked.

"What?" Sandy questioned. Using a long stick, she arranged the fire, the birds on a spit over it and potatoes, wrapped in banana leaves, rested in the coals. Once again, Ginny handled the cooking now that Palenaka and Weniki were gone.

"Isn't it weird that we've been separated by circumstances?" Amanda asked looking from Ginny to Sandy.

"What do you mean?" Sandy hadn't thought about the group as separated, just that the individuals left and why they were gone.

"Put it together," Amanda led her through an explanation. "We've tried to stay together. Now, Bear and Spyder are with Weniki and all of a sudden, Keith runs off because something's wrong. That leaves you, Hal, Ginny, Wind and me here. We're now separated in a way we would've never been before."

Sandy thought about the circumstances that had arisen. Everything made sense to her, but she could see what Amanda meant. Was it all coincidence or something planned to get them apart?

"I understand what you mean," she conceded. "What do you think's going on?"

"I don't know anything for sure," Amanda admitted. "But what if the Nāki are trying to get us apart? What if they know about us and know we're a threat if we're still together?"

Sandy hadn't considered that possibility, Amanda could have a point. What if the Nāki wanted them separated so they could attack. "I agree it's strange," she said. "It could still be only a coincidence though. I'll let Hal know what may be going on. We need to keep our guard up, just in case."

"I don't think so," Ginny said. "According to Weniki, this valley is still invisible to the Nāki. They'll never find us."

"I forgot about that," Sandy admitted. "You may be right, as long as we stay here, I simply don't know."

"There's no way anyone could find us with the entrance disguised the way it is," Ginny assured her.

"Maybe not," Amanda said, "but we're still separated and I'm not comfortable with it."

"Wait a minute," Sandy said alarmed. "If no one can find this place, how will Bear, Spyder and Keith be able to get back in here?"

"There's a way to come back through the cave," Hal said emerging from the path to the pool with Wind following. "Bear said Weniki would show them how to find the way back inside."

Sandy sat back in her chair relieved. She hadn't thought about the problem of their return until Amanda brought it up.

"We were listening to your conversation for a little bit," Hal said. "As for the Nāki, they had no way to know we were here. Only Weniki and Palenaka knew about us. We're safe."

"You're right," Amanda agreed. "Only Weniki and Palenaka are psychic. There's no way for the Nāki to know about us."

"We just have to get the weapons ready and wait here for them to return," Hal said and sat in a chair beside Sandy. Wind planted himself beside Ginny. "Now, when will that food be ready?" Hal said rubbing his hands together. "Tonight, I don't have to worry about Bear eating it all before I get a chance at it."

***

After running eight hours with only two rests, Keith stopped by a pool and sat down. It was only three or four hours until sunrise. He would rest until the sun came up and then start again. A feeling deep inside urged him to keep moving, but he knew he would only run himself into the ground if he kept going. Besides, he needed to have strength and energy when he caught up with whoever it was he was after.

Stopping for the night, he filled two empty canteens, laid out a blanket and settled in to sleep until the sun woke him.

When he jerked awake, it was because of a nightmare and not the sun. As with his meditation, his sleep was haunted with scenes of war. Though he couldn't remember specifics, something about them reminded him of stories of knights of the middle ages.

Shaking sleep from his head, he quickly packed his things, ate some berries and fruits and started again. Unknown to him, he slept less than half a mile from the entrance to the valley of Weniki's Ohana.

***

Bear traveled the rest of the night until frustration and fatigue forced him to rest. Anything faster than a slow walk and he lost the trail. He knew there was no way he could catch up to Spyder and his captors before they reached their village.

Unwilling to sleep on the ground, he found a tree where the lowest branches crossed about ten feet overhead. After climbing to the branches, he wedged himself into where they met and quickly fell asleep.

In his dreams, he floated among the clouds. *He saw a figure ahead of him and was sure it was an angel. By willing himself forward, he glided up behind the figure. From its hair and shape, he knew it was a woman. He reached out, tapped it on the shoulder. As she turned, he knew he would once again be able to look at Davata. There was no person he wanted to see in his dreams, other than her.*

When she turned, he was face to face with a grinning skeleton. He jerked away from the aberration and, losing his concentration, felt himself falling.

Abruptly, he slammed into the ground. In fact, the dream had caused him to fall from his perch in the tree. He was lucky he hadn't broken his neck on impact.

From behind him, he heard laughter. Not simply a snicker, but a full-blown belly laugh. Turning, he saw Keith red faced with tears coming from his eyes.

"What the fuck's so funny?" He snorted embarrassed.

"I saw... " Keith was laughing too hard to finish the sentence. Soon, he rolled onto the ground. For what seemed like an eternity to Bear, he continued, holding his stomach and curled into a semi-fetal position.

Finally regaining control of his emotions, he wiped the tears from his eyes and sat up. "I saw you slipping from about fifty feet away," he explained. "There was no way I could stop you from falling. You slipped to the side and dropped like a ripe cocoanut." He burst into another fit of giggles. "I'm sorry to laugh," he apologized, "but you looked like some sort of cartoon, especially when you looked up so surprised." Another fit of giggles erupted even though he fought hard to keep them down.

"You think that's funny?" Bear asked recovered from the shock of the fall and the embarrassment of Keith laughing at him.

"Hell yeah," he answered fighting more giggles. "I'm glad you're not hurt," he said, "honestly I am. I've been traveling hard for over a day and I'm glad to find you in one piece, but... " he let loose with more snickers and covered his nose and mouth with his hand.

"Okay, you've had your laugh," Bear said still aggravated. "You make the fire for coffee."

"Coffee," Keith repeated. "We don't have time for coffee. We need to get on the trail."

"What trail?" Bear asked defiantly. "There's no trail to follow after the rain yesterday."

"I can follow it," Keith insisted. "Something's showing me where to go."

Bear looked him appraisingly. "You still make the fire and coffee. We'll get going soon enough."

Keith knew better than to argue with him and began gathering wood.

***

"That's why I'm here," Keith said finishing the story of his feelings and the urge, which drew him to where they sat.

Bear had said nothing of Spyder's disappearance. He wanted to hear everything the young man had to say before telling him the situation.

"I'm glad you're here," he said. "There's a problem going on and we have to set it right."

"What kinda problem?" Keith asked.

"Spyder's been taken hostage by the Nāki." Bear cut straight to the core.

Keith sat up in reaction to the news. "Did they kill him?" he asked.

"I said he's a hostage," Bear corrected. "I'm not sure if he's still alive. They may have already killed him and done something with his body. I just don't know."

"We gotta find out," Keith said raising his voice. "We can't leave him with them. They'll kill him for sure."

"I agree," Bear said. "But, the first thing we have to do is find their village."

"It's about five miles ahead," Keith said, "and up the side of a volcano."

"A volcano?" Bear questioned. "Do you mean Lua Pele?

"I don't know the name, but it's a volcano," Keith said. "There's also something else there we need to watch out for."

"That's probably the Kalekona," Bear surmised. "Weniki said they were the dragons that breathed fire."

"Do you really think they breathe fire?" Keith asked. The idea of an animal spewing fire from its mouth seemed far-fetched to him.

"With the other animals they have here, I wouldn't doubt it," Bear confessed. "We have no idea what type of things we might encounter. With what's happened, I'll believe almost anything."

Keith was silent. Nothing in his life before taught him to expect the things that had happened to him and the human race. "Sensei," he said barely above a whisper, "what's happened to everything? Nothing's the way it's supposed to be. First, we lost electricity and had to live as our ancestors did. And, just when things started working out, we were attacked and had to fight. Then, we found ourselves here, a place where the people have no idea of what civilization is."

"You don't think Weniki and Palenaka are civilized?" Bear questioned.

"Yeah, I guess they are... in a way," Keith conceded and looked down at his lap. "But, it's not like what we're used to. What the hell's happening to us?"

"I can't answer that," Bear said. "All I can do is advise you to be open minded. Things are happening to us and we have to accept them and not dwell on the why's and how's. We obviously can't change what's happened, just the outcome, or at least I hope we can."

Keith sat looking at his crossed legs. "I don't know how you do it," he confessed. "It's about to drive me crazy."

"Follow me in this Keith," Bear said. "Are we in Rollingblock?"

"No," Keith said still looking down.

"Are we in a foreign world of some sort?"

"We sure as hell are," he answered with resignation. "We're stuck out here, who knows where."

"Stay with me," Bear told him. "Can you change the fact that you're here?"

"No." Keith's voice registered almost total loss.

"Are you the Keith I love and care about?"

Keith looked up into Bear's face, stunned. He had never heard his teacher talk like this before. "I'm still the same person I was before," he admitted.

"Then tell me what's changed." Bear instructed.

"We're not in the same place. There're no cities. There're people that want to kill us for no reason." He hesitated as the pressure built. Suddenly he blurted out, "We're lost and we won't ever get back home."

Bear sat quietly and let the young man's words drift through the trees and echo off the nearby cliffs.

They were no different from some of the thoughts that had run through his mind. He waited on Keith's understanding to settle amongst the fear and confusion. How could a person expect to accept the circumstances they had faced without questioning their own sanity?

Breaking the relative silence of the countryside, he asked, "Where is home?"

"It's back where I lived in Texas," Keith said totally dejected. "It's where I was raised. It's back where things were normal... " he paused, "When I was young."

"Keith," Bear waited until he had the young man's attention. Finally, Keith looked up. "The only differences between then and now are your age and location. You're still the same person. It doesn't matter when or where you are. You're still the same entity - the same person, just simply misplaced somewhere. If I take a grain of sand from one part of a beach and move it to another, isn't it still the same? Doesn't it still serve to make up the entire beach?" He paused a second. "The same as if I pluck you from your time and place, and put you in another time and place. Aren't you still the same?"

"Yeah," Keith agreed. "I'm still the same, but the time and place is different."

"So?" Bear let the question settle in the quiet of the forest.

Keith looked up. His expression slowly brightened. "That's what you were trying to teach me before!" He exclaimed. "I see what you meant. I'm the same. Only the world or situation has changed. I'm still the same part of the universe I was, I'm just *in* a different part of it."

"Pour me another cup of coffee," Bear said holding his cup out. "I may make a real student outta you yet."

Keith poured the coffee, excited over his acceptance of this complicated ideology. "I think I understand Sensei," he exclaimed. "It makes sense now."

"Not yet," Bear said sipping the brew. "You've only realized how the belief begins. But, there *is* hope for you."

CHAPTER TWENTY-TWO

Even in the sunshine, the trail was gone. The only thing they had to follow was Keith's feelings. Bear allowed him to lead the way and as they trudged along, he saw the peak of a volcano partially obscured by a line of lower mountains. It really was about five miles in the distance.

Keith soon entered a valley, which wound its way through the mountains. The further they traveled, the less dense the vegetation became. Heat and gasses from eruptions and volcanic vents seemed to prevent the growth of vegetation. Before long, they moved along a landscape that looked more lunar than earthlike. The land was grayish black with huge lava boulders and fissures that had once been lava flows.

"Look over here," Keith said excitedly.

Bear followed him to an obvious regularly used trail. "I think we've got a way to find Spyder," he said. "Thanks to you and your feelings, that is."

"I hope he's still alive," Keith said, worry in his voice.

"He's alive," Bear assured him.

"How do you know that?"

"I can feel it," he explained, "like you feel other things, I guess."

Keith nodded, understanding the man's feelings, and continued following the path.

A few yards later, Bear told Keith to hold up. "We'll wait here for dark," he said. "I don't wanna travel across that open space in broad daylight."

***

Hal snapped awake, jerked from sleep by something growling outside the house. Listening, he heard a thump and another deep growl, then another thump followed by something that sounded like the roar of a lion, deep and throaty - but much larger.

Sandy sat straight up beside him. "There's something out there," he said and started to get up.

She grabbed his arm. "Wait," she warned. "It's wrong."

"What do you mean wrong?" He asked.

"I don't know," she answered. "Something's not right about this. We're supposed to be hidden from animals as well as people."

"Well something's out there," he argued.

A bang sounded on the wall near the door to their room and Wind said, "You two awake?"

"Come on in," Hal said. "We're up."

As he walked in the room, another roar sounded outside. Looking at Hal and Sandy's faces he said, "Okay, I'm not the only one hearing this shit."

"We need to get out there," Hal said. His voice betrayed the conviction of his statement.

"And do what?" Sandy asked. "You gonna fight whatever it is?"

Hal ran his hand through his hair. "I don't know," he said honestly. "But whatever it is sounds big enough to tear this place apart."

"If it was gonna do that, it would have already started," Sandy argued still feeling that something wasn't right about the situation.

Hal stood and quickly dressed. "I still gotta see what it is," he said.

"I'm with you," Wind said.

232

Moving toward the door Hal said, "They may not be any use, but we need weapons."

Both men took shoulder holsters with 9mm pistols and donned them like jackets. After fastening them to their belts, they each took an M16, checked it for ammo and placed more clips in their pockets.

Hal nodded to Wind and quickly stepped out of the house. As they stepped outside, Sandy hurried past the door to Amanda's room. She would get her up, then gather some weapons and join the men outside.

Hal and Wind stood close to the outside wall of the house. Something massive moved among the bushes and trees, on the other side of Weniki's house. The trees swayed, some of them bowed as some gigantic creature passed between. Another roar, almost deafening outside the building, echoed throughout the valley.

Hal and Wind hurried across the space between theirs and Weniki's house. Both men snuck into the underbrush. Hal motioned for Wind to stay near the clearing's edge and went deeper into the forest. They traveled a distance apart until reaching the secret entrance to the valley. Crossing the path near the opening, they returned in the same search pattern.

Sandy and Amanda were armed and stood in the clearing when Hal and Wind returned. Ginny sat in a chair beside the embers in the fire pit.

"Did you see anything?" Sandy asked. She had heard no shots or animal sounds in the distance to tell what was going on.

"Nothing," Hal said.

"There wasn't anything out there," Wind reported.

"Bullshit," Amanda said with conviction. "There was *something* out here."

"We checked both sides of the path all the way back to the hidden entrance," Wind explained, "and there was nothing there. Not even a footprint or disturbed bushes."

"Then you missed something in the dark," Sandy said turning back toward the center of the clearing. Holding a torch in front of her, she revealed a giant three-toed footprint.

Ginny continued to sit in the chair as if nothing had happened.

***

After dark settled in, both men cautiously made their way across the barren stretch of land. Soon a boulder appeared in the distance and it looked as though it teetered on the edge of the world, the ground black beyond the huge rock. As Bear approached it, the trail dropped sharply and the terrain a few yards ahead of him disappeared into more darkness, as if the land abruptly ended. With no moon out, he couldn't tell if he faced a cliff or a steep slope. Nothing in the darkness yielded a hint of what lay before him.

Keith crawled up beside him, poked him with his elbow and pointed to their left. Lower, in the distance, was a soft glow. "That has to be individual fires," Bear whispered. "A single large one wouldn't show throughout the forest like that. We're near a village."

234

Bear moved to the boulder and motioned Keith to join him. They would wait here to see the lay of the land before them. If there was a village, they didn't need to move in closer and risk discovery. Daylight would disclose any traps or sentries posted to protect the settlement.

Positioning themselves on the high side of the boulder, they used the few bushes they could find to cover themselves and waited for the sun to climb above the volcanic slope. In the twilight, they saw three different sets of guards pass en route to the valley below. As the sun rose above the valley, another group passed along the path and disappeared into the trees on the slope ahead.

Waiting another two hours and experiencing no more pedestrians, Bear led the way down the slope of the trail. Before them was a dell covered with lush vegetation. Trees of various types rose above the landscape as tropical flowers and plants filled the rest of the ground. A tropical paradise lay in the valley surrounded by the devastation of a volcano.

They moved quietly down the slope, through the trees, watching for traps or trip wires. As they approached, Keith could smell food cooking. In the distance, he heard the sounds of village life. The clank of metal, conversations and the occasional sound of laughter echoed among the trees.

"I hope we've found the right village," he whispered.

Bear motioned for him to be silent. He motioned ahead and to their left. Looking in the distance, he eventually located a pair of sentries standing among the trees.

He nodded and lowered himself closer to the ground. If sentries were there, more had to be stationed at intervals around the camp. Some might even be close to them now. Not sure what to do, he lay still waiting for Bear to make a move. Surely, he had some sort of a plan.

***

Bear waited motionless. He wanted to see what the sentries would do. If they stayed together, where they were, he and Keith could move directly toward the village from their position. If the men separated to patrol the forest, that would present a more difficult problem.

Below, the men were talking. Both were animated and acted as if there was no real worry of detection. Neither of them watched the area away from the village. In fact, they never looked at anything in particular.

Both were dressed in shirts and trousers covered by a dark tunic with swords hanging from their belts. From this distance, Bear wasn't sure, but thought they might even have chain mail covering their chests and backs. He wasn't a student of history, but something about them was familiar. They actually looked like they were part of medieval Britain.

Even in the quiet of the forest, he was unable to understand what the two men said. In a couple of minutes another man approached them, said something and the three men walked away.

"Stay low and quiet," Bear said as he moved forward.

A wall of cliffs stood to their right. On two separate levels were paths along the face. *I hope they don't use those on a regular basis,* he thought. With Keith following close behind, he maneuvered to the top path.

About a quarter of the way along its course, they found a cave. Like the others on the island, it was too deep to explore without a torch. From inside its entrance, they had a view of most of the village nestled in the valley below. "All we can do is hope nothing's using this for a home," Bear said once inside.

The village consisted of numerous wooden structures of all sizes. There were men, women and children moving around the area, none of which appeared to be from a race of giants. As with the guards from last night and this morning, none of them seemed to be abnormally large.

"Do those look like giants to you?" Bear asked.

"No," Keith said. "But they might be considered large by Weniki and her people. None of them are taller than five foot six or seven inches with most of them around five-four or five-five. Those down there are dressed in clothes that make them look bigger and bulkier. That might be why they look like giants to Weniki's people."

"That could be," Bear admitted. "But, there're children down there."

"Where do you think the adults come from?"

Bear looked at Keith to see if he was being a smartass. He saw however, the young man was simply responding to his statement.

"Do you see Spyder anywhere?" Keith was looking intently at the community.

"Not yet," Bear answered. "But from here, we can't see the whole village either."

"There're more people there than I expected," Keith admitted. "Even if we found him, I doubt we could get him out."

"You're right about that," Bear agreed. "But we need to scout the area around the place. If there's a weakness, we need to know what and where it is."

Keith nodded and started removing his pack. "There's no reason we can't leave this stuff here until we get back."

"We don't leave anything," Bear disagreed.

"We can travel faster if we're lighter," Keith argued.

"This cave might be used for something," Bear pointed out. "It could even be a place for a night guard or something else. I only chose it so we could get a safer look at the village. If we leave anything here, it might be gone when we get back. If one of them found it, they'd know we were here and return for the things. We don't need any ambushes. No, we take 'em with us."

"I hadn't thought of that," Keith admitted.

While on the path, Bear had noticed that it disappeared behind some bushes about a hundred yards ahead. Motioning Keith to the front of the cave, he pointed to the bushes. "We need to get to those," he said. "We'll have to move slow and hope no one looks up at the path. If anyone comes up from behind, we double time toward 'em. If someone blocks the path, we charge - no shooting unless absolutely necessary. That would only draw more unwanted attention."

CHAPTER TWENTY-THREE

It took over two hours to cover the distance to the bushes. As Keith crawled up beside him, Bear patted the young man on the shoulder. "You did a good job," he said. "You got here without raising any dust or making noise." Grinning, he added, "You've passed your crawling test."

Keith grinned back, "That's nice, but for a little while, can we learn walking?"

Bear shook his head, "Nope."

"Figures," Keith said, "You're probably gonna make me crawl all the way back home."

"Now you get to practice tracking," Bear said seriously.

"Tracking?" Keith questioned. "Who are we tracking?"

"Anyone or anything that's not us," Bear said. "If we find fresh tracks, we know we're not alone. It's better'n stumbling up on someone."

Keith understood what he meant. He should have thought of that himself. It still amazed him how the man kept everything like that in his head. When he asked about it before, Bear had shrugged and said, "I've done it a couple of times before."

Bear moved into the bushes to their right. Following him, Keith mumbled, "Here we go again."

To Keith's surprise, Bear only went into the bushes a couple of yards and stopped. Using his knife, he cut small branches from the bottom of some bushes and stripped them of their leaves. Holding a bunch of leaves in his hand, he said,

"Roll these in your palms and smear them on all exposed skin."

Keith watched Bear to make sure what he meant. Following his example, Keith rolled the leaves briskly between his hands until they became sticky with sap, which he smeared on his skin until he had coated every inch.

Bear cut some more leafy branches from other plants. He was careful to cut the branches pointing away from the small path. He didn't want anyone to see the cuts if they were walking along it.

"Lay on your stomach," he instructed.

With Keith lying flat, he stuffed the branches under his clothing. When he was finished, he instructed Keith to do the same to him.

Returning to a sitting position, he said, "Hopefully this'll kill our scent. Now, redo your face paint."

When he was satisfied, he moved a little further into a particularly dense growth of bushes. "Take a rest," he said. "Drink some water and let your muscles relax, water the plants if you need to. It's gonna be a long day."

"Water the plants?"

"Take a piss," he said. "If you don't do it here, you will have to later on. Here, there's no one around to kill you for it."

Keith grinned, "I've still got a ton to learn."

"So have I," Bear responded and leaned back against a tree.

A while later he stood up. "How far from the valley do you think this forest goes?" Keith asked.

"I've got no idea," he answered. "It depends on how the lava flowed on this side of the slope."

"Where do we go from here?" Keith asked.

"I'm gonna go along the edge of the valley," Bear said. "If you noticed, the valley is bound by a cliff on this side too. I wanna see if I can spot Spyder anywhere down there."

"What about me?" Keith asked. "Do you want me to follow you?"

"No, I want you to follow the path. Stay at least twenty-five yards from it, on the left. Stop when it runs out or into something. Stay where you are when that happens. I'll find you. This is one test you better pass - your life depends on it."

Keith was surprised Bear was putting that much trust in him. If he screwed up, there probably wouldn't be a second chance. "I won't let you down," he said.

"The only way you can let me down," Bear said, "is if you get killed." Without another word, he moved back toward the path and in a couple of seconds disappeared in the bushes beyond.

A startled Keith stood, checked his surroundings and crossed the path. He wouldn't let his Sensei down.

***

Bear stayed about five feet from the edge of the cliff. He was close enough to see the village below, yet remain hidden against and among the bushes. He slung his rifle across the pack on his chest knowing he would only use it as a last resort.

He was able to travel easily and used a quick mixture of sap and dirt to chart the village on a piece of paper from his wallet. Soon, he spotted a long wooden structure below with a thatched roof. He settled in to see if he could identify a pattern to the movements of the villagers below.

One thing that stood out was that all the adults wore swords or shorter knives of some sort. Most of the men not only had swords, but carried long spears as well. He was sure this was not a village of peaceful people.

The village, however, did remind him of the medieval England of books and movies. The only thing missing were horses. *These people are willing and able to fight,* he thought. Then the difference between Weniki's people and these struck home. The people below him had weapons and tools of metal. Weniki's people used wood, their spears tipped with formed rocks.

He continued along the edge of the cliff until coming to an abrupt angle. The valley curved sharply to the right and even though the cliff followed the curve, it sloped downward. *At this angle, it won't take long to be level with the valley floor,* he thought.

Not wanting to be near the edge, as it grew closer to the village, he angled back into the brush. Before losing site of the buildings, he saw Spyder. His hands were tied in front of him and he walked between two men wearing tunics with bright red sashes at an angle across their torsos.

Bear watched as the men walked Spyder toward the long building. He backtracked along the edge of the cliff, keeping the men in sight. Sure enough, they kept Spyder between them as they entered the structure.

242

At least he's still alive, Bear thought. *There's no way Keith and I can get him out of there, though.*

He hurried back to survey the building where they kept Spyder. It was in the center of a cluster of structures with more on each side. There was no way to get in and out successfully without detection.

It was time to find Keith and mull over what he had found. Moving away from the cliff, he silently slipped through the brush, pausing to look, listen and smell.

After about a hundred yards, he found the path. The trail ran down a slope at about the same angle as the cliff. Following the trail only a couple of minutes, it turned sharply to the right. *Same as the cliff,* he remembered.

After another couple of minutes, he saw Keith. The young man was in a ball among a small group of banana plants. About fifteen feet away two sentries stood talking. Bear lay in a prone position and readied his rifle. *Let's see how he does,* he thought. He didn't want to shoot unless the guards discovered Keith. Even then, he didn't want the sound. But, there was no way he would let the boy be killed while he lay watching.

***

The footprint was at least five feet long, three feet across at the widest point and consisted of a heel portion and three toes. "Ho-ly shit!" Wind exclaimed.

About ten feet away was another, identical to the first. Hal held a torch closer so he could see the print in more detail. It was two inches deep with

243

claw marks extending from each toe. "We've got a problem, folks," he said. "Whatever made this, weighs tons."

The line of tracks went from the waterfall, between the houses toward the secret entrance of their valley. "That must be what we heard out here," Wind guessed. "The sound seemed to come from above the houses."

"If what we heard made these prints," Sandy said, "then what were the two of you tracking in the bushes?"

Hal realized what she was saying. "There was more than one," he said.

"That can't be," Wind said. "Nothing could come in the valley, walk through the camp and leave without us seeing something. Where the tracks came from and went to are solid walls, except for the cuts in the rocks. There's no way a creature that size could fit through one of those openings."

"Did anyone hear the growl after Hal and Wind went into the bushes?" Ginny asked.

Everyone shook their heads.

"Did either of you find any tracks or signs of anything away from the camp?"

"I didn't," Hal said. "What about you?" He looked at Wind.

Wind shook his head no. "There wasn't anything there."

Ginny nodded, turned and walked into her hut.

"What the hell was all that about?" Wind asked.

"We've got more to worry about than her right now," Hal said. "We need guards out at night."

244

Sandy couldn't shake the memory of Amanda's observation that something may have intentionally separated their group.

Hal brought the fire between the houses back to life. He knew the only purpose it served was to help in alleviating their nervousness. *Anything leaving a track like that could step over this fire with ease.*

"I'll take the first watch," he said. "Wind, I'll wake you up in about four hours. You take it from then 'til sunrise."

"I can take it now," Wind said. "There's no way I'll get any sleep tonight."

"Are you sure?" Hal was willing to take the first watch. He didn't want to ask Wind to do it if he wasn't able.

"Hal," he said, "I've never been able to go straight to bed after being excited. I was up until three in the morning after a track meet, imagine how long I'll be up after something like this?"

"Thanks man," Hal said, "I need the sleep."

"He'll even snore," Sandy said smiling. "He beats anything I've ever seen."

"You've got it then," Hal said. "Wake me up if you need to." He shook hands with Wind and headed back to the house with Sandy.

"Are you gonna be okay by yourself?" Amanda asked. "I can stay up with you if you want."

"No, you don't have to do that," Wind said. "I'll be fine."

"I'm gonna try to get some rest," she said. "There's no chance of sleep, but maybe I can rest."

"You go take care of yourself," he said. "I'll make sure nothing sneaks up on us."

Amanda smiled and kissed him on the cheek. "Thanks," she said. "I don't know what we'd do without you." She turned and walked toward the house leaving him standing beside the fire.

Wind added a couple of pieces of wood to the fire and decided to take a turn around the clearing. These people, his friends were all he had left. He knew he cared about them before, but never realized just how much. They had become family to him.

After circling the edge of the clearing and finding nothing, he sat under a banana tree and leaned against a rock beneath it. From this vantage point, he could see and hear the surrounding area. The crickets buzzed, the frogs near the pool croaked and night birds chirped as they flittered from branch to branch in the trees.

Everything had returned to normal. It was as if nothing had happened. No giant creature had walked through their homes, growling and leaving footprints the size of a dinosaur. How could nature be that forgiving? How could it return to normal as if nothing out of the ordinary had happened? *It's not out of the normal for here,* he thought.

Sitting under the tree, he relaxed and realized just how tired he really was. He leaned his head back against the rock and closed his eyes. In his martial arts classes, Bear taught how to close his eyes and see his surroundings in his mind's eye. He wasn't nearly as good at it as Keith was, but he did enjoy the exercise. Employing the technique, he allowed the stress and excitement of the night to slip away.

Almost immediately, he drifted off to sleep and his thoughts slipped into dreams. In his dreams, he and Palenaka were sitting by the pool laughing and talking. The day was warm and small animals came to the water to drink. The valley was invisible to the outside and their world was safe.

As he slept, Wind failed to see Ginny leave her hut. She carried a large machete and walked quietly toward him. The depth of his dreams blocked the outside world and she was able to slip up behind him undetected. Standing directly behind him, she raised the machete over her head.

***

The two sentries seemed completely unaware of Keith's presence. Both were dressed in the same black tunics as the others, however these wore green sashes diagonally across their upper bodies.

The sashes designate some sort of position, Bear silently surmised. *Probably jobs rather than rank.*

As they carried on a conversation about some female back in their village, they moved toward him. When they stopped, they stood less than five feet from where he lay concealed.

From his position, Bear could see Keith clearly. His camouflage made him look like a green lump among the rest of the foliage. As he watched, he saw a slight ripple under the mound. *Take it easy on the movements,* Bear silently warned Keith. *Movements can cause sound.*

One guard stepped away from the other apparently to relieve himself behind a tree. Under his disguise, Keith had gathered his feet. Quickly and silently, he stood and with his left hand,

247

grabbed the man across the mouth. With his right, he drove his knife into the man's kidneys. Without hesitation, he cut the man's throat and moved to the other.

Bear couldn't see exactly what he did, but the other man dropped soundlessly to the ground. When Keith turned around, Bear stood about ten feet away.

Keith's face was pale, his right hand coated with blood and he had a lost look on his face. He almost glowed white under his camouflage. It looked as if the blood on his hands had drained from his face.

Bear knew how he felt. Keith had experienced killing in a battle. However, this time, he had killed in a very personal way.

"Are you okay?" Bear asked just slightly above a whisper.

"I... I think so," Keith answered. His hands shook and he looked as if he would pass out.

"Take a few deep breaths," Bear instructed.

Keith looked at him doubtful.

"I'm serious," Bear insisted. "Take some deep breaths and let them out slowly. What you're feeling is normal. The bitter almond taste in your mouth is adrenalin. It and the shakes will go away in a few minutes."

"I just took the life of another person," Keith said, his voice cracking, "twice in fact."

"You've done it before, Keith. It just wasn't this personal. You've got to compartmentalize it, put it in the back of your mind. You can work it out later. Right now, you have to focus on the present."

Keith nodded. "I'll try."

"You know what Yoda says," Bear said. "Try not. Do, or do not, there is no try. It may seem silly, but it's true."

"I'm not sure I can," Keith said honestly.

"What do we need to do now?" Bear asked.

"Huh?" Keith answered. He knew he was dissociating unable to pull his thinking together.

"Describe our situation."

He hesitated, thinking. "We've got two dead men lying on the ground. Someone'll find them when their relief's come out. If not, someone is certain to miss them when they don't return. Both were knifed, so the Nāki will realize someone is around." It was obvious that his thoughts were becoming clear again as he spoke, more focused, not so scattered.

Bear waited, he could see Keith's attention gathering.

After a hesitation, Keith said, "I think I know what we can do. There's a vertical shaft about a quarter mile over there." He pointed a location where the path disappeared ahead. "It's deep enough that I couldn't see the bottom. We can drop the bodies in there. They'll still be missing, but no one will know what happened to 'em."

Bear nodded in agreement. "It's a good idea," he said. "We'll have to carry the bodies and use the trail."

Keith was already lifting one of the dead men. "I'll show you were it is."

Bear, picked up the other body and followed him down the trail.

CHAPTER TWENTY-FOUR

"They are outside the village," Weniki said. She sat in a building with Palenaka and Lopaka. "They are both safe. Something happened to disturb the younger one named Keith. He is overcoming his emotions with Bear's help."

"Last night, I felt a disturbance with the others," Palenaka said.

"It was a Kōtha," Weniki explained. "It is gone now."

"What of the other two?" Palenaka asked. "Can you see them?"

"No," Weniki said. "I can only feel their emotions. If I try anything stronger, the Nāki will know of them."

"Will they be able to help us?" Lopaka asked.

"They will," Weniki answered, "if they save their friend. If the man called Spyder is killed, I cannot say what they will do."

"Would that not place them on the path of vengeance?" Lopaka suggested.

"It might," Weniki agreed. "However, it may cause them to avoid the Nāki. When I shared with Bear, I saw that he wants to leave wars and battles behind."

"... and yet, he kills for his friends," Lopaka argued.

"Not him," Weniki corrected. "It was the young one, Keith."

"What of the others?" Palenaka asked. "What will they do?"

"They will follow Bear," Weniki said. "They will do what he says. You worry about the ones still at our hale. Are you interested in the one called Wind?"

Palenaka bowed her head and smiled. "I must confess," she said, "he is very nice. I hope we might be close in the future."

"That is too bad," Weniki said. "It will not be."

"What do you mean?" Palenaka asked looking up. "What has happened?"

***

Keith led Bear to the edge of a deep hole. It was at least ten feet across and partially covered in vines, limbs and leaves. Peering down, Bear was unable to see the bottom.

"Do you wanna throw a torch down and find out how deep it is?" Keith asked.

"What do we do if there's brush at the bottom and it catches fire?" Bear answered.

"I didn't think of that," Keith admitted. "Let's get rid of the bodies."

Both bodies disappeared into the darkness of the pit. Gauging by the length of time it took them to reach the bottom, Bear estimated its depth to be at least seventy-five feet.

"We need to scout the area to see what else is here," Bear said turning from the hole.

"You're not gonna believe what I found," Keith said taking the lead.

"Show me," Bear said following him across the trail.

Traveling through thick brush for ten minutes brought them to the edge of another cliff. Breaking through the vegetation, they saw a giant lake about

251

a half-mile away. The cliff where they hid was at least a hundred feet higher that the water's surface in the distance affording them an unrestricted view.

The lake extended from left to right at least ten miles and three from the closest side to the opposite. About a mile to their right, the foliage ended and barren lava coated ground extended down the side of the mountain to the water. On the far side, mountains rose from the beach to a series of peaks. As with the rest of the mountains on the island, their sides displayed deep crevices carved by centuries of water flow. The view was magnificent.

On the left, the Nāki's valley seemed to flow from the mountains to the edge of the lake where they had erected jetties. The piers jutted into the water with a number of boats tied to them. Other boats floated in the water and Bear could see people fishing with nets.

"It looks like a normal village to me," Keith observed.

"Even cannibals need to supplement their diets," Bear growled. "It sounded like long pig was only taken in intervals. Maybe it's used during festivals or celebrations."

"Long pig?" Keith questioned.

"Humans," Bear explained. "It's a term for human meat."

"Oh yeah," Keith said. "I forgot. I've heard that before."

"We need to get back to Weniki's Ohana Nui," Bear said and began walking toward the lava-coated slopes.

Keith hurried to catch up. "What about Spyder," he asked.

"He's alive for now," Bear answered. "But, if we take too much time, he might not be."

"Did you see him?" Keith pressed.

"He was tied up and being escorted by two men," Bear answered. "Now, it's time we stopped talking and started moving."

"Lead the way," Keith said following close behind.

"No more talking," Bear instructed. "Save your breath and your water. We're moving fast."

Bear moved along the edge of the cliff until reaching the lava flow. Once there, he turned right and ascended the rocky surface, staying above the vegetation. About three quarters of the way up the mountain, the vegetation reached its peak and descended the other side.

Bear was fairly sure they wouldn't meet any guards up here. No one would brave the dangers of an active lava flow to lead a band of soldiers against the Nāki in the valley below. Keith was having problems following and keeping up as they moved along the terrain.

Bear stopped near the peak of the volcano. A river of lava blocked their path. Keith was panting when he arrived. Looking at the flowing rock before them, he asked, "How do you expect to get past this?"

"I'm not sure," Bear answered. "That depends where it runs. We didn't have to cross it on our way to the village."

The lava flowed down the slope toward the tree line about fifty yards away. Following the flow down the side of the slope, they found that it poured into a tunnel and disappeared underground.

They turned and again traveled across the mountain. "We have about two hours until sunset," Bear said stopping for a break. "We need to get off this mountain before then."

"Wouldn't we be safer up here at night?" Keith asked. "It doesn't seem like the Nāki come up here."

"They must have a reason for avoiding the place," Bear cautioned. "Remember the Kalekona Weniki described before? They may be the reason the villagers shun the area."

"Those were the fire-breathing dragon things, right?"

"Right," Bear confirmed.

"Don't tell me you really believe in those," Keith said.

"Everything she's told us so far has been correct," Bear pointed out. "We've seen other weird animals here, there's no reason to doubt her about those."

"Shit, we've gotta get off this mountain," Keith said.

"Wish I'd thought of that," Bear said walking off, along the edge of the vegetation.

***

Ginny reached above Wind and cut the bunch of bananas from above his head. As she did, she bumped against his shoulder, pulling him from the depths of his dreams. Feeling a presence close behind, he dove forward hitting the ground in a roll, twisted and stopped on his knees facing Ginny.

"Very impressive," she said. "What do you do for the second act?"

Wind smiled sheepishly. "You surprised me. I must have dozed off."

"It's okay," she said. "We're the only ones in the valley."

"I must be a lot more tired than I realized," he said rubbing both hands over his face as he stood.

"It's time for me to start my gathering," Ginny said. "I'll keep watch. You go get some rest."

"Hal wants me to get him up," he reminded her.

"Let him get some sleep," she urged. "I've got a feeling, you're all gonna need as much as you can get soon."

"What makes you think so?" Wind asked.

"I don't know," she said. "But, something's not right. Something feels off."

Wind thought about it a couple of seconds, nodded and started toward the house. "Wake us at sunrise if you don't mind," he said, "and thanks, I appreciate the break."

She smiled and carried the bananas toward the fruit baskets.

As the world lightened in the east, Ginny knocked on the edge of the front door with a piece of wood. It took three times before, Hal pulled the flap back.

"Ginny," he said surprised. "Where's Wind?"

"I sent him in for some rest when I started my gathering," she explained. "Everything's fine out here." Turning to walk away, she added, "There's coffee over the fire."

"Thanks," Hal said to her back. Returning to his room, he woke Sandy.

"I'm awake," Sandy mumbled in response to his shaking her shoulder.

255

"I'm gonna check the valley for more tracks," he said buttoning his shirt. "I wanna see if I can figure out what that thing was last night."

"Take Wind with you," she said a little more coherent this time.

"He just went to bed a little while ago," Hal said. "He needs some rest."

Sandy rolled to her side and sat up. "You're not going alone," she said. "Hang on a minute and I'll come with you."

"It's okay," he said. "It's daylight and Ginny says there's nothing out there."

"Ginny!" Sandy exclaimed. Sleep immediately dropped from her. "You trust her?"

"She hasn't given me any reason not to yet," Hal admitted. "She may have an attitude problem, but she's been honest."

Sandy had to admit he was right. As she dressed, she said, "We need to leave here."

"Why would we leave here?" He questioned. "This is where the others will expect us to be."

"I understand that, but we need to leave," she insisted. "We need to get everyone back together. We shouldn't be apart."

The look on her face told him that she was following her feelings and wouldn't be able to explain it to him. He nodded silently and waited for her to finish dressing.

Wind and Amanda were in the large room when Hal and Sandy exited theirs. "You're up," Hal said surprised. "Wind, I expected you to still be asleep."

"Ginny relieved me when she started getting fruit early this morning."

"We need to talk," Amanda said.

Hal nodded, "Let me get something to drink," he said, "I need caffeine."

Wind led them out of the house to the fire where they all poured themselves a cup. Everyone sat in chairs as their morning ritual dictated.

"We need to go to Weniki and Palenaka's Ohana," Amanda said.

"Sandy says we need to leave too," Hal said.

"I don't mind going," Wind interjected. "But how do we get to the Ohana? None of us know where it is."

"Can either of you find it?" Hal asked looking at Amanda and Sandy.

Both shook their head no. "I don't know how," Amanda said. "But we need to get there."

"I feel the same thing," Sandy said.

"If it's because of that thing last night," Wind said, "I'm not sure it's reason enough for us to leave. It's the first danger we've seen since we got to the valley. It may have been just passing through."

"That's true enough," Hal agreed. "But when we got up this morning, the first thing Sandy said to me, was that we should leave. Now, Amanda says we need to go to Weniki's Ohana. I don't know how we'll find it, but I have no doubt we need to try."

"I can," Ginny said from a distance. "Weniki told me how to get there."

"When?" Wind asked. "Why would she need to tell you how to get there?"

"She told me last night," Ginny said. "She sends me thoughts every now and then. She must have felt the danger around us last night. I can get

257

us there. It'll take a couple of days, but I can find the valley."

"If she's contacted Ginny and told her how to get there, she must think we need to go too," Amanda surmised.

The last statement made sense. If Weniki was using her ability to help them, there was a chance to locate the valley and then the village.

"I vote to get going as soon as we can gather our things," Wind said. "We don't need to take a chance on seeing that thing from last night."

"Did you check the horses last night?" Hal asked looking at Wind.

"Nope," Wind answered with conviction. "I thought about it, but I wasn't willing to risk my ass by going over into that corner of the valley alone."

Hal was grinning and shaking his head. "I would give you a hard time about that, but there's no way I'd have gone myself. I'll go get 'em now."

"They aren't there," Ginny said. "I looked just before dawn. The only thing left is a bunch of blood. Even the pen was broken up and scattered."

Hal didn't look surprised. "It figures," he said. "That's probably why that thing last night didn't attack us. It was full from eating the horses."

Amanda rose to her feet. "We need to take all the weapons and ammunition."

"Right," Wind agreed. "We can get food along the way."

"There's no way we can lug all the weapons and ammo," Hal said.

"Weniki says not to worry about it," Ginny said. "It'll be taken care of."

"Menehune," Sandy said. "I forgot about them. I'll bet she'll ask them to help."

"Okay, we all carry four nine millimeters and the rest of the M16s," Hal said. "Use the clip and magazine bandoliers and carry three clips for each pistol and four for the rifle. Take two changes of clothing. The rest we leave in the house."

Everybody began collecting the items to prepare to leave. No one really wanted to stay and risk going the way of the horses.

***

Spyder sat with his back against a wall. He wore leg-irons with a short chain between them and a longer chain attaching them to a ring on the wall. His hands lay in his lap, secured by a smaller pair of manacles.

He sat in a large rectangular room with one door and no windows. A small fire burned in the center, vented by a single hole in the roof. He regained consciousness in his present location and had no idea how long he had been here before that.

Someone had left food and a spoon in a bowl. The food was a beef stew, which he ate hungrily. *I hope they're not trying to poison me,* he thought. *If they are, I'm dead.*

After eating, he stood to see if everything worked properly and if he hurt anywhere. He seemed to be in good condition with only minor aches and pains. Nothing was broken and he couldn't find any wounds.

All his weapons, including his knife were gone. The chain allowed him to move to within a couple of feet of the fire. Hearing voices outside the door, he retreated to his previous place along the wall.

The wooden door opened and two armed men walked into the room.

***

Ginny informed everyone that there was another way to leave the valley. She led the small group to the pool and showed them the cave Weniki, Bear and Spyder used when they left.

"This has been here the whole time," Wind mused. "I wonder what other things there are in the valley we don't know about."

"There's no telling," Hal said. "I'm learning to expect something new every day. Nothing is what it seems. We just have to trust and rely on each other."

A couple of hours later, they walked out the other end of the cave. Once outside, Wind looked back and the cave was invisible. "Would you look at that shit," he said. "The damn thing disappeared again. How do we get back if we need to?"

"We don't," Hal answered. "Lead us outta here, Ginny."

Taking the lead, she led them along the base of the mountains. With numerous fruit trees along the way, they would have no problem finding food. Each also carried canteens in case they were unable to find more waterfalls or streams.

At sunset, they stopped at the edge of a stream. "I still wish we could've brought at least a sleeping bag," Wind said. "I hate sleeping on the ground."

"Are you sure you wanted to add even an additional five pounds to the weight of the ammunition?" Amanda asked. "These tarps will just have to do." She spread her tarp on some leaves she used as a makeshift mattress.

They would sleep without a fire tonight. They didn't want to draw attention to themselves. The camp, if you called it that, was bare of nonessentials, with only their personal items in piles beside their tarps.

The meal that night consisted of fruits, berries and water. To everyone's surprise, Sandy produced a strip of jerky each. "I figure we could stand a little protein along with the rest."

After eating, the evening passed quietly and about ten o'clock, they decided to get some sleep. No one was actually sleepy, but all were tired.

"We alternate watches tonight," Hal said. "We switch every three hours as long as it's dark. I'll take the first one. I'll wake Sandy for the second."

"I'm not arguing with you tonight," Wind said. "Wake me when it's my turn. Amanda, I'll wake you for the one after me and then it's Ginny's turn."

Everyone understood the rotation and climbed onto their respective tarps. After last night, no one would sleep soundly.

CHAPTER TWENTY-FIVE

The sun dipped below the mountain peaks as Bear and Keith reached the vegetation on the lower slopes. An eerie twilight surrounded the men as they continued toward level ground.

"This place looks weird in this light," Keith observed.

"It's just because we're in the shadow of the mountain," Bear explained.

"Yeah, then there's the darker ones of the trees," Keith agreed. "It gives the place a strange look."

Bear stopped to take a break. They had descended the mountain using one of the vertical fissures created by years of erosion. They had descended between two sharp ridges, using the floor of the fissure for safe footing. From their present location, he knew it would take at least a full day's travel to return to the village.

"We need to get away from the mountains before setting up camp," he said.

"We need to find it fairly soon," Keith said. "I'm beat. Using the fissure to come down was faster and easier, but it was a long way to travel at one time."

"Let's find some water and stop there," Bear said. "We need to get going. If we stay here too long, it'll just be harder to get started again."

"It can't be much harder than it is now," Keith admitted. "This has kicked my ass."

Bear grinned and moved away. He knew exactly how Keith felt. The only thing keeping him going was the thought of the Kalekona living on the volcano. Neither of them was up to fighting something like that.

About twenty minutes later, they happened upon on a stream. The water gurgled along its bed and a small clearing provided a respite. "This should do it," Bear announced removing his pack.

Keith dropped his pack and sat down beside the water. "I'm glad this is it," he said. "I'm not sure how much further I could've gone."

"I know the feeling," Bear admitted. "It's been a long day."

Keith looked him surprised. "I don't know how you do it," he said. "You seem to be able to keep going no matter what."

"It's getting harder the older I get."

Keith didn't know how to handle the admission. He had always thought of Bear as being around his own age even though he knew better. His Sensei getting tired was something he never imagined. In fact, none of the group had ever allowed fatigue to influence any of their decisions or actions.

Keith lay his canvas on top of a pile of leaves for a cushion. He doubted he would notice the difference, exhaustion was about to him down.

"You need to eat," Bear said.

"I'll eat tomorrow," Keith answered. "I'm too tired to even think about it tonight."

"If you don't eat, you'll pay for it tomorrow," Bear explained. "Your body needs it."

"Okay, if you say so," Keith said.

Bear could see that he was fading fast.

"I need to go find some fruit," Keith said starting to rise.

"Look to your left," Bear said grinning.

263

Keith did as instructed and saw a banana and an orange tree less than six feet away. "You're a life saver," he said going to pick the fruit.

When he returned, he had enough for both of them. Bear produced some sugar cane from his pack and handed them to him. "These will help rebuild your energy."

Keith didn't look forward to the work involved in removing the outer husks, but his body needed the sugar.

The two men ate in silence, glad to be off their feet and looking forward to a night of rest.

***

Amanda was on watch when the first growl rolled through the forest. The thing from the night before was back. She hurried to wake the others and found them up and arming themselves. All of them, that is, except for Ginny. She was sitting, watching the others, making no attempt to get a weapon.

"Arm yourself, Ginny," Wind called to her.

"I'm a cook and a guide, not a soldier," she answered.

"Goddamnit woman, we need your help," Wind growled.

Ginny smiled and turned her attention toward the sound of a roar in the distance. The animal was following the path they left during the day.

"Ginny, get a gun," Hal ordered.

"If you all shut up, it won't find us," she said adamantly, still sitting.

264

They could hear the destruction of foliage in the distance. The creature was definitely back and seemed to be looking for them.

The sound moved closer. "Everybody gather your stuff," Hal ordered. "We're going downstream."

A few minutes later, he led them along the stream. He ordered them to stay in the water, hoping to disguise their trail and scent. Everyone carried their weapons and ammunition, the rest of the items left behind in their hurry.

A short distance later, Hal said in a loud whisper, "Everyone slow down. Don't make any extra noise. We may get away with this."

The sound of the animal came from behind them, in the direction of the camp they had just abandoned. Hal held his hand up signaling them to stop.

The creature was moving again - coming toward them. "The son of a bitch is following us," Wind declared. "How the hell does it know where we are?"

"We gotta go," Hal said and began moving.

From ahead, they heard the scream of a saber toothed tiger. "We're trapped," Amanda said.

"Turn left," Ginny said sharply. "Weniki says to go left."

Without hesitation, Hal turned left and plowed through the brush. A resounding roar of the creature answered another scream from the cat.

"Maybe they'll fight each other," Sandy suggested.

"Keep going," Wind said stopping. "I'll follow your trail."

"No," Hal barked. "We keep going together."

"I'll find you," Wind insisted. "If either of those things get close, I'll try to slow 'em down. No time to argue, just go."

Hal nodded and continued with the rest following him. A few minutes later Ginny said, "Turn left, go back toward the mountains."

Hal again followed her directions. *Thank God Weniki's helping us.*

A few seconds later, they heard gunfire. From its sound, Wind was using the M16 on full automatic. Short bursts echoed through the trees.

"Turn right," Ginny instructed, "then left again after the flowing water."

"What water?" Hal asked panting.

"Keep going, you'll find it," she said.

A few yards later, Amanda hit the ground, her right foot tangled in a vine. The more she struggled to free herself, the more it trapped her.

Hal grabbed her by the shoulders and pulled as Sandy tried to free her leg. The vines seemed to have a will of their own and refused to release her foot.

"Grab her arms and pull," Hal said dropping her to the ground.

Sandy grabbed Amanda under the arms and heaved. At the same time, Hal pulled his machete and hacked at the entanglement, freeing her leg.

Regaining her feet, Amanda re-joined the dash for safety.

About fifty yards later, they arrived at the bank of a small river. "How deep is it?" Hal asked.

"Not deep," Ginny answered. "We can wade across it."

With Hal leading the way, they crossed, still hearing gunfire from Wind in the distance. On the other side, Hal turned left. What he heard from Wind's direction was the sound of two animals fighting, but no more gunshots.

Hal charged along the river, moving toward the mountains as Ginny instructed. Bursting into a clearing, he came face to face with Bear. Keith stood a short distance to the side.

Amanda rushed to Keith and grabbed him. She clung to him desperately with her head buried in his chest.

"What the hell's after you?" Bear asked.

"One of those tigers and another animal," Hal answered. "We don't know what it is, but it's massive."

Bear looked at everyone, taking inventory of his friends. "Where's Wind?" he asked.

"He's back there," Hal said pointing his thumb back over his shoulder. "He's trying to slow 'em down."

"Let's go," Bear said looking at Keith.

Keith pulled away from Amanda, "We'll be back soon," he said.

"No, she screamed. "You can't go back there."

"Stay here," he said calmly, "We'll be back in a little while. Wind needs our help." He pulled away and moved to follow Bear.

"I'm coming too," Hal said. Then to Sandy he said, "The rest of you go where Ginny says. We'll find you."

Sandy knew there was no time to argue and simply nodded.

267

"There is a cave farther up the river, at the base of the mountain," Ginny said. "We'll be there."

Bear was off and running with Keith and Hal close behind. He could see their trail in the moonlight and had no trouble following it. A few minutes later, they met Wind racing toward them.

"How close are they?" Hal asked.

Wind was gasping for air. Between gasps he stammered, "I don't know. It sounded like they started fighting each other. That's when I took off."

"Smart move," Bear said. After looking around, he added, "Let's get back to the others. Maybe we can put some distance between us and the animals."

The rest nodded and followed him back along the trail they had just traveled. It took half an hour to find the cave and re-join the others.

***

Sandy used a torch toward the back for light. The cave was large enough to shelter all of them away from its opening. A small breeze flowed through a crack in the back wall to either another chamber or the outside.

Sandy placed the torch beside the crack allowing the smoke to flow out of the chamber. "Just like home," she said sitting down and leaning back against the wall. "Now we wait."

About half an hour later, Hal and the rest joined them. It was obvious Bear and Keith was done in. They had reached their limits. As both sank down the wall, Amanda sat beside Keith and put her arm around him. "I love you," she whispered in his ear.

"I love you too," he whispered back.

"Glad the two of you are still alive," Hal said standing in front of the men. "We were getting worried." Turning his attention to Wind, he asked, "What did you see back there?"

Wind had regained his breath and was calming himself. "I'm not sure," he answered. "I think I saw the tiger."

"What about the other one?" Hal pressed.

"I have no idea," Wind said. "It was within fifty feet and I could see all the trees swaying and the bushes being trampled. But, there wasn't anything there."

"How could all that happen if nothing was there?"

"That's just it," Wind hesitated. "The only thing I'm sure of is that I saw was a shimmer."

"A shimmer?" Hal repeated.

"Yeah," he confirmed. "A shimmer was causing all that noise and destruction -- and it was at least as tall as the palm trees."

***

Sandy felt restless. The rest were asleep, but she couldn't shut her mind down enough for sleep to take her into its sanctuary.

She stood, quietly walked to the mouth of the cave and looked out at the night. *How can paradise hold so many dangers?* She questioned silently. *We've seen prehistoric animals, heard giant monsters, met people who do magic and have to avoid cannibals. All of this in a place so beautiful, it takes my breath away.*

The dark beyond the cave appeared to have to normal. Except for the sounds of the night animals, the night was silent. Bear said he relied on the sounds of the animals to tell when danger was near. Chirps, croaks and buzzing filled the night and it sounded beautiful.

She went back into the cave to the back corner, ten feet behind the others. She leaned against the sidewall, pulling one of the pistols from a shoulder holster. To clean the weapon she had to release the clip and pull the slide back to lock it. When she pulled the slide to eject the bullet, the cartridge flew over her hand, hit the floor of the cave slid to her left and disappeared where the back wall met the floor.

"What the blazes?" she mumbled softly.

Bending over she reached down and was startled when her hand disappeared in the wall. She quickly jerked it back and looked at it. It was normal, all fingers in place and she didn't feel anything different. Turning her hand, she looked at the front, then the back alternately.

"What the... " she whispered.

Even a close inspection of the wall produced no visible sign that it was anything other than the wall of a cave.

Slowly, she extended her hand again and, as before, it disappeared into the back wall. *Another illusion,* she thought. *What's going on?*

Quietly, she went back and picked up another torch careful not to arouse anyone. The rest were sleeping with Hal and Bear snoring. After lighting the new torch from the other, she returned to the back of the cave. Slowly, she tried to place the torch

270

against the wall and it disappeared as her hand had before. She wasn't even able to see the fire through the illusion of the wall.

Again, she returned to the equipment. This time, she picked up a pack and a rifle. Returning to the back wall, she slid the pack forward until it disappeared through whatever this was. Taking a deep breath to steady her nerves, she stepped forward and watched as her foot disappeared.

She stood there with one foot on each side of the barrier. Still there was no pain, no sensation or feeling to cause concern. Leaning forward she allowed her head and half of her body to pass through the image.

Opening her eyes on the other side, she saw more of the cave illuminated by the torch she held. Turning her head as much as possible, she looked back at the wall. She could see nothing through the barrier. Still standing half in and half out, Sandy pushed the pack all the way through. Once it was on the other side, she used a rifle to slide and return it to the side where the others were.

It allows things to pass both ways, she thought.

She again slid the pack through the image. Taking another deep breath, she stepped through the wall carrying the torch.

The cave on the other side was more of a tunnel than the part where the rest lay sleeping. It extended into darkness straight ahead. She walked slowly along the tunnel, tapping on the walls as she went. She didn't want to have another passageway veer off without her knowledge.

Twenty feet later, a room opened up to her left. Pushing her torch through the opening, her jaw

271

dropped in astonishment. She couldn't believe what she saw.

In the chamber before her, were clothes, boxes labeled as canned food, battery powered lanterns, muskets, bows and arrows, a large piece of equipment and other cardboard boxes containing who knows what. Inspecting the piece of equipment, she found a plate that declared it a generator.

Looking at some of the other boxes, she found cigarettes, lighters, "C" rations, swords, spears and hand grenades. *Hand grenades,* Sandy thought looking around. *Where the hell did all this come from? There's enough here to keep us supplied for months.*

***

Hal awoke with Sandy shaking his shoulder. She was obviously excited and babbling on about some nonsense.

"Hang on," he said, "slow down. What the hell's wrong?"

"Nothing's wrong," she said. "You gotta see what I found. There's things we can use. We've got enough to keep us supplied for months. You won't believe what's back there. Get up. Come on. You've gotta see this." She spoke in a rapid staccato pace.

Hal sat up. "Okay, slow down. Just tell me what's going on."

"You've gotta wake the others up," she said. "You've all gotta see this."

272

"Okay," he said shaking the sleep from his mind. "Get the rest up and we'll take a look at what you've got."

Sandy hurried from person to person dragging them from sleep. In a few minutes, they were all up and grumbling. Keith could barely rouse himself enough to stand. "This had better be good," he said. "After the day I've had, I need all the rest I can get."

Amanda was up and much more coherent than Keith. "Sandy," she said, "what's going on?"

"I'll show you in a minute," she answered. "Help me get the rest up and going."

Finally, they had gathered their wits about them and stood facing her. "Good," she said looking from face to face. "Follow me."

She led them to the back of the cave and waited until they all stood near the back wall. Turning, she said, "Follow me."

Hal watched as she turned and abruptly disappeared through the back wall.

A few seconds later, her head protruded back through the rock. "Well are you coming or not?" She asked. Immediately, her head again disappeared behind the wall.

Hal looked at Bear. "What the hell?" He said a stunned look on his face.

"It's another illusion or hallucination of some sort," Bear said. "She's on the other side of that."

Without another word, both men walked through the image. On the other side, Sandy stood holding a battery-powered flashlight. "Welcome to my world," she said grinning. "You haven't seen anything yet."

Following a short wait, Bear stuck his head through the wall and looked at his stunned friends. "It's safe," he said. "Come on through." He pulled his head back and in a couple of seconds, the rest reluctantly joined them.

Sandy handed flashlights to everyone. With them all on, lights shone in every direction.

"How the hell did you find this?" Hal asked.

"I'll tell you later," Sandy answered. "You've all gotta see this." She turned and led them down the tunnel until reaching the room to the left. She passed it, turned around and with a sweep of her arm, motioned into the space.

Bear walked into the center of the opening. He saw boxes stacked on top of boxes. Supplies of all kinds were stored there. He saw armament of all sorts still in boxes along the wall. Weapons ranging from bows and arrows to hand grenades sat in the room.

Flashlights flitted from box to box. Hal couldn't believe what he saw. His attention froze on the generator. "We've got electrical power," he cried.

Ginny found a cook stove complete with a butane bottle attached. "I'll be able to fix proper meals," she said.

"There's coffee over here next to the "C" rats," Wind called out.

Hal and Sandy surveyed the boxes of food. There was enough to support them for months to come.

***

Bear looked at his friends, watched their reactions and realized something was wrong. He stepped back, squatted and leaned back against the wall of the room.

Sandy snapped her head toward him. *He's right,* she thought. *Something's not right with this.*

She went toward him with Hal beside her. There was no danger here, but something was wrong. As they approached Bear, he rose. "What do you think's going on?" Hal asked.

"I don't know," Bear answered. "My question is; why was this hidden?"

"I think it was hidden by Weniki," Sandy surmised. "I don't know why, but she's the one with the ability."

"Maybe she's hiding it from the Nāki," Hal suggested.

"That'd make sense," Bear agreed. "She shared with or contacted Ginny and gave you directions to this cave. She's helped us stay alive. Maybe she's trying to keep this out of Nāki hands."

"That makes as good sense as anything else," Hal said. "We'd probably all be dead if she hadn't helped."

Sandy stood quietly listening to the men. "I think you're partially right," she said, "but there's something missing. I don't know what it is, but I do know it's something important -- very important." She looked back at the supplies.

Bear walked away from the others and entered the tunnel. Following it, he found two more rooms to his right. Glancing in, he found nothing dangerous. Another fifty yards along, he found a pool of water near the back. He tested the walls and found them to be solid except for a crack in the back wall. As with the other crack, air flowed through to another location. *We can stay here a while,* he thought. *If we stay behind the imaginary wall, we should be safe.*

He returned to the others and told them what he'd found. Everyone agreed that safety lay behind the false wall. They all needed rest and this was the best place to get it. In less than fifteen minutes, all their supplies sat in the storage room in Sandy's World, as she called it, abandoning the outer room. They left nothing behind to show that they had ever been in the cave.

"I'm getting some rest," Keith said. "If there's any more emergencies, handle 'em without me and let me know how it goes."

CHAPTER TWENTY-SIX

Bear returned to the water in the back of the tunnel. He carried an M16, which he leaned against a wall. He shone the large flashlight down into the pool. The water was crystal clear and he could see at least thirty feet down, to where the bottom curved out of sight. He thought back about the village where Spyder was.

Obviously, the people in the settlement didn't expect anyone to be able to get close enough to spy on them, he thought. *... and the only indication of violence was the guards and Spyder with his hands tied in front of him. If what Weniki said was true, the guards could just as easily be to guard against the Kalekona. The village seemed to be nothing more than a group of people living together.*

He sat back against the wall to think. The cave was cool, damp and quiet. Even with the light out, the walls produced a slight blue glow. Once his eyes adjusted, he could see the cave back to the storage room. There were two additional rooms on the other wall, which he could clearly see.

Bear only glanced into the rooms on his way to the pool to make sure there was nothing dangerous there. He closed his eyes to relax.

Hal and Sandy walked up. "How did you do that?" Hal asked.

"Do what?" he answered, surprised that they had reached him without his knowledge as well as the question.

"You were thinking about the village where Spyder is," Sandy said.

"How did you know that?"

"I don't know how it happened," Hal said. "I had something flash through my mind and a couple of seconds later, Sandy rolled over and told me she had just experienced the same thing. We compared what happened and they were the same."

"What are you talking about?" Bear asked, still confused.

"I'll bet both of us can describe the Nāki village exactly as you saw it," Sandy said.

Bear finally understood what they were saying. However, with the strange things they had all seen here, this most recent experience was only a mild surprise.

"Keith went looking for you because of feelings," Hal said. "I just thought it was Weniki or Palenaka sending him thoughts or feelings."

"I thought so too when we were trying to find Spyder." Bear admitted. "But think about it. How could Weniki or Palenaka do that? Weniki told me she couldn't reach into the Nāki village. She said, if she did, they'd know where she was and their Kupua could block her."

"I also knew when Keith needed to leave," Sandy said. "I could feel that something was wrong, I didn't know what, but I felt he was needed."

"All this just goes to show that we've all acquired some sort of ability since coming here," Bear said. "How strong, how accurate or if we can control it are things we need to work out. Has Ginny said anything about it?"

"Nothing to me," Hal said, "you?" He looked at Sandy.

"Ginny barely talks to me," she said. "I remember Amanda saying something about unusual feelings."

"If you don't mind, ask her about it tomorrow," Bear said to Sandy.

"Sure, no problem," she agreed. "Oh, by the way, there's an opening to another cave room behind some of the stuff we found."

"Turn your light off," Bear instructed.

Hal turned the flashlight off.

"Now wait and watch what happens," Bear said.

A few moments later, their eyes adjusted to the dim light.

"Is it phosphorescence?" Hal asked.

"I don't know," Bear said. "It may be the same thing we were warned about not eating. The main thing is, we can save the batteries and still see in here."

"This makes washing our hands before touching food important," Sandy said.

"Good thinking, we need to be careful with that," Bear cautioned. "Be sure you don't wash them in any water we'll use for drinking." He shifted his position and rose to his feet. "I'm gonna get some rest," he said. "On the way back, I'll check the rooms on the left."

"You check the first one," Hal said. "We'll check the second."

Bear nodded and walked toward the room. He was exhausted and needed rest. However, safety had to be their main concern at all times. They had to make sure nothing or no one was hiding anywhere. He turned into the room.

279

There was also a dim light illuminating the space. He searched the walls for any signs of danger or another opening. On the right side of the far wall, he noticed an opening. He went to it and looked through. The room on the other side was small and seemed to be brighter, even without a flashlight.

Looking at the other walls, he noticed something different near a corner. He went over for a closer look and found another visible barrier. The wall looked solid, but he could reach through it with his hand. Pulling his hand back, he thought, *I'd better keep my parts on this side until I know what's over there. I damn sure don't wanna get drug through by something grabbing hold of me.*

Bear returned to the tunnel and hurried to the room Hal and Sandy was searching. Sandy stood alone in the room and jumped as he entered.

"Where's Hal?" Bear asked looking around.

"He's on the other side of that," Sandy said pointing at a wall.

He could see that part of the wall was dimmer than the rest. It was the same as the room he had just left. "He went in there alone?" He heard himself asking before he realized what he was saying.

Sandy looked at with a sly smile. "Nah, he's got the Secret Service with him," she said. As he started through the wall, she asked, "What are you doing?"

"I'm going to get my sign." He said and disappeared from sight before Sandy could comment. "I can write stupid on two pieces of paper and give them to both of you for signs," she said.

The light was the same on the other side. He could see Hal in the distance. "Hey man," he called out and started walking toward him.

"Stop right there," Hal called back. "There's a hole in the floor right in front of you. As he walked, he prodded the ground with a long stick. About fifteen feet away, the end of the stick disappeared in the floor. He left the stick in the hole and slid it to his left. The edge of the hole extended to within two feet of the sidewall.

Hal walked around the hole leaving the end of the stick in it to mark the edge. "I don't know about you," he said, "but I just found some new energy. I want to get some rope, more sticks and do some searching."

"I'm with you on that," Bear answered. "His energy store felt as though it had been refilled.

The two men lay the piece of wood a foot in front of the false floor. They didn't want to take a chance of mistaking its location.

They exited through the wall to find a nervous Sandy waiting for them. "It's another tunnel," Hal said putting his arms around her and giving her a hug.

Sandy never showed a lot of emotion in her actions, but she was obviously shook up. Hal kept an arm around her as they returned to where the others slept.

On the way, he explained that none of them should walk around inside the cave without some object to test the floor. "Not only are there false walls," he explained, "but, there are false floors. Right now, we don't know how deep they are. We could fall two feet or two thousand."

Back in the first hidden room, Hal and Bear gathered some wood, rope and other supplies. Their searching through the newly found supplies awoke Keith.

"Is it morning already?" He asked.

"Not yet," Hal answered. "Go back to sleep and get some rest."

"I don't think so," Bear countered. "Keith, you need to get up and help us. It's time for some more training."

Without hesitation, Keith rose and picked up his M16. He already had two 9mms in shoulder holsters. "What do I need to do?" He asked.

Bear explained about the other tunnel and the hole in the floor covered by the same type false vision guarding Weniki's valley and this cave. "We need things to mark their locations. You also need something like a walking stick to make sure you don't step into a disguised hole."

Keith nodded and began searching through the supplies. "By the way, I checked that smaller room before lying down. I think a group of people used it as a bathroom. There's smears of faeces around a visible hole in the floor."

"I'm glad you found it without killing yourself," Bear said. To Sandy, he said, "Will you please wake everyone else, tell them what we're doing and about the new bathroom?"

She nodded and went to shake some shoulders.

Keith found some tent stakes in a box. Pulling them out he said, "We can use these to mark things."

"Good idea," Hal agreed.

A while later, their items gathered, Hal kissed Sandy and gave her a hug. "We may only be gone a little while," he said. "On the other hand, we might be gone several hours."

"We won't be gone longer than a day," Bear said. "If we're gonna do this, we're gonna do it as completely if possible."

Sandy nodded and hugged him. Before they could leave, Amanda grabbed Keith in a desperate hug. "You take care of yourself," she said. "I thought I'd lost you before. I don't want to lose you now."

Bear watched as she held on to Keith. He could remember instances like this in his past. *He has no idea how much something like this will mean to him in the future,* he thought with slight envy.

He turned and walked away with Hal falling in behind. By the time they reached the false wall had Keith caught up. "Sorry about that back there," he said a little embarrassed.

"Never be sorry about someone caring for you young man," Bear said. "Her love and caring is something you need more than you know." He turned and stepped through the false wall.

CHAPTER TWENTY-SEVEN

On the other side, the men walked to where Hal left the stick. He picked it up and led the way around the hole. As he passed it, Keith laid a tent stake on the floor with its point toward the hole marking its location and did the same thing on the other side.

"I've checked the walls and floor for a distance," Hal said. I don't know where I was when Bear called me back, so I guess we start from here."

Bear took the left side of the tunnel, Keith the middle and Hal the right. They tapped the floor and the walls with long sticks as they moved down the tunnel. Keith made sure the floor was solid in front of all three men. They looked like three blind men trying to pick their way along an empty alley.

Eventually, Hal found another hidden room. He leaned past the barrier and looked around. It appeared to be the same as the others with the exception of a pile of objects in one corner. *Another cache of supplies,* he thought.

Before stepping through the wall, he checked the floor. There was none. Moving his stick around the edge, he found that it covered the entire entrance and extended further than he could test. His stick was a seven-foot tent pole and he couldn't reach the other side of the concealed hole with it.

"We aren't going in there," he said to Bear and Keith. "I can't find a floor from here. But, there's something piled in the far corner."

Bear nodded. "Let's keep going."

Hal laid a tent stake on the floor with the point toward the room. He crossed the first stake with a second to show that the entrance wasn't safe.

A couple of yards along, Keith found another entrance to the same room. He checked the floor and found it solid. He entered the room checking the floor and walls for openings as he proceeded toward the pile of objects in the corner.

Hal found the hole in the floor and traced it all the way across the room where it disappeared under a real wall. "The room's divided by a crevice in the floor," he reported as he re-joined the others. "Don't try to go to the other side."

Bear and Keith were staring at the pile in front of them. It was a collection of roman armor. There were metal headdresses, shields, swords and clothing. The things had been there for a while, but not long enough for the clothes to rot or disintegrate.

"What the fuck is all this stuff?" Keith asked.

"What does it look like?" Bear answered.

"I know what it looks like," Keith said. "But, there's no way it's armor from a Roman army."

"Why not?" Hal asked. "Would it be any different from some of the other shit we've seen?"

As Keith thought about the answer, Bear picked up a sword and looked at it. The weapon was heavy, sharp and had a mild layer of corrosion, which easily rubbed off. "These haven't been here that long," he observed. "With the dampness, they would have completely rusted in less than a year." He turned back toward the door. "We'll figure this out later. For now, we need to keep going."

Back in the tunnel, Keith marked the doorway and followed Bear and Hal. Further along, Hal found another tunnel running to the left.

"Do we split up and search both of 'em?" He asked.

"I think we should stay together," Bear said. "We don't know what may be in some of these. We may need each other's help." Hal and Keith both nodded. "Besides, we could get lost if we split up."

The tunnel ran for about another four hundred yards. They found four more rooms and two more tunnels. The rooms were empty and contained no more exits. The main tunnel appeared to end until Keith put his hand through the far wall.

He looked through the image of a wall to find that the cave opened to the outside world about twenty feet away. He pulled back and said, "It looks like another entrance to the cave system. I'm gonna take a look. I'll be back in a minute."

Before Hal or Bear could stop him, he stepped through the wall and disappeared. Both men poked their heads through the image in time to see Keith fall into a concealed hole.

Both men hurried through the illusion and upon reaching Keith, found him hanging on to the edge. If it hadn't been a desperate situation, Bear would have been able to find humor in the site. Nothing but Keith's fingers was visible from their prospective.

Bear and Hal each grabbed an arm and hauled him up and out of the hole. As they got him on firm ground, he collapsed, visibly shaken.

"There's lava at the bottom!" he exclaimed between gasps. He began shaking and his nerves seemed frayed. Bear pulled a canteen and held it to his lips.

Keith drank deeply, almost desperately. Finally taking a breath, he said, "There's a river of lava a couple of hundred feet down."

"Lava?" Bear questioned.

"If I lay on my stomach, maybe I can get a look at it," Hal suggested.

"NO!" Keith shouted and grabbed Hal's arm. "You can't breathe down there." He paused, took a breath, looked at both men and continued. "There are things living on the walls."

"What the hell are you talking about?" Hal asked. He looked at Bear as if to say, "He's lost it."

"There are things on the walls that look like spiders," Keith said. "They're huge, at least the size of a human. They're grey with red stripes and they were coming after me."

"Either he saw a lot, or his imagination ran away with him," Hal said. He knew Keith was usually a level-headed person. However, if he had actually seen a river of lava below him, his mind might make up the rest through fear.

Bear pulled his shirt off and told Keith to do the same. Both shirts had snaps and he thought they would work for his experiment. He snapped the garments together, pushed a long stick through each arm, and extended them to the bottom of the material. When he pulled, the wood separated forming a rectangle, he could see through the top of the gadget as if looking through a fabric box.

"I don't know if this will work, but it's worth a try," He said.

"I see what you're doing," Hal said. "If that image doesn't penetrate the fabric, you can see down the insides of the shirts."

Bear nodded. "Let's hope the image can't pass through the material. It's the same as using glass and four boards to see into water from the surface."

He turned back to the location of the hole and pushed the gadget into it. When he pulled the sticks apart, he was astounded at the scene.

About two hundred feet below was indeed a river of lava. The walls of the hole angled outward to a width of about fifty yards and strange creatures crawled on the walls. At first glance, they did look like spiders. However, on further inspection he saw that they also had wings.

Flying spiders, he thought, *that's all I need.* Spiders were his only phobia.

The river of rock below flowed slowly along the bottom of the crevice, glowing a combination of yellow and red. Flames occasionally flicked from the mass and the smell of sulfur and heated gasses assaulted his senses. *If there's such a thing as hell,* he thought, *this is probably what it would look like.*

Even though he was unable to discern their shapes, smaller creatures crawled along the walls. A spider grabbed one of these and after a brief struggle, ate it much the same as a dog ate a treat. Bear started feeling lightheaded, quickly sat up straight and removed the homemade viewer.

Leaning backward until he rested against a wall, he tried to make sense of what he'd just seen.

"You okay, man?" Hal asked.

"He's right," Bear answered. "There're spiders down there -- flying spiders." He looked around and saw Keith against the other wall, far away from the hole, still shaking and staring at where he had previously fallen.

Gathering his wits, Bear went to Keith. "You need to pull yourself together," he said. He thought for a moment, not sure how to continue. Even he wasn't sure what he'd seen. Obviously, there were strange animals living below the surface of the island, creatures he had only heard of in nightmares.

"Keith," he continued, "don't let this chew you up. We've seen other things here that aren't normal. Things that could never happen in the world we knew."

"We're not in the world we've always known," Hal said. "Remember, Amanda is back there waiting for you to return. You have to be strong for her."

"Bullshit," Bear said forcefully, almost in a voice of anger. He stood and stepped back. "Keith," he said in the same voice.

Keith kept staring at the floor.

"Keith," he repeated, hesitated a couple of seconds, then demanded, LOOK AT ME."

Keith's gaze moved slowly across the floor to the man's feet, then up his body to his face.

"On your feet Sempai," Bear ordered. After another couple of seconds, he growled, "Now."

Keith slowly made his way to his feet and faced Bear.

"Standing position," Bear ordered.

Without thinking, Keith assumed the attentive position for all verbal instructions and information in a class. He held his fists at waist level about four inches apart and waited.

"Pay respects," Bear ordered.

Keith bowed to him and he returned the bow.

"Center yourself," he continued. He waited a couple of minutes until Keith opened his eyes. The young man's breathing was steady and he appeared relaxed.

"We're returning to the others," Bear said. "You will protect us from a rear attack. Make sure nothing sneaks up from behind."

Keith nodded, bent and gathered his tent pole.

Hal was surprised to see the change in his attitude. At first, he thought Bear was being too harsh. He soon realized that giving Keith a job allowed him to concentrate on something other than what he had just seen.

The three men headed back toward their friends at the other end of the tunnel.

***

"Where are they?" Palenaka asked. "I cannot feel them anywhere."

"Something happened last night," Weniki said. "I felt fear from Ginny. Bear and Keith re-joined the others and they went to an ana along the edge of the mountains. I cannot sense them now."

The two women sat in the large structure with Lopaka. The building was a rectangle with windows to allow light and a door on one end. They sat around a table in the center of the room having a breakfast of fruit, bread and strong tea.

"Kimo says the man named Bear is a compassionate healer," Lopaka said.

"He is also a warrior," Weniki said. "When I shared with him, I saw many battles. I felt fear, pain and suffering."

"A warrior and a healer," Lopaka said thoughtfully, stroking his beard. Lopaka was a man in his sixties. White streaked his long black hair, the same as his beard. He was about five feet, six inches tall with a regal bearing, the obvious leader of the village.

"I shared with all of the newcomers," Weniki explained. "They are as strong an Ohana Nui as any blood could create. Even though they are from different bloodlines, they have a bond formed of adversity, fear, love and mutual support."

"What of the man called Spyder?" Lopaka asked.

"He is in the Nāki village," she explained. "Unless the rest are able to remove him, he is lost."

"How do they come by these strange names?" Lopaka queried. "They are not usual."

"They are an entertainment troop," Weniki explained.

"Not all of them," Palenaka corrected. "The ones named Wind, Amanda and Keith are new to the rest. But, they have been totally accepted by the others."

"Why can you not feel them?" Lopaka questioned.

"That is what I do not understand," Weniki admitted. "The Nāki Kupua have never been able to blind me that far from their village," Weniki said. "I fear they are in danger."

"What kind of danger?" Lopaka asked.

291

"I fear they may be in danger from others of Farn."

***

Bear, Hal and Keith returned to the rest without further incident. When they walked back into the room, everyone assaulted them with questions of what they had found. All three men were bone tired and promised to explain everything after some sleep. Even though the rest insisted, they laid out cots from their new stash of supplies and went to sleep.

For a short while, Sandy stood guard to insure the men's rest. No one asked her to do it, but she knew they had to sleep.

Five hours later, Hal awoke. Almost as if on cue, Bear sat up. "Rise and shine boys," Sandy greeted them.

Hal looked around and saw Bear stretching. "You do that every time you wake up," he said. "What're you doing, trying to get taller? Or is it just hard for an ole man to get moving after sleeping?"

"I'm just not willing to be as old and stiff as you are yet," he answered.

"Ask Sandy if I'm old yet," Hal said grinning. "I think she'll disagree with you."

Hal had done it again. There was nothing Bear could say. Hal was a good man and enjoyed teasing Bear about his and Sandy's relationship. He understood their friendship and supported Bear's feelings for her. He felt the more people that cared about her, the happier and more secure she would be. Besides, he knew Bear loved Sandy as a sister and would protect her as such.

Bear shook his head and grinned. "I want food," he said changing the subject.

"I've got some K-rations," Sandy said. "Sorry, but that's all we have in here. We can't cook inside the cave."

"If you've got some ham and eggs, I want 'em," Bear answered. Contrary to most people, he liked that particular serving of the food.

Sandy handed him what he'd asked for and found another breakfast meal for Hal.

As the men finished, Keith awoke, stretched and stood up. He saw Hal and Bear eating. "Are there any more of those?" He asked motioning to the food.

Sandy handed him a food packet. "It's all we've got," she said.

Keith took the meal and sat down, very interested in the food.

"Okay, will someone tell us what the three of you found?" Wind asked. "I don't wanna to sound too pushy, but there are some weird things happening here. Spyder's a hostage in some village and we're in a weird cave of some sort.

***

Spyder was back in the smaller building and, once again, chained to the wall. The day before, he was led to the building the locals called "The Hall of Justice".

Two guards led him into the building. Inside was a throne at the far end flanked by two guards.

Three long rows of seats ran along both sidewalls. Near the center of each wall were smaller thrones with staves standing to their right. In the center of the room was an altar to which the guards led him.

Once there, one of his guards said, "Kneel."

Spyder glared at the guard, remained standing and looked at the man in the throne thirty feet away.

One of the guards slammed a staff into the back of his knees causing him to drop to the ground. As he started to turn, a sword pushed against his throat. "Remain," the guard ordered.

"You hit me again and you'll have to use that thing," Spyder said, "or wear it up your ass."

"Sir," the man on the throne spoke in a firm voice.

Spyder slowly returned his attention to the man sitting before him.

"Please take no exception to our rules," the man said. "All who enter this room remain at the altar where you are. I am Aka, king of the Nāki."

Spyder stared back defiantly.

"May I hear your name?" Aka asked.

Spyder hesitated. He didn't want his captors to have any more information about him than necessary. "My name is Henry," he said. Henry was his real name, which he hated. He had gone by the name Spyder for over twenty years.

"I welcome you to our home," Aka said.

"You've got a strange way of inviting someone here," Spyder said. "I was attacked, captured and carried here. I had nothing to say about it."

"That, I regret," Aka said. "However, you were in the village of the Alaea. We did not think you would come to us if we simply asked."

Spyder nodded agreeing that he was probably right. "Why would I want to come here?" He asked.

"To learn of us," Aka responded. "We only want one thing here."

"I'm sure," Spyder had said sarcastically.

Now, sitting in the small hut, he wondered how much and exactly what Aka had said was true. He knew he was bait to draw his friends into the village. He couldn't allow that to happen, but he wasn't sure how to stop it. He had a lot to think about.

CHAPTER TWENTY-EIGHT

"So that's what we found," Hal said. Between him, Bear and Keith, they had explained their trip through the tunnel.

"Do you have any idea what the creatures were in the crevice?" Amanda asked.

"I've got no idea what they were," Bear said, "and I don't wanna find out."

"That makes two of us," Keith agreed.

"You said you found two other concealed holes," Sandy said. "Did you look in them?"

"No," Bear answered. "We needed to get back and get some rest. I was thinking about checking them out in a little while."

"But you did find another way in and out of the cave, right?" Sandy asked.

"Right," Keith confirmed. "We didn't make it to the exit because I fell through the floor."

"It wasn't your fault," Sandy said. "It's not like you did it on purpose."

"How the hell did it happen, by the way?" Bear asked. "By the time Hal and I looked through the barrier, you were on your way down."

"I got sloppy," Keith said. "I saw the outside and walked toward it without checking the floor. It was stupid, I know."

"Not stupid," Bear corrected. "You just followed your emotions rather than your head."

"Yeah but... "

"We'll talk about it later," he interrupted. He didn't need Keith beating himself up. The incident was over and the main thing was that he learned from it.

"I checked the entrance we came in after sunup," Ginny said. "Everything looked normal out there."

"Why?" Bear asked. "Someone could've seen you and found us."

"I was careful," she said, "and no one did. Besides, you're not my father. You can't tell me what to do."

"Do you want us to get Spyder back?" Bear growled at her.

"Of course, I do," she answered. "But me looking out has nothing to do with that. It's not like any of you are in any hurry to get him back. Sure, you went up and looked at the village. So, why don't you men go there and sneak him out?"

"Ginny," Bear was trying to control his voice. "It's not that easy. There're over... "

"Don't hand me that," Ginny stormed. "If you're as good with all that military bullshit as everyone says, there's nothing stopping you."

Before anyone knew it, Amanda was up and drove her fist into Ginny's face. She stumbled backward, lost her footing and landed flat on her butt.

As she scrambled to get back to her feet, Sandy stepped between the women. "You can get up Ginny," she said. "But, say one more word and what Amanda did will be minor compared to what I'll do."

"Try it," Ginny said. "And I'll... "

Hal stepped between the two women. "That's enough from everyone," he said looking at everyone in the room. Then, to Ginny, he said, "I understand you're worried about Spyder, we all are."

Ginny started to protest but Hal held his hand up. "Hang on a minute," he said. "Hear me out." He paused and looked into her eyes. "Ginny, the only way we can get him back is if we all stay safe and know what's around us. If we're found here by the wrong people, we lose the element of surprise."

"I believe that most of you care about Spyder," she said. "But that asshole," she pointed at Bear, "only cares about being in charge and ordering people around."

"Okay," Hal said. "I can change that. From now on, we'll follow what you think's best. The only way we won't is if it will put us in danger."

"You think I can't do that," Ginny said. "But, if he can then I can."

"Great," Hal said. "What should we do next?"

She thought a second. "We need to figure out a way to get Spyder out of there."

"Okay, how do we do that?" Wind asked.

"We need to know what the village looks like," she answered. "Keith and Bear have seen it. Maybe they can draw a picture."

"Bear's the only one who saw all of it," Keith said. I only saw one end."

Bear produced the drawing of the village and gave it to Ginny. "Let me know if there's something I need to explain."

She took the paper and looked at it. "What are these wavy lines on each side of the village?"

"It's the terrain around it. I figured we'd need to know the lay of the land so we could make the best approach," Bear explained. "The structure with the X on it is where I think they're keeping Spyder. At least, it's the one I saw him come out of."

298

"You saw him?" Ginny asked.

"I did," Bear answered.

"You son-of-a-bitch, why didn't you tell us that?" Ginny snarled.

"We haven't had a chance to talk as a group," he explained. "The most important thing is that he appeared safe and well."

"You should've told me," Ginny said. "He's my husband."

"You're right," Bear said. "I had other things on my mind and should have made time to tell you."

"Don't do that again," she ordered. "If I'm gonna run things, then you can't keep secrets from me. You have to work with me, not against me."

"I promise, I'll give you all the help you've given the rest of us."

Ginny glared at him, then looked at the paper in her hands. "What do you think is the best way to get to him?"

"I'm not sure yet," Bear said. "But that's not up to me now, is it?"

"I think we should go back to Weniki and Palenaka's village and show them what we have," Ginny said. "We can show them how to get Spyder out."

"They want us to teach them to fight," Hal said. "What makes you think they care about getting Spyder back?"

"They'll have to help get Spyder back," Ginny argued, "if they want our help to fight the Nāki."

"Blackmail," Keith said, "that's a good way to get their help."

"It's the only way I can think of to get Spyder back," Ginny said. "That's what we should be thinking about now. It doesn't matter how we get it done."

"What if they refuse to help once they've learned more about defending themselves?" Wind asked.

"They won't do that," Ginny said. "If they give us their word, they won't break it."

"Then, what do we do next?" Bear asked holding his hand out for the paper drawing.

"We need to gather our things together and get back to the village," she said, grudgingly handing the map back to him.

"What do we take with us?" Hal asked.

"Everything we can carry," Ginny answered. "We'll need it while we're there."

"What's the most important," Bear pressed, "weapons, food, clothes, water or what?"

"Weapons, water and food," Ginny answered. "The rest, we can come back for if we need them."

"May I make a suggestion?" Bear asked.

"What?" Ginny said.

"Keith, you go back and start teaching self-defense. Wind you help him. Hal you teach basic gun safety. The three of you forget where this cave is." He walked away, to the store of supplies.

"What're you doing?" Ginny asked.

"I'm gonna take a walk," Bear said.

"We'll need you with us for some of the training," Ginny said.

"I'll catch up with all of you later," Bear said, "in a couple of days."

"I want you to come with us," Ginny said.

"I'll join up with you at the village," Bear said. "I'm gonna take a different route there. It'll take me two or three days."

"I'm telling you to come with us," Ginny demanded. "Hal put me in charge. What's the matter, don't you like someone else ordering you around?"

"May I make a suggestion?" Wind asked.

"Only if you talk some sense into this hardhead," Ginny said.

"I don't have the training Keith does," Wind pointed out. "I think I would do better taking a break for two or three days."

"We need you with us," Ginny argued.

"To do what?" Wind countered. "What in particular do you want from me?"

"You can help Hal," she said. "He can use your help with the weapons."

"I think I'm gonna take a few days." Wind's voice carried a note of finality.

Ginny turned and faced the others. "What about the rest of you?" She asked. "Are the rest of you going to turn on me too?"

"I don't think anyone's turning on you Ginny," Hal said. "As for the rest of us, I think we need to get things gathered up." He went to the supplies and began rummaging around for things he needed.

CHAPTER TWENTY-NINE

Bear and Wind left while the others gathered their supplies. Both carried a rifle and pistol. With Bear leading the way, they headed away from the cave.

They stopped after about an hour. "What are we doing here?" Wind asked.

"I want to look into the other holes in the cave," Bear said. "But we need to let them leave first."

"Why did you and Hal let her take charge?" Wind asked. He knew there was no way Ginny had any idea how to lead the group effectively.

"If they go back and Weniki thinks we left in revolt, she won't come looking for us," he explained. "Right now, the only people I trust are those of our group."

"You trust Ginny?" Wind asked incredulously.

"I trust her to do what she said she would," he explained. "It'll get her out of the way, help Weniki's people and give us some time to check things out."

Two hours later, Bear and Wind returned to the cave. Inside, past the imaginary wall, Bear and Wind assembled another viewer.

Bear formed the rectangle and pushed it through the false floor. The space below was deep blue. The bottom was about fifty feet below. A stream flowed along from left to right. Strange animals used the water to drink. Some had four legs, some six, some had many like a centipede and a couple moved like caterpillars.

A creature with the head of a cat, the body of a dog and a barbed tail, walking on two legs, crossed the stream and disappeared into the red, green and silver foliage on the other side. Thin veins of gold ran down the sides of the cliffs to the floor. The place was beautiful. He saw no violence even with all the different animals using the stream at the same time.

He pulled the viewer from the hole. "Did you see that shit? He asked.

"That wasn't the same thing you saw before, was it?" Wind asked.

"No," he answered. "It's totally different. I'd describe the other as a view of hell. This one, in comparison, is the Garden of Eden."

"How can two, such different, things be beneath the surface of this island?" Wind asked, a glazed look on his face. He sat back against the wall and ran his hands through his hair. Even though the air was cool and comfortable, beads of sweat rose on his forehead.

"I don't know," Bear answered. "But we need to check the others we found."

"You want to go back and look at the other holes?"

"Not that I necessarily want to," Bear corrected, "but we need to. Something weird's going on here."

Thirty minutes later, they entered the room with the second false floor. After fashioning another viewer, they both peered into the hole.

Less than five feet away was the nose and mouth of some sort of dinosaur. As it opened its mouth, both men jerked back. A loud growl started and ended when Bear yanked the viewer out. The noise stopped instantly as if turned off.

"What the hell was that?" Wind asked.

"Your guess is as good as mine," Bear answered. "It looked like a dinosaur."

"Okay, then I'm not crazy," Wind said. "Because, that's what I thought it was."

"Did you notice the buildings in the background?" Bear asked.

"All I saw was teeth," Wind said, his eyes still wide.

"They looked like those in any city in the U.S.," Bear said. *What the hell are these things?* He thought. *Holes in the floor of a cave disguised with images of solid rock.* He stepped away from Wind and the hole, walking back and forth between the walls of the cavern. *The terrain, atmosphere and beings are all different. It's like windows to other worlds, other places.*

Wind watched him pace. "I don't understand why the holes are so important. They're no different, more or less, than any of the other things we've seen here. Where else can a person see a woman disappear, a saber toothed tiger, amphibious dragons and rock walls that don't really exist? Wind was essentially talking to himself.

Bear quickly picked up his gear. "We need to get going," he said.

"Why, what did I say?" Wind asked.

"Nothing," Bear answered, "but I think I've got an idea."

Further down the main tunnel, they found another branch to the left. The passage was unexplored since Hal, Keith and Bear had kept to the main tunnel. It took over an hour to explore the two hundred yard passage. Near the end, they found two more openings. Unlike the others, these were in the walls rather than the floor.

One opened to a desert. As they watched, a giant centipede crawled by. The animal was at least fifteen feet long with a long whip-like stinger protruding from its front. It probed the sand before it, evidently looking for food.

The second revealed a scene similar to pictures Bear had seen of Antarctica. However, the penguins in this place had usable wings that beat the air the speed of humming birds. As one flitted above where the ice met the water, a tentacle snapped out of the water and jerked it from the air.

They returned to the main passage and followed it to another room. In the corner of the room was a hole or window, as he had begun to think of them, that opened to show a city floating on clouds. The city was silver, gold and blue with tall spires rising from some of its buildings. The people he saw were no more than two feet tall with wings and flew among the spires.

The next room had a window in the opposite corner, which revealed a city of futuristic design. Hovercraft traveled along its streets. Other craft flew in numerous tiers, one over the other in opposite directions.

Further along, another tunnel branched to the left. After about the length of a football field, the tunnel ended with another pool of water. "We'll need to rest here for the night," Bear said. "It's six o'clock and there's more to explore tomorrow."

"I'm all for that," Wind answered. "I didn't realize how tired I am. This exploring kicks my ass."

"If you're anything like me, it's nerves," Bear said. I'm claustrophobic and having a little problem myself."

"I'd forgotten about that," Wind admitted. "Are you doing okay?"

"I'm alright," he said. "There's something about this cave that's different than the other. I imagine it's the fluorescent light. It doesn't seem to be so enclosed. Also, these windows we're finding help some."

"Windows?" Wind questioned the name.

"They're either windows or doors. I'm beginning to think they're openings to other worlds," he explained.

"Are you sure you're okay?" Now the man was talking about other worlds.

"I know it doesn't sound realistic," he said. "But how else do you explain 'em?"

"I can't," Wind admitted. "I'm not sure it's within our ability to explain."

"You may be right," Bear agreed. "But somehow, I think they're important. Don't ask me to explain why. It's just something inside that tells me they are."

Wind nodded and rummaged through a pack. He produced two cans of K-rats and offered Bear one.

"Only if you have ham and eggs," Bear said. "I can't stand any of the others."

"Yeah, I heard you say that the other day. That's what it is."

Bear shook his head. "You're a good man Wind Jefferson," he said with a smile. He pulled out a flask, took a drink and offered it to the young man.

306

Wind took the flask, lifted it to his mouth and drank. His eyes watered and he coughed at the strength of the rum. "Do you think we'll ever find out where we are," he asked, "or a way back home?"

"There's no way to answer that."

"Then we may be stuck here the rest of our lives." Wind sighed dropping his gaze to the floor.

Bear understood what he was feeling. The uncertainty of finding their way back to their own world, the loss of friends and family and no modern conveniences, created stress for all of them.

Bear knew the sun would soon set outside, yet inside the cavern, the light never varied. A constant blue glow emanated from the smooth walls. Someone or something other than nature had constructed the cavern. Both, the walls and floor were smooth unlike the pocks and ridges created by nature. Only water could create a smooth surface naturally and he doubted water was the architect of this domain.

They sat in silence a couple of minutes. "Have you ever explored any caves before?" he asked.

"Nothing like this," Wind answered. "I've been in a couple of small ones and we went to Carlsbad Caverns when I was a kid."

"That's about the extent of my experiences too," Bear said. "Think about all the ones you've been in. Did the inside of any of them look like this?"

"I know what you're getting at," Wind said. "This is nothing like any I've seen before. The rooms are too square and the floor, ceilings and walls too smooth. It's like they were made on purpose, as if they were made for some specific reason."

"That's exactly what I was thinking," Bear said. "I think we're... "

The ground shook violently as a roaring sound filled the tunnel.

"Get away from the water," Wind shouted scrambling along the wall.

Without a word, Bear copied his movements on the other side.

The cave continued shaking with the rumbling growing louder as if coming closer. The sound seemed almost like a growl rather than the shifting of the ground. Wind was still scrambling back along the tunnel when a creature about three feet long with a four-foot tail flew from the pool of water. It made a tight circle and dove toward Bear.

As it passed above him, it reached out with the talon of one of its three toes and sliced the strap of his rifle. The bird thing swooped up and a single shot from Wind's M16 dropped it in mid-flight.

Bear scrambled to his feet and pointed a pistol at the animal. It took a couple of seconds before he realized the shaking and sound had ceased.

"Are you okay?" Wind asked.

"Yeah," he answered. "I was lucky, it missed." He picked up the rifle.

As he inspected the weapon's sling, he turned toward the pool. "It didn't miss," Wind said. "Hang on, let me look at your shoulder."

"My shoulder," Bear said. "What's wrong with my shoulder?"

Upon inspection, Wind found a razor-like slice in the back of Bear's shirt. The skin underneath was also sliced. Beads of blood stood along the nine-inch line. "It gotcha," Wind said. "It's deep, but razor-thin. As long as we keep it clean, you shouldn't have a problem."

Bear nodded and walked toward the creature. "Thanks man. There's some tape back at the supplies. When we go back there, we can make some butterfly stitches out of it."

The animal on the ground looked like a miniature pterodactyl. The end of its tail looked like an arrowhead. "That was one hell of a shot," Bear said. "The top of its head's missing."

Wind walked over to see the results of his shot. Sure enough, the bullet had torn the top of the animal's head off. "You know that was a miracle shot," Wind admitted. "I've only shot one of these a couple of times."

"Miracle or not," Bear said, "You probably saved my ass."

"You're lucky man," Wind said shaking his head. He pointed at the three-toed feet. Each toe had curved claws ending in pinpoint tips. The inner edge of each claw had a razor edge.

"You got that right," Bear said. "Imagine if it had decided to bite me."

Wind looked at the beak. Inside were two rows of needle sharp teeth on both the upper and lower jaw. "Damn," he said. "That thing was made for some serious hunting." He looked around. "I'm not sure we should stay around that water."

"You may be right," Bear said. "Maybe we should go back to the supplies. There's no reason to be foolhardy."

Without further discussion, they gathered their gear and started back.

***

It took three hours to return to the room, which held the supplies. They took their time and probed the floor all the way. Neither was willing to bet whether the earlier quake had opened more windows in the floor or not. However, it had not.

Once there, Wind used tape to close Bear's wound. Afterward, Bear repaired the sling on his rifle then both men settled down to rest.

"Do you think they made it back to the village?" Wind asked.

"I doubt it," Bear said. "Hal was gonna wind his way there, so the others couldn't remember how to get back here."

"Why don't you want them to know how to get back here?"

"I don't trust Ginny when it comes to Weniki and Palenaka," Bear said. "I would hope she wouldn't do anything on purpose, but she might by accident."

"You would hope she wouldn't do anything?" Wind said.

"I'm trying to be nice," Bear said. "I've known Ginny a long time. She can be vindictive and cause other problems without meaning to." He hesitated, running his hand over his face. He didn't want to badmouth someone who wasn't there to defend herself. "There's something about her now. She's changed since coming here."

"You don't think she'd do something against us do you?" Wind asked.

Bear was quiet for a long time. "She wouldn't have before coming here," he said. "Now, I'm not sure. As I said, she's different. I don't think she'd intentionally do anything to put Spyder in danger."

Wind lay silent with his eyes closed for a while. A snore from Bear told him all conversation was over and it was time to sleep.

***

They made camp a while after the sun dipped below the mountains. "We'll rest here," Hal said. "Then we can make it to the village tomorrow morning."

"You don't make those decisions," Ginny corrected. "I don't agree with staying here tonight. We need to get to the village as soon as we can."

"Unless you can find it in the dark, we're staying here," he said. "I have to be able to see certain landmarks and I can't in the dark."

"We need to get closer before setting up camp," Ginny argued.

"I'm not sure where that is," Hal said. "We may already be past the valley entrance as it is. I also don't think we need to take a chance on meeting another of those giant creatures."

Ginny knew Hal was right in his decision. She just didn't like him making the decisions for the group. "Okay," she said, "we'll stay here. But remember that you put me in charge and I'll make the decisions from now on."

311

Hal shook his head and smiled. "Sure, no problem."

As they established a campsite, Sandy and Hal laid their things away from the fire. "I'm gonna kick her ass," Sandy said. "What the hell is wrong with her?"

"This is probably the first time she's ever been in charge of anything," he guessed. "She's in over her head and she knows it. Bear got tired of hearing her gripe, so he put her in charge. She'll either learn or shut up."

"After she gets someone killed," Sandy said angrily.

"I hope it doesn't get that far," he said. "We'll be in the village tomorrow and she won't have to make a lot of decisions then."

"Where is the village?" Sandy asked.

"About two miles over there," Hal said motioning to his right with his head.

"I thought you knew where we were," Sandy said.

"Let's get some food," he said and grinned at her. "You might wanna be careful that the food's not poisoned."

Even though she was in charge, Ginny insisted on fixing the food. As she did it, the rest sat around the fire. Sandy sat with the others and Hal stood watching them.

"We'll be at the village tomorrow," he said. "Bear said he wanted to keep the cave a secret for now and I agree. There's something strange going on here and until we know what it is, we shouldn't say anything."

Still working on the food, Ginny said, "The people in the village are our friends. I don't think we need to keep secrets from them."

"No one tells anyone about the cave," Hal repeated.

"If Weniki or Palenaka wants to know where we've been, I'll tell them," Ginny said stubbornly. "If we're to be allies, we have to trust each other."

"Anyone tells about the cave and I'll kill them personally," Hal said. "I hate to put it that way, but it's the way it is." He looked at the others in turn. "Are we in agreement?"

As the others mumbled among themselves, Keith rose to his feet. "I don't understand what all's going on. But if Hal and Bear say that's the way it is, I agree a hundred percent."

The rest voiced their agreement and waited for Ginny to say something. She was angry enough that she was shaking where she stood. "You can all kiss my ass," she said throwing a spoon to the ground. "When Spyder hears about this, he'll kick your ass, Hal." As she stomped off, she called over her shoulder, "Fix your own goddamn food."

***

Before Wind woke up, Bear went outside. The sun was barely above the horizon and shadows dominated the area. From the outside, he would never have imagined the secrets hidden deep within the grotto. The air was warm and a light rain had fallen sometime during the night.

He pulled a piece of jerky from his pocket and bit some off. As he chewed the tough meat, he let

313

his mind wander. *That cave has to be a meeting place of different worlds. We got here by some mysterious means and those windows are apparently different worlds. The two have to be connected somehow. There has to be a way to get Spyder...*

A scream came from inside the cave. "Not again," Bear growled and ran into the entrance. Another scream echoed and ended as if choked off to a gargling sound that quickly faded.

Bear rushed into the supply room and saw a creature on top of Wind. It was an ape of some sort and the size of a grizzly bear. Both were struggling in a death match. Before Bear could reach them, the creature fell to the side and Wind rolled on top of it. He had a death-grip on the knife now deep in the animal's throat. He twisted back and forth, pulled it out and plunged it into the chest and the creature stopped moving.

Bear, now standing beside the two, saw the knife buried to the hand guard. Wind had driven eight inches of blade into the creature. "Wind," Bear said, "are you hurt?"

He looked up. Without hesitation, he lunged at Bear who sidestepped in time for him to miss and land awkwardly on the floor. Before he could rise, Bear was on top of him.

"Wind," Bear shouted. He had seen battle rage before. Wind was reacting to an overload of adrenalin and nerves.

Wind's struggles slowly subsided and he regained control of his emotions and actions. His glazed stare returned to normal and he recognized Bear sitting on top of him. He looked around and

314

saw the mound lying beside him. "Goddamn, what the hell is that?"

Bear climbed off, allowing Wind to struggle to his feet. "I haven't had a chance to check it out."

As Wind inspected the creature, he said, "I woke up when it jumped on me. Luckily, I was able to get my knife out and the son-of-a-bitch screamed when I stabbed it in the side."

Bear let him talk. It was the best way for him to calm down and work things out in his mind.

"We struggled a little bit and I was able to get the knife in its throat," he explained. "When it fell to the side, I stabbed it in the chest." He looked at Bear realizing he had attacked him. "I thought you were another one," he said. "I didn't recognize you. Shit, I tried to stab you too."

"If you hadn't done such a good job on that thing, you'd have been able to," Bear said. "The knife was deep enough that you couldn't pull it out when you came at me."

Wind looked at him and his face sagged. "I'm sorry man. I didn't mean too... "

"Don't worry about it," Bear interrupted. "It happens."

They turned their attention to the thing on the floor. It was larger than either of them and weighed at least four hundred pounds. Coarse dark-brown hair covered the body and its head was a cross between a gorilla and a Bear. Its giant paws had four fingers tipped by enormous claws and an opposable thumb.

Wind noticed something different about its waist. He felt the body and discovered a belt covered in the same hair as the animal. "Look at

315

this," he said hooking his fingers in the belt and pulling.

The bear-gorilla thing lay on its side and Bear pushed it onto its back. It had been lying on a short dagger in a sheath. Wind looked up at Bear. "A dumb animal wouldn't wear something like this," he said. "This is an intelligent being."

Bear couldn't believe what he was seeing. Wind was right this was an intelligent being. "I wonder why it attacked you, not that it really matters," he said. "It may have simply seen you as food."

Wind shivered and looked back up at Bear. "I've had about enough of this place," he said. "I know there's more to the cave and I'll go with you if you want. But I vote that we go back to the village."

"I agree it's time to leave here," Bear said. "But not to Weniki's village. We need to go see about Spyder." He tried to read Wind's expression. "Are you willing to go with me?"

"Of course I am," he said. "You shouldn't even have to ask that."

"Then let's get some supplies and get going," Bear said.

316

CHAPTER THIRTY

Hal led his group into the village about nine in the morning. Weniki and Palenaka met them as they walked along the stream.

"Aloha," Weniki said. "You are welcome here."

"Thanks," Hal said. "It's good to be here."

"I was surprised you stopped so close to our village," Palenaka said.

"We weren't sure where the valley was," he explained. "We didn't want to miss it in the dark."

Weniki nodded, "We have a place for you," she said and walked toward the center of the village.

She paused at a large hut and motioned at its front door. "This is for you," she said.

As they entered, Weniki stopped Ginny. "This is not for you."

"I'm the leader now," Ginny said proudly.

"Not here," Weniki said. "You still have much to learn."

"I won't be treated any differently than the others," she argued.

"You have the choice to stay under our rules or leave," Weniki said matter-of-factly.

Ginny looked at Hal, "You're not gonna allow this are you?"

"It's their rules," he said, shrugged and went to check the inside of their new home.

When the rest were inside, Weniki looked at Ginny and said, "You will come with me."

***

The sun rose over the horizon earlier on top of the ridge than it had on the plains below. The climb the day before left them exhausted. The night passed uneventfully and both men were rested and ready for what lay ahead.

"Are we gonna scout the village again?" Wind asked.

"Maybe," Bear said. "It depends."

"Depends on what?" Wind asked.

"On them," was all Bear said as he started walking along the tree line.

An hour later, they found where the lava flowed into the ground. Three hours after that, they reached the cliff overlooking the lake where they stopped to rest.

"I never would have dreamed of something that pretty," Wind said chewing on a piece of cocoanut.

"It is beautiful," Bear agreed. He motioned to his left, "This cliff runs all the way to the edge of the Nāki's valley. It slopes down the last half-mile or so to the level ground. At that point, the village is to the left with the lake to the right."

"Is that where you and Keith went?"

"It's one of the places," Bear said. "I want us to get near there by nightfall."

"How far away is that?"

"About five or six miles," he estimated. "We'll have to travel fast and quiet. There may be guards out."

"I'll try to keep up," Wind said.

"If anything happens to me, you need to get away," Bear said. "Come back the same way we've traveled and return to the others at the village."

318

"I'm not about to leave you here," Wind protested.

"If they take me, it's because I'm dead," Bear said. "There'll be no reason for you to stay."

Wind understood what he meant and nodded. "We just need to make sure neither of us is caught."

Bear grinned and slapped him on the shoulder. "Good thinking," he said. "Now, let's get going."

***

They encountered no guards as they traveled along the edge of the cliff. The foliage was thick and hid them on the left. The only people to their right were sailing on the lake a half-mile away.

Just before sunset, Bear told Wind to make camp but keep his gear together. "If we have to move, we won't have time to gather it up."

"Wanna try some of this?" Wind held out a piece of meat.

"Salted fish," he said. "I salted and dried it at the first camp after you and Spyder left. I ate some a couple of days ago and it didn't kill me."

Bear took the meat and bit off a piece. It was slightly salty but sweet at the same time. "Damn, that's good," he said. "You've had this all the time?"

"I thought we might use it for traveling," Wind said. "But, with all the fruit and stuff, we didn't need it."

Bear shook his head and rubbed a hand over his face. "If you don't beat all," he said. "You were so anxious to get out of the cave, I didn't expect you to remember any of the important stuff."

"I had it all stuffed in one pack," Wind explained. "All I had to do was pick it up and remember to get the guns."

The sun was below the mountains to the west and the sound of the nocturnal critters was growing.

"Did you ever notice how loud it gets here at night?" Wind asked.

"I rely on it," Bear said. "When it gets quiet, something's up. That's when I get nervous."

That makes sense, Wind thought. *They'll shut-up if something comes around.* "I heard 'em, but never thought of it," he said.

"If you're gonna survive here, you're gonna have to learn to be aware of your surroundings," Bear said. "Almost everything around you will tell you what's going on."

"I guess I've been too worried about not getting killed to look for signs," Wind admitted.

"You'll get the hang of it," Bear said. "All you have to do is pay attention to things around you. For now, you just need to remember a few things. There are essentially no right angles in nature. Plants usually grow or point in one direction and the wind carries sound and scent. Use all your senses not just your eyes and ears."

"I understand the wind thing. But I hope you're gonna explain the rest sometime," Wind said.

"I will if I have to," Bear assured him. "But once you start observing them closely, I doubt I'll have to."

Wind's expression brightened. "No right angles in nature," he said. "That's why you were questioning the rooms in the cave. They all had square corners."

Bear smiled and nodded, "See, it's not as hard and confusing as you thought."

"I don't know about that," Wind said. "But I still feel jumpy about that thing this morning. I'm not sure if I'll sleep for a month."

"Believe me, that feeling's normal," Bear assured him. "That was a hell of a way to wake up." He paused and then held his finger up to his lips in a shushing signal, pointed to his ear and then pointed further along the cliff.

Wind strained to hear what he was motioning to. In the distance, he heard the faint sound of voices. "They're a ways away," Wind whispered.

"About fifty yards," Bear whispered back.

"Where are they?" Wind asked. "Can you see 'em?"

Bear pointed in the same direction again. "You're gonna have to move quietly," Bear said. "We'll follow 'em at a distance." Wind nodded and grabbed his pack. Bear placed a hand on Wind's, "Leave it here," he said. "We'll come back for it later -- bring your weapons and stay behind me."

They moved in close enough to see the men, guards from the Nāki village. Like the others he'd seen previously, these walked down a path with no attempt to conceal themselves. *Why do they bother to have guards if they're not worried about intruders?* Bear thought. *It's like they want to be seen.*

Bear immediately stopped and signaled for Wind to stay where he was. "This isn't right," he whispered.

The two guards turned and drew their swords. At the same time, four other men armed with swords and spears rose from the bushes behind them.

"Remain where you are," one of the guards ordered.

Wind quickly pulled his rifle up, ready to fire. Bear put his hand on the weapon, "No," he said and pushed down on the barrel. "There's more."

Three men stepped from the trees on each side. A dozen men armed with swords and spears now surrounded them.

"We can't get 'em all," Bear said.

As Bear and Wind rose from their crouched position, the guard said, "You will come with us." With that, he and his companion turned and continued down the trail.

***

Bear and Wind followed slowly behind with the rest of the guards flanking and following them.

"Sling the rifle," Bear ordered.

Wind put his arm through the sling and hung the rifle over his shoulder. "What the hell's going on?" He asked unable to believe the men hadn't taken their weapons.

"I've got no idea," Bear answered. "But for now, we go with 'em."

"Did you hear the accents?" Wind asked.

Bear nodded. The men spoke like Weniki and Palenaka in their choice of words; however, the accents sounded slightly British.

The small group wound its way down the path to the valley. After entering the village, they proceeded toward the large building in the center.

322

At one smaller building, Bear nodded to it and said, "That's where Spyder was."

As they traveled along, Bear noticed similarities to Weniki's village. Fruit was stored in pots along the outside walls, meat hung from racks and all of the houses had tables in front of them.

When they reached the large building in the center, the guard knocked on its door. When the door opened, he and a man inside exchanged words Bear couldn't hear. The door closed and the guard turned back to them. "When you enter the Hall of Justice, you will walk to the altar in the center and kneel. You must leave all weapons here."

So they did know these were weapons, Bear thought. *They must've felt confident that they could take us. They're either naive, arrogant or know something we don't.* Bear was sure it was the latter. He removed his rifle and pistols.

Wind followed his example. They leaned the rifles against the wall and placed their pistols next to them.

The door opened and the man inside said something. The guard led them into the room and walked toward the altar in its center.

Bear was a Master Mason and the room looked very familiar except for its size. It was at least twice as large as any lodge he'd seen in the past. He and Wind walked up to the altar.

A man sat on a throne at the end of the room, in front of them. "Kneel," the guard ordered from beside them.

As Wind followed the order, Bear made some motions before he knelt. The man in the chair said, "Will the elder please rise?"

Bear rose to his feet and stood erect. The man in the chair nodded and said, "I am Aka, King of the Nāki."

Bear nodded in return, "I am Bear," he said, "and this is Wind." Bear had to use the nickname, he couldn't remember Wind's real name.

"You are a brother or our beliefs?" Aka asked.

"I am," Bear answered.

"What makes you a brother?" Aka pressed with his questions.

"My friend isn't," Bear answered.

Aka nodded, "I thank you," he said. "Are you friends of Henry?"

At first, Bear was surprised Spyder had told Aka his real name. Then he realized Spyder was keeping the Nāki at a distance, not allowing them to become friendly. *Smart move,* he thought. "We are," he answered.

"Your friend is well and safe," Aka said. "He is resting in a special place."

Aka noticed Wind shifting from one knee to the other and looked at the guard standing beside him. "Take him to his friend," he said.

The guard stepped up and took hold of Wind's arm to help him up. "Please come with me," he said.

Wind stood and jerked his arm from the guard's grasp.

"Take it easy," Bear cautioned. "They're not being aggressive. Don't give them a reason."

Wind nodded and followed the guard from the room.

***

Wind was ushered into the building where Bear saw Spyder a couple of days before. A fire burned in the center, under a hole in the roof. In a corner, Spyder sat, leaning back against a wall.

"Spyder," Wind called out and hurried toward him.

Spyder stood and gave Wind a hug. "It's good to see you man," he said. "What happened? Are you okay? Are you alone?"

Wind noticed the chain attached to his right leg. Pointing at it, he said, "I can see they're treating you well."

"Hell, that's nothing," Spyder answered. "I could probably slip it off my leg, it's so loose." Spyder returned to his position sitting in the corner.

"I'm here with Bear," Wind said sitting against the wall next to him.

"Bear's here?" Spyder asked. "Where is he?"

"He's talking to that Aka person."

"Yeah, I met him," Spyder said. "Not sure what I think of him."

"He's the leader of the Nāki," Wind said. "I know what I think of him."

"Don't be too quick to judge," Spyder cautioned. "I've seen him every day in the village. He's always friendly and allows me to go for walks twice a day. I have to wear loose shackles, but only have two guards with me and almost no restrictions."

"You sound like you trust these people," Wind observed, "like you've made friends with 'em. Maybe that's what they want."

"It could be," Spyder agreed. "But it doesn't fit. Everyone stays five feet from me so I can't do

325

anything. At the same time, none of them seem afraid of me or threatening in any way. When I meet one, they always nod and say hello. Hell, they're as friendly as those in Weniki and Palenaka's village." Spyder noticed the guard had failed to manacle Wind. "Let's try something," he said.

"You're not wearing one of these." Spyder pried his right boot off with his left foot. He slid the manacle down, and with some wiggling, removed it from his leg and replaced his boot. "Let's see what they do when they see me without mine."

"Aren't you asking for trouble," Wind asked.

"Maybe," Spyder admitted. "But I don't think so."

"Have you tried to escape," Wind questioned.

"There're four guards outside," he said. "And I hear 'em walking around the building all the time. But, now that you and Bear are here, we may be able to.

***

Bear had answered some expected questions proving he knew certain secrets of this society. "We accept you as a brother," Aka said. "You are welcome here."

"What about my friends?" Bear asked.

"They will be brought here immediately," Aka answered and nodded at a guard in the back of the room. The man left and Aka continued, "We knew of your presence before. You and your friends were with the ones called Weniki and Palenaka. You then went to the forbidden cave. We were surprised that

326

you left the cave safely. There are many dangers in it."

"We found some of 'em," Bear said. "I've got some questions about that cave."

"Please wait until your friends join us," Aka said. "Then, if I find you worthy, I will answer what you ask."

"I understand," Bear said nodding. "I need to let you know, though, that the man you call Henry isn't a brother either. He is, however, a close and trusted friend of mine."

Aka nodded his understanding, "We will not speak of our ways," he said.

"We also call him Spyder," Bear said trying to fill the time until his and Wind's return. "It is a nickname the same as Wind is a nickname."

"What is a nickname?" Aka asked, confused at the reference.

"It's a familiar way to refer to someone," Bear explained. "Bear is a nickname. My real name is Raphael or Rafe, for short."

"Since we will be friends," Aka said, "may I call you Bear?"

The door in the back of the room opened and Spyder and Wind walked in. "Bear's fine," he answered.

When Spyder and Wind reached the altar, Aka motioned to the benches on their right. "Please sit, we have much to discuss."

Bear held his hand out to Spyder who shook it then hugged him. "It's good to see both of you safe," Spyder said.

327

They walked to the benches and sat down. "It is nice to meet two animals and an element," Aka said chuckling.

The men grinned; all three were surprised at Aka's sense of humor. "We are honored to be here Worshipful Master," Bear said.

"I am only called such in ceremonies," Aka said. "All other times, I am Aka."

"Thank you sir," Bear said. "May I ask questions about this island and the cave we discussed earlier?"

"First, I must ask you of the other village," Aka said.

To Wind and Spyder's surprise, Bear said, "If I find you worthy, I'll answer what you ask."

Aka took no exception to the statement and nodded in agreement. "What do you know of the people there?"

"They seem to be peaceful," Bear said. "They also seem to fear the people in this village."

"They say you're... "

"Hang on Wind," Bear interrupted. "We're discussing the people in the other village."

Wind understood he was about to say something Bear didn't want said, at least not yet. He closed his mouth and looked back at Aka.

"You have well trained people," Aka said.

"They're just friends," Bear countered. "We're not part of an army. We don't even know how we got here."

"That may be explained later," Aka said. "My seers describe you and your friends as well trained."

Bear noticed Aka's use of the word seer. Along with the dress of the Nāki, the name made sense. If

328

Weniki's people were descended from ancient Polynesians, the Nāki had to be from England's history.

Two groups from earth's history, Bear thought. *This place has to be some sort of crossroads of various times in history. That might explain the windows in the cave. I understand the dinosaurs, but when did we ever have any of those other creatures?* This flashed through Bear's head more as feelings than individual thoughts.

"We're all good friends," Bear explained. "We're like a traveling entertainment troupe. As friends, we'll help and protect each other in any way we can."

"Two guards are missing," Aka said. "Is this because of you?"

Bear hesitated, then stood, "That was me," he admitted. "Neither of these men was with me."

"There were two of you," Aka said. "The other is in the valley of desire."

"The valley of desire is the name of Weniki's village, Hana O'Makemake," Bear translated. To Aka, he said, "Yes he is. He's with the rest of our group."

"Did those called Weniki and Palenaka tell you we are at war?" Aka asked.

"They didn't use the word war," he said. He wasn't sure how to explain the accusation of the Nāki being a war-like people and cannibals. He decided on an end around approach. "I saw women and children in your village. If you're at war, how do you keep them safe?"

"We will not speak of such things now," Aka said. He rose from his chair and stepped from the

329

riser it sat on. He looked at the other Nāki in the room and said, "You may leave us now." The others immediately left the room. As he stood, Bear rose from his chair. Before Spyder and Wind were able to stand, Aka motioned for Bear to sit back down, "There is more we need to learn from you first." He slowly paced the floor and stroked his chin in front of them as he spoke.

Bear knew the discussion was about to become strained. Both men wanted to trust the other, but the safety of two villages were at stake. At the same time, Aka was demonstrating trust by remaining in the room with strangers.

"We are not the same race of the others," Aka said. "It seems that there are many things you do not understand."

"Careful," Spyder whispered.

"Will you explain some of it so we can understand?" Bear asked. Spyder was right; he should use extreme caution here.

Aka briefly stopped pacing and looked at him. He appeared to consider the request. "If we speak as brothers, I must tell you of things which may confound and astound you. Your race is not part of the Confederation of Worlds. I am not sure I can make you understand."

"Confederation of Worlds?" Bear questioned.

"What the hell's that?" Spyder asked.

Aka looked at Spyder. "I am sorry," he said. "However, I will only answer questions from an outsider if he is a brother. Please do not take offense to this."

"None taken," Spyder said. "I'll wait."

330

Aka turned his attention back to Bear. "The Confederation of Worlds is a government consisting of solar systems within our galaxy. We know of your planet, but it's not technically advanced enough for us to approach yet."

"Wait a minute," Bear said interrupting him. "You've changed the way you speak."

"There are certain rules we have to follow in a conflict like this," Aka explained. "The language we use here, is foreign to us. It's complicated, but right now, I'm using a translator so I can speak to on your level. Neither of the villages is allowed to operate above the level you have seen."

"Hold on," Bear interrupted again. "I don't see a translator."

"Like I said it's complicated," Aka assured him. "It involves technology beyond your current level of understanding. Please don't think I'm talking down to you. It's simply a fact. The English language is the assigned language as the median for us to use, the same as the level of advancement. It was chosen by, how do you say it, the luck of the draw."

"You'll have to excuse our surprise," Bear said. "We're hearing that not only are there other people in the universe, but there're galaxies full of 'em. This is beyond any reality we've ever known. It's nothing more than science fiction to us." He thought a second. "I guess the first thing we need to know is how did we get here?"

"The one you know as Weniki brought you here," Aka said. "She manipulated a portal to bring you to Farn."

"Can we get back?" Bear asked.

"It's possible," Aka said. "The openings in the cave you talked about earlier are portals. They're doorways to other worlds and times. You would probably think of them as dimensions. Besides those in the cave, there are many others on this planet."

"I'm not sure I'm ready for this," Wind said running both hands through his hair. "None of this makes any sense. Are you telling us, we're on a different world then our own?"

Aka looked at Bear. "It's a good question," Bear said. "One of our friends looked at the night sky and saw familiar stars. How can we be in a different place, if she located known constellations?"

"This will be hard for you to understand," Aka said.

"Like the rest isn't, Wind said sarcastically.

Aka seemed to ignore the comment and continued. "This is one of many such places used to settle disputes between worlds. This was once a small-uninhabited planet in your solar system at a different time than you come from. The confederation changed it, modeling it in the image of a part of your planet. That's why Weniki was able to bring you here."

"Another time?" Bear questioned. "In our solar system? When and where the hell are we?" He was becoming overwhelmed and exasperated.

Aka hesitated, obviously thinking about his answer. "This is your planet Earth, one hundred thousand of your years in the future."

"Bullshit," Spyder said standing. "You said this was an uninhibited planet."

Again, Aka looked at Bear.

332

"If you talk to them, it is the same as talking to me," he said. He hoped this would satisfy the secrecy requirement. All three men had questions and Bear didn't want to have to simply restate Spyder and Wind's questions.

Aka nodded, "That's acceptable," he said. "The matter of keeping our secrets is now in your hands. Remember your obligation."

"That's fine," Bear said nodding. "I trust these men with my life."

"Yes, you do," Aka acknowledged. To Spyder, he said, "This planet was barren for ten thousand years before being changed. It's the law."

"What happened?" Bear asked. "Why was it barren?"

"I'm not allowed to answer that question," Aka said.

"Why?" Wind asked sounding dejected. "Why can't you tell us what happened to our planet? It's where we lived."

"Because it's in the future," Aka explained. "It's far enough in the future that things may change. It's also why we never go into the past. In the past, one could change events and cause a paradox. In the future, that can't happen."

"What if the people of Earth changed their paths?" Bear asked. "What if they weren't destroyed and continued beyond this time?"

"That's why we go into the future," Aka said. "If Earth continued, our actions would simply be erased as it progressed. However, because our actions weren't tied to the past, there would be no consequences."

333

"Hold on a second," Spyder said, "We are tied to the past. We're part of this planet's past."

"That's correct," Aka said nodding. "That's why what Weniki did is forbidden. No one from your world, from any time, is to be involved."

"The people of both villages are stuck here until they die," Bear said.

"Yes we are," Aka said.

"Why?" Wind asked. "Do you mean you're stuck here forever?"

"Earlier, he said none of them were tied to the past," Bear explained. "If the winner could go back after the conflict or war or whatever you call it, the actions here would be tied to the past."

Aka nodded silently.

"Since they leave their world forever, there're no consequences for them in winning or losing," Bear said. "Think of it this way. If the U.S. and China got into a conflict, they could each send a group of people to a deserted island to fight. The winner of the fight would decide the outcome between the two nations."

"If that's true," Wind said, "You must send your best soldiers."

"All circumstances for the resolution and the people involved are randomly selected by a computer," Aka explained. "None of us choose where we go or when, what the setting will be or who will be with us. It is simply by chance. The only requirement of those who go is that they are adults. The children you see were born here."

"How long have you been here," Spyder asked.

"In Earth years, about six hundred," Aka said, "time is different here. I was on Earth a short time

334

to learn the culture I was to operate as. I was in Britain and known Arthur. This is why I speak differently than Weniki."

"Arthur?" Bear repeated. "You were King Arthur?"

"That was my title," Aka confirmed. "Aka is the translation of that name for this place and culture."

"I thought you couldn't change history," Bear challenged. Arthur surely did."

"Only in mythology," Aka corrected. "Steps were taken to remove any proof of my presence there."

"Holy shit," Spyder exclaimed, "King Arthur and the knights of the round table -- that was you?"

"It is now only a myth on your world," Aka said.

"It may be a myth," Spider conceded, "but, it influenced Britain's history a lot."

"The government watched it closely," Aka said. "Fortunately, the effect was positive. Weniki also visited Earth in the past. The Hawaiians knew here as Po'ele. Her influence was less than mine."

Bear's head was spinning, "I've had enough for now," he said.

"Are you sure?" Aka asked. "This is the only time the confederation will allow me to speak on this level. All translations will be reduced to the level you experienced when you first arrived."

"Before that," Bear said. "What about the doorways? Do we use those to return to our time and place?"

"Yes," Aka said. "You must find the one to your time and place on this planet. There is only

335

one. I cannot tell you where it is. When you arrived, a portal was created to your time and place. You will have to find it yourselves. It remains attached to when and where you left. If you find it and return, it will be as if you never left. Everything there will be the same, as will you. The doors for the rest of us are gone. We must remain here."

"You said this was one place of many," Bear said. "Can or will it be used by others from your time and place?"

"No," Aka said. "However, other parts of the planet may be used by other times or places. At the same time, once this dispute is resolved, this place may then be used by others."

"And the doorway back for us may be on some other part of the planet," Bear said. Things just went from bad to worse.

"That's correct," Aka confirmed. "I'm sorry, but I can't help you find it. I have to keep my attention here. My world depends on it."

"I understand," Bear said. "Does Weniki know all this?"

Aka nodded, "She does."

There were a hundreds questions Bear wanted to ask, but stress etched Aka's face. *It's probably from the translation,* he thought. He'd seen a change in the man since he started speaking on a level Bear thought normal. "I thank you for helping us with the information," Bear said. "The only thing I can promise you is that none of us will ever tell Weniki or any of her village what we have learned here. If you wish to keep us here as captives, I will assure you we'll escape as soon as we can. If you let us go, we will never speak of this meeting."

336

Aka seemed pleased with the statement. "You are free to go as you choose," he said. "If you wish to remain here tonight, you are welcome. We will lead you out of the valley tomorrow. I know you want to re-join your friends."

All three men smiled. As Bear started to speak, Wind interrupted as he rose to his feet. "We are well met in this place," he said. "As for my part in this triangle of friends, your secrets are safe with me."

"As with me," Spyder said standing.

Bear stood and bowed, "I'll complete the triangle of friends as Wind called us," Bear said. "I just hope we never have to face each other in combat," Bear held himself straight and faced Aka, "because I will defend my friends with my life."

"As you say, we are well met and friends here," Aka said and bowed. When he straightened, no stress registered in his features. "We have a place prepared for you if you wish, a place of honor." He clapped twice and the guards returned to the room.

337

CHAPTER THIRTY-ONE

The place of honor was a large wooden structure. Over the front door was a crest comprised of a shield with a dragon's head inside and a lion on each side facing the shield. Inside, were five smaller and one large room. Each bedroom contained a large bed and a chair. The large room contained four large and three small padded chairs. A cook-stove sat in a corner with three shelves above it. The shelves contained spices, flour and other supplies for cooking. Red and blue material adorned the walls matching the cushions on the chairs.

After the first night's comfortable rest in a week or more, the three men met in the living room the next morning. "That beat the shit outta sleeping on a dirt floor," Spyder said grinning.

"Does anyone else think something's not right with any of this?" Wind asked. "I don't mean just this village, but the whole thing."

"Both sides seem passive," Wind said. "But that can't be if what Aka said last night is true."

"I think it's true," Bear said. "It would explain the things we found in the different rooms. I wouldn't be surprised if others had been brought here in the past."

"What things, what rooms?" Spyder asked.

"We'll tell you about 'em later. For now, we need to get back to the others," Bear said starting a fire in the oven. "I want some tea and something to eat before leaving, how about the two of you?"

"Food," Spyder said. "That sounds good to me."

"You're not gonna cook it are you?" Wind asked looking skeptically at Bear.

A knock drew their attention to the front door. Wind opened it and Aka stood outside. "Greetings," he said stepping in. "We have prepared a meal for you this morning. I and my captains will have you eat with us if you agree."

Wind looked at Bear and grinned, "That'd be better than taking a chance here."

"We'd be happy to accept," Bear said. "Is that okay with you Spyder?"

Spyder grabbed his hat. "I've tasted your coffee and I've tasted their food," he said. "You lose."

Stepping from the hut, they found their weapons lying along the front wall. "I don't think we'll need those," Spyder said shaking his head in disbelief. This place and the people weren't anything like Weniki described.

They enjoyed the breakfast on a large rectangular table. Aka and eight other men joined Bear, Spyder and Wind. None of the men spoke of danger or fighting. Instead, they discussed the events in the village the day before.

Eventually, one of the men reported a man missing. "He was to return last evening," the man explained. "He was to the east on the plain."

Aka paused in his eating, a thoughtful look on his face. "How long has he been gone?"

"Four days," the man answered.

Looking at Bear, Aka asked, "Did you see a man dressed as we are on your journey here?"

"Nope," Bear answered. "The only thing we saw in the last couple of days was a creature that attacked Wind."

"How did this creature appear?"

"It was larger than a man, had dark brown hair and wore a knife around its waist," Bear explained. "It attacked Wind while he was asleep."

Aka nodded and motioned for one of his captains to stand. "Show these men your true self."

The man stepped away from the table. His body shimmered, rippled and morphed into the creature that attacked Wind in the cave. It stood looking at the others showing no aggression even though it still wore a sword. A few seconds later, it returned to its image of a human.

Wind stared in shock and Spyder had armed himself with a knife from the table. Aka seemed to expect the reactions, "Please do not worry," he said as the man returned to his seat. "It is our true appearance. The other villagers must keep this appearance", he motioned to himself, "the same as us."

Spyder put the knife beside his plate, but looked skeptical. Wind still stared at the man, his mouth open in disbelief. Spyder nudged his shoulder and flipped him under the chin with his finger. Wind closed his mouth and continued staring at the man a moment.

"Are you saying I killed a man?" Wind said.

"If you killed in defense of yourself, you did nothing wrong," Aka said. "That is what Brother Rafe said so it must be."

"Why did it attack?" Bear asked

"I do not know," Aka said. "Maintaining our current appearances cause problems in some. That may be the case."

"We'll need to leave this morning. It has nothing to do with this," Bear said. "We have friends at the other village and need to get them."

"Will you return?"

"I don't know," Bear answered honestly. "We all need to discuss this further."

Aka nodded his understanding, "You are free to leave when you wish," he said.

"Thank you," Bear said. "We'll leave soon.

When he stood, Spyder and Wind joined him. It was time to go.

***

Guides led them to the end of the valley, where they continued on their own. The rest of the way to the cave, Bear and Wind filled Spyder in on what had taken place during his absence.

Even after Bear explained the first wall in the cave, Spyder was hesitant to walk through it even though Bear and Wind went through without hesitation.

He finally eased himself through and followed the others to the storeroom. They didn't want to spend any more time in the cave than they had to. After gathering more supplies, they left, heading for Weniki's valley and their friends.

The sun was below the mountains three hours when they entered the valley. "Remember," Bear reminded them, "we snuck Spyder out and know nothing about what's going on here. No discussion of what's going on or what we plan on doing."

"Except for the sneaking part, it's not far from the truth," Wind said. "I'm still not sure what's going on or who's a friend and who's not."

"I think that's the way all three of us feel," Bear said. "We need to get our people out of the valley and back to the cave. For some reason, neither group can read our minds in there."

"Do we leave tonight or tomorrow?" Wind asked as they reached the edge of the village.

"Tomorrow," Bear answered. "Tonight would cause suspicion."

Weniki and Palenaka approached from the center of the village. "Aloha," both of them said in unison. "You have returned," Weniki said smiling. "We were worried for your safety."

Palenaka looked at Spyder. "You have returned with your friend. That is wonderful."

Hal led the others as they hurried up to greet the three men. He grabbed Spyder and gave him a tight hug. "I thought we'd lost you man," he said stepping back. "Damn, it's good to see you," he took Wind's hand, "and you too."

Sandy grabbed Bear in a big hug as soon as she reached him. "It's good to have you back," she said, her eyes glistening with tears in the torchlight. "We didn't know if you were okay or not."

Ginny was hanging on Spyder, unwilling to let him go. "How did they get you back?" She asked with her face against his chest.

"How *did* you get him?" Keith asked shaking Bear's hand.

"We'll tell you about it later," he answered. "Right now, is there any food?"

As they ate, Bear told a story about how they had rescued Spyder. Wind even inserted some imaginary details making the tale believable. Spyder added some things about leaving the village. No one spoke of the cave or meeting the other villagers and the rest seemed to accept the story.

"It's good to be back," Bear said to Weniki. "There're a lot of people in the village. It's gonna be harder than we thought. Wind and I ran into some sort of creature that looked like a cross between a bear and an ape. The damn thing even wore a knife."

"That was one of the Nāki," Palenaka said. "They have the ability to change the way they look. They can become animals when they choose to."

"What about you?" Keith asked. "Can you do that?"

"No," Weniki answered. "I can make it appear as if I have, but it is not real."

"We have to make plans," Bear said. "We need to go back to our supplies in both places. We have to go back to the first place as well as Weniki's valley. We have things there we'll need. Since we got Spyder back and a long way to go, we'll have to leave tomorrow. The Nāki will surely come after him."

Weniki nodded in understanding, but Bear thought he saw something in her expression. *She's not buying it,* he thought. *She's going along with it, but there's no way she believes what I'm saying.*

"What about crossing the canal?" Sandy asked. "How do we get across?"

"Can the Menehune make another bridge?" Keith asked.

"I do not know if they are willing," Weniki answered.

"We can make a raft," Hal said. "That's not a problem. Then we can use it both ways."

"Good idea," Bear agreed. "That way, there shouldn't be a problem with how long it has to be there."

Palenaka was looking at Wind all through their meal. When Bear made this last statement, she frowned slightly. "Is something wrong with that?" Wind asked her.

"It is just that I had hoped you could remain longer," she said. "You return only to leave so soon."

"If we're to teach you how to fight the Nāki, we have to," Wind explained. "Bear explained some of what we need to do and it'll take most of the supplies we have back there. We'll also need the horses we have here and the ones back there."

Nice touch, Bear thought.

"We will have things ready for you tomorrow," Weniki said. "Tonight, you must rest."

Soon Bear and the others went to the hut, supplied by Weniki and her people, to rest. Tonight, Weniki allowed Ginny to accompany Spyder to his room.

***

After breakfast the next morning, Bear led the rest out of the valley. Soon, they turned left and headed toward the cave. As they did, Spyder said, "We'll explain everything to you later. There're some things we need at the cave."

344

Following five hours of traveling, they reached the cave. They removed the Nāki from the storeroom and then Bear, Spyder and Wind explained what had really taken place at the Nāki village.

After answering a number of questions, Bear said, "We don't have all the answers folks. We've told you what we know. Now, it's time for us to put our heads together and try to figure out what's going on."

"Actually, using Earth in the future makes sense," Amanda said. "That way, the actions of the combatants don't have an effect on Earth or the other planet's future other than who wins and who loses. There are no paradoxes from the future, only the past."

"That doesn't help us now," Keith said.

"Sorry," Amanda said. "I was thinking like a scientist. You're right, it doesn't change our situation."

"Who do we help?" Sandy asked. "Who's our friend and who's not?"

"I don't think either of them are our enemies," Bear said. "I think we're nothing more than pawns in a game of chess."

"Then we just stay out of it," Spyder said.

"I don't think they'll let us do that," Wind argued, "especially if Weniki brought us here to help them."

"I think he's right," Hal agreed. "If others have been brought here before, then we're stuck in the middle."

"The only difference I've seen between the two is that Weniki denied being a shape shifter. According to Aka, they all are."

"Maybe they're not," Amanda said. "Maybe they have other powers like the disappearing thing."

"That could be," Sandy suggested. "But, who do we believe?"

"Neither and both," Bear said. "I'm not sure how, but we've got to stay out of this." He looked at the others in the cave, "We have to be willing to do anything necessary, even kill, anyone trying to drag us further into it."

Everyone went quiet after the last statement. None of them wanted to kill another person, no matter whether he or she looked like a creature or not.

"That's a bit strong isn't it?" Ginny asked. "Just because you don't agree with someone, you want to kill them."

"Goddamn it Ginny," Bear said. It was obvious his patience had about run its course with her. "I don't agree or disagree with either of them. I don't know enough to make a decision like that."

"Right," she said. "So why would you be willing to kill people without knowing everything?"

"Ginny, it's very simple," Sandy said. "He doesn't want to join either side since he doesn't know which is right and which is wrong. He's suggesting that we be willing to kill to avoid taking sides -- to stay neutral, in other words."

"Leave it to you to take his side," Ginny snorted and glared at her.

Sandy took a step toward her.

"Don't touch her," Spyder ordered.

346

Sandy stopped and looked at him, turned slowly and, never removing her gaze, returned to her position beside Hal.

"Ginny, I just kept you from getting your ass kicked," he said. "I'm not sure but that it might be justified. You know what Bear meant. You're just being stubborn. Now knock it the fuck off."

Ginny's eyes grew wide with surprise. He had never talked that harshly to her and she didn't like the fact that he had now. *Every one of these assholes are acting like they're better than I am and that bitch Weniki only adds to it.* To Spyder she said, "You're just like the rest. You think you're so much better than I am. Who do you think was trying to get you back? It was me. They only worried about how to get back to the real world. They didn't care if you were here or not. They were willing to go back without you. Bear only went back when Hal made me the leader.

"Made you the leader of what?"

"The group," she said. "He put me in charge just like Bear was in charge before."

"Good God Almighty," Spyder said shaking his head. He pulled his cowboy hat off his head, ran his hand through his long hair and replaced the hat. "First, Bear was never in charge. We followed his suggestions because he was the most knowledgeable. Nobody elected him leader. Second, he and Wind were the ones that came to rescue me. I'm sure that was by design. Third, if you did what you usually do, complain about everything, they probably put you in charge to stop the complaining. It's what I would've done."

347

Ginny stared in disbelief. She knew he was right. They had simply moved her out of the way and done what they wanted.

"There was more to it than that," Bear said. "I thought we needed to find out about the Nāki and not let Weniki know what was happening. Making her think I was mad about something seemed the best way to throw her off. Since Ginny didn't know about it, she didn't have to try and conceal anything."

"Makes sense," Spyder said. "It would have worked fine if you hadn't gotten yourselves caught."

"It was all part of the plan," Wind said grinning sheepishly. "Right Bear?"

"You lie and I'll swear to it," Bear said with a smile.

"Hal and Sandy told me about trying to communicate through thought," Amanda said trying to change the subject. "We've been trying it a little since then, and something seems to be working. We can't read each other's thoughts, but sometimes pictures come through from the other person."

"I've felt the same thing," Bear admitted. "Some of it seems to be from you guys, but I'm sure some of it's from Weniki or Palenaka. I don't know if they were doing it to make sure I was safe or if they were spying on me."

"Both sides seem to at least partially tell the truth," Wind said, "at least enough to justifying our trust of 'em."

"Neither of them have been threatening in any way, Keith said. "We can come and go as we please."

348

"For now," Sandy pointed out. "That can't continue if we choose a side. Actually, Weniki and Palenaka already think we've made a choice."

"She's right," Hal said. "As it stands now, we haven't made an enemy of either side."

"We haven't made enemies, but Weniki isn't sure if she trusts you," Ginny said.

"How do you know that?" Hal asked, a cautious look on his face.

"Any time I'm close to her, she shares with me."

"How close?" Hal asked.

"A couple of miles," Ginny said.

"What about outside the cave?" Bear asked.

"No," Ginny said. "That's too far. Besides, it's none of your business. Sharing is personal and between the ones sharing. That's something you have no control over."

"Nobody wants to control your sharing with Weniki," Spyder said. "But we, as a group, need to make sure why she's contacting one of us."

"She never tries to tell me what to do," Ginny explained. "She only cares about all of our wellbeing."

"How so?" Keith asked. "What makes you think that?"

"She never tries to tell me what a person should do," Ginny said defensively. "She only asked about everyone to make sure we're all alright. She was very concerned when Bear and Wind left and struck out on their own."

"Wait a minute," Sandy said surprised at what she just heard. "How did she know Bear and Wind were gone before we got back?"

"Don't be so suspicious," Ginny snapped back. "Members of her village are always out hunting. When they are in the area, Weniki will use them as a conduit of some sort and can contact me."

"How often does this happen?" Hal questioned.

"Not often," Ginny said, becoming irritated at all the questions. She stood and started to pace. "Sometimes once a day, sometimes twice, it just depends."

"She's spying on us," Bear said looking around at the others.

"That's just like you," Ginny's emotions exploded. "You take everything negatively and become suspicious and confrontational of anyone who doesn't do what you think they should. I've had it with you and your shit." She stormed out of the room. When Spyder looked after her, she passed through the barrier to the outside.

"She's gone," Spyder said.

"I'll go talk to her," Amanda said.

"No," Spyder stopped her. "She just needs time to sort things out. She'll come back when she's ready."

***

Ginny stomped out of the cave wanting to get some space between her and the others. *Spyder has no idea what those assholes are really like.* She kicked at a rock. *He actually thinks they care about him. All they give a shit about is their precious Bear. That son-of-a-bitch doesn't care about anyone but himself.*

350

She walked away from the cave, toward the beach. Few rocks or insects in her path were safe from her wrath. In her rage, she failed to notice the people to her right and left. They watched her rant and rave, each unaware of the other.

"I ought to poison every fucking one of 'em," she said stripping the leaves from a small limb. "Goddamn, I hate putting up with this shit."

From the right, three men stepped out of the foliage dressed in a Polynesian style. "You seem angry," one of the men said.

Startled, she jumped and faced him. As a reaction, her hand rested on her pistol. "What're you doing here?" She asked.

"We are hunting for food," the man answered. "Are you well?"

"I'm fine," Ginny said. "We were... "

From the left three men rushed into view carrying swords. "Get away from her," one of the men said.

Ginny was surprised at the appearance of the other men. They wore red and blue clothing covered by metal breastplates, with sheaths hanging from their belts.

"Are they Nāki?" She asked the Polynesian.

"They are," he answered, his friends stepping up beside him.

You are in danger. The Nāki must die. The thoughts flashed through her mind uninvited. "They must've come here to capture me," Ginny said. "They did that to my husband. You have to kill 'em."

351

As the Polynesians started forward, Ginny hurried to her right, removing herself from immediate danger.

"Kill the animals," one Nāki yelled and started running toward the others.

Neither group hesitated. They charged each other with Ginny in the middle. When they clashed, they blocked her way back to the cave. In panic, she pulled her pistol and fired a shot, into the air, hoping to draw the attention of everyone in the cave.

Even though the Polynesians had no swords, they possessed excellent fighting skills. The two groups were evenly matched and fearsome fighters. Spears expertly blocked swords, which in turn parried the thrusts and slashes of the longer weapons. Bodies mixed until it was impossible to tell one side from the next except for dress.

Bear, Spyder and Hal, with the others close behind, rushed from the cave in response to Ginny's shots. They located the fight about a hundred yards from the cave with her on the opposite side holding her gun ready to shoot again.

Spyder fired an M16 into the air in an attempt to get the attention of the fighters. Immediately the two closest combatants turned and attacked them screaming as if insane.

Spyder lowered the rifle as Bear pulled a pistol. Both men fired one shot at the same time. The others scattered into the bushes as both attackers dropped lifelessly to the ground. In less than two seconds, the area was empty of Polynesians and Nāki except for the bodies on the ground.

Ginny ran to Spyder, "What the hell happened out here?" He asked.

"I don't know," she answered. "I was walking along thinking and before I knew it, people were screaming and running at each other. I shot at the Nāki, but missed."

Hal knelt to check the men on the ground. "We've got a problem now," he said standing. "They're dead." He removed his hat and slapped it across his leg. "The others saw us shoot them before they left." It was rare for Hal to express anger. He usually kept such feelings to himself until he worked through them. "Goddamn it Ginny," he barked, "why couldn't you just stay in the cave. Now you've got us in deep shit."

Bear removed his hat and ran his hand through his hair as he tried to clear his thoughts. "I doubt she did it on purpose Hal. Our problem now, is that we've killed people from both sides. Even if we want to be, we're no longer considered neutral by anyone."

"You don't know that," Ginny argued. "Weniki's people may still trust us."

"What were her people doing here in the first place?" Keith asked. Something didn't seem right about the situation to him.

"They said they were hunting," Ginny said. "Then all of a sudden, the Nāki attacked."

"The only thing that matters now," Bear said, "is what we do from here. I've got a sneaking suspicion that both sides were either looking for us or have been watching us all along."

"That makes sense," Wind said. "That would be a hell of a coincidence for them to arrive here at the same time."

"I think he's right," Amanda said.

"I think we're caught between and on our own," Sandy said. "We'd better decide what we're gonna do soon."

"Let's get back in the cave for now," Hal suggested.

Everyone agreed and they all returned to the storeroom.

"I think something about these false walls stops Weniki or Palenaka from sharing with us," Bear said. "All planning and serious discussions should probably be conducted inside here."

"I agree," Hal said. "We've... "

"I don't," Ginny interrupted. "Wind was attacked in here. How did they know he was here?"

"I've got an idea about that," Sandy said.

"We're open to ideas," Spyder said sitting on a wooden case.

"Bear said Wind was attacked by one of the Nāki in its natural state. He also said holding their human form caused a strain on 'em. I think it's possible that the Nāki accidentally stumbled upon Wind, probably from the other end of the tunnel, and attacked him. If the rules say they have to be in human form, there had to be a reason he wasn't."

"I see what she means," Keith said. "The attack was due to a physical or psychological stress on the thing. It's not something it would normally do."

Bear nodded in agreement, it made sense. "If that's true," he said, "I wanna know what's at the other end of the tunnel."

354

Keith stood up, "I'll go with you."

"I didn't say I was going anywhere," Bear countered.

Wind snickered, looked at Hal and shook his head. "When will you be back?" Hal asked.

Bear knew his friends could read him all too well. "Probably in a couple of hours," he said.

Keith joined him as he went to the door of the storeroom.

CHAPTER THIRTY-TWO

Bear and Keith made it to the opposite end of the tunnel without incident. On the other side of the false wall was the hole in the floor with the flying spiders. Bear wasn't happy about being near it, but somehow they had to find a way across to the other side.

The hole was about six feet wide, which both men could jump across, However, it was unnerving to jump from one side to the other and not be able to see what you were jumping. Both men made it with no problem other than a little anxiety.

On the other side, the cave ended on a shelf. A vertical drop plunged from the shelf at least five hundred feet. A narrow trail coursed along the face of the cliff to the right.

"Why don't you go along that and see where it leads," Bear suggested.

"Why don't you kiss my fuzzy ass?" Keith answered with a grin. "I'll go back and tell everybody we shouldn't try it if you fall."

"Mighty kind of you," Bear said and stepped toward the trail.

Keith grabbed his arm, "I was joking man. You'll kill yourself."

"So was I," Bear said. "A person could get hurt doing that."

"You know who could do it?" Keith asked. Then without waiting for an answer he said, "Wind."

"Better yet," Bear countered. "What about Amanda? She has climbing experience."

356

"I forgot about that," Keith admitted. "But she's a... " He hesitated, not sure if he should finish the sentence.

"If you say it, I'll tell her."

"That's why I didn't say it," Keith said. "I don't need two women hating me."

"I'll wait here," Bear said. "You go back and get her." Then, remembering the holes along the way, he said, "You can get back without killing yourself, can't you?"

"I'll be back in a couple of hours," Keith said with an unfavorable look. "You sure you want to stay here until I return?"

"I'll be right here."

Three hours later Keith and Amanda jumped across the disguised hole in the floor.

"Keith says you have a six inch ledge you want me to walk," Amanda said to Bear.

"If you're willing," he answered. "It's a sheer drop and there's no way for us to keep you safe. There's a bend on the path about twenty feet from here, so we can't tie a rope to you."

"I wouldn't want you to," she said. It might get in the way and cause me to lose my balance." She looked at the narrow ledge. "That's no problem. It just depends what's on the other side of that outcrop."

"Now listen to me," Bear turned serious. "That ledge is there for a reason. You can see footprints on it, so it's used for something. You have to be careful and not let anything surprise you. This place has... "

"I won't Daddy," Amanda said smiling at him. "I know you're only worried about my safety. But,

357

this isn't a problem by any stretch of the imagination."

"You wanna rest before you try it?" Keith asked.

Amanda leaned over and kissed him on the lips. "I'll be back soon."

Without hesitation, she stepped on the narrow ledge along the face of the cliff. She seemed to float along the path as if she weren't inches from a plunge to her death. It took her less than a minute to reach the outcropping in the cliff.

Over her shoulder, she yelled back, "It continues on a long way. I'll be back in a while." A pause then, "Don't wait up," and she disappeared from sight around the jutting rocks.

"We might as well sit down and wait," Bear said sitting and dangling his legs over the drop-off.

Keith sat further back with his back against the edge of the cave.

"Don't you want to come out and look at the valley?" Bear asked.

"I'm quite comfortable here," Keith said. "I can see all I need to where I am."

"Don't like heights?"

"I'm scared of 'em," Keith said.

"Like me and close places," Bear nodded, understanding what he felt.

***

About an hour later, a voice from behind them made Keith jump and almost sent Bear off the ledge he was sitting on.

358

"You won't believe what I found." Amanda stood just inside the mouth of the cave.

"How did you jump over that hole without me hearing you?" Keith asked astounded that she had snuck up on him.

"I told you, you won't believe what I found," she repeated.

Both men stood and followed her as she re-entered the cave. About five feet in, she turned left and walked through the wall.

"Well, I'll be kiss my ass," Keith said following her.

Bear shook his head as he followed Keith. After crossing the hole in the floor, he never thought to check the walls.

Inside this tunnel, the walls shone like the other. As Amanda led the way, they were able to move along quickly until she reached a curve in the tunnel.

"Stay to the side," she instructed, "there's a hole here."

She had placed three rocks with a fourth on top, next to the lip of the hole. The same configuration of rocks marked the opposite side. Once on the other side, she walked a few yards away and pushed her hand through the wall.

"This is where I came in," she said. "I don't know what's further down the tunnel. When I came in, I immediately went toward where the two of you were."

"Outstanding job Amanda," Bear said. "We need to... " He reached out, grabbed Keith by the arm and pulled him away from the hole.

A tentacle reached out of the floor and felt around the lip of the hole.

"Son-of-a-bitch," Keith said stunned by the sight.

"Okay," Bear said rubbing his chin as he watched the thing search the floor. "We don't stand beside the holes anymore."

"We're lucky it was a narrow opening," Keith said thoughtfully. "If we'd taken too long going around it, we might've been caught."

"It's something to remember," Bear agreed. "Let's keep going and see where this leads." One behind the other, the trio continued along the tunnel.

They traveled in this fashion for three hours, finding and marking two more holes in the floor and three in the walls. Eventually, the tunnel reached a dead end.

Keith stepped up beside Bear, "I'll bet it's a false wall," he said.

"Ya think?" Bear said sarcastically. He raised his hand and pushed it forward. It passed through the barrier. Leaning forward, he pushed his upper body to the other side. After a short hesitation, he pulled back and said, "You won't believe what's on the other side."

Amanda started forward and he placed a hand on her shoulder to stop her. "When we go through, we need to stay low. There's a ledge and some bushes we need to hide behind. Keep the noise to a minimum and no quick movements. It's overlooking the Nāki village on the opposite side of the valley where Keith and I were before."

He led Keith and Amanda through to the ledge beyond, where they found thick bushes providing

360

enough cover to keep them from the sight of the people two hundred feet below.

"This is where the Nāki live," Bear said nodding at the valley. "That's the lodge they use for formal ceremonies and official business. It's where we met Aka and found out what we did about the Nāki and the other group."

Keith looked around their position. They were about halfway between the top of the cliff and the floor of the valley. There were no guards or lookouts in view, so they were safe where they were.

Bear pointed out that no paths led away from the ledge. "It wouldn't surprise me if the Nāki didn't know about this ledge. The only way here is behind us. There're no fresh footprints. It's been a long time since anyone's been up here."

"I'll bet there's another tunnel down near the valley floor," Amanda said.

"What about the cave we saw on the end?" Keith asked looking at Bear.

"Let's get back in the tunnel," Bear said turning around and passing through the image of rock.

Back inside the passage, he waited until Keith and Amanda entered. "We need to get back to the others," he said. "This is information they all need to know."

***

Three hours later, they entered the storeroom. "We were beginning to wonder about you," Hal said, looking up from a stew he was eating.

361

"It was a long trip," Bear answered. "It took a little longer than we expected."

"Well, get some food while you tell us about it," Sandy said stirring a pot over a lit can of sterno. "It's not much, but it's something."

Keith waved a hand at her, "Nah, we've already eaten, thanks though."

Sandy looked up in surprise. "I didn't know any of you took food with you."

"We didn't have to," Keith assured her. "We had steak, potatoes and a salad."

Sandy looked at the half-warm pot of stew. "Well, I just thought... "

"If she throws that stew out, I'll kick your ass," Bear said to Keith.

The look on Sandy's face spoke volumes. She had taken the time to fix a meal, and now she thought it was for nothing. She said nothing, but she also had to wonder why they didn't bring food back for the others.

Still kidding, Keith said, "Well maybe we can have a little... "

"Keith," Amanda interrupted, "If you don't shut up, I'll slap the taste outta your mouth."

"We haven't eaten since we left," Bear assured her. "I can't speak for him, but I'm starving and that stew looks like a feast."

Sandy realized Keith was teasing. "Glad to hear it," she said. "Now, you and Amanda come on over here and get yourselves some food." She dipped the oversized spoon into the pot and filled two bowls.

Keith was at the end of the line and stepped up when Bear and Amanda moved off to sit down and eat. He picked a bowl up and held it out to Sandy.

"I'm sorry," she said, "I didn't think you wanted any. They got the last of it."

"Okay," Keith said, adding what he thought was the proper repentance to his voice. "You win. I was wrong. I shouldn't have teased you."

"Thank you," Sandy said sweetly. "But that doesn't make more stew."

Keith grinned, "I'll be nice from now on and there's more stew in the pot."

"It's for seconds if anyone wants it."

"I'll have seconds," Hal said rising to his feet.

"Me too," Wind said as he rose.

Keith's face sagged. *She's serious. They're gonna get seconds and I'll have to eat K-Rats or MREs - that sucks.*

When Sandy dipped the spoon into the pot, Hal grinned at the look on Keith's face. "I was just messing with you," he said. "You can have the rest."

"Me too," Wind said. "But that stuff is good. I wouldn't wait too long for someone else to have a chance to get it. You might go hungry."

Keith realized they were all harassing him. With a big grin, he said, "I won't make that mistake again," and held his bowl out. After Sandy filled it he added, "Thanks, I'm starving."

It was dark outside and time for Bear, Amanda and Keith to describe what they found earlier.

***

Kawika and Waiaka returned to the Nāki village and reported to Aka. Standing at the altar, Kawika finished his story.

363

"When we neared the forbidden cave, we saw one of the foreigners. She held discourse with members of the Alaea. When we stepped forward, she commanded them to kill us. Surely, she has power and authority over them."

"Can you be certain that she commanded them?" Aka asked.

"I have no doubt," Waiaka supported his leader. "I heard her words. She said, 'They have come to capture me. They did that to my husband. You must kill them and the Alaea attacked."

"During the attack," Kawika continued the account, "Brother Rafe and the one called Spyder shot a member of each side." Neither Kawika or Waiaka had seen the two combatants rush Bear and Spyder in fits of battle induced rage. Both fixated on their enemies with a concern for protecting themselves.

"This sounds most unlike Brother Rafe. However, by his own word, he was the only member of his band who knew our beliefs." While Aka stroked his chin thoughtfully, Kawika and Waiaka waited patiently at the altar. "I suppose it is possible that we were outwitted," Aka admitted, "Or Brother Rafe has no power to control the others."

Aka didn't want to declare his newly found brother to be an enemy. At the same time, he had to think of the survival of his people. "We must treat Brother Rafe and his friends with caution. Trust them not, until such time that they prove themselves worthy of our faith. Of this command, all will take notice and let it so be done."

Both men at the altar bowed and left the room. Aka's order fell just short of pronouncing Bear and the others enemies, which meant they were not to be sought out and attacked. However, they were also, not to be trusted.

**

At almost the same time Aka received his information, Kini reported his version to Lopaka, Weniki and Palenaka who sat around a large table in Lopaka's hut.

"When the Nāki appeared, the female you share with, commanded us to attack. As she is your 'akiu, we followed her order. During battle, her friends appeared and killed a warrior of each side."

"She told you to attack because I sent her a message for that purpose," Weniki explained. "We must keep them from the Nāki, whose lies could turn them against us. Did you say the battle was near wahi kapu?"

"That is correct," Kini answered. The others came from inside the ana and attacked us as we defended the female."

"Mahalo," Weniki said. "We must speak among ourselves now."

Kini bowed and left the hut. "Is she your 'akiu?" Lopaka asked looking at Weniki.

"No," she answered. I do not use her to gather information. She thinks more of herself than of others, which I hoped to change. If successful, I would have used her to assist us in acquiring the assistance of the others."

"What makes these different than the others that were brought here before?" Lopaka asked.

"Except for Bear, none are taught to follow the orders of their leaders," Weniki said. "All of the others brought here were warriors and taught to follow their leaders without question. I could easily lead them through sharing. Ginny and Bear are the only ones in which I can leave a suggestion. I can contact them if the need arises."

Lopaka looked calmly at her, "Is that the only reason you left a thought with Bear?" He asked.

Weniki held his gaze, "What do you imply?" She asked in return.

"I understand that you bonded with him," Lopaka said.

Weniki looked sternly at Palenaka, trying to read her expression. Palenaka looked serenely back. To Lopaka, she said, "I wanted a bonding. That is all, it meant nothing."

"As you say," Lopaka said accepting her explanation. "You and Palenaka are important to us. If it is as Kini says, we cannot put off defeating the Nāki any longer. We must deal with these haoles if they become involved in our war. We are nearing the end of the time of preparation.

***

"There's another tunnel we haven't checked out which goes the other direction," Bear said. Hal and Keith were drinking instant coffee with him while the others still slept. Bear insisted everyone get a good night's rest. He knew things had to be taken care of today when they awoke.

"It's strange that neither group is willing to come in this cave," Hal said. "With the supplies

366

here, it's obvious others have come here through the different doorways. I would think they should know the place pretty well."

"I'm not sure either group is controlling the false walls and floor," Bear guessed. He had spent a lot of time thinking about the subject. "I think they're somehow controlled by the federation Aka talked about. Both of them probably had a separate doorway they came through, but a cluster like this is most likely controlled by an outside source."

"That makes sense," Keith agreed. "But, what does that do for us?"

"For one thing," Bear answered, "it gives us a place of relative safety. We can use it as a base of operations. There's another tunnel we haven't checked out yet and I wanna check it out today."

"I'll go with you," Keith said.

"I'd rather you stay here," Bear said. "I'd like Hal to come with me. While we're gone, you and the others should keep watch in the tunnel and near the outside of the cave."

We'll do it," Keith said. "Do you know how long this might take?"

"I've got no idea," Bear said. "But if it goes where I think it does, it's worth the time."

"You think it goes to Weniki's village don't you?" Hal said.

"It might," he answered. "If it does, we've got a great advantage."

Hal nodded in agreement. Using the tunnels shortened a trip to the Nāki village by three hours. If there was one to the other, it might do the same thing.

Hal and Bear gathered supplies in packs. "We might be gone over night," Bear said to Keith. It just depends on how far it is and the number of holes in the floor."

"You two take care," Keith said. "I'll let everyone else know what you're doing. If you're not back by the morning after tomorrow, we'll come looking for you. Be sure and mark the holes in the floor so we don't fall in." He shook hands with both men as they left and sat down with a cup of coffee.

CHAPTER THIRTY-THREE

Bear and Hal carefully made their way to the tunnel and proceeded to the point where Bear previously turned back. From there they proceeded slowly, using sticks to probe for holes.

"Oh, by the way," Bear said stopping to get Hal's attention. "If we find more holes, don't stand near them. We saw a tentacle come out of one yesterday. It seems that some of the inhabitants will reach out and try to touch others."

"Cute," Hal said. "I'll bet the yellow pages never saw anything like these things." He chuckled shaking his head, "In fact I'll bet no one from our time and place has ever seen anything like any the creatures and people here."

"No bet," Bear said and continued along the tunnel. Hal followed him; the last conversation was sobering and caused both men to remember where they were, and the dangers surrounding them. They were living a true nightmare if ever there was one.

Bear moved slowly forward, probing the ground with a stick. Searching the tunnel was time consuming and nerve wracking. At any time, they could fall through a hole or as Bear found out yesterday, possibly have something reach out and drag them in.

Twenty minutes later Bear found a hole in the floor. They anchored a strip of cloth near the edge and after finding the edge, circled it and placed another piece of cloth on the other side. Within fifty yards, they found two more empty rooms. Finding no other doorways in the rooms, they marked them and moved forward.

369

It took another two hours to reach the end of the tunnel. As with all the others, it ended in a false wall. "Do you remember any ledges or anything like that on the valley walls?" Hal asked.

"Nothing I can remember," Bear said. "I've been thinking about it, trying to picture it in my mind and I can't remember a thing."

"We'd better take care," Hal advised. "We don't want to stick a head where someone could chop it off."

"I don't worry so much about yours, it ain't that good looking," Bear said. "But I'm kinda partial to keeping mine."

Hal grinned, "Asshole," he said stuck his head through the wall and looked around. Like the others, the cave extended another fifteen or twenty feet. He reached forward with his stick and probed the ground, it was safe. Moving forward, he checked the floor to the edge of the cave.

When Bear came through, he checked the walls for doorways and found none. They were at least a hundred feet above the valley floor. As they suspected, Weniki's village lay below.

People in the village were going about their daily routines, everything there appeared normal. In a clearing to their right, a number of men and women practiced with weapons.

Some of the weapons appeared to be long staves, the last six inches of each end was about twice the size of the rest of the weapon. As Bear scanned the training area, he saw other people using the same weapon on practice dummies. However, their weapons glowed blue at the ends. When the ends came in contact with something else, sparks flew with the sound of a small explosion like a large firecracker.

Bear looked at Hal, "Never expected that," he said.

"Look behind that large hut over there," Hal pointed to a structure further to the right.

Other people were spinning slings, similar to the one Palenaka had, over their heads. They threw objects against a rock wall where they exploded like hand grenades.

In a space between the two, people practiced a style of unarmed martial arts. They defended themselves against weapons such as knives, swords and spears as well as hand to hand fighting.

"We've got trouble right here in River City," Hal said, a solemn look on his face.

"We need to go back to the Nāki valley and check it out better," Bear said.

"I agree," Hal said. "Either we're looking at a one-sided massacre or a war none of us are ready for."

"For some reason, I don't think it's one-sided," Bear said and walked back through the false wall.

***

A little over four hours later, Bear and Hal were on the ledge overlooking the Nāki village. Both were extremely wary as they approached the hole where Bear saw the tentacle, but passed without a problem.

With only a couple of hours before sunset, the Nāki village appeared as it did when Bear was there. As Bear watched, Hal searched the ledge for a trail of some sort.

"It looks like a trail runs across the cliff about ten feet below this ledge," Hal said when he came back.

"Maybe we can use it to scout the village," Bear suggested.

"Possibly," Hal said. "But with all the false things we've seen, I'm not sure I wanna jump down on something that might not really be there."

Bear hadn't thought of that. "That might be a rude awakening," he said. "Glad you thought of that. It's a long way down." He looked at the valley below.

They heard voices from somewhere to the left. Both men quietly moved back into the mouth of the cave as the sound moved closer. Two men walked along the path below. They passed under the ledge and continued around a bend.

Bear and Hal moved back into the bushes on the ledge. "I guess that means the path is real," Hal said.

"It's real," Bear agreed. "I still have a problem using it though."

"I know," Hal said. "I'd hate to meet those guys on it. Not only that, but if we drop down there, how do we get back up here?"

"That's a good question," Bear said. "We need to find a way to check the village out. Let's look the ledge over again and see if there's some place to lower a rope or something. Maybe there's another doorway or something."

Bear moved to one end as Hal checked the other. A few minutes later, Hal hurried up to him. "I think I've found something," he said excitement edging his voice.

Bear followed him to the other end of the ledge. "Look at the face of the cliff from the edge down to the path," he said.

Bear peeked over the edge and saw hand and foot holds carved in the face. Someone had chiseled them out to give access to the cave.

"We can use those?" Bear said.

"It doesn't change the fact that we have a problem if we meet someone on the path," Hal reminded him.

"I think we need to take the chance," Bear said.

"I'm willing," Hal said. "I don't like the idea of having to fight in the first place. In the second, I don't like the idea of it happening on such a small path and so high up, but lead on McDuff."

More voices came from where the others disappeared. "Go to the other end and stay behind the bushes," Bear said softly. "See if they continue on."

Hal quietly moved to the other end of the ledge and crouched behind the bushes there. The men passed beneath Bear's location and shortly emerged below Hal. They continued along the path until rounding a bend a few yards away. A couple of seconds later, Bear appeared on the ledge below.

Looking up at Hal, his voice barely above a whisper, he said, "I'll be right back."

He quickly went to the bend in the path and carefully looked around it. The guards, clad as the rest he'd seen, continued along the path in the distance. *Must have been a changing of the guard,* he thought. *We'll probably be safe for a while.* He returned to the ledge where he found Hal waiting on the path.

"They're probably replacements for the others," Hal said.

"Exactly what I was thinking," Bear agreed. "Let's see where the path goes and what we can find out."

The path wound along the face of the cliff and they were able to hide behind bushes in most places. In a few others, they had to crouch low to remain out of sight.

A short time later, they found an area where the Nāki practiced with weapons of their own. Even though the weapons were different, they practiced the same as their counterparts in the other valley.

The swords and spear-tips glowed red and resulted in the same shower of sparks when they struck something or someone else. In addition, they had catapults used to launch glowing objects that exploded on contact.

"Dragons that breathe fire," Bear observed.

"Could be," Hal agreed.

Below, they heard commands issued. However, because of the distance, they couldn't understand them.

"Let's get back," Bear said moving back toward the ledge.

Upon reaching it, Bear found that he was alone. Hal was nowhere in sight. He waited ten minutes and was about to start back when Hal rounded the outcrop of rocks.

"I was starting to worry," Bear said.

Ignoring the statement, Hal said, "They're planning to attack the day after tomorrow."

"You went forward a little further along the path," Bear guessed.

"I wanted to see if I could hear what they were saying," he explained. "They're doing what they call a final test before fighting the other village. It looks like both sides are evenly matched."

"Let's get back to the cave," Bear said. "We don't need to be caught before we can tell the others what we know."

***

Three hours later, they met Keith near the storeroom who told them Spyder was at the mouth of the cave. As Hal entered the room, Bear went to get Spyder and bring him back.

When he entered the chamber with Spyder, Bear said, "We won't be needing guards. Neither of the villages seems to have scouts out."

"They're too busy getting ready for war," Hal said. "This is some serious shit folks."

"There's no reason for us to get involved is there?" Sandy asked.

"Can't we just stay here, in this cave, outta the way?" Amanda added.

"I think they're both right," Hal agreed. "It's not our fight."

"I've got no problem with that," Bear said. "But, we have to be ready in case any of them come inside."

"What do we do then?" Amanda asked. "Do we just let them in, or do we defend ourselves?"

"That's a good question," Bear said, "and I don't have an answer. I don't know."

"Why don't we put a sign up and warn that anyone coming in will be killed?" Ginny asked.

"Don't be ridiculous," Wind said. "That would only tell them where we are."

"It's not as ridiculous as it sounds," Bear corrected. "It would tell them where we are, but, at the same time, would give fair warning to both sides that we don't want to be involved."

"It's not a bad idea," Spyder agreed. "But, I'm not sure they need to know where we are. There seems to be rules to their war and we don't know what all of 'em are. The other thing is that I'm not sure we should bottle ourselves up in this cave."

"We wouldn't be bottled up," Hal explained. "We can go a number of places in the tunnels."

"If neither of them use the tunnel that is," Bear said. "If they do, we're in trouble."

"What if we simply go back to where we arrived in this time and place?" Sandy asked. "There wouldn't be any reason for them to follow us and we'd be outta the way."

"That's where Weniki thinks we are now," Keith reminded them. "We told her we were going back to get supplies."

"He's right," Amanda agreed.

"They know we're not there," Ginny said.

"How could they know that?" Hal asked.

Ginny looked at the others and her face sagged.

"Weniki's been in contact with you hasn't she?" Bear said.

Ginny was quiet for a moment. She wasn't sure how to tell them what happened. "Weniki has contacted me three times since we came here." She paused and quickly added, "Not since the attack by

376

the Nāki." She looked at the floor and tears filled her eyes. "I can't control when she contacts me. I don't tell her anything, but I can't stop her from getting in my head."

"She's a goddamn spy," Keith said stepping toward her.

"Hang on," Bear said stepping between them and putting his hand on Keith's chest.

"Fuck you," Keith said slapping the hand away and took another quick step forward.

Bear turned and slammed his palm into the young man's chest knocking him backward off his feet onto his back. "I said hang on," Bear repeated.

Keith started to get up angrily. "Don't," Bear warned pointing at him. "Not unless you wanna wind up there again."

Keith stopped, still kneeling on one knee. There was no way he would force Bear's hand. He took a couple of deep breaths and forced himself to calm down.

Turning back to the others, Bear said, "She said she couldn't control when Weniki contacted her. She may not be the only one. Weniki shared with all of us, what's to say she didn't set all of us up the same way?"

"What do you mean?" Amanda asked.

"While we were sharing, she might've planted something making us receptive to suggestions from her or Palenaka," Bear suggested.

"If that's true, we can't go anywhere, outside this cave, without them knowing where we are," Sandy said.

"It was not Weniki that contacted you," a voice from the storeroom door said. Bear spun and saw

Palenaka standing in the doorway. Everyone jumped to their feet as she said, "It was me."

"What the hell are you doing here?" Wind asked.

"I mean you no harm," she said stepping further into the room. "I am here in spite of Lopaka's order to prepare for battle."

"We know your people are getting ready for a war," Hal said.

"I saw you and Bear on the path above the village," Palenaka said. "I knew then that I must come to warn you."

"Warn us of what?" Bear asked. "We already know your people are going to fight the Nāki."

"Lopaka has ordered Weniki to take you as captives so you cannot help the Nāki. He no longer trusts you."

"What about Weniki, does she trust us?" Bear asked.

"It does not matter," Palenaka said. "She will do as Lopaka says -- he is our leader."

"Why are you going against your leader's orders?" Bear asked.

Palenaka looked at Wind, her gaze lingered for an instant and then she looked at the others. "I do not agree that you should be involved, even if it is only as captives. You would not be harmed; however it is not your fight."

"If we wouldn't be harmed, then why do you think it's wrong?" Amanda asked.

"I do not think this war should take place," she said. "I cannot explain it now. I must leave here."

"What do you suggest we do?" Sandy pushed for another answer.

"I cannot stay in this place any longer," she said. "I must stay beyond the vision except for short times." Palenaka turned and walked out of the room.

The rest followed her into the front of the cave past the false wall. Palenaka stood waiting for them and the rest took seats around the room.

"There are things about us that you do not know," Palenaka said. "We are not as we seem."

"We know about the requirement of the war," Bear said. "Your worlds settle disputes through wars fought here."

"That is true," Palenaka said. "However, that war is over. There is no reason to fight now other than the remaining Nāki and Alaea are enemies."

"You mean the ones that remain here?" Spyder asked.

"Those of us here are the only remaining people from our worlds," she said. "Both our worlds were destroyed when our sun exploded. We were left here because no people of warring nations may go to another world until the war is ended."

"So if there's no reason for the Nāki and Alaea to kill each other," Wind said, "Then why do they still want to fight?"

"It is because Aka and Lopaka have the same father," Palenaka explained. "When they chose their warriors, they took those that supported them."

"Hatfield and McCoy's," Sandy said, "and we're caught in the middle."

"There's nothing we can do to help that situation," Bear said. "It's outta our hands." He looked at Palenaka, "What do we do?"

"You must stay hidden," Palenaka said. "If you are found, you will be taken."

"There's no way for us to leave without Weniki finding us," Hal said. "If we stay here, she'll find us here."

"What if we go deeper in the cave?" Sandy asked.

"You will be removed from the cave by a Kōtha," Palenaka said, "or you will die by it."

"What the hell's a Kōtha?" Amanda asked.

"It is a creature, created by thoughts, which lives only as long as its creator wishes it to live. You experienced one before."

"When?" Hal asked.

"You were all threatened by a large creature. A creature that remained unseen by any of you. You saw only a shadow, the movement of trees and large footprints in the ground. You heard its scream as it approached."

"The first time we heard it, you and Weniki were gone," Hal said. "The second was when we found Bear, Spyder and Wind."

"That is correct."

"Then we were being herded where Weniki wanted us," Hal surmised.

"Herded?" Palenaka asked.

"Forced to go where she wanted us to go," Hal described what he meant.

"That is correct," Palenaka said.

"Then that thing chasing us wasn't real," Keith said.

"It was real," she corrected. "But it does not live now."

"If we stayed in the cave, this Kōtha would force us out," Bear brought the subject back to their present situation.

"It would."

"... and if we didn't come out, it would kill us."

"It would," Palenaka confirmed.

"Then what do we do?"

"You allow me to hide you," Palenaka said.

"Where?" Hal asked. "Where could we hide and not be found?"

"At the beach," Palenaka said. "There are rocks extending into the water not far from this place. You may hide on those."

"That'd put us out in the open," Spyder said.

"In the open, but if we take weapons, they can only attack from one direction," Hal said.

"I will try to cloak you as well," Palenaka said. "However, I cannot assure you that I will be successful."

"I think it's worth a try," Wind said.

Palenaka looked at Ginny. "You will be the most difficult to hide. Weniki has left traces in your mind. Through these, she can talk to you. I will try to prevent her, but may not be able to."

"What about you?" Wind asked. "Will you be coming with us?"

"If it is acceptable to you I will," she said. "Otherwise, I will hide on the mountain."

"You're not going back to the village and your people?" Bear asked.

"I cannot," she said. "I have made a choice to warn you. The Alaea would kill me if I return or they find me. I have broken the laws of my people."

"When do the Alaea plan to leave their valley?" Hal asked.

"Tomorrow after the sun rises," Palenaka said.

"When will they get here?"

"Just after midday," she said.

"Then we need to be on the rocks by then," Spyder said, "and you're coming with us li'l lady."

"I thank you for allowing this," Palenaka said.

"What are your feelings about being against your mother?" Keith asked.

Palenaka looked down a moment and then looked at him, "She is not my mother. She Lopaka's sister. Before leaving our world, she received the powers you know of. She can also create the Kōtha as well as move objects with her mind. Some of those powers she gave to me. I can also control animals."

"What about the Nāki?" Bear asked. "Do any of them have powers like you?"

"Only that, for them to die, they must be killed twice, or have their head removed," she answered.

"Damn, they're serious," Spyder said surprised. "That makes things more difficult."

"If we're gonna make a move tomorrow morning, we're going to have to get things together tonight," Amanda said. "We'll need food, clothes and fresh water to take with us."

"I can't go back in there," Palenaka said.

"I'll stay out here with you," Wind said. "I can get my things tomorrow morning."

"Let us know if there's a problem," Hal said as they walked back past the barrier.

CHAPTER THIRTY-FOUR

Hal and Spyder made a trip to the room where they had previously found the roman style clothing. From there, they took eight swords, one for each of them. Spyder wanted something to cut the Nāki's heads off if needed. He didn't like the idea of having to kill them twice.

"In fact, there're a lot of things I don't like about this," he said.

"While we're here," he said bending over to close one of the two bags they had the swords in. "How do we know we can trust Palenaka to really be on our side?"

"We don't know it for a fact," Hal said. "But I'd rather trust her, especially if she's right about that thing Weniki can create. I don't need to be in here with that thing. Just call me a coward."

"Coward," Spyder said picking up one of the bags.

When he turned around, Hal was holding a sword toward his chest. "Shit, you told me to say it," he said.

"You know what I could do with this?" Hal asked.

"Walk back to the storeroom with it up your ass?" Spyder guessed.

Both men laughed as Hal dropped the sword, picked up the other bag and they both left to re-join their friends. Stress was building throughout the group with the possibility of being involved in a war. None of them could find a reason to fight. Not even Spyder who the Nāki had earlier held captive.

By ten o'clock, everyone was ready to go. Palenaka led them out of the cave toward the water to the east. She made them pick their way carefully and show no sign of their passing.

As Bear and Spyder left the cave, they rigged one of the claymore mines from the weapons stashed deep in the cavern. There was no way they wanted anyone to find the other weapons to use against them. At the same time, they didn't want to destroy those weapons if they didn't have to.

Once at the beach, Palenaka used a palm frond to erase their tracks on the soft sand. From there, they headed north and proceeded just inside the water's edge. That way, the water would erase the evidence of their passage.

She's good at deception, Bear thought. *If she continues to help us, we've got one hell of an allay.*

Almost instantly, a thought flashed through his mind as if he heard a voice. *I will be true.* He knew it was either Palenaka or Weniki. *It is Palenaka,* the voice said.

He looked at her and she nodded to him. *Yes it is me,"* it repeated. *Do we have a chance?* He asked. *I am not sure,* it said. *I can promise nothing.*

Ahead, a large pile of lava rocks extended into the water. The rocks were fifty feet wide at the base angling upward to about ten feet at the top and at least two hundred feet long.

"We will use those rocks," Palenaka said pointing at the rocks jutting into the ocean.

"There's nothing wrong with those," Hal said. "We can probably hide near the back outta sight."

"Doing that, and with Palenaka's help, they may never see us," Spyder said. "Hell, I may just move there."

"There may be ants Spyder," Bear said.

"Kiss my ass Bear," he growled back.

The ocean lapped the beach and around the end of the rocks closest to the sand. The water they crossed to get to the rocks was about six inches deep and ten feet wide.

All of the previous members of the gunfighter's group wore western clothes. They carried black powder pistols, 9mms and M16s. The rest carried everything but the black powder weapons. Spyder had insisted on the replicas 'just in case'.

They laid out their weapons and provisions on top of the rocks. For food, they had MREs, fruits and vegetables since a fire would give them away. They were prepared to stay hidden three or four days if needed.

"I will try to keep us hidden," Palenaka said. "If I am to do this, no one may leave this place."

"That's not a problem," Keith said. "We're set to stay here a while.

"Weniki and her people are getting closer," Ginny said. "I got a flash of something in my mind."

"They are less than one of your hours away," Palenaka said. "They are searching for you."

Gray clouds gathered in the sky over the mountains and moved slowly toward the shore. "If those keep coming, it'll help hide us," Sandy said to Palenaka.

"I hope that is true," she replied.

"Are you doing that?" Sandy questioned.

"I can only make the air heavy," Palenaka said. "I cannot control the weather if that is what you are asking."

"I don't understand," Sandy said. "But, thanks for what you're doing."

"We must remain low on the rocks, in hiding," Palenaka said to Bear. "We must also remain silent."

"Listen up folks," Bear called to the others. "From now on, Palenaka says we have to stay low on the rocks and keep as quiet as possible."

"We're in the open, on a pile of rocks, waiting to watch two different groups of people go to war," Sandy observed. "This just ain't right."

***

Weniki and Lopaka led their people through the thick underbrush. They were in a line over a hundred yards wide and two hundred yards deep. As they approached the area of the cave Palenaka and her group had departed only a few hours ago, Lopaka called to Kini.

"Take ten warriors and search the wahi kapu," he ordered "If Palenaka and the haoles are there, return and we will remove them."

Kini bowed his head and went to gather his men. With fifteen other men, he moved into a close position to the cave. They circled the entrance and in unison moved forward. No one could escape the net they formed. About ten yards from the front of the cave, they stopped. "Palenaka," Kini shouted her name. "If you are here, you must come out."

There was no sound from the opening. "Palenaka," he called again, "we mean you no harm. You and your friends may go in peace. This is not their fight."

Still no sound came from the cave. On Kini's command, the men moved toward the center of the opening. About five yards from it, one of the men triggered the trip wire on the claymore mine.

The majority of the group stood in the kill zone of the blast. A deafening roar echoed through the area as the blast threw dirt, leaves and branches into the air to join the flying shrapnel. Only three of the group survived the deadly debris and they frantically retreated to Lopaka and Weniki.

After receiving their report Lopaka said, "Palenaka as well as the haoles must die. They have chosen to fight against us and killed our people. We must not allow this to go unpunished."

Weniki felt a twinge of sorrow for Palenaka. She was a good student and friend. *I will miss her,* Weniki thought and as quickly as the feeling came, she dismissed it. Palenaka was now her enemy.

A light rain began falling on the army of Polynesians as they continued through the thick forest. "The rain is her doing," Weniki said to Lopaka. "She does not want us to see where they are.

"Can you stop it?" He asked.

"I cannot," she answered. "Palenaka has assisted nature to bring the rain. It should not last long."

"Where do you think they are?" Lopaka asked.

"I do not know," Weniki admitted. "However, they have not traveled far. We must widen our line.

We can reach from mauka to makai. They must not be allowed to escape."

On Lopaka's order, the line stretched from the mountains to the ocean. None of the warriors attempted to hide their presence. They advanced noisily through the brush, driving all living creatures before them.

***

Bear heard the claymore as it delivered its deadly cargo. "They found our gift," he said to Spyder.

"That's one way to start a party off with a bang," he returned. Both men knew to keep the gallows humor between them.

Hal crawled up beside Bear and Spyder. "There's no turning back," he said. "We're their enemy now." A look of understanding and commitment passed between the three men.

The group slipped in together near the back of the rock island. Bear looked at each of them slowly. "We may be able to stay hidden for today," he said. "But if they stay near here tonight, we may have a problem. Actually, we want them to keep going."

"They will not," Palenaka interrupted. "They will stay near wahi kapu this night."

Bear thought about what she said. She knew the people better than he did, so there was no need to question her judgment. "Do what you have to do," he said, "to get yourselves in the mind to kill people. We all know it's not easy. We won't unless we have to, but you have to be ready just in case -- tonight'll be a long one."

In less than an hour, they saw animals running from left to right. Boars, rabbits and other animals fled before an advancing line of people.

"They're trying to find us by using tactics the early Mongols used for hunting and fighting," Bear said lying on the rocks between Hal and Spyder. "They form a line and drive every living thing in front of 'em. If we were there, they'd eventually find us."

The line of Alaea stopped just before passing the rocks in the water. It took them an hour to set up camp and post guards. Sentries walked along the water's edge while others could occasionally be seen entering and leaving the forest. There had to be more hidden from view. This was war and the Alaea would take no chances of being surprised.

When the sun set over the mountains, the air over the water turned cold. "Everyone needs to wrap in a blanket," Amanda said. "It's gonna feel colder than it really is, the humidity will see to that."

"I'm gonna check the area out," Bear said. "We need to know what's going on."

"You can't," Spyder said. "They might catch you."

"I can get in there and back without being seen," Bear argued.

"They do not have to see you," Palenaka said. "Weniki will feel you if you leave these rocks. Of that, I am sure."

Bear thought about what she said. *She's probably right. Weniki might've left some sort of thought when we shared like she did with Ginny. If I go, I'll probably have to fight and give this location away.*

"You're right," he said. "I just don't like being without recon info."

Amanda was right, the night was very cold -- and long.

***

As the sun rose over the ocean in the east, the Alaea broke camp and moved slowly to the north. The band of outsiders watched the army's movement from the relative safety of their rock island.

"If we give 'em a little time and space, we can go south, away from the fighting," Hal said. "Let them have their war. Maybe we can find the doorway back to our time."

"There are no doorways to the south," Palenaka said.

"That's where we were brought through to this place," Spyder reminded her.

"You did not come here through a doorway, as you call them," she said. "Weniki created a ripple and brought you here as she did others."

"We saw evidence of the others," Hal said. "What happened to 'em?"

"None of them accepted where they were and what had happened," she explained. "Every group was soldiers and warriors from different places and other times. They would not accept being here and fought everyone not of their kind."

"They were all killed," Bear interpreted.

390

"That is correct," she said softly, lowering her head.

"Aka said there were doorways to the north," Bear said. "Do you know if that's true?"

"There are many doorways to the north," Palenaka confirmed. "All are in caves like the one we slept in the night before."

"How big is this island?" Sandy asked. With all the mountains, there could be thousands or millions of caves.

"This is not a true island," Palenaka said. "Before coming here, I saw maps of this world. This land joins what, in your language, is a continent. I think its name was Floder before the world ceased to support life. It matters little now. This world is not as it was before."

"Floder?" Keith asked.

"Florida," Sandy said. "I'll bet this was Florida."

"That makes sense, if this was North America," Bear said.

"How can we possibly find the right cave, much less the right doorway back to our time?" Sandy asked. "There must be millions."

"There are many thousands," Palenaka confirmed. "Since you look for a place previously of this world, you must go to that place. There you will find many passages to many worlds and times. You must find the correct one and the secret to use it."

"Why can't we just use one of these and travel to our home after that?" Amanda asked.

"You came from a certain place and time," Palenaka explained. "You may only go back through the passage to that time and place. No other will take you to your time *and* place."

"Ain't that a helluva note?" Spyder said. "We gotta go fifteen hundred miles, find the right cave, then the right doorway so we can get home. That sucks."

Bear sat quietly listening to the conversation. He cleared his throat, "If that's true, we gotta get away from this war first. After that we have a long walk ahead of us."

"I've got a question," Wind said. "Why don't we make a boat and sail from here to as close to where Texas was rather than walking around the Gulf of Mexico?"

"That's a good idea," Keith said. It could cut months off the trip. All we have to do is cross these mountains to the gulf."

"This gulf you speak of is not safe," Palenaka said. "Creatures which live there will prevent you from making the journey. Also, there are man-animals which live on the water. If you escape the sea creatures, the man-animals will kill you."

"Okay, sailing is out of the question," Bear said. "Now back to the present. We need to get outta here and around the Alaea and Nāki. How are we gonna do that?"

"I do not have an answer," Palenaka said apologetically. "However, I will help you any way I can."

"We believe you," Wind said, "and we thank you for your willingness."

Palenaka nodded her acceptance of his statement.

"When the men on the shore go north, we'll go south," Bear said. "We'll go around the south end and up the other side of the peninsula and avoid having to fight. Does anyone object or have a better idea?"

They all remained silent.

***

Four hours later, men returned from the north. They rounded up the remainder of the back guards and headed north where the Alaea had disappeared.

Hal reached over and shook Bear's shoulder to awake him. "They're leaving," he said.

Bear sat up and rubbed the sleep from his eyes.

"It's time to go folks," Spyder said.

"Did they all leave?" Bear asked.

"I think so," Spyder answered. "There were a helluva lot more than we could see."

"Let's get outta here," Bear said.

Ten minutes later the entire group had gathered their supplies and gone to the beach. From there, they entered the forest and moved southward. Wind traveled ahead of them as a point man to insure they didn't walk into a trap.

Less than an hour into their trip, Wind returned, running toward them. As he ran up, he said, "There's another force of the Alaea coming this way. They're doing the same as the other and there's no way around 'em."

"Goddamn it," Spyder spat the words as he spoke. "Can't we catch any breaks?"

"We must return the way we have come," Palenaka said. "There is no place to hide. We will not have time to climb the rocks again."

"So we stay ahead of 'em until they drive us into the other force," Hal voiced what everyone else thought.

"We do for now," Bear said, "until we figure something else out. Let's get moving."

They headed northward moving quickly but quietly. "Angle toward the mountains," Bear said. "We need to be near high ground in case we run into the other force."

Before long, they skirted the base of the mountains and came up on the cave and the bodies of the men killed by the claymore mine.

"Why don't we just get in the cave?" Amanda asked. "They'll never expect us there."

Almost as an answer to her question, a low growl filled the cavern.

"I don't think so," Sandy said backing away from the entrance.

"We keep going," Hal said and started moving.

"We must stay together, if I am to cover us," Palenaka reminded them. "We must not be felt by Weniki."

With never more than three feet between them, they continued along the base of the mountain range. They could hear the noise of the following force as they unknowingly followed behind. The second force was no more than a couple hundred yards behind, driving them into the first, wherever it had camped for the night.

The people behind them seemed to be gaining. The warriors didn't have to stay in a group and worry about being felt while they moved. As the sun dipped behind the mountain peaks, they seemed to put distance between themselves and the army following them.

"We keep going," Bear said. "We need as much space between them and us as we can get."

Even as the shadows and distance grew, the noise from the army seemed to stay with them. "They don't seem to care about being heard by either us or the Nāki," Hal observed.

"Something's wrong," Bear said. "Is Weniki anywhere around?" He looked at Palenaka.

"She is nearby," she said. "I cannot tell where without Weniki feeling us."

"Let's keep going for a while," Bear suggested.

"Lead the way," Spyder said motioning forward.

A few hundred yards along, Ginny grabbed her head and stumbled. "Oh my God," she said and fell to the ground.

Spyder knelt beside her, "What's wrong? Are you okay?"

"She's trying to contact me," Ginny said holding her head.

A few seconds later, she looked around puzzled. "It's gone," she said. "The pain's gone."

"Weniki has found us," Palenaka said. "I am sorry, but I could not stop her."

"Don't worry about it," Bear said. "I'm sure you did your best. We need to get to high ground to make it harder for them to take us."

"There is a valley ahead where we can hide," Palenaka said.

"Lead the way," Bear stepped aside and motioned for her to pass.

Less than five minutes later, men broke into song in front of them. Palenaka stopped, "The Nāki are between us and the valley," she said.

"We're trapped between the armies," Bear said.

"Talk about being between a rock and a hard spot," Sandy said shaking her head.

Bear looked up at the mountain beside him. "We check the slope of the mountain for ledges and other places to fight from," he said. "We can't give up. None of us is safe; all of us are enemies of both sides. They may take us, but it won't be without a fight or a high price for them. We check the slopes and meet back here in two hours. Stay away from both camps."

CHAPTER THIRTY-FIVE

The outsiders sat in a circle. Palenaka had assured them that a fire would bring no danger. "This is the night before the battle," she said. "Both sides will perform ceremonies. No attack will take place until the sun rises above the horizon. At that time, a warrior from each side will meet in the clearing below. They will do battle. By custom, the winner will not fight in the war. He or she will be the messenger to tell the rulers of the outcome. Even though this is not a battle for worlds, both sides will honor the custom. The war will end only when all are dead on one side."

Bear nodded contemplating her statement. *This is a battle to the last man, woman and child,* he thought. "How many rounds of ammo do we have?" He asked no one in particular.

"I'm only guessing," Hal said, "but probably two thousand for the M16s and a thousand for the 9mms. I don't know about the black powder weapons."

"That'll be enough if we let them kill each other before we have to engage 'em," Bear guessed.

"Don't forget these," Spyder dropped the bag with the swords they took from the cave room. "There are eight swords in that. If we have to take the heads of the Nāki to kill them the first time, we'll need those."

Palenaka looked at the weapons in the bag. "Do not clash those with the glowing weapons, it will do no good."

"Figures," Spyder said. "They're useless as hell."

"Not so," Palenaka corrected. "They do not work against the weapons, but do work against the people."

"What about those glowing things your people use in their slings?" Hal asked. "Can we throw them with your hands?"

Palenaka reached into a pouch hanging from her belt. "If you mean these," she said producing a round object the size of a golf ball, "the answer is yes." The object was black with a red dot. "After you push the red area, you must rid yourself of the dart. If you do not, it will explode if dropped or shaken."

"If you kill or find one of the Alaea dead, and they have a pouch of these, take 'em," Bear instructed. He looked at Palenaka, "Sorry, it's nothing against your people in particular. But, now that we know how to use 'em, they'll come in handy if we can get our hands on 'em."

"The glowing weapons will do you no good if you do not have the belt the person carrying the weapon wears," Palenaka explained. "The belt and the weapon must be together to make the energy."

"Everyone got that?" Spyder asked. "If you run outta ammo, those could save your life."

"I hope none of them ever get that close," Bear said. "But if they do, using the enemy's weapons has turned the tide of many battles." He looked at the rest of the group, "You're gonna need all the sleep you can get tonight. I know it'll be hard, but all of you must rest."

"I will assist you in this rest, if you will allow," Palenaka said.

"What do you mean?" Bear asked. "Won't you need rest too?"

"I will be fine with a short meditation," she said. "I can, however, assist you in your needs, if you are willing to trust me in this matter."

Bear looked at Wind, "If Wind trusts you, that's good enough for me. I have no reason not to right now."

Wind smiled in appreciation.

"So there's a way for you to help us relax?" Bear questioned.

"There is," Palenaka answered. "It is a simple matter."

"It may be simple," Sandy said, "But I'm gonna need all the help I can get."

Everyone voiced their agreement.

As each finished eating, Palenaka assisted them in sleeping. The exercise took only a couple of minutes before she moved on to the next.

Bear was last. "Wake me before the sun rises," he said. "We need time to prepare."

She nodded and placed her hands on both of his temples.

***

Bear awoke to Palenaka shaking his shoulder. As he sat up, he was surprised at how well he felt. "Thank you for your help in sleeping last night," he said. "It worked."

"I am pleased to have been of assistance," she said smiling.

"We need to wake the rest," he said and rose to his feet. As he turned toward the sleeping group, he

399

saw Weniki standing on the other side of the embers of the fire. She stood with a man dressed in Polynesian attire, his face partially painted with black and carrying a spear.

"Everybody up," Bear yelled as, in a flash, his pistol was out of its holster, cocked and pointed at Weniki.

She held up her hands, palms forward. "I mean you no harm," she said.

The others, jerked awake by his warning, scrambled to their feet. In a couple of seconds, they all stood, pointing weapons at Weniki and her companion.

Thoughts and feelings flooded Bear. He remembered Weniki relieving him of the burden of a lifetime of emotional pain and sorrow. He could feel her soft touch and the warmth of her essence as he and Weniki bonded in the water beneath the falls.

The feelings turned to ice and chilled his soul as he realized she only used him toward her own end. She had no feelings for him other than what he could do to help her defeat the Nāki. A feeling of rage grew inside.

"What do you want?" he asked, controlled anger in his voice.

"I am here to offer you the opportunity to join in the ku'ia-lua," Weniki said.

"That is the single combat before the war," Palenaka said.

"So you are offering one of us the opportunity to participate in the ku'ia-lua," Bear said. "If we did that, we would be one person less, win or lose."

"Hell no lady," Spyder said. "Are you outta your fucking mind? We stay together."

"What stops us from killing you where you stand?" Keith asked.

"This is a matter of custom," Weniki said.

"Yours not ours," Keith said.

Weniki's companion stepped forward and every gun shifted toward him. "I'll kill you where you stand and laugh when you fall," Keith growled.

Weniki placed a hand across his chest. "We come in peace and you threaten us. I do not understand this."

"That's probably because we've been drawn into a war we have no part in," Hal said.

"You entered the war when you attacked our people as they defended Ginny," Weniki said.

"We didn't attack anyone," Bear argued. "Two people came at us with weapons and we defended ourselves."

"Our hunters said that they found Ginny walking in the woods and while talking to her four Nāki approached," Weniki said. "The hunters told me that Ginny said she was in the same danger as her husband from the Nāki. She then told them to kill the Nāki. During the battle, you killed one of my hunters and a Nāki. We will not simply stand by and allow this to go unpunished."

"That's not how Ginny said it happened," Bear argued.

"I am sure," Weniki said. "But, that is the way it was." She gazed at Bear with a stern expression. "Do you wish to join the ku'ia-lua?"

"Nope," Bear said. "If I have to kill, I want kill a lot rather than just two." He looked at the others,

401

then back at Weniki. "It's time for you and your pet to leave now."

Weniki looked at Bear trying to assess his intention and resolve.

Bear raised his pistol, pointing it toward the companion. "Do you leave now or does he die?"

There was no doubt that the man meant what he said. She turned and walked off, her companion following close behind.

Bear looked at Ginny, "We'll talk about this later."

"There's nothing to talk about," she said defiantly.

"Ginny, shut up," Spyder said harshly, "or I'll shoot you myself. We've got enough trouble, we don't need you adding to it or brooding over the past."

"It won't be long now," Bear said. "We need to get to our positions. Before you do, you have to listen to me." He looked slowly at each member of the group. "I started to tell you on the rocks. We're about to face something none of you have ever had to face before. This is gonna get gruesome. If any of them make it to our locations, you're gonna get bloody. You have to make sure the blood is theirs and not yours." He searched the faces of his friends. They had to understand what they were up against.

"You may have to do things you have never thought of doing. Remember the Nāki have to die twice or have their heads cut off. Anything short of that, and they'll come after you again." He took a deep breath and let it out. He was sure he wasn't getting the gravity of the situation across to everyone. "I love and care about every one of you.

Because of that, I can't overstate how nasty and debilitating the sights and sounds may become. You could see heads ripped from bodies, intestines hanging out and people will be screaming from pain and fear. You have to turn it all off and get mean. It's time to get junkyard dog mean. Nothing matters but your survival and you'll only survive if you lose all concern for people, literally lose your humanity for the duration of the battle. Don't let 'em get close. Kill 'em as far away as you can without missing your shot." Everyone stared straight ahead, the facts seemed to slowly sink in. *Maybe some of them will survive,* he thought.

Taking another deep breath, he said, "Imagine the worst you can think of and understand that will probably not be bad enough. I'm serious." He bent over and picked up a rifle, "Now get to your positions, good luck and I wanna see all of you after this is finished."

CHAPTER THIRTY-SIX

Anger grew inside Bear as he ascended the side of the mountain to his defensive position. *That bitch worked all of us, especially me,* he thought. *She'll pay if it's the last thing I do. If I have to hunt her for years when this is over, I'll kill her.*

Each of the group was in position at about the same level on the mountainside. All positions rested above vertical drops with treacherous approaches on each side. The enemy would have to work, not only to fight, but also to navigate the steep slope at the same time.

Bear laid out his weapons and ammunition. He arranged the clips near the weapons so that he could reload in minimum time with minimum effort. He had intentionally taken the most vulnerable end of the defensive line. He had more experience and felt it gave them their best chance for survival.

From his vantage point, he could see the army of both sides. *These boneheads fight the way the British did against the colonies in the American Revolution. Each side lines up facing the other with a field between 'em, then they move in and fight. I can't imagine advanced civilizations settling disputes like this, much less by this level and style of fighting.*

"We are not as advanced as you think." Bear jumped at the sound of the voice behind him. Palenaka laid a bag on the ground and opened it.

"How the hell did you get here?" He asked looking to make sure they were alone.

"I used my gift," she said.

Bear remembered how she had disappeared from one place and reappeared in another the day he first met her. He nodded and looked at the bag. "Whatcha got there?" He asked.

She reached in and pulled out one of the exploding balls. Bear's face lightened up. "How the hell did you get those?" He hesitated, "Never mind, it doesn't matter. I'm just glad you did."

She put ten on the ground beside him. "I must take the rest to the others," she said.

"I know this has to be hard on you," Bear said. "It's not easy to take a side against your own people."

"There has been too much killing," she said and bowed her head. "It must end."

As he watched, she faded from view and he knew she was on her way to distribute the rest of the bag to the others. He arranged the darts, as she called them, beside the clips of ammunition.

A cheer rose from both sides of the open field below. One man from each army stood apart from their forces. At least a hundred yards separated them as they raised their weapons above their heads and shook them in an obvious display of bravado.

Both men lowered their arms and began walking to the middle of the field. When they stood about twenty feet apart, they stopped. Both men knelt and bowed their heads. After a few seconds, they rose to their feet and, once again, raised their weapons, this time in salute.

Lowering their weapons, they assumed fighting stances and began circling. Cheers erupted from both sides supporting their combatant.

***

The Alaea used a spear, the Nāki a sword and both were expert with their weapon. The hand-to-hand combat was over in only a few of minutes. When the weapons clashed, sparks flew accompanied by the sound of clashing metal and loud pops. The small explosions reminded Spyder of electricity arcing across a 220-volt circuit.

The men slashed, thrust and parried against their opponent with a speed that was almost a blur. In a couple of seconds, showers of sparks engulfed them with a constant pop-pop-pop coming from inside the melee. Abruptly the sound and shower of sparks stopped and the Nāki stepped back. He held his sword in front of him with both hands, its point toward the heavens.

He circled it twice above his head, and sharply brought it down with the point toward the Alaea. A red ball of light flew from its end and struck the Alaea in the center of his chest, blowing the man backward, off his feet to the ground.

A cheer arose from the Nāki as the winner knelt facing the dead man and bowed his head.

Spyder couldn't help but be impressed with the man's actions as he paid tribute to his fallen enemy. *This is one strange place,* he thought. *Not only the place, but the people and the customs as well. They kill someone and then honor the fucker.*

The Nāki rose and faced his people, once again raised his sword above his head and to a roar of cheers walked to the near side of the clearing.

***

Immediately, both sides approached to where only about fifty yards separated them. As if receiving a silent command, a roar erupted from both sides and they attacked.

Everything happened so quickly that Bear was unable to keep up with all the combatants. The middle third or so of each army surged forward at a run while the outer third on each end, ran off the field into the forest.

*"What the hell... "*he thought. He'd never seen anything like this. Both sides formed in ranks facing each other only to have most of them separate and disburse away from the field of battle. *Shit, they're gonna be everywhere.*

A ball of red light flew from the left of the clearing and landed behind the Alaea with a loud explosion followed by another and another.

The clashing armies on the field, was incredible to see. Sparks and smoke rose to the sound equivalent to a dozen machine guns firing at once. Even Bear was surprised at the sight and sounds. Nothing in his military training prepared him for this.

He looked to both sides and could make out vague movements in the thick trees and foliage. Flashes of light marked the positions of warriors and soldiers as they fought.

The sound of an M16 came from a position to his right. "Hold your fire until they're close enough for every shot to count," Bear yelled.

Another shot immediately followed his statement. Ginny was determined to kill as many of the others as she could before they had a chance to get close.

"Stop shooting Ginny," Spyder called to her.

She ignored him and continued firing at the group below.

"Ginny goddamnit," Spyder yelled, "save your ammo."

"Shoot in the middle of the group," she yelled back. "We're bound to hit someone." She fired again.

Ginny knew nothing of hunting or fighting. If she did, she would know what any hunter knows. If you shoot into a flock of birds, even with a shotgun, you'll miss them all unless you're very lucky.

Palenaka appeared beside Bear and dropped more darts. Bear looked from the battle below to her. "Is there any way you can knock that crazy bitch out?"

Palenaka looked at him surprised. "You want me to make her sleep?"

"If you can, I do," he said. "Don't hurt her, but knock her out and give her ammunition to the others."

Palenaka nodded and disappeared, which still amazed him. He intended to ask her if any of the others could sneak up on him in that manner, but she was gone before he could.

After one more shot, the firing ceased and only the sounds of the battle could be heard. The familiar smell of ozone wafted to his location dredging up long forgotten feelings from his past. Feelings he thought he'd left far behind.

A few minutes later, Palenaka reappeared, "She will sleep for a long while."

"Thanks," Bear said. "I didn't expect the armies to go into the forest. How long does a battle like this last?"

"Until the last one is dead," she answered.

"I know you may not know, but how long could that last?" Bear pressed.

"Many days," she said. "The deaths include the ones in the village also."

The answer shouldn't have surprised him, but the implication of future death and destruction astounded him as it sank into his psyche. The understanding that one side or the other would cease to exist -- and he, and the people he loved and cared about, were trapped in between served to drive the enormity of the situation home.

They had to get out of the area, however, fierce fighting raged on both sides as well as on the field before him. Right now, he couldn't see a way to escape. They waited, trapped in their defensive positions. He had unwittingly placed them in positions of no escape.

At the bottom of the mountain, individuals and small groups fought, drawing ever closer to the slope upon which they hid. He could see Spyder and Amanda a short distance away. He knew that Ginny was unconscious somewhere between them and the rest were scattered further along with Hal at the other end.

A single Nāki scrambled up the steep slope toward Spyder's location. To his credit, Spyder let the man continue without alerting either side of his location. There would be plenty of time to shoot the man before he made it to the ledge.

About half way up an explosion erupted at his back, almost tearing him in half. *Alaea darts,* Bear thought. *They're a helluva lot more powerful than I thought.*

Another man began up the slope near the first. Again, about half way up the slope an explosion erupted, this time almost under his feet, took him apart.

A group of both Alaea and Nāki emerged from the forest below in a running battle. None seemed intent on climbing the mountainside with the purpose of attacking the outsiders spaced across the slope above. Their fight simply carried them in that direction as they attempted to gain an advantage over the other.

An explosion a short distance away drew Bear's attention back to his left. Two Alaea were scrambling from the trees below when another dart ripped both of them to pieces. *The Nāki have 'em too.* He thought.

He hadn't seen them in the village before, but it shouldn't surprise him that the weaponry was fairly evenly matched.

As more people emerged from the trees below, the fighters on the clearing broke apart and scattered, entering the trees in different places. *So much for the formal fighting,* he thought. *They're everywhere now.* Three people still stood on each end of the clearing. *The leaders must be directing the fighting from there. I've never seen anything like this.* He surveyed the entire scene closely. *We're in deep shit.* This last thought was more of an understanding of fact than just a possibility. They were outmanned, out gunned and had nowhere to go.

Groups of fighters emerged from the trees at the edge of the clearing. The battle spread, encompassing the entire area below. Smoke permeated the trees obscuring the fighters from view and there were no existing lines of defense.

Palenaka squatted, her arms wrapped around her knees behind him watching.

He turned around, "Palenaka, is there any way you can use your gift to move us from here?"

"There is not," she answered. "I could only take you away one at a time. However, as I said before, the vanishing removes much of my strength."

"Then it would take twice the strength away if you took someone with you," Bear surmised.

"That is not right," she corrected. "If I touch another to include them with me, it takes no more strength than if I was alone."

"How far can you go while invisible?"

"I cannot go beyond the Nāki or the Alaea if that is what you ask."

Bear thought a couple of seconds and then looked up at the mountain.

Palenaka followed his eyes. "Yes," she said seeming to understand the question without him asking it. "The top is within my ability. However, to include the time for me to regain my strength will take most of the daylight time. I did not mention this because, when I take one away, it reduces your ability to protect yourself by one. When you are reduced to one or two, you will be in grave danger."

"I understand the danger," he said, "but if we can save some of us, we need to do it." He hesitated

411

only a second, thought about the order and said, "Take Wind first. Don't give him a choice. Just take him and explain it to him when you get him to the top."

Before Bear could realize what was happening, Palenaka, in a smooth flow of actions removed her sling, placed her knife between her teeth, loaded and spun her sling above her head. About two seconds after she let the dart go, two Nāki died as it hit the ground between them. The men were sneaking up on the position from the side.

Bear looked at where the two men once crawled. *They know where we are,* he thought. When he turned back, Palenaka was gone. He turned back to the fighting. *I hope this works.*

More people spilled from the trees, both on the side closest to him and the other one. The battle seemed to be spreading wider as glowing balls of energy flew through the air. They came from different locations and flew in various directions.

There were valleys on both sides of the mountain. The one to the north went deep into the range through the Nāki village to the large lake beyond. The one to the south was shallow and ended against a ridge where Bear figured the underground tunnel ran.

If we can cross that ridge and get to the other side of the Nāki village, we may have a chance to work our way up the coast of the lake, he thought. *Maybe we can get outta here that way.*

The combatants below were getting closer and he knew they'd soon have to start shooting.

***

Hal looked at the fighting below. *Just a little closer,* he thought, *I don't wanna miss.*

He looked over at Wind to make sure he was still okay. As he watched Palenaka appeared behind him, placed a hand on his shoulder and they both faded from sight. "What the hell... " Hal couldn't believe what he saw. Palenaka was stealing them one by one. He didn't know where she was taking them, but he was sure it wasn't somewhere nice.

He was a little confused. Palenaka did things to get them ready to defend themselves. She'd even brought some of the darts to him an hour or so ago. Why was she now taking people away? *Sure, we're in a tight spot here,* he thought, *but, she's weakening our position when she takes someone away.* A few seconds later, a possible answer fluttered into his mind. *She's found a better place and moving us one by one. Shit, I hope that's it.*

Hal looked back at the men below. They were slowly moving closer as they fought. He would wait until they reached a certain large rock before he started shooting. That way, they would be well within his effective range with the M16.

Looking to his right, he saw two Alaea sneaking up the slope trying to hide behind the sparse bushes there. They were only about fifty yards away. *They're gonna be the first to die,* he thought as he brought the rifle up to his shoulder. He sighted on the closest one and slowly squeezed the trigger. The rifle punched against his shoulder and the man released his weapon as he hit the ground.

413

The other did much the same, as Hal's second bullet slammed into his head just above the left eye and tore the back of his head away as it exited.

He heard shots from the others. *They're gettin' too close,* he thought, *now's the time to get mean.*

As he turned again to the front where the various groups of people fought below, he saw that the gunfire had attracted the attention of a few. The ones not engaged in a fight were looking up trying to identify where the sound came from.

A Nāki threw something at Keith's position and a few seconds later, the ground exploded below him. The man had thrown a dart and missed. As Hal got him in his sights, a rifle fired and the Nāki dropped to the ground.

As long as we can keep them in a cross fire, it gives us an advantage, he thought and looked to his right again. He and Bear had the largest areas to cover and he couldn't afford to forget the space to his right. They were lucky the Alaea and Nāki were more involved with killing each other and didn't center their attention on the outsiders.

***

Keith heard a shot from his right followed shortly by one from his left. Hal and Bear were already taking people out. It was different than it was when they had to defend Rebel's Revenge. He hadn't had time to think about what was happening or going to happen. Now, he was watching two armies tear each other apart.

Before, he was able to dissociate from the violence. Even in the movies, it was different with

414

the deaths and explosions. The hero always took fantastic chances and did seemingly impossible things to win the fight. However, this was real life, people were dying before him and he did not intend to try anything heroic.

he felt sick at his stomach. The violence below was unbelievable. The screams both of fear and of pain were real. He could smell the battle in the very air he breathed. The atmosphere seemed charged with something other than electricity. *It has to be emotions,* then another thought came to him, *or spirits. People are dying here. How can anyone find glory or honor in any of this?*

He could see Amanda about ten yards away. She was hidden behind a rock and staying out of sight. Spyder kept watch around a rock of his own. It would be hard for anyone to get to him short of using one of those dart things. He couldn't see Wind, but with no place to go, he was sure his friend was waiting behind a rock of his own. Besides, Wind wouldn't leave until told to. He was loyal, reliable and took friends seriously.

Keith saw an Alaea crawling directly toward him in a vertical crevice. He knew the others couldn't see the man's approach. *It's up to me,* he thought and placed the man in his sights. As he did, the Alaea looked up and even though fifty yards below, he was sure the man looked directly at him. Keith imagined he could see determination in the man's face.

He has nothing against me personally, he's just doing what he thinks he has to, he thought. *He's a warrior. This is nothing more than a job for him. He'll kill us and never think about it again. We're nothing more than an obstacle.* He tried desperately to justify killing the man below, but nothing he could think of would allow him to take a life casually.

Keith closed his eyes and relaxed his mind, letting his thoughts flow randomly. He allowed his emotions to drift away and forced himself into a thoughtless state. He knew it was the only way he could survive this.

When he opened his eyes, he targeted the man and squeezed the trigger without further thought. The rifle bucked slightly, the man slumped against the mountainside and slid backward, into a deeper part of the crevice and mercifully out of sight.

***

The men below Spyder were almost to a place he'd marked in his mind. Once they were there, he would start shooting. He wanted to give them every chance he could before giving his position away and taking their lives. He didn't like the idea of killing, but if they came closer, he would defend himself and his friends.

A small group reached the mark. They were fighting each other, but Spyder didn't want to get in the habit of making excuses for not shooting. He took aim at one man, but before shooting, an idea came to him.

He turned his aim to two of the Nāki fighting side by side. He shot the two men in rapid succession weakening their side enough for the Alaea to quickly defeat the four remaining Nāki.

Two of the Alaea started up the slope while the rest went back toward the forest.

Spyder waited until the men were near the trees to kill the ones coming toward him. *It worked*, he thought. *I didn't have to use as much ammo.*

He looked over to where Sandy was and saw Palenaka appear beside her. In less than a second, both women faded away. *What the fuck?*

"Bear," he yelled to the other side.

"What?" Bear called back.

"Palenaka just took Sandy away."

"I know," Bear called back. "She's moving us. You'll see why later."

As long as someone knew what was going on, he was satisfied to let things happen. If Bear knew where she was taking people, he must have something in mind. Spyder knew the best thing he could do was keep the area clear of danger. That meant more people had to die. He turned his attention back to the problem at hand.

***

Sandy felt a hand on her shoulder and as she glanced from the battle, the world shimmered around her. The next thing she knew, she was sitting on top of a mountain. She could hear the battle below as she looked at Palenaka.

"What the hell did you do?" She asked her head turned away from the edge of the cliff.

"I will return," Palenaka said and vanished.

"She'll be back," a voice assured her. She turned and Keith stood to her blind side. As she struggled with her confusion he continued, "She and

417

Bear found a way to move us up here. We can travel along that ridge, he pointed along the top of the mountain to their right. Bear and Palenaka think we can reach the lake he saw before and follow it to the north. Maybe we can avoid this bullshit that way."

"But if we're up here, we can't help them out down there," she argued.

"She said she and Bear discussed that and Bear thinks it's worth the risk."

"I don't like being up here and not able to help," she insisted.

"I know the feeling. I feel as useless as lips on a duck," he said. "Palenaka said it's gonna take most of the day to get everyone up here."

"Maybe we can find a path along the ridge," Sandy suggested.

"Bear and Palenaka wants us here when she brings Ginny up. Bear wants you to keep her in line and quiet."

"I don't think anyone can keep her in line, short of kicking her ass," Sandy said. "I'll do my best, but I'm not willing to put up with too much of her shit." Explosions below drew her attention to the battle. "Maybe we can throw some of those darts if they get too close."

"Do you have any?"

The only thing either of them had was their rifles. "It's gonna be a long day," Sandy said and looked around for a place to sit and wait.

CHAPTER THIRTY-SEVEN

Bear had little doubt that he could take out either of the leaders of the two groups. *That won't change anything though,* he thought. *With the mindset of everyone involved, nothing will change until one side's totally exterminated. It's their idea of honor. Even if Weniki and Aka are brother and sister, the reason for their war is gone. They'll gain nothing other than the genocide of one group or the other.*

"You are correct," Palenaka said from behind him. Bear spun around at the sound of her voice. "It is now a belief, a way of life for both sides. It does not matter, the cause."

"Who's at the top so far?"

"Sandy and Wind," she said. "I think Amanda is next."

"I'd rather you take Ginny next," he said. "Now that we have two people up there, she should be okay." Before Palenaka could disappear, he grabbed her arm. "Give her rifle to Sandy. Tell her to hang on to it until I get up there."

Palenaka smiled and faded from view. *If we're lucky, she'll still be unconscious when I get there,* Bear thought as he watched her vanish.

Below, more fighters emerged from the trees. Bear heard an explosion to his right. When he looked over, he saw a shower of dust and rocks. Someone had sent a dart toward Wind's previous location.

He saw a flaming missile coming from the catapult to his left. The object struck the slope below with a thunderous explosion.

419

That ain't good, he thought and aimed at one of the men working the catapult. He adjusted the site for five hundred yards, took a deep breath and relaxed. Timing the shot to be between heartbeats, he squeezed the trigger. The first shot splintered wood beside the man, the second slammed into his chest. Two more shots dropped the other men working the catapult.

Bodies of fighters from both sides littered the slope below. The ferocity of the battle drove home the fact that one side or the other faced complete annihilation. Each represented the last remnants of their civilizations. In the end, the population of one world would totally cease to be, removed from existence by a single useless battle. He could only shake his head in disbelief.

***

Shadows bathed the slope below. Everyone stood atop the mountain except Hal and Bear. "Palenaka, I'm sorry, but you look like death warmed over girl," Sandy said.

"The individual trips left have almost weakened me so that I require sleep," she said.

Periodically, they could hear either Hal or Bear shoot, keeping the aggressors away. They had no idea how long they could remain safe.

Palenaka needed about forty-five minutes to recover after each trip now. With the last two, she only spent about thirty minutes between them. She sat with her legs crossed, back straight and eyes closed. She relaxed, rebuilding her energy in order to remove the two remaining men from danger. She reached deep inside and joined with the stream of nature around her.

Using a method taught her by Weniki, she gulped the energy from around her until it burned deep inside. She settled her mind and allowed the energy to flow throughout her body. With the cycle completed, she repeated it four more times.

"I must return," she told Spyder as she rose.

"We all appreciate what you've done li'l lady," he said, "but you look like hell. You need to rest before you go back down there."

"They haven't much time," Palenaka argued. "They must be brought here or they will die."

Before Spyder could say anything, she disappeared. He looked over at Sandy, "She doesn't listen any better than Ginny."

Sandy nodded grinning, "She's definitely one of us now."

A few minutes later, a ripple appeared in the air beside Keith. Palenaka flickered into view and two other outlines accompanied her, then all three disappeared again. A couple of seconds later, they appeared again almost as ghosts. All three were transparent and again flickered as if cast by a dying projector. Slowly, they solidified and held their form. Immediately, Palenaka collapsed between Bear and Hal.

***

"She's in trouble," Sandy said reaching her in two quick steps.

Bear knelt beside her and felt her neck for a pulse. Her chest barely moved.

"She's got a pulse and she's breathing," he said.

"She's pale as hell," Hal observed. "Getting all of us here was too much for her."

"She was worn out before she brought the two of you here," Wind said. "She only took fifteen or twenty minutes to recover. Then she brought two of you at once."

"She's one hell of a woman," Amanda said.

"We need to cover her and elevate her feet." Ginny was awake and looking at Palenaka from behind the others.

"She's right," Bear said after looking up, surprised by the concern in her voice and the knowledge she displayed. "She's in shock. If we move her now, we'll kill her."

Bear pulled his duster from his pack and covered Palenaka with it as Sandy placed another pack under her feet. "This should help," she said.

He looked around the top of the mountain, his vision limited by more trees and brush. "We've got to make sure there's no way for any of them to sneak up on us," he said.

"We're safe here," Spyder spoke up. "I checked and there's only one way safe to travel from here and that's along the ridge to the west. The sides of the ridge are too steep for a person to climb. The ridge goes beyond the valleys on both sides. We're safe."

Bear nodded. He knew if Spyder said it's safe, it was. They could stay here until Palenaka recovered as long as it didn't take past dawn tomorrow. The problem with being on top of the mountain with only one direction of attack was that, it was also their only way of escape. Bear didn't expect an attack, but he didn't want to stay in any one place too long.

**

Palenaka's consciousness sank deep within her body. In her mind, she stood on a cliff overlooking a beautiful valley. Below, she watched the spirits of nature as they glided through the valley. These were the healing entities flowing through every conceivable thing including the world itself.

As she watched, Bear and Spyder appeared to her left, the rest, except for Ginny, appeared to her right. She slowly looked at each of them. "How are you here," she asked. "I did not bring you to me."

"You're one of us now," Hal said. "We're worried about you and wanna help."

"There is nothing you can do." Motioning toward the spirits below, she added "They watch over me now. It is up to them as to what will happen to me."

"There has to be something we can do," Sandy argued. "Maybe we can give you energy in some way."

Palenaka looked back at the spirits, "It is their decision alone," she repeated. "I must ask that you not interfere." Bear faded from view and one at a time, the others disappeared.

In the physical reality, Bear was shaking each individual to disrupt his or her meditation. While they orientated themselves, Ginny said, "Everything's okay here. I haven't seen anyone or anything."

"Thanks for keeping watch," Bear said. In fact, Ginny had insisted on keeping watch while the others attempted to help Palenaka.

"I had to," she said. "I think Weniki might be able to read me. We can't take that chance."

"Good thinking," he said. She had actually shown concern for the rest and put them first. His appreciation was sincere.

"I'm gonna get some rest," she said. "You guys are gonna have to fend for yourselves food wise.

Bear looked at the sun setting beyond the mountains. He could hear the battle as it continued in the shadows below. According to Palenaka, the fighting wouldn't stop until the bitter end. Essentially, once the fighting started, the warriors were on their own. Individual leaders would control those under their direct command, but there was no central command and control.

Bear had no idea how the leaders of each army would know when the fighting was over. Theoretically, there would be no one left to tell them. The whole thing left him confused.

Spyder stepped up, "I'll take the first watch," he said. "You and the others need to get your rest. Send Keith out in four hours."

"You got it," Bear said. He was too tired to argue or discuss the situation with any detail. If Spyder was willing to take the first watch, they were safe, he could sleep and Palenaka could mend.

***

When Bear awoke, Hal was sitting a short distance away, obviously having just awakened

424

himself. He looked around and rubbed the sleep from his eyes. Spyder stood over him holding out a cup of coffee. "It's instant," he said, "but, it's better'n nothing."

Spyder went to Hal and gave him a cup. "We figured both of you needed to get some rest," he said.

Palenaka is conscious and says we need to get moving," Ginny said coming up.

"She's okay?" Hal asked.

"She looks like she's back to normal," Ginny answered. "But, she thinks we need to get outta here."

"Sorry guys," Spyder said. "If Palenaka says we need to go then I think that's what we should do."

None of them was willing to question her at this point. She had saved their collective asses and she probably knew something they didn't, which at this point wasn't saying much.

In a few minutes, Palenaka joined everyone gathering their things together as they prepared to leave. "We must go," she said. "The war has almost reached both villages. The fighting grows more intense."

Moments later, they left the top of the mountain, traveling along the ridge with Spyder leading the way. "Are you alright?" Bear asked. He felt uncomfortable that none of them had talked to Palenaka about her experience.

"I am well," she answered. "Because of Ginny, I was returned to this existence."

"Because of Ginny?" Hal questioned. "What did she do?"

"She offered herself in my stead."

"What do you mean, offered herself?" Hal pressed as they followed Spyder among the trees.

"It is a personal thing," Palenaka said, "a thing between her and the spirits."

Ginny was ahead of them, a couple of feet behind Spyder. She traveled in silence watching the ground where she stepped.

As Spyder explained, the trail traveled along the ridge until connecting to another ridge. The traveling was easy as they worked their way among thick brush. Turning right, they followed the new ridge until they overlooked the Nāki village. The village below was empty; however, they could hear the sound of fighting in the distance.

"They've emptied the village to fight the Alaea," Hal said.

"Do not mistake the apparent emptiness of the paths," Palenaka said. "Many people still remain in the village. They stay hidden in case of attack from the other side."

"They're hid in the houses," Spyder guessed.

"In the homes and much of the land around them," Palenaka corrected.

"Will others come back at night?" Bear asked.

"They will not," Palenaka answered. "The village will be defended by the people left behind."

"We need to go down after dark," Bear said. "We'll try to get past the village without having to confront anyone."

"Guards will be hidden around the village," Palenaka said. "There will be many and it is doubtful that we will pass without detection."

Bear nodded, understanding that people would probably have to die. He didn't want to kill, but if

426

his and the lives of his friends were on the line, he would. There was no way Palenaka could get them past the guards in the little time they had. They would have to do it on their own.

"You and I take the lead," Spyder said. "With Hal and Keith in the rear and Wind in the middle, we might have a chance."

"I like that," Bear said, "except for Wind being in the middle. I want him in the lead."

"He's not as experienced as you or me," Spyder said. "He'll probably get caught."

"Right," Wind said interrupting. "When they come for me, the two of you take them out."

Spyder looked at the young black man; he was loyal, courageous and tough. He still had the exuberance of youth and the self-myth of invulnerability. "That sounds great," he said, "but, if something goes wrong, you're probably the one who'll suffer the consequences."

"What's to go wrong?" Wind asked. "If you or Bear let something happen to me, who would you have to pick on?" He grinned. Sure, he was nervous. However, he had no doubt in either man's ability to keep him safe.

"We need to rest," Bear said. "We'll go when it's completely dark."

Without further discussion, everyone looked for a place to rest for the next few hours. Bear and Spyder took positions at either end of the camp. Palenaka sat in a meditation position in the middle of the rest. Even though she was meditating and regaining her strength, she reached out with her feelings to the edge of the ridge and the ends of the camp to keep them safe.

Weniki looked up at the top of the mountain where Palenaka and her new friends were. She had been successful in getting them out of the reach of the battle here. *Palenaka will, no doubt, go to the Nāki village,* she thought. *She will try to lead them around the Nāki and escape north.*

The thought saddened her. Palenaka had no way of knowing that as many Nāki were in or around the village as were fighting here. *She will lead the others to certain death.* She lowered her head at the thought.

"What troubles you?" Lopaka asked. "We are winning the battle. Soon we will use the Kōtha to disrupt their entire army."

"It is Palenaka," Weniki explained. "She is trying to take the strangers around the Nāki village to safety."

"You knew when she was sent here that she was not one of us," Lopaka argued. "At least she did not turn to the Nāki. I will mourn her loss, but it is not totally unexpected."

Weniki nodded. She knew he was right. Palenaka was a judge from the Confederation. She came to Farn to ensure that neither side used weapons more advanced than they agreed to. An accident had left Palenaka with amnesia and Weniki took advantage of it. Ten years of training resulted in an ally with growing powers. Palenaka had no idea of the abilities she possessed. Weniki knew she was at least as powerful as herself. Now, she would be lost.

A race of Weniki's people still resided underground. They were the flying spiders Bear had seen when he looked through the internal window and the true warriors of the Alaea. In a short time, many of the Alaea would gather in a group and the warriors below would leave their domain for above ground. Unknown to Weniki, Lopaka planned to kill anything not under her sphere of protection.

When all the Nāki were dead, Lopaka planned to order Weniki to use her power to force or trick the warriors into returning underground. Then he would seal the passage, making it safe for all the remaining Alaea.

Around them, the battle raged. Fire flew through the air and as swords met spears, miniature lightening flashed with the sound of small explosions. The Nāki gave way as the Alaea overwhelmed them in and around the plains. They backed toward their village. Once there, the chosen Alaea would join together in a group and the flying warriors would kill anyone outside the group including the unfortunate Alaea still involved in the battle.

CHAPTER THIRTY-EIGHT

Hal opened his eyes to Bear shaking his shoulder. "It's dark," he said.

Hal looked around. "Good," he said. "I was wondering what was wrong. I thought I was going blind."

Bear shook his head smiling. *He's nervous and covering it with humor.*

In a few minutes, everyone was up and ready to travel. "How far ahead do you want me?" Wind asked.

"We'll maintain the distance," Bear said. "You can't worry about that. If you do, someone may know we're behind you."

"I'll do a slightly slower than regular pace."

"You need to be as quiet as possible," Spyder said. "We still don't want to draw attention to ourselves. Just try to get past without being seen. We'll do the rest."

"Keith and I'll pull up the rear and keep the rest between you and Bear," Hal said. "We can do this."

"Lead the way," Bear said to Wind.

They continued along the ridge as it descended toward the lake. The night was dark with only pinpoints of stars for light. They moved slowly and cautiously so the animals around them continued their songs in the dark.

Bear noticed that Wind moved effectively through the bushes. If a limb bent with his passing, rather than allowing it to whip back, he eased it back into position. He watched his foot placement, avoiding anything that might make a loud noise. *He's learned well,* Bear thought.

As they neared the place where the ridge met the plain, two men stepped out ahead of Wind.

"What business have you here?" One asked pointing a spear at the young man.

"I'm just trying to find a way to get away from the fighting," Wind said. "I don't mean anyone any one any harm."

"He's one of the Alaea," the other said.

"No sir I'm not," Wind said timidly. "I'm just someone caught in the middle."

"Do you know the one named Bear?" The first man asked.

"Yes," Wind answered. "He's a friend of mine."

"Where is he?" The first man edged closer.

"I'm supposed to meet him near the lake," Wind lied, pointing ahead of him.

"You will go with us to Aka," the man said motioning to the side with his spear.

"I can't," Wind answered. "Bear'll be looking for me."

"You go with us or die," the second man threatened.

Bear and Spyder each rose behind a man and in the blink of an eye dispatched them both, cutting their throats. As they let the bodies slip silently to the ground, four more armed men rushed toward them.

Bear parried a spear thrust and drove his knife into the man's throat. As he turned toward the next, a shot rang out. The man grabbed his face and went down. Instantly the side of the ridge was full of moving bodies.

Nāki fighters emerged, moving in mass. Bear saw a hoard of people before him. A second shot

431

and a man near Spyder dropped. Bear looked back at the other warriors. They seemed to ignore the gunshot and continued moving toward the Nāki village. They seemed to ignore the humans and passed by without attacking.

Bear turned, looked up and saw his worst nightmare come true. Flying spiders circled the Nāki village. He froze in his tracks and stared at the scene. They were the creatures he had seen when he looked through one of the holes in the cave. The spiders were the size of a human, dark grey with red horizontal stripes on their legs.

Their wings beat the air like a bumblebee and as they circled the village, some of the animals swooped down to land beside the houses. One misjudged and crashed into the roof of one building. Immediately, five Nāki ran onto the path beside it.

When the sixth tried to escape, something grabbed him from behind and jerked him back inside. A scream followed and a few seconds later, the spider left the building. The knowledge of what just happened made Bear's skin crawl.

"We've gotta get outta here," he said, a quiver in his voice.

The Nāki warriors rushed toward the village. None of them seemed surprised by the flying spiders and none of them hesitated as they ran toward, what Bear believed was, certain death.

In the village, flaming arrows soared into the air illuminating the scene. Some struck the creatures while others fell back to the ground. Of the ones that missed, a few landed on the wooden or grass roofs, igniting them. It took only seconds for flames to engulf the structures.

The sight in the village was horrendous. Nāki and Alaea clashed with spears, swords, knives and staffs. Flashes of light followed closely by mini-explosions. Along with the flaming arrows balls of fire soared through the night. Screams of pain, fear and anger punctuated the scene. Men and women on both sides were dying in the fierce battle a short distance away.

Bear led the others down the rest of the slope toward the lake in the distance. Emerging from the vegetation, they rushed onto a flat area covered only with grass, which went to the edge of the water about a hundred yards away.

To their right, more of the spider things raced toward the village. They were coming in behind the Nāki reinforcements. There was about to be a slaughter.

Bear looked at Palenaka who stood facing the full moon, her head tilted up and her arms in a now familiar position. "Palenaka," he whispered.

The young woman remained still and quiet as if she hadn't heard him.

"Palenaka," he repeated a little more loudly.

The rest of the group looked toward where she stood. As they did, a red glow emanated from her body.

***

This cannot be, Palenaka thought as she watched the battle below her intensify. *There was an agreement that they would not use flying warriors.*

433

Palenaka followed the others to the flat land beside the lake. There, she saw more Alaea warriors approaching to trap the unsuspecting Nāki in the village. *This is not allowed.*

Palenaka faced the moon for strength. Bringing her hands into the meditation position, she cleared her mind and called to Weniki.

Seconds later, Weniki answered. *Are you safe, my friend and student?*

We are in no danger, Palenaka answered. *But there are flying warriors attacking the Nāki.*

That cannot be, Weniki returned.

I am watching them at this time.

It is Lopaka, Weniki responded. *I know nothing of this.* She looked at Lopaka. The man was sitting on a log. She now understood why he could send no one out to check on the battle. The flying warriors would kill anyone not in this group. He had tricked Weniki and Palenaka. He was using flying warriors and he looked serene. Palenaka had many questions, among them where did the warriors come from. However, if she asked such things, Lopaka would know she knew of his treachery.

This must not be allowed, Weniki sent back.

It cannot be stopped, Palenaka reminded her. *The warriors are loose.*

Remain hidden, Weniki sent back. *You must all remain hidden until this is ended.* She broke off the mental connection with Palenaka.

Try as she might, Palenaka was unable to communicate with her again.

***

434

The glow from Palenaka's body dimmed and another transparent ripple flew from her engulfing the small group in the blink of an eye. She turned to them, "We are safe here," she said. "We cannot be seen by anyone."

"What the hell's going on?" Spyder asked. "We gotta defend ourselves."

"That is not required," Palenaka said.

As if to prove her point, a spider scurried by completely oblivious to their presence and continued toward the village.

"If anyone leaves this small area they can be seen."

"You've made us invisible," Sandy said.

"I have."

"Why?"

Palenaka looked at her sadly. "The Alaea have broken the agreement of the confederation and are using the flying warriors. This is not allowed."

"What's gonna happen?" Bear asked. "You can't keep us invisible forever."

"I do not have the answer to that," Palenaka admitted. "Weniki said that we must stay here until the battle is finished."

"... and you trust Weniki?" Hal asked.

"She says she didn't know about the flying warriors," Palenaka said. "I believe her." The last statement held enough conviction it left no question in anyone's mind of its validity.

Wind walked to Palenaka and put his arm around her. "How safe are we here?" He asked.

"We are safe if none of the warriors happen into the protected area. They cannot see us, but they can pass through the wall by accident."

"Form a circle and face outward," Bear said.

It only took a couple of seconds for them to form a small circle, each facing outward. "How far does the protection extend?" Keith asked.

A spider flew from the village, circled overhead and flew back toward the village. Obviously, the protection was in place and it couldn't see them even from above. Fireballs arched through the air and a few flaming arrows still streaked in the distance. However, the majority of the battle consisted of clashing weapons. Sparks and small explosions filled the scene.

"Look for a color change of the ground," Palenaka answered.

They found a very subtle difference in the color of the ground about ten feet away. The protected area was a circle about twenty feet across.

"If a warrior comes inside the area, you will be in danger," Palenaka said.

With the aid of the full moon, they could see combatants from both sides clearly. It was obvious the Nāki would lose the war. Some of the spiders shot or spat fire from their mouths. However, it was only the ones on the ground with that ability; none of the ones flying had it.

"This is a massacre," Amanda said shocked at the sight.

"That it is," Hal said taking a deep breath and letting it out slowly, "that it is."

A spider approached directly toward the group, attempting to reach the fighting. The thing traveled on eight legs. Its grizzly head could only move a small amount in any direction which explained it's large black eyes. The green teeth in its mouth were humanoid and clicked as it constantly opened and closed its jaw. As it entered the protected area it stopped, only for a second, but that was enough. A hail of lead slammed into its body. The thing moved forward a couple of steps and dropped to the ground.

"She is dead," Palenaka said looking at the creature.

For some reason, Bear was surprised to hear her call the thing 'she'. "We need to get it out of this place," he said moving forward.

"Wait," Palenaka called out.

Bear looked at her, "What for?" he asked.

Palenaka pointed past the giant spider and he saw three more moving toward them. They gave no indication of seeing the humans. Of course, he had no idea how he would know if they did.

The creatures passed dangerously close to where he thought the edge of Palenaka's protection extended. The hideous things passed without noticing the people standing in a circle. "There may be many warriors away from the fighting," Palenaka said. "Not all of them are in this battle. Some will be looking for Nāki elsewhere.

Bear nodded. *Typical battle tactics,* he thought. *Hold troops in reserve or use them to sweep the countryside for outlying combatants.*

"Then, there's no telling how many individual warriors there are running around?" Keith asked.

"That is correct," she answered looking around. "They may be in any direction."

"Why did that warrior come from the south?" Hal asked. Hal was thinking about where the spider had come from as Palenaka and Bear discussed the

437

situation. "That's the direction of the Alaea. There's no Nāki there."

Palenaka lowered her eyes as if ashamed to answer the question. "When the warriors are released, they cannot be controlled," she explained. "They will kill anything which appears as enemy." She hesitated, "Even the Alaea."

"Oh my God," Amanda said in a stunned voice. "What kind of people would do such a thing?"

"Only someone in a blood feud," Palenaka said. "Lopaka and Aka hate each other and will stop at nothing short of killing the last of their enemy."

Two Nāki forced a warrior back toward the group. The warrior lashed out with one of its two short forelegs, trying to make contact with the men. The Nāki used their swords to block the blows and force the creature backward.

Bear saw another Nāki about fifty yards away spinning a sling over her head. She released the dart and a second later, an explosion flipped the spider on its back. Its legs flailed wildly in the air a couple of seconds and stopped when one of the Nāki buried his spear in the thing's grisly head.

***

The position of the battle seemed to be shifting as the Nāki retreated. More and more members of each side moved toward the small band of people made invisible by Palenaka.

The Nāki, fighting fiercely, backed away from the overwhelming number of Alaea troops and warriors. As Bear watched, he saw the spider warriors kill Alaea as well as Nāki. It was as if they

438

were on a killing spree and it didn't matter who or what died.

The Alaea backed the Nāki until they were less than fifty yards away.

"This is gettin' a might close," Spyder said. "We're gonna need to move unless we want all that in our laps."

Bear checked his pistols assuring himself that they were in their place and ready for use.

Suddenly, a blue shimmer wavered beside him and in a second Weniki appeared. She looked tired, but at the same time, she carried herself with resolve. "The end is near," she said to no one in particular.

Spyder, Wind and Keith had turned their M16's on her as she shimmered into view. Palenaka placed her hand on Wind's rifle, "She is here to help us," she said.

Bear stepped back toward the group away from Weniki. "Is that true?" He asked. "Are you here to help us?"

Weniki looked at him as if she were staring into his soul. "I should not have brought you here," she said. "It was wrong of me. None of you should be part of this. I was wrong and I am sorry."

The battle now raged along one side of them and threatened to block any possibility of leaving to the north. The last thing Bear wanted was to have that route cut off. He didn't like the idea of everyone trapped on the southern end of this peninsula, even as large as it was.

His gaze lingered a second then he said, "We're about to be trapped here. When the Alaea win, we're not gonna be able to escape to the north."

"It is not a problem," Weniki assured him.

From beside Wind, Palenaka said, "I understand."

"You understand what?" Wind asked looking at her.

"We must move into the Nāki village," she explained. There is a cave near it where we may hide."

"There're two caves," Bear said. "Which one should we use?"

"The one at the other end," Weniki said serenely. "The closer one is filled with more Alaea warriors."

"How the hell are we gonna get through that shit?" Spyder asked looking at the battle now almost close enough for them to spit on.

"You must follow Palenaka," Weniki explained. "She will travel ahead of us." She noticed Wind looking doubtful. Before he could protest, she said, "She will be safe -- and she must be away from us."

"Why?" Ginny asked. Surprised, everyone looked at her. She had said nothing for a long time and the rest seemed to have forgotten she was there. "Why should we trust you?"

"We have to trust her," Spyder said sternly. "She's about all we got."

"Bullshit," Ginny retorted. "She's done a lot more than she's saying. Do you remember when she was gone from her valley and something huge roamed through it one night?" She looked around at the others. "That was her. Not her in person, but something she created. There never was a monster, just something to make us leave. It was just something to make us go to her. I knew it, but couldn't tell any of you. She kept me quiet by threatening to take my voice away, as she put it."

The rest looked at Weniki for confirmation. She said nothing, but her face showed that Ginny was telling the truth.

Ginny continued. "I was the one she had the least mind control over so she threatened me physically. But, I'm not about to stand here and let her put all of you in any more danger. I don't trust her any more than I can fly to the moon." She turned toward Weniki, "Now bitch, do what you want, but the rest know about you."

"We will speak of this later," Weniki said. "Now we must leave."

"Not a chance in hell," Spyder snorted and raised his rifle. "Is what she said true?"

Weniki hesitated only a second, then slowly nodded. "What she says is true," she admitted. "I will explain when we are safe. If we stay here you are all in grave danger." She nodded to Palenaka.

Palenaka pulled her arm away from Wind and quickly stepped away before he could protest.

He started for her and Keith grabbed his elbow. "She's outside the protection," he said.

"If she's outside the protection," Sandy said, "what's protecting us now?"

Weniki smiled sweetly as if nothing had happened, "I am," she said. "We must move slowly. If we hurry, it may cause problems."

"What's to stop them from coming into the protection area?"

"No one can enter the protection," Weniki explained. "However, if we do not move slowly, they may notice us."

"We'll follow you for now," Bear said. "But, you have some explaining to do later."

Weniki nodded and started walking toward where Palenaka stood among the fighting.

As they moved among the combatants, the battle raged all around them. Many times a fighter backed against the force field surrounding them. Feeling the pressure to their back, they would instinctively move to the side as they continued fighting. Once, an Alaea warrior slashed a Nāki and backed against the field. It turned its body, using its legs to swivel, and looked to see what pressed against its back.

An instant later, it exploded. Bear saw Palenaka look away and continued leading them toward the far end of the valley. *Yes, it was Palenaka* flashed through his mind and he knew Weniki was answering his unspoken question.

From the uncertain safety of their protective bubble, they witnessed humans torn apart. When the spiders ripped the heads from bodies, they seemed to bathe in the blood that poured from it. When a spider lost its head, a thick yellow goo pulsed from the body.

They continued following Palenaka toward the north end of the valley. As they proceeded, they encountered fewer soldiers of either side. Soon they appeared alone and moved rapidly until finally reaching the path winding up to the cave Bear and Keith had found earlier.

As they started their climb up the path, they had to walk in single file. Bear led the procession with Spyder and Ginny following last. Still at the bottom of the trail, an Alaea warrior appeared to their right. It stepped forward and, with a single swipe of a short front leg, slashed Ginny across her chest opening a deep gash, from her right shoulder to her left hip. Blood instantly gushed from the wound.

Spyder's hand flashed and he emptied eight shots in the head and body of the warrior. The creature's legs collapsed and it dropped to its stomach and lay motionless.

More spiders appeared behind it clambering along the slope, over boulders and the fallen body. As Spyder and the others fired at the advancing warriors, four of the creatures shot fireballs in return, while three attempted to circle the humans. Bear, Hal and Sandy blocked their approach with automatic weapons causing a brief retreat.

It took a direct head shot to kill one of the warriors. Their bodies were surprisingly resistant to bullets and a single shot did little or no damage. When one dropped in front of Bear from above, he emptied his M16 into it.

Before he could reload, the others charged forward. He pulled both 9mms and began firing. Hal and Sandy both picked their targets carefully. Behind them, everyone were quickly emptying their weapons.

A warrior reached Wind and knocked him to the ground. Before Spyder could react, the spider started to vibrate, smoke rose from its body in thin wisps just before it exploded.

443

Weniki stumbled and shaded her eyes with a hand. Palenaka grabbed her shoulders to stabilize her. Weniki looked back up and stared at another of the approaching warriors. It exploded a few seconds later. Bear swung a pistol toward the last spider. It stopped advancing, began vibrating and black liquid and slime erupted as it exploded. He looked at Palenaka and she shimmered as if her body produced extreme heat.

I didn't know she could do that, he thought searching the rest of the area for danger.

Spyder rushed to where Ginny lay on the ground. Blood soaked her as it poured from her body and he could tell in one glance that she had no chance of survival. Cradling her head in his arms, he watched helplessly as her life ended. With his face buried in her tangled hair, she breathed her last breath.

When he looked up, a transformation had turned his features to stone. Bear recognized the man's feelings for what they were. He had experienced the same thing with the death of Davata. Revenge would be in the front of the man's mind.

"We gotta get to the cave," Bear said placing a hand on Spyder's shoulder.

He pulled away. "They're gonna pay for this," he said. Then looking at Weniki he added, "You're part of this shit too." He slowly raised his rifle toward her.

Bear gently placed his hand on the barrel. "We need her," he said. "When we get to the cave, you can kill all the warriors you feel you need to."

"I've got no reason to go up there now," he argued. "She may have been a pain in the ass, but I loved her." He looked down at his wife lying on the ground.

"I'll help you get her up there," Wind said stepping forward.

"I'll carry her," Spyder said bending down and scooping her into his arms. Without another word, he started up the path and the rest followed.

Once inside the cavern, they relaxed and took turns watching the valley below. Spyder lay on the floor at the front of the cave. Periodically, his rifle would bark and another warrior from one side or another dropped lifelessly to the ground.

Weniki understood the man's need for retaliation, created a wall shielding him and cave from view.

CHAPTER THIRTY-NINE

Weniki sat calmly with her back against the inside wall of the cave maintaining the veil at its entrance. Bear could see that the effort of protecting them and the veil had drained her of much of her strength. When she looked at him though, her smile appeared genuine and warm.

"It was never my intent for harm to come to any of you," she said. "I wanted only to receive knowledge."

"That may be true," he said. "But you kidnapped us and brought us to this place where a war was about to start. You had to know that there was a chance some of us would be killed."

Weniki spoke softly, barely above a whisper. "I did not expect to care for you."

Bear knew what she meant by the statement. Until his bonding at the falls with her, his feelings for Davata were as strong as the day she died. Afterward, and not just because of the experience, his feelings of loss had lessened. He still loved Davata, but the pain that dug deep into his soul had eased.

Another shot sounded from Spyder at the cave entrance. The sound echoed to the unseen back of the cave and returned.

He hadn't expected to care for another woman for a long time to come. However, during their bonding, Bear had learned much about Weniki and he liked what he knew.

"I'm not sure what's gonna happen," he said, "but Spyder's a strong willed man. He also holds the respect of the rest of the group. I'm not sure what they're gonna think about you being here."

As Weniki started to answer, Wind called out from beside Spyder. "Bear, Hal, come up here. You're not gonna believe this shit."

Arriving at the front of the cave, Wind pointed to the main part of the village. There, the battle continued. However, now the Alaea spiders were killing the other Alaea fighters.

"The Nāki are gone," Weniki said.

"What do you mean gone?" Sandy asked having followed Hal up.

"All of the Nāki in the village are dead," Weniki explained a touch of sadness in her voice. "When all of the Nāki are dead, the warriors will kill the rest of the Alaea."

"Didn't Lopaka think of that when he released the warriors?" Amanda asked.

Weniki nodded, "He did," she said. He planned to use me to return them to their place." She turned and looked at the people beside her. "But I am not there now."

"You did this on purpose, didn't you." Sandy said more of a confirmation than a question. "You left your people to help us."

"I told her of the warriors," Palenaka said. "It was then that she told me to keep you where we were."

Bear had started to understand. Weniki hadn't expected Lopaka to break the agreement and use the warriors. When he did, she chose to open him and her people up to the killing attacks of the spiders. Soon there would be no human forms, other than themselves, on the southern end of the peninsula.

"How do we get away from the warriors?" Sandy asked. "Once they kill all the people, they'll go looking for others."

"They will all come to the Nāki village," Palenaka explained. "Once they are here Weniki and I will stop them."

"Goddamn," Spyder exclaimed looking toward the remains of the village. "Will you look at that shit?"

Giant spiders almost covered the main part of the village. They searched through the empty buildings, looking for human survivors. Overhead, hundreds of spiders flew, obviously looking for the same thing. More of the creatures poured in from the entrance of the valley as the number of flying ones grew.

Weniki and Palenaka stood, faced each other and raised their arms to the meditation position. A rainbow of colors surrounded them extending into the dark depths and out through the entrance of the cave.

Almost immediately, the Alaea warriors turned on each other. The killing was brutal and merciless. Balls of fire flew skyward from many on the ground. It seemed that the ones in the air now fought the ones on the ground.

The battle in the village raged for over an hour. In the end, less than a hundred spiders circled the destroyed structures in the air and all the earthbound arachnids were dead. Suddenly, the rest turned on each other and the killing began anew. Twenty minutes later, all but one was dead.

The one remaining animal flew higher into the air as the sun peeked over the top of the mountains.

The battle had lasted the entire night. The warrior soared up and up, climbing farther until it reached about five thousand feet. There, it folded its wings and plunged toward the ground. Without opening its wings again, the creature slammed into the ground at full speed killing it instantly.

Weniki and Palenaka both lowered their hands and slumped to the floor of the cave. Both women were unconscious from exhaustion.

***

Sandy pressed a wet cloth to Weniki's forehead. Amanda watched over Palenaka a short distance away. Both women were unconscious but thrashed and mumbled as if being assaulted by horrible nightmares.

Spyder, Hal and Bear stood on the path in front of the cave. "We need to go down and check the village," Spyder said.

"You're probably right," Hal agreed. "There may still be some of those things left."

"You can go if you want," Bear said. "But I'm staying here. I'm not sure I could stand to be around that many spiders at once, much less spiders the size of a man. I almost lost it last night walking through 'em when they couldn't see us."

"We can check on 'em," Spyder said. "You don't have to go. I know how you feel. If they were giant ants, you couldn't get me near there."

"We'll check it out," Hal said. "You keep guard here."

"If you're gonna go," Bear said. "Take Wind and Keith with you. They'll be help if you have to fight your way back here."

"I doubt we'll have to do that," Spyder said. "I don't think Weniki and Palenaka would've stopped if any were left alive."

Bear was surprised that Spyder showed so much trust in the women's abilities. "Not to bring up a sore subject," Bear said. "But I can't figure out how that warrior was able to see Ginny last night. We were supposed to be protected and Weniki and Palenaka were both effective before."

Spyder pulled his hat off and wiped his face with a bandana. "I've been thinking about that," he said. "It happened just as we formed a single line. Ginny and me must have been outside the protection without Weniki realizing it. When Ginny and I appeared from nowhere, it attacked the one closest to it - Ginny." His face was grim, but not like previously and there was no accusation in his voice.

This change in attitude shocked Bear. The man had obviously been thinking a lot about the incident. Not just about what had happened, but how it happened as well. Spyder never ceased to amaze him.

"I was trying to give both of you time to think about what we do with Weniki and Palenaka," Bear said.

"What is there to do with them?" Spyder asked. "They're part of us now."

"I agree," Hal said. "They both gave up their people and their lives to protect us. Granted an

450

accident happened, but I don't, in any way, think Weniki did anything on purpose."

Bear was glad to hear that the men felt essentially the same as him. He still had to check with the others for their opinions, but he felt better about the possible outcome.

"I'll go get Wind and Keith," Hal said. "We'll get going as soon as we can." He entered the cave to tell the young men of the plan and enlist their help.

Spyder looked directly into Bear's eyes. "I was pissed at Weniki when Ginny was killed," he said, "but that was just a reaction. I know she wasn't to blame. You and her seem to have something between you, and that's good. You seem better since you met her. I know she can't take Davata's place. Hell, I doubt she wants to, but I think you'll both be good for each other."

Bear nodded and placed a hand on Spyder's shoulder. "Bullshit," Spyder said and grabbed him in a strong hug.

Bear knew the pain Spyder must be feeling. He knew of the gut-wrenching loss and the feeling of helplessness. *This too shall pass my brother,* he thought. *This too shall pass.*

A few minutes later, the others walked up. Hal handed Spyder a bag. "Here's some food," he said. "I don't know how long this will take."

Spyder took the food, nodded and walked down the path away from the cave. Wind and Keith followed close behind.

"We'll be back as soon as we can," Hal said and followed the other men.

***

451

When Spyder reached the edge of the village, an eerie silence lay over the area. They had passed what was left of a few humans as well as bodies of spiders on the way. Adding to the feeling of strangeness was the sight of hundreds of bodies, both human and spider. To top it off was the smell. The destruction was immense with most of the bodies torn to pieces. Few remained in tack.

"We'll need to check each building as we go," Spyder said. "We can't afford anything or anyone to wind up behind us."

The rest nodded in agreement and wordlessly spread out to perform their gruesome search. There were bodies in almost every building Spyder looked into -- all were dead. As he moved from one building to another, he checked on the other men. By the looks on their faces, they were finding the same.

It took them two hours to work their way to the main building where they previously met Aka. The other men joined Spyder as he approached the front door, which was intact. Upon checking the outside of the building, they found it to have sustained little damage.

"Stay to the side," Spyder said. "Remember, there's a large room and I doubt there's any light in it. If we can't see, we don't go in until we can."

Hal moved to the opposite side of the door where Keith joined him. Wind stepped up beside Spyder. Taking a deep breath, Spyder flipped the latch and still standing to the side, swung the door inward.

When he peeked around the edge, he could see the entire room lit with six torches, three along each sidewall. He could see no one inside from his vantage point. He slowly slid around the doorframe and entered the room.

The other men followed close behind him and formed a line across the end of the room. There was no one, human or spider in sight. They slowly made their way toward the throne where Aka sat when they first met him. The silence in the building was so complete it was loud.

Something didn't feel right to Spyder. His nerves were on edge and his senses sharp. *We're not alone here,* he thought. He stopped, closed his eyes and listened to the quiet around him hoping that he could pick up on something out of order.

A snap from behind the throne sent him and the rest silently into hiding among the long benches on each side. In a couple of seconds, Aka rose from the floor behind the large chair. He had no weapons and moved with confidence. It almost looked as if things were exactly as he expected.

He's been hiding underground, Spyder thought. *The son of a bitch hid from the fight and now he's coming out to see what's left.*

Aka moved around the throne and started toward the door when Spyder and the others rose from their hiding. He stopped, staring from man to man. Suddenly, he broke into a broad grin. "My friends, you're alive!" He exclaimed with his arms held open wide. "I trust your friend Rafe is well," he said walking toward them.

"He is," Hal said from across the room. "But for right now you need to stay right where you are."

453

Hal fidgeted on the other side of the room.

Aka stopped with a surprised look on his face, "What is wrong?" He asked. "You have survived the war, I have survived the war. Even the Alaea warriors couldn't kill us."

"Just how did you get away?" Spyder asked. "How did you manage to live through the war that killed all your people?"

"When the Alaea warriors attacked, my guards hurried me into hiding," he explained. "I heard the battle raging above me. There were screams and explosions, it sounded horrible. Finally, the sound quieted. When I heard nothing for a time I came up to find you here."

"It's strange to me that there are no dead humans or spiders here in this building," Wind said.

"It doesn't even look like the building was attacked," Keith observed. "How did you and this building avoid being attacked?"

"For this, I have no answer," Aka said shaking his head and looking at his feet.

"I think it's because of something you're not telling us," Spyder said looking suspiciously at the man.

"I assure you sir that I do not know the answer to my survival besides what I have said."

"Bullshit," Wind said emphatically. "You're lying."

In less than the blink of an eye, a shimmer passed over Aka and he transformed into a hideous winged creature. To Spyder he looked like pictures he'd seen of gargoyles sitting atop old buildings in other countries. He stood before them bent and misshapen with sharp talons on both his hands and feet. Tiny horns protruded from the top of his forehead and his smile framed razor sharp teeth.

Before the men could break from their surprise and react to the transformation, Aka spread his wings and flew rapidly to and out of the door. When they did gather their senses, they hurried from the building in time to see the creature disappear over the slopes of the volcano.

"We gotta get back and let the others know about this," Spyder said.

"You're right," Hal agreed, "but we still have to be careful. There's no telling what else might be left around here."

With Spyder leading and Keith taking the rear position, they started back to the cave and their friends.

***

Weniki and Palenaka were sitting in the cave sipping herbal tea when the men returned. After a description of finding Aka and an explanation of what had happened with him, Weniki nodded as if she understood.

"It was told that one of the brothers was a Wakoka," Weniki said. She looked around at the uncomprehending faces, "a winged creature said to feed on souls," she explained. "Many thousand years ago, a dim but powerful sun exploded and created Wakoka from people of nearby worlds. Following many generations, few Wakoka remain. It was said that either Lopaka or Aka was one. No one dared to question either leader. Also, few people believed the story about the creatures."

"What will it do now?" Amanda asked.

"I cannot say for sure," Weniki answered. "It will almost certainly assume a shape that will allow it to join others and create another village or community. It feeds on the fear, anger and souls of others."

"Speaking of myths," Sandy said. "What about the Menehunes? Are they real?"

Weniki smiled and shook her head, "No, they are not. I knew of the belief in them and used it to get you to our valley. I am sorry for the deceit. Also, the giant animal which forced you to leave the valley and come to the Alaea valley was a Kōtha. It is an image cast by either Palenaka or myself. We used it as a way to get you to the Alaea valley without having to ask and bring suspicion."

"At least it allowed us to discover the cave and all the supplies," Hal said.

"Speaking of which," Bear said, "how did all those supplies get here?"

"They were brought by groups to use in wars to decide the fates of many worlds. This has been done for many hundred generations."

"Aka told us about the wars and the reasons for 'em," Bear said. "What we want to know now is how do we get back to the time and place where we belong? Is there some way you can send us there?"

"That is difficult," she said. "There are many windows in the cave you found. Some lead to other worlds and others lead to different places on this world. There are many such caves on Farn. You will need to find the one that leads back there."

"Then Aka told the truth," Spyder said. "We need to get back to where Central Texas was thousands of years ago."

"What can you tell us about the rest of this world?" Bear asked.

"It has been used for many generations for settling world disputes," she answered. "There are survivors of those worlds now trapped in this place. Some are peaceful and some are not. Many still wage war on any person they meet."

Amanda had been sitting quietly, listening to the conversation. "If this is truly the Earth thousands of years in the future, then the land and seas have changed," she said looking at each of the others. "What Central Texas was before may be at the bottom of an ocean now."

"When this world was reformed, the land and waters were reformed to their shape when the world was inhabited. It should be as you remember."

"If that's true, then we have over a thousand miles to travel," Amanda said. "That's gonna take a long time."

"There is said to be a cave to the north that has windows to other parts of this world," Palenaka said. "We must find the cave and the proper window."

"We'll rest today and head out tomorrow," Spyder said looking at Bear and Hal.

Bear nodded. "We can stand guard at the entrance of the cave. It should only take one at a time," he said.

"That is not needed," Weniki said. There is nothing of danger here now."

"What about the Kalekona here on the volcano?"

"They remain higher on the mountain," she said. "They are not a danger this close to the bottom."

"What about something from the back of this cave?" Sandy asked.

"There were three windows here," Palenaka explained. "But they have been blocked. Nothing may come through them."

"I'm satisfied," Bear said, "and I plan on getting some sleep tonight. It's time for a rest. We'll worry about the rest tomorrow.

Everyone began unpacking their supplies to get comfortable and have a much needed night's sleep.

***

From deep in the cave he watched the people as they lay their things along the walls. He would watch and see where they went tomorrow. Perhaps then, if he found them worthy, he would approach them.

CHAPTER FORTY

Bear awoke to the smell of coffee. The events of the previous day were hazy and it was hard to believe that just a few hours before they had seen a battle resulting in the deaths of almost five thousand people and a couple thousand of those horrific spider warriors. The smell of coffee reminded him of better, more peaceful times.

He lay on his back looking at the ceiling of the cave listening to Hal and Sandy already up and moving around. The sooner they left the valley, the better he would feel. It wasn't just all the death, but the fact that so many were animals that he feared -- spiders. He shivered and sat up forcing the thoughts of the animals from his mind.

"Well if it ain't Sleeping Ugly," Hal said with a grin. "Welcome to the world of the living."

"You feeling any better?" Sandy asked.

He looked around and saw the others still sleeping. "I'll be much better after we leave here."

"I'm not in any hurry to wake the rest up," Hal said. "We're gonna need our strength if we plan to look for the cave Weniki told us about."

"I am not sure where to look," Weniki said from the other side of Bear.

"I didn't see you there," he said looking back at the woman. "I thought you were asleep."

"I remained here during the night," she said. "Palenaka is gathering food."

Bear looked around. It was just as he thought; Wind was gone too. "Wind's got it bad for that girl."

Sandy handed him a cup of coffee, "Do you blame him? He's young and so is she."

"They seem to be good for each other," he admitted. "He's been through a lot. I just hope she's as serious as he is."

"Palenaka takes very little in a light manner," Weniki said. "She is careful in all that she does."

As if on cue, Palenaka walked into the cave carrying a bag. A few steps behind her, Wind arrived carrying two leave-wrapped bundles. The bundles hung from each end of a limb slung over his shoulder.

"We've got meat," Wind said setting the load down. Leave it to Palenaka and her sling to bring down food."

Palenaka ignored the statement and emptied her bag on a tarp. "If we remain here today, we can prepare the meat for travel," she said.

The activity, roused the rest from their sleep. "Coffee," Keith declared. "I smell the nectar of the gods."

"You and your morning coffee," Amanda said. "I'd hate to be around you if we ran out of your daily dose of caffeine."

This is a resilient bunch, Bear thought. *They never cease to amaze me. Even Palenaka and Weniki act as if nothing happened yesterday. They seem to have forgotten about Aka. But, I wanna know where he is and if he's still a problem.*

He is no problem. He knew the thought flashed through his mind from Weniki. *The war is over and he has nothing to keep him here.*

Bear looked at Weniki and saw the woman gazing at him, a smile on her face. He knew he had to control his thoughts and feelings about her. She

460

always said she wouldn't read a person's thoughts without their permission. But, still...

"I suggest we take the day to rest and prepare the food so we can travel tomorrow," Hal said. "I could stand to be lazy another day."

"You got my vote," Amanda said. "It's been a while since we lazed around."

Bear saw Spyder come in the mouth of the cave. He'd failed to notice that the man was gone. "It's done," Spyder said to Hal and Sandy.

"She'll rest well here," Sandy said. "I just wish you would have let us help you."

"It was something I had to do alone," he answered.

"You didn't let me face it alone," Bear reminded him. "This was right," Spyder said. "It's the way she'd have wanted it. She was a private person."

"He is correct," Weniki said. "Ginny was a good person. Even when threatened, she did what she could to help others. I too think she will rest well here."

"I guess we'll stay here for the day," Bear conceded. He was willing to try to put his feelings aside about the dead spiders in the village.

They spent most of the rest of the day doing nothing more than healing from the trauma of the battle before. They spoke of better times as they ate the food Wind and Palenaka supplied.

That afternoon, Bear ventured to Ginny's grave. There, he stood motionless for a long while. *She is at peace here,* he not only thought but felt as well. When he started back toward the cave, he found a fighting staff of the Nāki. Picking it up, he continued to his friends.

One by one, for the rest of the day, people left the cave to visit Ginny's grave and say their good-byes.

*****

At twilight, Weniki and Palenaka stood side by side on the path beyond the cave. Both women held their arms in the meditation position. A green glow shone around their bodies, then rapidly grew until it filled the village below. The spiders and human bodies glowed brighter than the surrounding area and then simply vanished. The women lowered their arms and walked silently back to the cave.

The sun had set beyond the mountains in the west and the stars twinkled brightly in the night sky when Weniki re-entered the cave. She passed Wind as he went out to join Palenaka where she sat on the path.

Bear had stood witness to the vanishing bodies and waited for Weniki to return. She smiled as she passed him. "Are they all gone?" He asked.

"Yes," she answered. "The village is empty."

"Thanks," Bear said. "They were giving me the creeps."

"I must rest," Weniki said. "May we speak back there?" She nodded toward the back area of the cave.

He nodded and followed her until she sat against a wall. He could see that the effort had drained most of her strength. *I don't understand how they do everything they do and still keep going. Their recuperative power is amazing.*

As he sat beside her, she said, "We needed to rid the land of the bodies. If they remained, they would cause disease for many seasons."

"Thanks just the same," Bear said. "I feel better about being here now. Like I said, spiders are the one thing that scares the hell outta me."

"Not the only thing," Weniki said.

Bear looked questioningly at her.

"You have a fear of being abandoned as well," she said. "You can leave or be by yourself. But, you fear others leaving you."

"You're the only one besides Sandy who knows that," he said. "It's not something I usually tell others."

"I understand," she said. Leaning her head back against the wall, she closed her eyes. "May we speak quietly?"

"Quietly?" He repeated the word. "You mean mentally?"

Yes. The answer popped into his mind.

He relaxed against the wall, closed his eyes and waited.

Sandy watched from a short distance away with Hal beside her. "Even though she's the reason we're here, I think she's good for him."

Hal grunted and looked at them. "It's strange," he said. "Weniki's the reason we're here, but I don't hold anything against her. The situation we left wasn't any better than the one we're in now."

"It was a more populated dog-eat-dog world we left," Sandy agreed. "Weniki has eased Bear's pain over the loss of Davata. Anyone who could do that for him is okay in my book.

With the meat cooked, eaten and the rest salted, the rest of the night was spent relaxing. Palenaka and Wind eventually came in the cave and Wind was singing a ballad a cappella. His voice was sweet and flawless, and the last thing Bear remembered as he drifted off to sleep.

CHAPTER FORTY-ONE

They had been on the trail for an hour or so following a late start. The coffee and breakfast was more tasty than usual and no one felt the pressure they had been under the last month or more. They needed to travel, but hurrying was no longer a necessity.

Bear led them to the edge of the lake where they followed the shore northward. The water was to their left and the volcano on their right.

"I think we should do some fishing," Keith said looking at the smooth surface of the lake. He remembered quiet days spent with his grandfather fishing from a pier. It never mattered if they caught anything or not. They were together and he told stories while Keith listened, wrapped in the sounds and smells of nature. His grandfather was a great storyteller and he could imagine he was a part of the story and not just listening.

"Maybe later this afternoon," Bear said. "Fish does sound good for supper."

After traveling along the lakeshore for three hours, Weniki said, "We must go into the mountains."

"Now?" Hal asked.

Weniki pointed to a valley, "We must go through there."

"I agree with Keith's suggestion earlier," Hal said. "I'd like to catch some fish before we leave the water."

When the others heartily agreed, Bear asked Weniki, "Is there a need to hurry or can we stay a while and do some fishing?"

"There is no hurry," She answered. "I only say that our path is that way."

Wind spotted a growth of cane a short distance away and volunteered to cut some for fishing poles. Palenaka went with him to get the cane. She had questions about this way of getting fish.

The rest dropped their packs and set up a temporary camp. It took only a short time to cut the cane and attach strings. After rummaging through the survival supplies from the cave, they came up with wire, which they fashioned into fishhooks. In very little time, they had baited the hooks and were trying to catch supper.

They used fibers from one of the nylon ropes to construct long lines and were able to get the bait a distance into the water.

"This is the life," Hal said. "Are you sure we gotta get back to our reality? I kinda like it this way."

"Nobody shootin' at us or causing problems," Spyder added. "I'm not sure but what we're better off here."

"There's just one thing I'm worried about here," Wind said gazing at the serenity of the lake.

"What's that?" Bear asked.

"I'm not sure we'll catch anything with that around," Wind answered.

Bear looked warily around for a possible danger. "With what around?" He asked.

"Spyder's face," Wind answered matter-of-factly. "It's no wonder we haven't caught anything yet."

Bear relaxed. He should have known something like that was coming.

"Hell, let's just sweeten the bait and use a black worm," Spyder countered. "Of course, it'll be a small worm... "

"Alright you two," Sandy interrupted. "This is going south quickly." Then thinking about what she'd said, added, "And I mean in more ways than one."

Both men chuckled and continued soaking their bait. Neither of them cared if they caught anything or not. It was nice simply to relax by the side of the lake.

Soon, Hal pulled in something that looked like a strangely formed bass. "Is this good to eat?" He asked holding the fish up for Weniki to see.

"It is very good," She assured him.

In no time, they were all catching the same type fish of varying sizes. "It must be feeding time," Amanda said watching the others. She didn't care for fishing. She would cook them if the others wanted, but fishing wasn't her thing.

Just as Sandy pulled the largest fish of the day from the water, a giant body leaped from the water and splashed back into it before anyone could see what it was. A second later, a large fin emerged heading for shore.

"Kalekona," Palenaka yelled. "Get away from the water."

Everyone dropped their homemade rods and scrambled away from the lake's edge except for Spyder. Bear noticed that he was slower to retreat. *He doesn't care about his safety,* he thought.

As a creature emerged, Bear saw the type animal he was sure had killed Dr. Hamilton. It had a slender body supported by four powerful legs, which held it at least four feet off the ground. A short dorsal fin ran the length of its body and along the top of a tail serrated on both sides. Its head, attached to a short neck, looked like a Komodo dragon with horns and canine teeth.

Weniki stopped, turned toward the animal and raised her arms. A ball of fire flew from her and struck the creature head on. The Kalekona staggered a couple of steps, shook its head and returned its attention toward the now retreating people.

Another fireball flew from Weniki with the same results. The animal was less than ten feet from Spyder when he started shooting with two 9mm pistols. After four shots, the creature dropped to its stomach, but Spyder kept firing until both pistols were empty. He calmly loaded another clip into each weapon and returned it to its holster.

"No more running," he said and went back to where his fishing pole lay.

The rest stood frozen in place, stunned at the man's actions. Slowly, Hal looked at Bear who returned his gaze and shook his head slowly and the men stepped forward.

"You think we've got enough fish for tonight?" Bear asked walking up beside Spyder.

"Probably," Spyder answered. "I imagine we've got enough for two or three meals. But that motherfucker ain't running me off."

Bear nodded his understanding. "We'll give it a little while longer." When he caught Keith's attention and nodded, the young man understood. He picked up an M16 and stood guard while the rest fished.

Bear looked at Weniki and asked, "Why didn't your powers stop that thing?"

"I do not know," she answered. "I have never tried to stop one before."

"Well, we know bullets stop them," he said and returned to his fishing.

An hour later, they agreed that it was time to go to the valley. Enough time had passed that Spyder didn't feel like he was running away and he was willing to go with them.

As they traveled toward the valley Amanda asked Weniki, "Is the valley safe for us to stay in tonight?"

"I am not sure," Weniki answered. "I will know more when we arrive."

***

As with most of the others, this valley had a stream running through the middle of it surrounded by dense growth and various tropical trees. The place was stunning in its beauty.

About a half-mile in they found a clearing. "What about stopping here?" Hal asked.

"It looks as good as any place," Bear answered. "What do the rest of you think?"

"I'm for it," Wind said and the others nodded.

"Do either of you feel anything dangerous here?" He asked looking at Weniki and Palenaka.

"I sense nothing here." Weniki answered. Weniki nodded in agreement.

"Let's make camp," Bear said to the others.

In no time, everyone was unpacked and fish were cooking over an open fire. Palenaka had seasoned and marinated the fish with herbs and berries she carried in a bag. Weniki searched the area around the clearing for specific plant leaves. These she ground with stones and mixed with water from the stream in a large gourd. She took banana leaves and perforated them with a small bone. In about thirty minutes, she strained the mixture into coconut halves through the perforated leaves.

She handed half a coconut to Bear. "What's this?" He asked.

"It is like your rum," she said. Then with a smile added, "But better.

Bear tasted the concoction and smiled. It tasted like a Bahama-Mama with vodka. It was delicious. "This is outstanding!" He exclaimed. Looking at the others, he said, "You gotta try this." He raised the coconut in salute and took another drink.

"Do not drink it too quickly," Weniki cautioned. "It will make you feel bad tomorrow should you do so."

"Watch out for the hangover," Keith translated.

Grinning, Bear said, "I could do with some alcohol and as much as I hate hangovers, I could even stand one of those."

Weniki poured the liquid into shells for everyone. After the first drink, they were all asking her to make more, which reluctantly, she did. Standing near Palenaka, she said, "We will stay here for another night."

Palenaka smiled knowingly. "You may be correct," she said and checked the fish above the fire.

They spent the rest of the night drinking the liquid Weniki made and eating fish and fruit. They all felt a warm glow when they went to sleep.

***

Weniki and Palenaka sat beside the stream, at the edge of the soft glow produced by the fire. They watched the water as it glowed softly in its bed. As in their valley, they created the illumination to help relax. Neither of them sensed danger in the valley and both were happy to have the last few days behind them. "We must help them return to their time and place," Weniki said. "I was wrong to bring them here."

"I sense no blame from any of them," Palenaka informed her.

"I blame myself," Weniki admitted.

"There is no need," Palenaka argued. "They come from the time of the last change of this world. In only a few seasons, their civilization would experience the upheaval and life would cease."

"You are correct. However, they do not know this."

"It is your decision to tell them or not," Palenaka said. "I will do as you wish."

Weniki looked at the water and changed its color from aqua to gold with blue streaks. Palenaka smiled at the change. Weniki always seemed to know which color or combination perfectly matched her mood.

"They must be given the choice," Weniki said. "We will discuss it with them tomorrow."

A figure slipped silently from the trees unnoticed by either woman. It reached out with a long staff and, in turn touched Weniki and Palenaka on the back of their head.

With a bright flash of light, each slumped and lay on the ground.

"There are things yet to be done," the figure said as it melted back into the darkness.

CHAPTER FORTY-TWO

Bear awoke to the sound of the stream babbling in its bed on its way to the lake. He sat up and looked around. The sun still below the mountain peaks submerged the valley in twilight while everyone else still slept.

Bear remembered the night before and assessed his physical situation. *Where's the hangover?* He slowly stood waiting for the headache and upset stomach to raise their ugly head. When they didn't he went about the task of making coffee.

I wonder where Weniki and Palenaka are. He pulled the top from the pot and dipped it into the water when a movement to the side caught his eye. Dropping the pot, he quickly stood and reached for a pistol.

Weniki sat up from behind a log, shook her head and looked around. She raised her hand to her head as he walked up.

"I thought I was the one that was supposed to have a hangover," he said.

"It is only a pain," she said. "It is not from lama."

"Lama?" He asked.

"It is a drink that makes one feel good today, but too much causes pain tomorrow."

"I know what kind of drink you're talking about," he said. He knew that no one had drunk enough for a hangover and they should be alright today.

Weniki rubbed the back of her head, a small glow came and went and she smiled up at Bear. "I am well now." Looking at the rest sleeping, she looked back to Bear and asked, "Are they not well?"

"They're fine," he answered. "I imagine they're just catching up on the sleep they've missed for a while."

Palenaka stirred and sat up. Immediately, she too raised her hand to her head and grimaced. Before she could say anything, Weniki placed her hand on Weniki's head. Following a similar brief glow, Palenaka smiled at her. "I thank you," she said.

"I had the same pain in my head," Weniki answered. "It is probably from a ground leak."

"A ground leak?" Bear asked raising his eyebrows.

"The ground around volcanoes can leak bad air. If it was blowing over us, it would cause a pain in the head."

"Or more than that," he added. If an odorless gas was seeping up through the ground, it could cause trouble for them all. "We need to get the rest up and see how they feel."

A short while later, the rest were up and drinking coffee none of them the worse for wear. Last night was what they needed to revive their energy and raise their spirits.

"Does anyone have any idea about where to find the cave we're looking for?" Hal asked no one in particular. He knew only Weniki or Palenaka could possibly know anything about it.

"I know it is in the side of a valley," Weniki said. "I do not know which valley it is in."

"Will it be covered or will we be able to see the entrance?" Keith asked.

The front of the cave can be seen," Palenaka said. "The window inside may not be."

"Hell, we'll just have to search every cave we see," Spyder said as if the idea meant nothing to him.

"That might take a long time," Amanda pointed out.

"Well missy, what have we got but time?" He asked. "I've got no place to go in a hurry. This place is good as any."

Something about the conversation struck a chord in Palenaka. She wasn't sure why, but it seemed that there was something she should say. She looked at Weniki who had a perplexed look on her face.

***

None of them was in any hurry to be on their way and it took over three hours to prepare. Now, an hour after that, they stood at the entrance of a cave. "How do we safely check it?" Hal asked.

"I guess we'll have to do it like we have all the rest," Bear answered.

"I have to agree with Amanda," Sandy said. "This could take a long time.

"I don't know of any other way to do it," Bear said.

"We can tell you if there are windows in them," Palenaka said. "We can uncover them if they are there as well."

"That makes it a lot easier," Wind said. "I didn't look forward to walking through every cave here."

Weniki walked to the entrance and raised her arms. When she turned around she said, "There is at least one window here."

"I'll take a look at it," Hal said. As he followed Weniki inside, Keith joined him.

The rest found places to sit and wait. It took almost two hours before the three returned. Weniki led them out and Hal said, "There were two in there, but you wouldn't want to go through either of them. One was a desert and the other looked like it was underwater."

"Shit!" Spyder exclaimed and everyone turned to see what was wrong. "Mix 'em together and we got mud," he said, hesitated and gave a big grin.

"You asshole," Wind said as everyone else laughed at the joke.

Palenaka looked perplexed. "How would you get mud?" She asked and the laughter increased. Still confused she said, "Sand and water does not produce mud."

"It was a funny missy," Spyder said laughing at her obvious confusion, "a joke."

Weniki reached into Bear's mind to find the humor and began to snigger. "I will explain it to you," she said as she started further along the valley.

That day and the next they searched three valleys and eight caves. Three of the caves had no windows while the rest hid one to four inside.

Weniki carried two of the Nāki staffs on slings across her back. Along the way, she taught Bear how to activate and use the weapon. She cautioned him about touching the ends once the staff radiated its power. To prove its power she had him strike a

476

tree. It went through the tree trunk like a hot knife through butter. After a little practice, he found it not much different from the bow he used in martial arts.

***

As was now the custom, they camped beside a stream and built a fire to cook any meat they trapped or shot that day. Weniki was surprised that these people could drink lama with no negative consequences.

She had picked up a reed along the way and periodically pulled a strange looking reddish colored vine from a tree. Using her knife, she stripped the vine into long strings not much thicker than a hair and tossed them across her shoulder.

When Wind asked what they were for she said, "A lola."

"What's a lola?" he asked her.

"You will see," she said.

When he pressed the subject, she told him to have patients.

Sitting by the stream, she cut the reed to a length measured by her sling. She drilled a number of small holes equally along each end of the reed.

When Wind kept bothering her about her construction, she stood and said, "I will return when I am done."

When she walked off Wind looked around and realized everyone was looking at him. "What," he said defensively. "I just wanted to know what she was making." When he looked at Sandy, she shook her head and went back to the sewing she was working on.

477

"Did you find out what it was?" Keith asked.

"You know I didn't," he answered screwing his face up.

"Sometimes patience makes things easier," Keith said.

When Wind looked at Bear, the man was nodding.

"Shut up," he said good-naturedly.

Bear shrugged innocently and went back to cleaning a pistol.

The same time the rabbits finished cooking over the fire, Palenaka returned empty handed. Wind looked up, but refused to ask if she finished the item.

Weniki produced two more gourds of lama for the meal. When they finished, their bellies full and spirits high, Palenaka left the clearing. When she returned, she carried an instrument that looked like a medium sized harp.

No one besides Wind paid any attention to her until she strummed the first chord. When she did, all heads turned and they stared in astonishment. She played a song Wind had sung the night before. Half-way through, he joined in and the sweet soft sounds combined and drifted through the trees.

Weniki picked up some of the strings Palenaka hadn't used. She tied each end of the bundle to short piece of wood. After searching a couple of minutes, she found a reed, dipped it in the stream and then smeared it with red mud.

When she drew it across the strings of vine, it produced a sound almost like a person humming. Weniki expertly increased and released tension, changing the notes as she drew the reed across the strings.

Together, Weniki and Palenaka played until past midnight. They were even able to play along with most of the songs someone else began singing.

The night was warm with a gentle breeze. The stars shone brightly above through the thin canopy of trees and even the stream seemed to sing with the music. When they decided to call it a night, they each went to sleep at peace with the world.

***

The next morning, Bear awoke to Spyder shaking his shoulder. When he opened his eyes Spyder simply said, "Get up."

By the look on his face and the tone of his voice, Bear knew something was wrong. He was instantly awake and hurried to his feet, retrieving his M16 as he did.

He smelled coffee, but when he looked at the fire, an old man stood beside it leaning on a staff. Upon seeing Bear, he stood up straight and held the staff beside him. He bowed as Bear approached and said. "Master, I have news."

The old man was the epitome of what the movies had shown of a Japanese or Chinese martial arts master. His posture was straight and long white hair cascaded down his back and over his shoulders. The same color of hair formed a moustache and a goatee at least as long as Spyder's. Though his features were gentle, his eyes belied a hidden strength.

A small gold square and compass embroidered on the breast of his brown robe drew Bear's attention.

Bear returned the bow. "Are you a traveler?" He asked.

"I am a traveler from the east," the man answered. "I trust I am among friends."

"You are among friends and a brother," Bear said.

"This I know," the old man answered. "I know of the treachery of the one who called himself Aka."

At the name, Weniki and Palenaka stepped forward. Bear held out his hand to stop them. He lowered his rifle and placed it on the ground. "Do you come in peace?" he asked.

The old man looked at his staff and smiled. "This is only for walking and a defense against rude animals."

Bear reached down and picked up the Nāki staff. "Will you sit with us?"

"It would be my honor," the old man answered and sat beside the fire on a log.

By this time the rest were up, wondering what was happening, and who this stranger was among them.

As Bear approached the fire he said, "My name is... "

"Master Edmonds," the stranger finished.

"And you are?" Bear asked without showing surprise. His military instincts now took over.

"I am Master Kikuchi."

"Do I know you?" Bear asked.

"You do not," Master Kikuchi said. "But I know you try to return to your time."

The rest gathered around interested in finding out who this stranger was. He sat; relaxed on the log, as if he had shared their company the whole time they were on Farn.

"Would you like some coffee?" Sandy asked. She had no idea who this was, but if Bear wasn't worried, that was good enough for her right now.

"I would prefer the tea," Master Kikuchi answered.

She looked at the spit over the fire and for the first time realized that there were two pots hanging there. "Sure, no problem," she said and went to the fire.

Amanda joined her and, after figuring out which pot was which by smell, started pouring cups for them all.

"You will find the cave you look for a short way up this valley," Master Kikuchi said. "I will go also if it pleases you."

"Do we need you with us?" Spyder asked.

"Not now," the old man answered looking at him. He looked back toward Bear, "But, you may soon."

"Do you know which window leads to... " Bear hesitated, trying to find the right words, "... the place we want to go?"

"It is not a problem," Master Kikuchi said. "I will take you where you need to go."

Everyone sat around the campfire sipping coffee or tea. Since there was tea, Weniki and Palenaka chose it as their morning drink.

"I would like to welcome you to our group," Bear said holding his hand out to Master Kikuchi.

The old man took his hand and shook it. "It is good to find you my brother," he said taking another sip of tea.

"How far away is the cave?" Hal asked.

"No more than a full sunrise," Master Kikuchi answered.

"About twenty minutes from here," Spyder surmised.

"We have much time," Weniki said. "The day is young."

"Not as much as you think," Master Kikuchi said. "Trouble is on its way and we should be on our way."

He held his cup out to Sandy, "Thank you for your kindness." Slapping both hands on his knees he said, "We must be off before it arrives."

Bear rose as the old man stood. He paused a couple of seconds thinking. "We need to get going," he said. "If Master Kikuchi says there is danger, then I believe him."

That was enough to get everyone moving. Weniki and Palenaka watched as they readied their gear. "Have you heard of this man?" Palenaka asked Weniki.

"Only as a myth," Weniki answered. "He has great powers and searches for a secret one."

"Who or what is this secret one?" Palenaka asked watching the others as they shouldered their packs.

"No one knows," Weniki said. "But he or she is said to bring peace to Farn. He is to stop the confederation from settling disputes here. Because of him, the world is to grow and flourish. He will be known as The Ancient One."

Palenaka looked at the ground thinking. Master Kikuchi was surely old enough to be the one in the stories. If he were the one then she and Weniki would have to do everything they could to keep him safe.

When the rest had their belongings slung on their backs, Using his staff as a walking stick, Master Kikuchi led the way down the middle of the valley.

***

This is the place, Master Kikuchi said standing before a cave. It looked like any other hole in the side of a mountain they had checked. In fact, there was another not a hundred yards further down the valley.

"How do you know this is the one," Amanda asked.

"I assure you that this is the one you must take, child," Master Kikuchi said looking at the opening. "There are two windows inside. Only one takes you where you must go."

"Weniki and Palenaka, would you check it out for us please?" Bear asked.

Master Kikuchi watched as the two women entered the mouth of the cave. A few seconds later, he spun on his heels and turned his face up at the sky.

"It is here," he said calmly, "everyone in the cave except Master Edmonds."

Bear stepped up beside him un-shouldering his rifle. "You will need the weapon from the Nāki village," Master Kikuchi said.

483

"This'll do good enough," Bear said gripping the rifle.

"It will not," Master Kikuchi said. "You're flying metal will not stop them."

Bear knew better than to argue with the old man and it seemed that time was crucial. He quickly dropped the M16, shrugged his pack from his back and removed the Nāki staff from his shoulder.

Three creatures descended through the air toward the men. All three looked as Spyder had described Aka when he flew out of the building in the Nāki village. They plummeted toward Master Kikuchi and Bear at unbelievable speed.

Bear stepped to his right and Master Kikuchi to his left. They left enough room between them so that one would not strike the other as they used their weapon.

All three gargoyles landed a few feet in front of them. Each of the animals had a staff of their own, which they produced and held before them.

Master Kikuchi bowed to the creatures and surprisingly, they bowed in return. Out of reflex, Bear bowed to them and spun his weapon into position.

As the first advanced toward Bear, shots rang out. Spyder and Hal weren't willing to let him face them without contributing something.

When the bullets struck the creatures, they ricocheted in various directions. "Stop shooting," Sandy cried as everyone in the cave heard the bullets whine as they bounced off the gargoyles.

A bullet sizzled by Bear's head as the gargoyle swung his staff downward. Bear blocked the blow and countered to the creature's side. The animal blocked the strike and thrust at his stomach. He parried and sidestepped with just enough room to have a button on his shirt disintegrate.

More shots rang out as Spyder aimed at the third creature's eyes. This time the bullets didn't ricochet. They struck true to his aim blinding the animal. It stumbled around, eventually dropping its staff and immediately stepped on it.

The gargoyle's leg exploded, it flailed its arms in the air until it fell directly on the end of the weapon. Body pieces flew in all directions. One even bounced off the creature Master Kikuchi fought.

Instinctively, the creature looked to its left and Master Kikuchi slashed at it with his staff cutting it in half "Go to the cave," Bear called seeing the animal drop.

The old man turned without a word and walked almost casually to the entrance as if nothing out of the ordinary was happening. When he reached everyone in the cave he said, "Come, I'll take you to the window."

"But Bear... " Sandy started.

"He will be along soon," Master Kikuchi assured her with a smile.

Below the opening, Bear blocked and countered using all his skills. He was in a state of satori, the warrior's mind. He neither saw nor thought about what he did. Completely relaxed, he let his body take over the fight.

The gargoyle struck side to side, then overhead. As their weapons clashed, small explosions immediately followed blue-white flashes.

As the creature advanced, Bear backed toward the cave entrance. The gargoyle stopped and stepped back. In a shimmer, it changed to Aka.

"I will spare you if you come with me," it said.

"Do you really think I would do something like that?" Bear countered.

"I will also spare your friends," he added.

Bear thought a few seconds about that. It was a sure way for the rest to survive. Maybe he could escape later. It might be worth a try. He lowered his staff. "Do you promise to let the others go?"

"You have my word on that," Aka said stepping forward.

Bear hesitated, "Do you find me worthy of granting my wish?"

Aka stepped up to where he stood less than five feet from Bear, "I do," he said. "You have my word."

Bear raised the spear to throw it to his right. As his left hand made contact, the spear glowed blue. Before Aka could react, his head flew from his body. Bear viciously slashed forward with his left hand and caught the creature's neck, severing its head from its body.

As he turned to walk to the cave he muttered, "Asshole."

Inside the cave, the rest gathered before a window. As Bear walked up Master Kikuchi said, "Go," and stepped aside. In rapid succession, Spyder led the way through the opening with Hal bringing up the rear.

Bear bowed to Master Kikuchi. "It's done," he said.

"I knew it would be," the old man said. "Now it is your turn."

Bear looked at the window, "After you," he said and motioned toward it with his hand.

Master Kikuchi bowed and stepped through. On the other side, he and the rest were wavering forms looking back.

Bear looked at the entrance of the cave. *There's more to come,* he thought and stepped through the window to join his friends and face an unknown future.

Epilogue

Bear stepped from the window. Hal and Sandy stood on a ledge looking out over a valley. They were obviously in the mountains, but not in Central Texas. Towering pines, oaks, piñon and palm trees covered the mountains and valleys.

White fluffy clouds floated across the sky on a light breeze. The temperature felt to be in the middle seventies.

Bear looked back where the window should be. In its place was the rock face of a cliff. "Where the hell are we?" He growled at Master Kikuchi.

"You are needed here," the old man said. "The danger is great and some of you may not survive. But there are those that need your help."

As Bear looked into her emerald-green eyes, Weniki stepped up and took his hand.

THE END

www.ingramcontent.com/pod-product-compliance
Lightning Source LLC
Chambersburg PA
CBHW011400010726
47495CB00009B/2711